AN EXCESS MALE

DISCARD

HARPER Voyager

An Imprint of HarperCollinsPublishers

AN
EXCESS
MALE

MAGGIE SHEN KING

This is a work of fiction. Names, characters, places, and incidents are products of the author's imagination or are used fictitiously and are not to be construed as real. Any resemblance to actual events, locales, organizations, or persons, living or dead, is entirely coincidental.

AN EXCESS MALE. Copyright © 2017 by Maggie Shen King. All rights reserved. Printed in the United States of America. No part of this book may be used or reproduced in any manner whatsoever without written permission except in the case of brief quotations embodied in critical articles and reviews. For information, address HarperCollins Publishers, 195 Broadway, New York, NY 10007.

HarperCollins books may be purchased for educational, business, or sales promotional use. For information, please email the Special Markets Department at SPsales@harpercollins.com.

Harper Voyager and design are trademarks of HarperCollins Publishers LLC.

FIRST EDITION

Designed by Suet Chong

Library of Congress Cataloging-in-Publication Data has been applied for.

ISBN 978-0-06-266255-2

17 18 19 20 21   LSC   10 9 8 7 6 5 4 3 2 1

for Mom

storyteller extraordinaire

and

for Dad

who made everything possible

And you O my soul where you stand,
Surrounded, detached, in measureless oceans of space,
Ceaselessly musing, venturing, throwing, seeking the
   spheres to connect them,
Till the bridge you will need be form'd, till the ductile
   anchor hold,
Till the gossamer thread you fling catch somewhere,
   O my soul.

—WALT WHITMAN, "A NOISELESS PATIENT SPIDER"

I

WEI-GUO

I sneak another glance at Wu May-ling, my potential bride and the guest of honor at this matchmaking lunch. It may be years before I get another opportunity to be so near a young woman, and my eyes dart from the plump curves of her pink lips to the delicate point of her chin to her narrow cheeks and lush eyebrows. I drink in the warmth behind her eyes, the feminine loveliness in her every gesture, the electric charge she produces in me. Both angular and soft, delicate and strong, her face could beguile me for a lifetime. I imagine myself her master and subject for an entire night at a time.

Someone clears his throat, and I jerk up to find my two dads glaring at me. My face hot, I sit up taller and glance around the table to see if May-ling's two husbands noticed my indiscretion. There is a scowl on Husband One's face, but he's been scowling ever since he sat down. Intent on transporting a soup dumpling to his plate intact, Husband Two appears to have mostly food on his mind. I suddenly understand what it's like to be Dad, my mother's second husband and my biological father. But then, he has only one husband who outranks him, while I will have two to mind if I marry into this Advanced family.

Dad bestows a fatherly smile upon May-ling. "Our Wei-guo has impeccable health habits. He weight trains three times a week and swims and runs as well. He can bench a hundred kilos. You should see his biceps."

Sitting on my other side, Big Dad stiffens. "You're embarrassing our guests," he says to Dad with forced levity. With both hands, he offers up the ribbon-and-lace-adorned tin of individually wrapped moon cakes Dad spent hours choosing.

We have honored MaMa's dying wish, staying together under one roof as a family. I think she would be comforted to know that my two dads have become steadfast companions and that through Dad, I continue to hear her opinions. Her two men have taken to wearing the same shirts, both pouncing upon whatever happens to be clean. Even their paunchy and stooped silhouettes have started to look alike.

May-ling beams at the gift, her good nature evident in her twinkling smile. "I have a very sweet tooth. Thank you." Her smoky eyes and translucent silk dress could not be a more enticing blend of intrigue and grace. Despite having birthed a child, her manners and air remain maidenly, a primed canvas awaiting defining strokes of paint.

Which, I admit, I desperately want to apply.

Husband Two, a software designer and what the establishment calls a prosperously sized man, takes the tin from her and scrunching his nose, examines and leaves it under his chair without thanking us. If I did not know from his casual shirt and uncombed gray hair that he is not on board with Family Advancement, I do now.

Ironic that someone with such disregard for social niceties should possess so cherubic a face.

Dad doesn't seem to notice. "Wei-guo has won three triathlons, the five- and ten-thousand-meter races more times than I can remember. He'll be thrilled to give all three of you a free assessment. Put you on a diet—" I elbow him. His enthusiasm knows no bounds.

Sitting half a head taller than everyone at the table, Husband One, a corporate accountant, wrinkles his brow, looking even more displeased. He is in dire need of a weight-*gain* plan. A cold could take him. He seems to be the Alpha, the way he sits there with his arms crossed in judgment, waiting to be buttered up. Too important, even, to eat. That said, I've yet to see a better-fitted suit on a man. A linen hanky in his jacket pocket, a watch fob hanging from his vest, and his silvery hair slicked back, he seems a relic from a bygone era.

Hero, our matchmaker, gestures at May-ling, his three chunky rings glittering. "Lee Wei-guo was voted one of Beijing's top master personal trainers the last five years in a row by *The Worldly Bachelor*." If this same webzine had not ranked our matchmaker top in client placement, we would not have hired him. The volume and frizz of his shoulder-length hair bring to mind disorder and bad judgment. Even in a profession dominated by registered same-sex lovers—the Willfully Sterile—he sticks out, a baboon peacocking among men. We pray his name is a good description of his abilities.

Our matchmaker is trying to help, but mention of *The Worldly Bachelor* only serves to remind May-ling and company that there are forty million more single men like me out there to choose from, that it has taken me until my forties to save up enough to enter matchmaking talks at this lowest rung. Furthermore, my living relies on such unmarried men. The government has awarded us—members of "The Bounty"—official status, investing in public campaigns to make the words "unmarriageable," "excess," and "leftover" in reference to men unpatriotic and backward. And for "The Bounty," fitness programs like those that I offer are State-funded and mandated. The distraction and physical exhaustion of a thoughtful exercise plan are as nonnegotiable for us as sleep, food, and weekly, State-arranged sex.

Husband Two seems uninterested in the conversation—above it even—focusing solely on shoveling down all the sliced beef shank on the table. He must be one of those jerks who considers his pot belly a status symbol.

"I don't like to brag," Dad says, "but Wei-guo really is the best in his field."

I didn't expect Wu May-ling to catch my eye. Before anyone notices, her flirty bangs fall back over her face, and she returns to sipping the shark's fin soup. We paid dearly into the Nature Preservation Fund in order to bring this dish to the table to signal our serious interest. Now that the right to propose matchmaking talks and marriage has become the prerogative of the woman's side, my dads dare not spare any expense. But even as they caution me not to settle for anyone less than right—"a bad marriage is worse than no marriage at all"—I know what they won't say: *our budget will not allow us many more of these lunches.*

"Comrade Lee." Husband One finally deigns to open his mouth.

"Please, call him Wei-guo," Dad says.

Husband One starts over with my given name. He asks how long I've been a master trainer, in what direction I hope to take my career.

"Our son earned his certification more than twenty years ago. Before he'd even graduated high school. He broke the program's record too, completing it in just under four months."

Big Dad frowns at Dad. "Let our son answer."

Wu May-ling makes eye contact again and smiles in commiseration. I like her. It can't be much fun to be married to these two grandpas. I feel sorry for her. Only the more financially strapped or money-grubbing husbands go the max to three.

I stare into her eyes even as I answer Husband One. "I cut my teeth on our city's elite at the Body Essential." Everyone who is anyone knows the Body Essential, the studio where the unmarried scions of our noted Party officials, financiers, and industrialists fulfill their exercise requirement. The owner's father (and chief investor) is a ranking member of the Politburo, but still, Husband One turns up his nose. "Those same clients followed me to my own studio eight years ago. My hourly rate rivals that of actuaries." At this, he raises a leery eyebrow.

I continue, "For my clients' convenience, I work early mornings and evenings, but my schedule is at my own discretion." May-ling nods, and I see the two of us with the middle of the day to ourselves. Strolling the streets hand in hand. Eating in bed. Rollicking.

Husband One asks again about my career ambitions.

"I like owning my own business. Being my own boss. I've worked very hard to get here." I smile at May-ling and can't help adding, "I'm looking for a special woman. A true love. A kindred spirit." I stop short of saying "play pal," extra emphasis on the word "play."

Big Dad shifts in his chair. "Wei-guo continually updates his program, his equipment, his gym. He's always innovating so as to gain competitive advantage."

Husband One crosses his arms. "I hope you don't mind me asking, but why not go to Vietnam, Burma, or on some marriage cruise, and bring back a woman? Why share?"

Big Dad answers again, "Wei-guo understands Advanced families. That's how he grew up. That's what he knows best. Like his father and me, he values literacy, shared culture and beliefs. And the preservation of our people." In private, Big Dad liked to contend that it took, at the very least, two husbands in friendly competition to keep up with MaMa and her robust chatter.

"Yes," Dad says, "we are staunch supporters of China First." My dads are eager to establish us as law-abiding patriots.

Husband One looks to me for confirmation, no doubt skeptical of the party line. These days, only fools speak freely among strangers. I nod yes, but do not elaborate. What do I care about the dilution of our blood and the increasing complexity of our society when my most basic need for a wife and child is not met? I do not say that I've grown weary of my weekly ten-minute hygiene session with my State-assigned "Helpmate," but trudging overseas requires even more money, bureaucracy, and governmental interference. Furthermore, casting one's lot with a foreigner, a "sign-language wife," brings its own set of problems.

Husband One asks how I like to spend my free time.

Dad says, "Wei-guo serves on the Strategic Games Council. He is also the founding general of his battalion."

Husband One's scowl intensifies. Dad forgets that much of the public fear that instead of providing a much needed outlet for unmarried men, our war games condone aggressive behavior and create opportunities for mayhem. The bludgeoning to death of six soldiers two days ago during a game is fresh in everyone's minds.

The clam at the end of Husband Two's chopsticks stops halfway to his mouth. Light clicks on in his eyes. "I've amassed 5,468,325 krps in *Metagalactic Domination*. I am Emperor Divine of Omega Centauri, Superior Warlord on Small Magellanic Cloud, Eunuch General of Messier 83 . . ."

I steal a glance at May-ling. Head down, she is now the one who doesn't stop eating. Husband One rubs his chin, his mouth an upturned grimace, as pained perhaps by his counterpart's rambling as by my choice of pastime.

Finally, Husband One cuts him off. "Our spouse is quite a fan of virtual warfare. But you like actual fighting."

Surprisingly, Husband Two returns to picking out clam meat and says nothing more.

Big Dad says, "Wei-guo spends most of his time on the governing board's Safety Council."

"I'd note too that there is no physical contact of any kind allowed in Strategic Games," I say. Our critics always overlook this fact. "It is high-level strategy, teamwork, and wilderness training using the most sophisticated technology. It is an intense workout in the great outdoors."

"That's terrific," Wu May-ling says to me. I think it's terrific too, the way she keeps trying to forge a connection.

I ask how she likes to spend her free time.

She glances at Husband One and hesitates. "We loved to salsa and merengue before our son came along."

I am immediately transported to her youth. To her pulsing hips. I've long dreamt of marrying a woman sophisticated in the ways of the world.

Big Dad says, "I understand you have just one child."

May-ling flinches. I quickly send her a look to say that I am on her side, that I do not find their situation odd. After my family saved the requisite two million yuan needed for me to enter matchmaking talks as a third husband, it has taken another eight months to get this nibble of interest, and Big Dad will not blow it for me with a careless remark. Every man is allowed one child, and negotiating the size of the dowry refund and a dissolution option if a baby is not born in three years is the matchmaker's first order of business. After six years of marriage, May-ling should already have two kids.

Husband One says, "Our son just turned two, and we intend for him to have our undivided attention for his first three years."

Big Dad leans toward May-ling. "May I ask—I hope you don't mind my asking—have you ever used an infertility specialist?"

"We have a child." Husband One covers May-ling's chopstick hand with his. "And May-ling is only twenty-two."

"The child is yours?"

My desperate position seems to be of little concern to Big Dad. Furthermore, he does not tolerate family disunity or my disrespect. He would kill me if he knew I would rather take a chance with a wife like May-ling and no child at all than drift along lonely and alone for the rest of my days.

"Our son belongs to all of us." Husband One sits up even taller. "And, no, we do not believe in sex selection."

"Nor do we," Dad pipes up. That is, of course, everybody's party line these days.

"We are a true family in name and deed," says Husband One. "Our son takes the Wu surname, as will all our future children."

My two dads' eyebrows shoot up together. In order to promote female births, the adoption of maternal surnames will become official in another year, and the birth rate has skyrocketed in anticipation. Supporters of China First fear that over time, the law will send more men offshore for wives and births, undoing all the gains made by ten years of Advanced family tax breaks.

Husband One continues, "We believe in sharing both our country's wealth and pain. Should it become necessary for our government to raise the unit spousal limit, know that we are prepared to go the max again and make that sacrifice."

May-ling starts at this proclamation, and my eyes follow the drops of tea tracing the curves of her bosom. I breathe easier knowing that going the max again after I join their family troubles her too. Big Dad fidgets, at a loss for words. Husband Two eyes the hairy crab, no doubt wishing for a lazy Susan rather than the intimacy of this smaller table.

"Every unit has its quirks, so let's not waste more time discussing our bad habits." Husband One promises that Hero will satisfy all our questions later. I am glad that it is not his inclination to keep pushing his views. "Today, I am most interested in getting to know Wei-guo. To see if a rapport exists."

May-ling's gaze snaps up. She stops dabbing at her cleavage. We find each other and grin.

Husband One stops short of the restaurant's door and pulls the hood of May-ling's gray coat over her head. He cinches the hood's drawstrings, and May-ling's shoulder-length hair sprouts like cat whiskers around her chin.

She smiles and stops him. "Let me." She loosens and throws back the hood, and I am heartened to see how graciously she handles her controlling husband and stands up for herself. We six men surround and wall her off, giving her some private space. She flips her hair off her shoulders. It catches the light in an undulating shimmer, gorgeous as a bolt of watered silk, and it's all I can do not to stare.

When I next look up, I am not surprised to find Husband One glaring as if I've violated her. He steps between us and pulls the hood over May-ling again before she finishes tucking away her hair. She takes hold of the strings this time and leaves them loose.

"We are so honored to meet you today." She bows to Big Dad and then Dad, thanking them for an elaborate and delicious meal and for the pretty box of moon cakes. Husband One has little choice but to stop fussing at her and do the same.

She turns to me next and squeezes my hand warmly. She closes my fingers before letting go, and a jolt of electricity shoots through me when I feel the sharp edges of a note. Despite the crowd around us, we've managed to reach each other. We've managed to establish a connection without speaking a single word. I barely have time to tuck the paper in my pocket before Husband One shoehorns himself between us and appropriates my hand.

After we say our good-byes, Husband One takes May-ling by the elbow and urges his counterpart to do the same. Flanked by her two tall sentries—one rail thin and the other hulking—she seems both their prize and prisoner. Outside, an expanse of blue windbreakers—a twentysomething martial arts club tour group from Guangzhou—blocks the flow of pedestrians. There seem to be more eligible bachelors every time I turn around. I locate lines of families with a wife or daughter sandwiched in between and fail to find another woman as covered up, as circumscribed. Overcome with an urge to run over and break May-ling free, I calm myself with a peek at her note. She has given me her contact information.

"They act as if we picked a restaurant in a seedy neighborhood," Big Dad says, no doubt reeling from the size of the check. "It's downright insulting."

"They are a very proper and very loving family." Hero links arms with Big Dad, and we head in the direction of my Strategic Games Safety Council meeting. (The government overseer of the council called an emergency session just this morning to discuss the six recent deaths.) Hero asks me what I think of May-ling.

"I like her," I say, my heart still soaring from the touch of her hand. "She's charming."

"I can walk fine." Leaning hard on his cane, Big Dad clops away rudely, surely trying to lose Hero's hold of his elbow. I'm certain my forthcoming reply also irritates him.

"You aren't going to deprive me of the chance to show my respect," Hero says in a flirtatious lilt, "to be of service?"

Big Dad has nothing against the Willfully Sterile, but his dignity will not abide an affected man hanging off his arm in public, even if the man is wearing a cream business suit. I have no doubt Hero, secure in his identity and his booming career, loves little more than to mess with a guy like Big Dad.

I support Dad's elbow and help him keep up, his clicking knee reminding me that his every step hurts. As much as I long to get married, I worry how my two aging fathers will get by without my daily presence.

After some jerky steps, people near Big Dad and Hero turn and stare, and Big Dad allows us to catch up. We continue four abreast down the wide, tree-lined street.

Hero sighs. "Isn't our city gorgeous?"

Backlit by the sun, gingko trees as far as the eyes can see reach from opposite sides of the sidewalk, their canopies bathing us in a golden glow. Neither of my dads comments, so I heartily agree with Hero.

Predictably, Dad adds, "It sure is crowded."

The whole of Beijing seems to be here jostling against us, trying to enjoy this beautiful sight, and I'm relieved when he doesn't say more. Stately, eight- and ten-lane boulevards crisscross our city, and we rarely walk down one without one of my dads pointing out that countless properties were seized and lives disrupted and, in the most egregious cases, cut short to make possible their construction. Relegated to tiny, stacked boxes, ordinary citizens pour into parks and scenic streets, thirsting for open air and elbowroom, so that our leaders could have their show of grandeur.

Big Dad says, "We are worried Wu May-ling may be barren."

Hero points out that she has a child. "I guarantee she's fertile."

I say, "If anyone can't have kids, it's Husband One."

Dad pats my hand on his elbow and stresses patience. "This is our very first match."

Big Dad adds, "There are more pretty girls than one."

Hero chortles, unable to keep a straight face at the ridiculousness of Big Dad's assertion. Intensely competitive, Big Dad cannot even acknowledge the scarcity of brides.

Hero cranes his head around Dad and catches my eye. "You should know you're Wu May-ling's first match as well. She just came on the market. She picked you out of about five thousand in my office."

My heart does a little jig. Big Dad snorts. A young man pushes between Dad and Hero, no doubt irritated by our creaky pace, and Hero links arms with Dad to shore up our line.

"I didn't want to color your judgment with talk of money. This is, after all, a marriage. A lifetime commitment." He reveals that they're asking a hundred thousand less than the basic dowry price. "I found you an amazing deal. The best one around."

"A good deal is the farthest thing from our minds." Big Dad is touchy on the subject of money. A man who loves tax savings more than his manhood is the public's favorite stereotype of the Advanced male. "What's the catch?"

"They want an honest man. Somebody they all like." Hero explains that the threesome is going the max because they have their sights on a three-bedroom apartment. "I'm not supposed to tell you that Wei-guo's name will be on the property title."

"It *should* be on the title," Big Dad says. "What's the catch?"

"Have I mentioned that the two husbands are brothers?"

"Is this a joke?" Dad says, breathing hard. "Wei-guo will be forever outvoted. What century do they think they're living in anyways? Brothers sharing a wife!"

Those brothers seemed an equal and opposite reaction to each other. I didn't sense much rapport and wonder if Dad's concern would really matter.

Dad stops walking and stares at the matchmaker. "That second husband is kind of an interesting fellow."

Big Dad adds, "He's a Lost Boy, isn't he?"

"Please," Hero says with a lowered voice. He glances around. "We mustn't make these accusations lightly. He's a top-earning programmer."

Hero is right to preach caution. Males with severe autistic, oppositional, or attention difficulties could be neutered and institutionalized, and a rumor is all it takes to start a messy investigation. My dads continue to stare him down, one from each side, and he releases their elbows. Some busybody tells us that non-moving pedestrians must stand to the side.

Hero clears his throat. "You already know about the maternal surname. Also, they want me to stress that they are a true family, that the children belong to all the fathers."

"Of course," Dad says. "We believe the very same."

"Let him finish," Big Dad tells Dad. We tighten our circle around Hero.

"They don't assign nights. May-ling decides who gets bedroom time."

A smile takes over my face. I can already see her choosing me over the two grandpas.

"That's outrageous," Big Dad says. MaMa kept a strict bedroom schedule, as do most Advanced families. She used to spend every other week with each of my dads, but they eventually talked her into alternating nights. My dads argued that too much closeness was lost over seven days.

Hero places one hand over the other and lowers his head. "They believe in fairness, in equality of all members. As the most junior spouse, Wei-guo will undoubtedly benefit from such thoughtfulness."

"How do we know for sure then if a child is ours?" Dad asks.

Hero says, "They are all yours."

Big Dad grimaces. Dad's eyebrows are almost at his hairline.

"I understand your concern." Hero promises to pursue the matter with May-ling's husbands.

"This is not a marriage," Big Dad says when the matchmaker finishes.

On the contrary, I want to say, it's *better*. I welcome this chance to win with my wits, my looks, my sperm. I suspect I don't want the tedium of scheduled sex for the rest of my life.

Hero says, "I know those folks, and I wouldn't propose them to you if I didn't think Wei-guo has a very good chance at becoming May-ling's favorite."

"That's too much pressure," Dad replies. "Marriage should be a sanctuary, not a popularity contest."

Hero bows daintily. "You are right, of course. I wanted you to have a shot at May-ling. She'll be snapped up by next week—" He waves, his hand a butterfly in flight. Not only will he continue to aggressively market me, he says he will re-feature me as the bachelor of the day.

Big Dad shakes his head in disgust. Finally, he asks if there's anything else we should know.

Hero says, "Just the usual." My STD panels, genetic disease profile, tax, bank, and asset statements should all be up-to-date. "And they also want an intelligence test. If you are truly interested."

A terrible scowl takes over Big Dad's face. My mediocre intellect has long been a sore spot for him. "We will let you know." He says good-bye to Hero, dismissing him unceremoniously.

"Absolutely not," Big Dad says, with Hero barely out of earshot. He jabs a finger in my direction. "You will not be falling for that minx or that"—I wipe his wayward spit from my nose—"that peddler of used goods."

I say nothing. Big Dad hates it when I argue, hates it even more when I refuse to engage. He has been telling me how to act and what to think for four decades. I've always tried to please him. I've been a filial son.

But he will not bully me from this rare opportunity at finding a wife.

I deposit my fathers at a teahouse, where they will wait while I attend my meeting. Saturdays are precious errand days for us. My fathers prefer to handpick their fruit, longevity snacks, and personal items, but public transportation is no longer safe for them. Our crowded buses and subways are the number one source of concussions and broken hips for elderly men who garner little consideration in a society overrun with men. There's a horrible joke out there: the easiest way to snuff out your father-in-law—put him on a bus.

I jog the rest of the way to the Ministry of National Defense, where the offices of Strategic Games occupy a portion of the bottommost basement floor. The game we play has more in common with laser tag than actual war. We shoot out of our uniform sleeves, handle no weapons, and receive no combat training. Yet the government classifies us as potential Enemies of the State. It insists that we be overseen by actual military men, midranking ones no less. It subsidizes a portion of our program, but it also caps us at fifty thousand participants, even though many more would like to play.

As I approach the fountain, our favored gathering spot, I count nine Safety Council members huddled around it. We like the high shooting water jets and their ability to muffle potential voice recordings. I am the last to arrive.

I say hello to everyone and clap the backs of the guys next to me. "What have we heard?" It is not the policy of the People's Armed Police to divulge names or the circumstances of the crime before the conclusion of its investigation, but there is always the possibility of rumor.

Little Sung, our youngest and most vocal member, leans in and quietly tells me that a friend of a friend knows one of the dead. "He said the man worked for the Commerce Department, that he had stepped on some high-ranking toes there." With his fist, he stamps a spot just below his heart. "And his body had a purplish black circle here."

"He was branded?" I ask.

Someone adds, "I heard more than once that this was about a woman, that the six fought and killed each other over her."

We are quickly inundated with gossip accusing the six men of blackmailing their boss about an affair, of being tax cheats culled in a government conspiracy, of trying to stage a protest over the immigration cap for foreign brides. . . .

Doc, our silver-haired council chair, shushes us. He points at Little Sung. "I want you to bring up the purple circle and the workplace run-in at our meeting. Can we name your source?" A physician whose dedication to Strategic Games kept him involved even after he married and lost the right to play, Doc is much loved and respected among us.

Little Sung says, "My buddy doesn't want to be mixed up in this. And the victim's family is understandably wary."

"All right," Doc says. "Do your best." He glances at his watch and says it's ten past our meeting time. "We've waited long enough."

We line up to enter the building, its cavernous lobby deserted on a Saturday. One by one, we place our right palms on the Safety-Check and name our meeting room. Doc surrenders his watch to the SafetyScan to be "debugged." Most of us know better than to bring our info rings, message pens, and pocket geniuses here, but Doc, our leader, is required to model transparency.

I pass under the SafetyGate and pause for a second as my body is swept for prohibited items. The bell dings when Little Sung enters, and he freezes for a count of ten while his implanted chips are temporarily deactivated. I've never understood why anyone would offer up his privacy for the convenience of not carrying identification and monies, for home and office doors that automatically swing open, or for a hospital to know his every change in mood, but Little Sung swears by it.

We wait for him.

The relentless expanse of red in the carpet, ceiling, and walls bears down on us as we cross the foyer in the direction of the stairwell. Little Sung breaks away toward the bank of elevators and presses his hand on another SafetyCheck. Neither our status nor our business here merits elevator rides, but he is resentful of our treatment and hard-headed. His best buddy on the council laughs and follows. The sensor soon beeps, and "access denied" is broadcasted in a polite female voice in surround sound. Doc and I share a look, shaking our heads. As we descend the dim, cinder-block stairwell, someone parrots the voice, and "access denied" in falsetto echoes along with our footsteps. Guffaws break out behind me, and I can just imagine the lewd, accompanying gestures. Finally, Doc reminds us that six men are dead and tells everyone to shut up. They do.

Our entrance into our small meeting room clicks on the harsh institutional lights as well as the red recording signal on the three cameras. Like schoolboys, the ten of us sidle into the three rows of plastic chairs with L-shaped desktops.

I check the time. We are sixteen minutes late. Major Jung, our pompous, government-appointed overseer, hates it when we are late. We hate that our Safety Council possesses only the right to recommend policy, that decision-making authority lies with Major Jung and his superiors—outsiders who care only to keep Strategic Games under their thumbs.

Lately, Major Jung has taken to spying on us with the cameras. He no longer arrives first, and we very much look forward to his lectures on tardiness when he is himself tardy. Today, seven minutes after us—we are all silently counting the minutes—he enters, his presence dark and hulking in military uniform, his sharp beak of a nose and beady eyes as menacing as a hawk on a hunt. Not bothering to remove his flat-topped cap, he lets us know just what he thinks of us.

We do not bother to rise and salute him; we are civilians. Many of the guys intentionally slump and sprawl out, their limbs limp jellyfish tentacles. We only dare attempt these pathetic forms of disrespect.

The major clears his throat. "What I am about to share with you will not be made public."

His failure to reprimand surprises me.

He continues, his gaze fixed on the back wall, "What I'm about to share is morally corrupting and soul-damaging, but it is my duty to inform you. It is your duty, your responsibility as members of this council, to know. To carry this burden. It is our combined duty to make certain that the participants of Strategic Games and the public are never again harmed in this way."

The major says that the People's Armed Police apprehended the killer this morning, a mentally imbalanced seventeen-year-old male who had tried his misguided best to defend the honor of his fourteen-year-old sister. The six killed had been harassing her with graphic photographs and disturbing messages detailing the many ways they were going to violate her.

Suspicion washes over me. His story matches none of the street talk.

"Her family, which also happens to be the killer's family, is also a victim, one that is scared, ashamed, and sorry. We will not incite or pollute the public's sensibility or further the pain of our many, many victims by broadcasting the specifics of this sad and filthy case." He crosses his arms as if there is nothing more we need know.

I will never understand why the government finds it necessary to shield us from such occurrences. It's ridiculous to think that hearing about a rape or murder makes us want to do the same.

"How were the men killed?" Doc says.

Major Jung clasps his hands behind his back, puffs out his gold tasseled and beribboned chest, and frowns. Doc did not raise his hand or stand as required by Jung and his "parliamentary" procedures.

"Oh. Sorry," Doc says with feigned sincerity. He sticks two fingers in the air and waits to be called upon before rising to his feet to ask again how the six men were killed.

"With a baseball bat. An aluminum alloy, to be exact. Again, that is privileged information." The major slaps some papers onto Doc's desk. "Pass this around. This will explain everything."

Still standing, Doc ignores the police report that we all know will be even less enlightening than the major. "What do the eye-witnesses say?"

"There are none." The major states that the killer lured his victims into a silo and clubbed them to death there.

"Six men were not able to overcome one seventeen-year-old kid," Doc deadpans.

"Do you have a question?" Our major abhors any hints at sarcasm.

Doc apologizes again. None of us can appear to intentionally offend. "Why were six men not able to overcome one?"

"Because they were lured to the silo one at a time."

"Why—"

"You've asked your three questions," the major says. "Let someone else have a turn."

Little Sung's hand shoots up. Doc sits down, but still does not pass the papers. The major glances around the room, surely wanting someone else to speak. Finally, he calls on Little Sung.

Little Sung rises. "A purple burn mark was found on the torso of every one of the dead men. Can you tell us about that?"

The major pulls back his chin and frowns. "Who is the source of this nonsense?"

Little Sung continues, "The dead men discovered last week that one of their superiors at the Commerce Department was having an affair." He employs our usual tactics—exaggerations that point the finger away from our sources and buried nuggets of truth to indicate that we are scrutinizing the investigation.

"Who is spreading these lies?" the major roars.

"A friend of a friend heard—"

"We do not deal in gossip."

"The father of one of the dead," Little Sung says.

"Which one?"

Little Sung shakes his head. "I do not know."

"You do not know or will not say?" The major's voice booms.

Little Sung shakes his head again.

He approaches Little Sung to tower over him. "Claims without named sources cannot be investigated. It is your official duty as a member of this council to divulge the source of this information."

Little Sung stares straight ahead. "I do not know."

Major Jung snarls in disgust. "It is also your duty as a member of this council not to advance gossip." He studies his documents, flipping through page after page of some report, making a show of diligence and fairness. "The medical examiner has noted no burn marks on any of the victims. Your claim cannot be true."

"You are right, of course." Doc raises his hand.

Major Jung looks at him, but does not note that he has spoken out of turn again.

Doc stands. "But this is what's circulating on the street. Unfortunately, this is what the public believes. As you are aware, I am a physician, and I would be happy to reexamine the bodies and put rumors to rest. At no charge, of course."

The major says, "The families will never allow the bodies of their loved ones to be violated a third time.

"Sit down," he says to Little Sung and Doc. "Our business is the safety of all the participants of Strategic Games. And this incident confirms that we do not have sufficient measures in place to help the mentally ill.

"The rate of detrimental mental illness among males eighteen to fifty is four point nine percent. The head of each team—the 'general'"—the major's tone turns sarcastic uttering the word—"knows their players best." He looks at Doc. "You will communicate to the 'generals' that they will submit to this council in one month's time the names of four point nine percent of their team—five men each—most in need of psychological help. These candidates will be evaluated and offered counseling if needed."

Doc jumps to his feet. "Please, that's—"

"That will be all for today." His papers already gathered, the major turns his back on us and swaggers out.

I slump back in my desk, my stomach a twinging knot. Putting anyone on a mental-health watch list would be the first step in sending him away.

I punch in May-ling's contact information. Dots of color scintillate on the screen and coalesce into her striking face.

"I was hoping you'd call." Her smile is warm, her gaze direct and genuine. I feel again our connection. I am reminded how long I've felt alone and adrift.

I dim the lights a bit before activating my camera, thrilled that she has opted for a face-to-face. "I loved meeting you yesterday," I whisper.

"I loved meeting you as well," she whispers back.

"I'd love to show you my studio tomorrow."

"Really?" Her smile brings out deep dimples.

"I'll pick you up at eleven." If she does not bring up their dating rules, I'll know we have something.

"I can be at your studio at eleven."

"Do you own a car?" It would be proper for her to come alone if she is locked inside the safety of a car.

"Don't you worry."

"All right then," I say. "I won't worry."

Unable to think of a way to keep her on the line, I let her go, but lunge for the button to capture her image. On my screen, she is a whir of creamy skin and flying hair. I save it to my desktop, so I can return again and again to this feeling of hope and of belonging.

I go beyond my usual vacuuming and trash-emptying routines to eradicate the kind of grime my mother would have noticed. Between clients, I wipe down, disinfect, and reorganize all the free weights. I dust and shine every machine, every exercise ball, every jump rope and flexibility strap. I stay late wiping the fingerprints and streaks off the mirror walls. I go through an entire roll of tape ridding the dark floor mats of lint.

I reassess my Wall of Fame and move the Happy Alumni section, the wedding and baby photos of clients who completed their exercise requirement here, more front and center. I want May-ling to see how I value the hope of family, how I encourage my clients to stay optimistic. I edit, rearrange, and square up the announcements—the promotions, birthdays, and newsworthy items. I pride myself on maintaining longtime clients. They are my second family. Finally,

I put the beefcake pictures of the men who've set studio records in squat, bench press, and deadlift well below eye level. There is no need to focus her attention on my competition.

At home, I study the advice on matchmaking sites. *Bathe. Arrive on time. Be a gentleman. Compliment.* I find the tips elementary until this: Learn to dance. If your woman is out on the floor with someone else, you might as well not exist. I imagine Husband One and Two left in the dust while May-ling and I shimmy, twist, and twirl together, communicating with our bodies our horizontal desires. I spend the rest of the evening studying up on salsa and merengue, listening to, downloading, and organizing Latin beats.

The music of a fourteen-piece orchestra will infuse my studio with sexy, hip-shaking rhythm when May-ling arrives. Casually clad in a form-fitting black tee and my shortest shorts, I will give her a tour of my facility. I will assess her flexibility, her muscular strength and endurance, her cardiovascular capacity, her body composition. I will coach her through the use of my equipment. I imagine that my wit, my charm, my virility will be everything her husbands are not.

Our last stop will be my basketball court/movement studio. A catered Cuban lunch will await us there, as well as mojitos that I will personally mix. I will tell May-ling that it is her turn to coach me. Though I've studied the steps online, I will play the uncertain, but ultimately brilliant, student.

Murmuring apologies, May-ling stumbles into my studio a half hour late, a sleeping toddler on one shoulder and a gigantic bag hanging off the other. Her hair is up in a messy ponytail, loose pieces everywhere. Whitish curds mottle the shoulder of her red shirt. Sweat rings her armpits.

This is not the date we agreed upon.

She groans when I relieve her of her bag and whispers that she walked all the way here. BeiBei was up all night teething. He is a light sleeper, and getting into a vehicle would have interrupted his much-needed nap.

I cannot help noticing the echo of Husband Two in the child's extraordinarily big head. "You walked here alone?"

"Not alone," she said. "I had my little man."

"Surely your husbands do not allow you out unescorted?" Stories of women abducted and sold on the black market appear all the time in the news. Mao's Mausoleum has become a sanctuary for a number of such disgraced and discarded wives. May-ling's flash of offense makes me back off.

"I need to wash my hands. Would you mind holding him?" She transfers her baby onto my shoulder. "I'll be fast."

The boy starts whimpering that very second and arches off me toward his mother. She croons and kisses his cheek. He wraps his arms around her neck and pulls her breasts into my elbow. I freeze. She tells me it always takes him a minute to wake up.

Shushing her boy, May-ling circles us with her arms, puts her cheeks to his, and rocks. Soon, both their heads are on my shoulder. I'm coaxed into swaying with them. Their warmth melts into me, and this sustained, whole-body consciousness of another is not something I know. I touch my head to May-ling's, BeiBei a ball of heat between us. I place a tentative hand on her back and sway like they are my loving wife and child. May-ling is a whisper of sweet almond, of sweat and soured milk. My neck is sticky with BeiBei's perspiration, but lulled and slightly euphoric, I hold on tight.

May-ling cups BeiBei's head with a hand. "Say hi."

He arches back to regard me and sticks his fingers in my mouth. Kissing him again, she tells BeiBei that MaMa is going to the toilet. Smiling, she peels herself away and waves. "Be right back."

BeiBei's mouth turns down and quivers. His eyes pool. I too feel a measure of loss.

"It's all right," I bounce and tell him again and again. "MaMa will be right ba-a-a-ck."

He is small yet substantial, a ball of nonstop movement and distress. His baby hands bang on my mouth as he howls *ba-ba*. It sounds like he's calling me daddy. I move my head like a New Year's dancing lion to make myself a more difficult target.

Nothing comforts him. He nearly pokes my eye out, and I chomp down on his fingers the next time his hand comes near. I flush when May-ling returns and finds my teeth around her son's hand and him alternately wailing and calling me daddy.

"He likes you." She cuddles her child. "He calls everyone he likes BaBa."

BeiBei mouths his fingers and pouts at me from his motherly perch. When he mumbles *ba-ba* again in between the sucking, May-ling grins at me, delighted.

B ack in my main studio, BeiBei shrieks and covers his ears. His sneakered feet pommel his mother's stomach.

Cooing all the while, May-ling faces him away from her and apologizes to me again. "I think it's the music."

He doesn't like music? It's not even loud.

"I think the beat agitates him."

There goes all my planning. What can I do but be a gentleman and turn off the merengue? I cross my arms and stand a distance away. I thought we had something, a special connection—the hots for each other even. I thought the two of us were in cahoots, securing a date without going through the proper channels. It turns out she's the one who's pulled a fast one on me. May-ling has apologized repeatedly, but not once has she said sorry for bringing BeiBei.

He nearly falls out of her arms lunging for the ground. His squat legs motor toward the stability balls. He crashes into the largest one, knocking it off the rack. The thing is bigger than he is.

"You found a purple ball!" May-ling claps as if he's managed the impossible. She asks if it's all right for him to play with it.

Before I can answer, BeiBei pushes another off its perch. May-ling stops it from rolling away and asks what the balls are for.

"I'll show you." I set one behind me, rest a foot on it, and put my hands on the ground. There is an extremely difficult maneuver—the ball pike—that I planned on executing for her. Toes balanced on the ball, my toned behind up in the air, every muscle taut—it is a dazzling display of strength and agility.

I hear another ball thump to the floor, and May-ling stops watching me in order to corral it. She bounces the thing. "Let's play."

BeiBei is too young to listen. He goes for a kettle bell next. When it refuses to budge, he pulls with two hands and makes as if to sit down. My heart skips a beat as I tumble off my ball and lunge for the sixteen-kilo weight.

BeiBei pushes away my hand and renews his bawling. He tries again to dislodge the kettle bell, and I brace his back so he does not pull the weight on top of himself. On the rack, there are a half a dozen more kettle bells with which he could off himself. I lift and fly him through the air like an airplane. I even make whooshing noises.

May-ling beams at us and spreads her arms to zoom alongside. "Isn't this fun?"

Eyes still wet, BeiBei looks alarmed, but game. It's clear his ancient dads do not do this with him. We careen around the room, and he tries to grab the lat pull-down bar. I allow him to bat it and hop back every time the bar swings at his face.

"You're good with kids," May-ling says.

Good at not allowing them to maim themselves on my turf. I wonder if all this is a test. I wonder too if I like her enough to go through the trouble of passing.

Finally, I say, "Why did you give me the note?"

That good-humored glint is back in her eyes. She cants a shoulder. "I liked you."

BeiBei twists toward the ground, and I ease him down. He approaches a stack of weights, pushes his finger into their pin slots. I kneel next to him, pick up the chained pin, and show him how to slide it in.

I look up at May-ling. "You make up your mind awfully fast."

"I'm a good judge of people."

I arch an eyebrow, not sure whether to be flattered or alarmed.

"Really. I get this feeling, this ticklish happiness in the pit of my stomach. It's excitement and also calm, like everything is the way it's supposed to be. It's like how I feel around my childhood dog. My favorite people all make me feel like this right away."

"I tickle you. Like a dog."

She bugs her eyes out at me. "I'm seldom wrong." She is serious. "There's something between us. Tell me you don't feel it."

I feel lust is what I feel. I pull the pin out of BeiBei's mouth. "What do you see in me?"

She considers my question. "A kindred loneliness. A loyal heart." Her eyes zero in on me. "A brave, but false front."

I frown. "Does your second husband tickle you as well?"

Her smile is tight. "He's really smart. A genius."

Yeah, a clueless genius. "Why'd you marry him?"

She is quiet for a second. "I don't regret it." She strokes the downy swirl atop her son's head.

I pause as well, trying to process her seeming honesty. "And Husband One?"

She tsks good-naturedly at the name. "He's a tickler."
I do not like her answer one bit.

The floor of my studio is littered with elastic bands, foam blocks, Ping-Pong balls, paper cups. Tired of luring BeiBei away from one dangerous situation after another, I sit him on my shoulder and usher May-ling into my movement studio. Maybe the boy can entertain himself with the mirrors.

"What's this?" May-ling approaches the table in the corner crowded end-to-end with beef empanadas, shrimp croquettas, pork cubanos, and rum cake.

"I was hoping that you'd teach me to merengue. Hence the music that we shut off. And this lunch is supposed to complement the Latin dancing." I rest my head ruefully on BeiBei's thigh. She should know what she's missing.

"You did all this for us?"

For you, you dumb egg, I want to say.

She approaches and tugs on BeiBei's foot. "Look. Yummy."

From my outer studio, a man calls out BeiBei's name.

"BaBa is here!" May-ling exclaims to her son. She scampers to the door.

Husband One comes floating in with a tray of meat buns. He hands the food to May-ling, stretches out his arms, and BeiBei kicks off my shoulder, leaping for a hug. That this old goat commands such affection from this child, a child who is most likely not his biologically, makes me see red. That he comes to my gym in yet another impeccable suit irks me further. I am a naked midget next to him.

He notices my spread in the corner. "We think alike." He shakes my hand. "It's good you called. It's best we get to know each other without intermediaries."

So, he's a cheapskate and a sneaky one at that. "Our match-maker is a longtime client of mine." He is no such thing, but I want to see Husband One's reaction. I have no intention of stiffing anyone.

"We like him too." This guy is smooth.

May-ling tells Husband One that I want them to teach me to dance. "He has music, and the Cuban food completes the theme."

Husband One's eyes light up with an enthusiasm uncharacteristic of the man I met at lunch. "We haven't danced in such a long time." Asking me to turn on the music, he hands BeiBei to May-ling and sheds his blazer. How is it possible for a shirt to stay so crisp under a jacket?

"BeiBei hates music," I say.

"No such thing." He glides toward May-ling, a panther on the prowl.

I could have let it go, but I make him take off his shoes.

"Of course," he says. "We mustn't scuff up your floor."

They sandwich BeiBei and begin to shimmy. They look practiced. Sleek. Like they belong together.

Feeling like a dunce, I crank the music, pounding it out louder than my ears can stand. Four fingers in his mouth, BeiBei drools between them, unperturbed. Happy even. They sway, dipping him side to side. Like the matchmaking site says, I might as well not exist.

Husband One spins May-ling out, pauses, and turns to me. "Come. Join us."

"I'm not much of a dancer," I say. That was the line that I rehearsed last night—the line I was going to utter with great humility and then prove wrong—but the words could not be more true. "I should go see if, uh," I stall, unable to recall his name, "your other husband is lost outside."

May-ling tells me he's at work and drags me by both hands to the center of the floor. Still holding on, she smiles into my eyes and shows me how to take side steps, to lead with my rib cage and then hips. Husband One circles us with BeiBei, modeling the move. She tells me I'm doing the merengue and repositions my right hand on her side just below her breast and straightens my left arm. My face is hot, my hands shaky, my armpits gushing. She encourages me to feel the music, to let the orchestra live inside me.

Just as I get the hang of it, Husband One butts in. May-ling wraps an arm around him, BeiBei on his shoulder between them. She drapes her other on me. Husband One does the same. Together, they smile at me.

"Okay. Let's go left first," he says. "Count of ten."

Their steps sweep me sideways. Husband One keeps count and encourages me to hold on to them. There is nowhere to put my hand except around his waist. Lest I be thought uncooperative, or worse—slow—I back up as much as possible and complete the stifling circle. My face is on fire, my limbs granite. I hardly know how to move, where to look.

"Close your eyes," May-ling says.

I could not be more grateful to shut them out.

"Rib cage, then hips," Husband One chants.

I block out his feline grace, loosen my shoulders, and try to feel the music again. I concentrate on my ribs and my hips, the rhythmic step and drag of my feet. I bump into Husband One as our circle changes direction. He steadies me.

"You move like an athlete," he says.

I suspect he's making fun of me, but the corners of his eyes crinkle with warmth.

"I'm so glad you want to dance," he continues. "I've forgotten the joy dancing brings. This togetherness, this intimacy, this common direction, and built-in safety net—all this is very much what I envision for our family."

His rhapsodizing reminds me of the little tidbit I learned last night to impress May-ling: merengue originated in cane fields among slaves who danced, dragging one foot, because they were ankle-chained.

I ask if he likes athletes. "Physical types?"

"Very much so. Athletes know discipline and hard work. They've learned to play fair."

I suspect that a dense workhorse is what he wants.

He pauses and catches my eye this time before leaning and easing me in the opposite direction. I can't deny that I feel welcomed, that he has extended his hand to me time and again. I wonder if my cynicism is the false front May-ling mentioned. I flash to my fathers practicing *qigong* together at dawn, challenging each other to *wéiqí* every night. To their decade of steady companionship since MaMa died.

BeiBei reaches for the floor.

"You want to dance too?" Husband One trills to the little guy and puts him down.

BeiBei runs over and wraps himself around my thigh.

"You like Uncle Wei-guo," Husband One says, both amused and a little taken aback. He offers a hand to his son. "Hold mine too?"

BeiBei tightens his grasp of my leg, and I am touched that our earlier play meant something to the little guy.

I take one of his hands and point to his father. "How about you hold hands with both of us?"

Together, we show him how to step one foot and drag the other. BeiBei wiggles his butt in imitation. He squeals as we count aloud and lean into each other ten times to the right, ten times to the left.

Quickly bored by the subtleties of merengue, BeiBei's short legs churn. He leads the circle, pushing up against his father. Our steps hurry into a shuffle, and soon, we too give up on the dance. May-ling catches my gaze as we gallop faster and faster, round and round. My neck and shoulders loosen. The orchestra drums and pounds inside me. In the mirrors around us, we are a whirl of red, white, and black, of big smiles and open faces. BeiBei's laughter rings and fills my studio, and at a deeper register, I hear myself join in.

2

HANN

May-ling tiptoes to the couch where Hann has settled for the night and nudges his feet with her knees. He thought she was already asleep. She hasn't spoken much to him the last few days, not since she agreed to the matchmaking lunch and then inexplicably threw him out of his own bed. He draws up his knees to make room and touches his feet down on her lap. She allows them to stay. He lowers the volume on the business report.

She yawns. Her eyes stay on the entertainment screen even as she stretches her arms skyward and wedges herself next to him. He scoots to the edge of the couch and makes room once again.

"Coming to bed soon?" she says.

An unexpected stab of jealousy pierces him. "Like our boy toy, do we?" She must have had a better time with Wei-guo, dancing at his studio, than Hann realized. He had thought his problematic little family safe when he offered up Family Advancement during a heated quarrel with May-ling. He did not expect her to take him up on the idea. With her fertility problems and Xiong-xin being Xiong-xin, Hann did not imagine that matters would progress beyond that matchmaking lunch.

May-ling says, "I like you better." She stares long and hard into his eyes.

"I know, sweet pea." He curls up a corner of his lip. "Are you welcoming me back to my own bed?"

She burrows into him. He kisses her forehead and hugs her tight. He lets her lips graze his.

She says, "We can still call it all off if you'll just love me."

"You are my one and only."

She kisses him fervently. He tolerates the slurping, her hungry nibbles. When her lower region begins its forward press, though, he stops responding. He had hoped to discourage her advances by agreeing to go the max. He regards her admiringly, sending all the love he can muster her way.

May-ling's face shuts down as she tosses back the blanket and crab-shuffles gracelessly over him. He looks away from the flash of nipples in the droop of her pullover. *His* pullover. They've had this exchange too many times, but he reminds himself to be patient. To be kind. He is the one in violation of the marital law. He is the one who has duped her. Sexual orientation is not something the young, sheltered brides of today understand, and May-ling is on the verge of truly grasping and accepting his lack of desire for women.

He's relieved when she drags her feet in the direction of his bedroom. Day in and day out, May-ling pads around their apartment barefoot, toes splayed and dirty, the butt of her sloppy sweats sagging to her knees. May-ling's mother, a notorious daughter breeder, used to insist that she and her sisters coat their faces with makeup like slutty foreign actresses. Sometimes Hann regrets convincing

May-ling that she is naturally beautiful, that the extraordinarily big-hearted woman he has come to love requires little such enhancement.

"You know you mustn't dress like that around a new husband." Ragging on her does little good, but Hann tries to lighten the mood.

"What do you care?"

"You're right." Praying that her invitation to bed is still good, he pushes to his feet, his back twinging. "It's not possible for me to care."

She stares at him, dead-eyed. He asks if Wei-guo is a possibility.

"I just can't understand why you won't consider a unit dissolution."

He sighs. These days, May-ling jumps from Family Advancement to dissolution in the same breath.

He says, "I can live with Lee Wei-guo. Or, if you don't like him, someone else. We'll find us a trustworthy man. One that meets your high standards. He exists."

"You know that I'll give you full access to BeiBei if you accept the truth and do what's right."

"I'm living my truth." Hann enunciates each word, his eyes flashing. "Tell me, what's more true and right than a father and husband, being here day in and day out doing everything he can for his child and family?" Despite his bluster, he is deeply aware that he has never been a true husband to her. He cannot shove aside the knowledge that in marrying her, he and his emotionally defective brother have wronged her in a most fundamental way.

Even as he thinks this, Hann questions his own sanity. No man in his right mind would risk so much to bring harmony to his household. To eradicate counterrevolutionary thought and challenges from its excess of dissatisfied men, their government has lumped homosexuality with mental illness and genetic diseases and classified everything heritable. It requires same-sex lovers to register their sexual orientation and undergo vasectomies. It is criminal for them to marry, reproduce, or raise children.

He regrets goading May-ling into matchmaking. Looking for a new spouse only increases the possibility that Hann's marriage could be exposed and forcibly dissolved, his paternity wiped from all records, his child and family taken from him. And that doesn't even begin to address his reeducation, the fines, the dire consequences.

May-ling says, "The truth is that you insist on being Willfully Sterile."

"I am not sterile, and there is nothing willful about the way I was born." He feels both disappointment and an overwhelming rage. "You know this is not a choice. And why would I opt to be subhuman? For the privilege of sneaking around just so that I could raise my own child?" How could she, after six years with him, still think this way? "And how sadistic is our government, believing the trait hereditary, yet calling us willful?"

There is not a trace of regret in her eyes. "We could divorce Xiong-xin and Advance with Wei-guo and Hero. I'm willing to do that for you."

"Don't be crazy." Where does she get this idea that he wants to marry Hero?

"We'd be upholding the family unit and reforming the misguided. We'd all be heroes."

He shakes his head at her. She thinks he's paranoid. People her age believe that the average citizen is sympathetic and accepting of same-sex lovers, that excessive regulations make rule breakers of everyone and band people together.

He knows that couldn't be further from the truth.

"You'll feel more fulfilled with Hero, and you know it."

"I can't stand that buffoon."

Hann wonders if she made him hire Hero in order to play matchmaker herself. Hero matched May-ling to Hann and his brother and is probably the most successful Willfully Sterile man she knows. But Hann doesn't want Hero—doesn't *need* Hero. She has no idea, would in fact be devastated to learn, that Hann's badminton team, a group of a dozen discreet married professionals who've pledged to limit their dangerous activity to one another, serves as his sexual outlet.

Hann says, "You forget that I spent most of my adult life 'being fulfilled.' I'd rather have a family."

"I won't think less of you for being drawn to him."

"I don't want him."

He was not loud enough to wake BeiBei, but May-ling glances pointedly in the direction of the bedrooms. There's a sliver of light beneath Xiong-xin's door, but they both know he cannot hear anything over the din of his virtual games. After MaMa, their last surviving parent, had passed away, they moved Xiong-xin and his multimedia consoles into her bedroom. Two years without pregnancy news and the four of them sardined into a small apartment had taken its toll. May-ling could not put up with another evening of virtual gunfire and explosions, and to tell the truth, neither could Hann. Without his MaMa to enforce sleeping arrangements, May-ling camped permanently in Hann's bed. It is up to him now to make her spend one night a week with Xiong-xin.

It was also after their mother died that Xiong-xin told them he was heretofore to be called Double X. He said "XX" were his English initials. The new moniker made Hann think of James Bond, 007. Hann supposed there was no real harm with Xiong-xin reinventing himself as a suave super spy while he calibrated a new equilibrium, especially since their mother's death demanded difficult, daily adjustments from his routine-obsessed brother. The new persona was all in Xiong-xin's head anyway.

"Your brother couldn't care less if he's married to me."

"Your *husband*," Hann corrects her, "may not show it well, but you know he loves you. It would kill him to lose our family." He hates it when she underestimates Xiong-xin, when she thinks she can tell Hann how his brother thinks or feels.

"It makes no difference to him if it's me who 'helpmates' him or someone else."

"Please stop."

She grabs both his wrists and pushes her face in front of his. "Dissolve our unit, or divorce Xiong-xin and bring on a spouse for each of us. Those are your choices."

He shakes her off. "We're not going to dissolve anything. Or divorce anyone. You haven't the funds for it." From time to time, Hann has to remind May-ling that divorcing Xiong-xin would be cost prohibitive. She has not produced a child for him and is in violation of their marital contract. It's not much of a threat—Hann's sexual orientation is a worse offense—but it is a cruel jab at her fertility struggles.

She mutters all the way to their bedroom.

Upside down in their bed, his feet atop the pillows, BeiBei has been doing gymnastics again in his sleep. May-ling moves the three guardrail chairs.

"Let me," Hann says.

His back stabs as he scoops their boy up and shuffles a half circle on his knees. He settles between BeiBei and the wall, giving May-ling the preferred outside spot on the bed. Hann curls himself around BeiBei, sinking into his baby-sweet warmth. All is right with the world if he can just hold on to their child, to the life they've built around him.

May-ling lowers her sweat bottoms and panties and tugs Hann's top over her head. Hann closes his eyes and pretends not to notice. It is going to be a long night. He keeps still, breathes evenly, and tries his best to bring on sleep. She climbs over BeiBei and squeezes between Hann and the wall. Sliding his undershirt up, she presses her breasts against his back and hugs him and BeiBei, completing their circle. She exudes a soft, not unpleasant animal warmth. If this were enough for her, Hann could die happy cocooned in their little nest.

She whispers, "Why did you say at the lunch that we'd go the max again?"

"I was just testing them," he says, relieved she wants to chat. "China First, my ass." He relishes the way she combs her fingers through his hair. He cannot resist pointing out that no man is easy to live with. "You won't regret having me around as a buffer."

She buries her face in his neck. "I'm afraid to have Xiong-xin's baby. What if we end up with a Lost Boy?"

"Xiong-xin's not Lost," Hann says in a hiss, "and being Lost is not heritable." He too worries about this and feels like a fraud trying to shut her down. Their government reserves the right to neuter and, if necessary, institutionalize Lost Boys, the growing 2 percent of the country's male population with severely violent or antisocial behavior. Their parents had paid plenty to make certain that Xiong-xin was not stuck with any labels, and Hann is not about to undo their considerable efforts.

"You don't really believe that," she says.

"Please stop." Xiong-xin may be difficult, but he is highly productive and skilled at his chosen profession and self-supporting. How can Hann deny him the right to reproduce when Xiong-xin has endangered himself by sheltering Hann within their family and allowing him to have a child?

May-ling sighs and tightens her arms around Hann. Images of Xiong-xin frantically plugging his ears against loud noises, Xiong-xin standing arms crossed insisting on getting his way, Xiong-xin rocking himself to ward off a misbehaving BeiBei parade across

Hann's consciousness. He too lets go a sigh. It evolves into a loud and weary yawn.

"I think Xiong-xin may be sterile," May-ling says. "I can't get pregnant with him."

It took May-ling five years to have BeiBei with Hann, and he is pretty certain the problem lies with her. He says, "It's impossible to get pregnant when you two hardly ever have sex."

She pries his arm off BeiBei, climbs over him spiderlike, and wedges her head into his shoulder. "Go get your fertility switched back on. Have another baby with me." The State inserted birth control implants into his arm after BeiBei's birth.

Hann turns away—how could she demand that he risk breaking more laws—and she whispers into his ear, "You and Xiong-xin share a mother. Your baby will be like his baby. Wouldn't it be wonderful to have another baby, you and me?" Her arms around him feel like a stranglehold. He imagines instead a newborn, the miraculous heft of a tiny body, its helplessness and its power to seduce, its all-engrossing scent.

"Don't you love me?"

"I do," he says.

"The way Xiong-xin acts around BeiBei. It's obvious he doesn't want to have a baby."

"Stop," Hann says, but he cannot disagree. As awkward as it is for Xiong-xin to interact with adults, he is many times worse with BeiBei. It would not be an exaggeration to say that the baby both irritates and scares him.

May-ling says, "I don't want to complicate our family further. Or endanger it in the process." Hann couldn't agree more. She holds his face between her hands. "Say you'll do what's right for all of us. Please?"

Hann doesn't answer. She gives him a quick kiss as if to seal the deal. She tugs down his boxers and straddles him. It's clear she will not give up tonight without a fight, so he grits his teeth, and he looks away from her swinging tits, her dark, hungry bush. It's been nearly three weeks since he's had sex, and the urge is there. He lets her grind. She shimmies before him, her eyes pleading, but he can't coax himself to touch her breasts, her advancing nipples. After a while, she lowers her weight onto him and clutches him tight. He lets her guide him inside. She is damp and sticky, the heat she generates smothering. Hann feels boxed in, claustrophobic, and it's all he can do to catch his breath, to not lose his erection, to not fight his way out of her grip and be free.

He squeezes his eyes shut. Wei-guo with his floppy, pop-star hair and his self-indulgent body-builder physique materializes. Hann was prepared to dismiss this inconsequential PE coach. But there was something quite endearing in the way he nudged his hair aside with the back of his hand, in the exposed earnestness in his eyes when he zeroed in on BeiBei and on Hann too, and acceded to their demands.

May-ling moans, her shoulder cutting into Hann's throat. He pushes her an arm's length away, his hands braced against her breasts. Remembering the man's damn puppyish eagerness to please, his sumptuous spread of Cuban delights, the heat of their merengue, Hann begins to move to the rhythm of Wei-guo's slim, snapping hips. Could he be the one for May-ling and their family? He has passed their first test: willing to bypass his parents and ignore the formalities of organized courtship, he has the makings of a rule-breaker.

Could Wei-guo keep their secrets safe?

Hann leaps out of the auto-drive cab, late again for his weekly lunch with Xiong-xin. He hates paying a premium for private transport, but there was no extricating himself from his accounting firm's partnership meeting and the mandate to make certain that their client, the State-owned ChinaCoal, saves face. A dying business in a dying industry, ChinaCoal has been absorbing other insolvent, State-run concerns for the last nine quarters and reporting positive earnings through negative goodwill. Chang, their firm's Party representative, rebuffed every one of Hann and a fellow partner's attempts to place limits on this illusory gain. At noon—Hann's appointed hour with his brother—the discussions were still going nowhere. He finally claimed a client lunch and excused himself.

In the small, crowded restaurant, Xiong-xin is the only customer without a companion. Hann hurries to him and apologizes again and again. He is more than twenty minutes late. Xiong-xin makes the tiniest wave with two fingers and keeps waving until a waiter notices and approaches. He asks the waiter to serve the food and tells Hann that he has already ordered beggar's chicken and hand-pulled noodles with XO sauce.

"Good," Hann says. Xiong-xin likes to eat. To induce him to attend these lunches, Hann lets him pick both the restaurant and the dishes. "No greens?"

Xiong-xin's eyes dart as if Hann has caught him red-handed. "Sorry."

"No need to be sorry." Hann finds his brother's timidity both heartbreaking and worrisome. "Tell me. What did you think of our matchmaking lunch?"

"I like what you said about sharing our country's wealth and pain," Xiong-xin replies. "It's good that we are doing that."

Hann stops himself mid-sigh. If nothing else, his literal-minded brother's heart is always in the right place. There is not a selfish or mean bone in him. "Remember what I told you about conversations?"

The waitress arrives with a tray of small appetizers, and Hann knows better than to continue. Xiong-xin chooses the seaweed and five-spiced tofu before he remembers to ask what Hann prefers. Hann picks the pickled radish. Xiong-xin must eat more vegetables. Xiong-xin dives into the tofu. It pains Hann how heavy Xiong-xin has become, how the bigger and bigger-sized pants they buy fail to faze him. They have important matters to discuss, and Hann suppresses his urge to remind Xiong-xin to chew thoroughly for better digestion, to savor the flavor of each bite so as to eat less.

When he finally looks up from his plate, Hann says, "There are two levels to every conversation."

"I know," he says good-naturedly. "There's what's said and what's not said."

"Exactly. Wanting what's best for our country was what I said to the Lee family. What I did not say, and this does not make it a lie," Hann points out, anticipating the accusation, "if certain things are understood or cannot be politely told, it can be left unsaid. And what I did not say was that May-ling is unhappy and wants a third, and hopefully, better husband."

Xiong-xin's eyes blink in succession. "She's not happy?"

"With me, mostly." Hann decides to spare him. "She wants a husband in every sense of the word, and I can never be that."

"She doesn't like me either." Xiong-xin peers up at Hann for confirmation.

"That's not true," Hann says. "And to be clear, this does not affect your bedroom time each week." Xiong-xin fidgets in his chair, and Hann asks what he thinks of Lee Wei-guo.

"He's a cool guy," Xiong-xin says. "We have a lot in common. I think we can be friends."

It's fortunate that Xiong-xin thinks well of most people Hann endorses. "Maybe you can work out with him." Xiong-xin visits a trainer weekly at Hann's insistence, but the man can't seem to get Xiong-xin to break a sweat, let alone lose weight. "May-ling and I had to know if he's good with children. We introduced BeiBei to him."

"Does he like the baby?"

"I think so."

Xiong-xin's face droops in disappointment, and Hann is pained that his brother's own ineptitude with BeiBei troubles him more than the fact that Hann did not include him on that date.

Hann says, "I have a plan to win back some of May-ling's affection."

Their waiter nudges aside teacups and slides the beggar's chicken onto the table. Xiong-xin stops him from pulling aside the lotus leaves. Xiong-xin relishes the chance to cut through the shell of baked mud and dissect the bird. Hann sighs. A dish like this has the potential of holding up the discussion for a good five minutes. He waits for Xiong-xin to expose the chicken.

"Ready to hear my plan?"

Xiong-xin draws the knife in sure, precise strokes down the breastbone. Hann repeats the question. It takes Xiong-xin another two seconds to hear him and grunt.

"Women like to hear about their men's achievements." Hann decides to clarify. "Real-world achievements. Not virtual ones." Xiong-xin is so intent on his carving that Hann nudges his foot. "The other day at lunch, you went on a bit too long about *Metagalactic Domination*."

He jerks up seconds later, alarmed. "I'm sorry. I didn't mean to."

"It's all right." How could Hann be mad when Xiong-xin apologizes so readily? "But what that means is, because you talk mostly about your games, May-ling never hears about your job. How can she be proud of you if she has no idea of its importance?"

Xiong-xin stops his knife work. "She doesn't know about my job?"

"No," Hann says emphatically. "How can she brag about you

if you don't explain the many ways your software safeguards our country and our largest corporations?" Xiong-xin beams, and Hann lets him bask in the moment. "This is what we're going to do. You will message me every day at four with the day's highlight. If it's substantive enough, we will craft something together to wow May-ling at dinner. And we'll keep it short. Three or four sentences."

"I know, I know," Xiong-xin says. "I should look for cues and not dominate the conversation." He whacks the chicken's thigh joint.

Sensing that Xiong-xin's patience is near its limit, Hann moves on to part two of his two-prong attack. "I think it would be great if you also bring May-ling a little present every few days."

"A present!" Xiong-xin sounds put out.

"Something simple," Hann says. "A chrysanthemum, a sweet bun, a toy for the baby. Something to show you care and are thinking of her. I'll help you."

"But there aren't any stores near my office."

"Don't worry. I'll help you," Hann says. "Now, tell me about your bedroom time last night."

He blinks. "It was fine."

"C'mon."

"Well." He stares at his hands. "May-ling had a headache because BeiBei was teething."

"That's not right," Hann tells him. "By contract, she has to have sex with you once a week. You must tell me when she doesn't."

Xiong-xin flushes red. He does not know where to look. "It's okay. I don't mind."

"Have you tried my tip? Did you ask what makes her feel good?"

"She said she likes it quick and fast."

Hann closes his eyes and rubs his face. "You're going to give her a massage next time. She's always angling for massages. Start with her feet. You know how to give one?" Xiong-xin looks horrified.

"Massages always put her in a generous mood. And then you can ask how best to please her." Short of an entirely new personality, there's probably no winning for Xiong-xin in the bedroom. May-ling would love it if he never touched her again, but that would not be right. Someone has to fight for him.

Xiong-xin reassembles the chicken—without bones—on an empty plate. There is a perfectionist streak in him that often feels pointless to Hann. He lets Xiong-xin eat in peace.

After some minutes, Xiong-xin notices that he's the only one eating. He puts a drumstick on Hann's plate. "How're you going to make May-ling like you again?"

Hann starts. Fair is fair. He doesn't say that she likes him fine. It's just that there's no fixing him. "What do you think I should do?"

Xiong-xin chews for so long Hann thinks he's forgotten the question. "She's always telling me how tired she is. Maybe we should hire a houseboy."

"What for?" Hann says. "You and I clean our own rooms. She just has the living room, kitchen, and bathroom, and all day to look after that."

"Oh." Xiong-xin takes another bite of chicken and chews. "What about a bigger household allowance?"

"She spends too much as it is."

Xiong-xin scrunches his nose. Hann regrets soliciting his opinion.

"How about a dog? May-ling loves dogs. She is always saying how her chow chow was her best friend growing up."

"For the umpteenth time, we barely have room for all the people in our apartment, let alone for a dog." Hann shakes his head, feeling both used and amused that Xiong-xin has managed to slip something from his own agenda into his suggestions.

Hann's watch vibrates. Hero writes: **Come after work?** The heat behind his words feels like a glimpse of sky, a lifeline to pull him from his drab days. It also feels like an anchor around his neck.

He has told Hero in no uncertain terms that they will not have sex again, but Hero seems to find resistance a challenge and a turn-on. Hann ought to bring May-ling and Xiong-xin along for an update. Hann drafts a message to them, returns to it again and again throughout the course of the afternoon to modify the arrangements. Even though he has resolved never to expose himself, his family, and potentially his badminton team again to this foolishness that is Hero, Hann knows deep down that he will not ask May-ling and Xiong-xin to the meeting. He does not want them there.

At seven, only the escrow man is left in Hero's front office, his headset askew and feet on desk, bickering over accumulated interest with some client. Hann mouths the word "*Boss?*" and the man waves him toward Hero's office.

Hann's shoes click across the marble floor. Carved mahogany shelves jammed with a dizzying display of colorful scrapbooks surround the room. Every potential groom is allowed one such book of baby and graduation photos, résumé, handwritten self-introductions, news articles, report cards, diplomas, and whatever else that best showcase his achievements and personality. Part of Hero's bullshit is that his is an old-fashioned calling where old-fashioned approaches work best. He differentiates himself by going retro, saving man-hours by not digitalizing anything. He claims that these scrapbooks are the next best thing to meeting the actual man, that women like to handle personal artifacts and study penmanship. It's surprising how many people eat this up. On any given day, potential brides and their families crowd his long library tables and spread out books to study their options. Because there is no other way to access his candidates except to park oneself inside his shop for half a day at a time, the place always looks busy and prosperous.

Hero's office door is ajar, his lights dimmed. Something jazzy and playful toots. Hann stands behind the door and watches him pour an amber liquid, Scotch most likely, into finely cut crystal. Hero brings the glass to his nose and savors the aroma before tipping it down in one gulp. Hann hopes he is hammered.

Hero shakes back his hair, twists his hips, and spreads his arms across the windowsill as if to embrace his personal panorama of city lights. The man is forever striking poses. Stuffed into a flaring, lavender coat, his considerable gut hangs over breeches and thigh-high boots. A parrot on his shoulder would complete the pirate-captain look. Hann feels an urge to grab Hero by his mop and chop it off, to yank the baubles from his fingers, to rip his embroidered costume to shreds, so agitated is he with the man's unfortunate taste, his insistence on furthering the most damaging same-sex-lover stereotypes. Hann would like to stake down every fluttery bit of Hero. It's ludicrous that such a queen (the child of a Japanese mother) should change the *i* in Hiro to an *e*, and the fact that he dares do this irks Hann like a splinter in his toe.

And yet, Hann can't seem to stay away. He clears his throat.

Hero slowly looks over a shoulder, lifts it, and leers. "Hey, handsome," he says, his voice gravel and smoke. He turns as if he were a slinky runway model. His shirt and silver waistcoat are unbuttoned to the bulging shelf of his stomach, the thatch of gray over his sternum exposed. The indecency of him grates at Hann. He wants to punch Hero in the gut. He wants to run his fingers through his chest hair and get stuck in its tangles.

"How about a drink?"

Hann grunts, closes the door behind him, and joins Hero in front of the window.

"Let's sit down." One could set fire to his breath.

Hann doesn't move. Ice clinks into a glass. Hero knows how Hann likes his Scotch.

"How was the date?"

Hann's sip lights up his throat. "I thought *you* were providing the updates."

Hero's narrowed eyes glint at Hann. "Your boy doesn't mind unassigned nights."

"He said that?"

"He's a cocky one," Hero says. "He thinks he can bed May-ling without the help of a schedule."

"So much for your foolproof personality matching."

Hero claimed to have done Hann a major favor, giving his family free testing and then allocating an employee's entire day to finding them optimal candidates. The fact that other matchmakers accomplish this same feat with a computer didn't seem to faze him.

Hero puts a hand on his jutted hip. "Don't forget that I had to work with Miss Stomach Tickle and the privacy Nazi." Their candidate pool shrank to unworkable after May-ling applied her sixth sense and Xiong-xin eliminated the men with body chips and indiscreet online footprints.

Hann ignores the dig and asks if Hero has dug up Hann's marital contract.

"May-ling's parents are entitled to twenty-five percent of the third-round dowry."

Hann curses. When he married, two spouses had been the max, the standard for two decades. The government allowing a third spouse did not seem like a remote possibility, let alone May-ling agreeing to it.

"I can try to negotiate for you."

Hann sneers at the absurdity of that. May-ling's parents are gambling addicts who lived off the fruits of their loins and their mahjongg winnings. While everyone was obsessed with producing a male heir to pass on the family name, they placed their bet on girls. Her parents must have paid staggering fines for defying their one-child limit. May-ling avoids the subject, but no one could have had six daughters in eight years without abortions, illegal sex selection drugs, or semen spinning. Rumor had it that the engagement of the four eldest (all by the age of three) helped finance their household. They had no need of a second husband and his income. The last two girls were allowed to come of age and auctioned off. A double contract to brothers, May-ling's engagement set records. Hann and Xiong-xin supported the household after that, the parents' life savings all but depleted.

Hero says, "I still think your dowry is too low."

Hann reminds him that they are asking for unprecedented discretion. "There's a price for that kind of silence."

Hero shakes a finger. "Not when king of the roost is the position you're giving away."

Hann hardens his expression to discourage further discussion. It's not Hero's hide that's at risk if Hann is exposed. Hero's not the one who'll be reeducated, his child branded a bastard, his family taken from him.

Hero cants a shoulder and bats his lashes. He asks how May-ling likes Wei-guo.

"I don't sense much upstairs with him."

"The easier to live with, no?" Hero reminds Hann that Wei-guo scored off the charts on agreeability.

"We're not going any further without genetic panels and intelligence scores."

Hero raises an eyebrow. "We can stipulate in-clinic fertilization. I know someone who can mix you a perfect little sperm cocktail."

"We're not out to cheat anybody."

Hero studies him, and his eyes soften. "Ahhhhh. I understand."

He places a hand over Hann's. "You have my word that I will find you a candidate with flawless genes, that you will not be burdened by a problem child."

Hann extracts his hand. "Don't get ahead of yourself. This match could be another of May-ling's ploys to turn me straight." Few things make him feel smaller than Hero's compassion. And few things irritate him more than assumptions about his feelings toward his brother.

"Oh, the poor, deluded little bitch," Hero says with a self-satisfied smirk.

Hann wraps a fistful of unruly hair around his hand and pulls. "Don't call her a bitch."

"Kiss me, and I'll call the bitch anything you want."

Hann yanks him so that they're eye to eye. Hero only wants to fuck, a straightforward transaction. He doesn't want to make trouble for Hann; he has no reason to. Hann breathes in the man's Scotch-laced breath—the badminton group be damned—lets the fumes dull his reservations, and bites into Hero's lip.

3

MAY-LING

XX is over half an hour overdue, and I am worried. He is only ever late when he is kept after work for a talking-to. The last time this happened, he spent the evening replaying the scene while raking welts into his arms and legs. Hann had to call his boss. The two of us spent a long night trying to reassure XX that he would not be fired if he took his manager's directives to heart.

I've been steering BeiBei from one quiet game to another so that he would not overwhelm XX the second he returns. I did not grow up in a nurturing household. Now that Hann has given me a taste of that, I want to create that feeling for my son. For all of us. I crave it like food and water.

Just as BeiBei upends a tub, sending blocks crashing and skipping in all directions, XX walks in the door. His shoulders jump to his ears and stay there.

"I'm sorry, I'm sorry," I say. "Is everything all right? Where have you been?"

A clumsy smile creeps over his face. His cheeks redden by the second as he crab-walks toward his room. He is hiding something large behind his back, a present of some sort. If I weren't so afraid of Hann's bedroom ideas and his endless stream of intimacy-enhancing gifts for XX and me, XX's efforts could almost be endearing. I appreciate that he keeps trying, but we'd both be better off with quickies. I tell myself that I am lucky: XX always tries to be nice to me. He hasn't the backbone to force me into anything in the bedroom. But all I feel are the holes in my heart. He is like a hapless brother to me, and who wants to lie around naked with her brother pointing out her erogenous zones?

BeiBei also notices the awkward walk. No doubt remembering the Super Ball and wind-up flipping monkey XX brought him recently, he charges at the package. I suspect Hann is trying to remake his brother into gift-bearing daddy to increase his appeal. I rush after BeiBei.

"No," XX says too sharply, and pushes away the insistent little hands. "It's not for you." He breaks away in an awkward waddle toward his room.

BeiBei's interest is now doubly piqued. He runs after XX and hangs on to his sweater with both hands. "Give me."

"Precious," I cry, wrapping my arms around his middle, "you're going to rip BaBa's clothes. How about we have some dried dragon eyes?" I keep a selection of treats for just such occasions.

XX makes it to his room and slams the door. It wouldn't be far from the truth to say that he's afraid of the baby.

"Mine," BeiBei howls. His arms claw at the air while his feet hammer my stomach.

I struggle to a couch. It takes all my strength to turn him around on my lap and keep him from flinging himself at XX's door. XX never means to provoke him, yet something invariably goes awry when they are together. I shake a tambourine to distract BeiBei. He bats it, clanging it across the floor.

BeiBei is required to attend Citizen Calisthenics twice a week at our neighborhood women and children's park. I take him every day to all the gymnastics, playground, and track time for two-year-old boys, and still he is feisty as ever. I can't help but feel that I'm getting my just rewards.

I was sixteen and naïve when I married Hann. Pregnancy was impossible, given what I thought were his patience and gentlemanly considerations in the bedroom. I was touched and grateful that he didn't hold me to our marital contract. Early each evening, we closed the door on his mother, holed up in our bedroom, and talked. He didn't have the no-nonsense, authoritative disposition of an important business executive. He was curious about my upbringing, about how my parents were able to produce and then manage six daughters, about my relationship with each of them. He shared stories about his own family and helped me keep his nosy mother at bay.

It was immediately apparent how supportive and caring he was toward XX. And how contentious, unkind, and self-serving my interactions were with my sisters. My dislike of XX, my impulse to hide my family, filled me with shame.

By the time we had sex seven months into our marriage, I was in love and hungry for him. My tummy ached with longing and tickled with bliss. I lived for Hann's touch. Lying next to him, skin to skin, was heaven. I wanted him to do things to me. I felt so close to him.

But sex was a once-a-month affair on the twelfth day of my cycle.

My older sisters complained endlessly about their abundant bedroom "chores" during their annual visits home on Married

Daughters' Day. When I asked Hann if he needed more, he told me that once a month was all old guys like him could muster. We spooned and snuggled. I tried to touch and excite him, but he inevitably stopped my hands and brought them to his lips, his kisses loving and apologetic. He said that we must save his meager strength for baby-making. My ache for him embarrassed me.

When Hann finally confided that he was what the government termed "Willfully Sterile," but that we would have a child, I didn't fully understand that our physical closeness had just one purpose, that he would want nothing to do with my body once I had conceived BeiBei. At first I had suspected he didn't want me because he was with other men, but Hann promised me that he was done with same-sex lovers. He told me his heart was mine, and I *knew* that was true. He was the perfect husband outside the bedroom. So I believed him. What choice did I have?

By the time I married XX a year after I married Hann, I was intimately familiar with his strangeness and his outbursts. Though not classified a Lost Boy, I was certain he was one. But there was no way out of that marriage. There was zero chance of my parents returning the dowry. Or of Hann forgiving such a betrayal.

It didn't dawn on me at the time that he was playing his own game of betrayal.

My mother-in-law made sure that I alternated bedrooms each night and that XX and I had relations at least once a week. Between a Willfully Sterile man and a Lost Boy, I knew enough to be afraid of what I might give birth to. I mustered up the courage to ask XX for money and keep quiet about it. I strong-armed him into accompanying me to the doctor (it thrilled his mother to see us connect over a bedroom issue) and stay in the waiting room while I secretly had my fertility switched off.

After my mother-in-law died, Hann in his grief became convinced that I needed an infertility specialist. I decided that I was only willing to chance it with one child and that I'd rather have Hann's. I got more money out of XX for pH-lowering injections and pills that ensured baby boys. For under-the-table income, some doctors offered these illegal treatments. A girl would have most likely suited our family better, but I knew Hann would only be appeased after I had a son to pass on his name.

And what a son we have.

BeiBei will not stop screeching. I can barely hold on to him. My shins are black and blue from his flailing legs, and it takes everything I have not to shake him. To throw him to the floor. I hate that he reduces me so often to my worst self. I flip through XX's *Gamasutra*, but the buxom manga amazons fail to soothe BeiBei. I feel around in the crevices of the couch and find the Super Ball. I wave it in front of him before tossing it. The ball boings away unnoticed.

Still crying, BeiBei arches and lunges in my arms as I stand up. I nearly drop him. I set him on the rug and leave him writhing—I hate to do this, but it's the safest option—and run for a snack, talking soothingly at him all the while. I fumble in the kitchen for something enticing enough to stop the tantrum.

Hann chooses that moment to step through the door. "What's the matter?" his voice booms. "Where's MaMa?"

"Everything is fine," I yell. I do my utmost to create a warm and inviting haven for my family, yet Hann inevitably stumbles into trouble first thing upon coming home. "I'm just getting BeiBei a little snack for not pulling at his Little BaBa's clothes." I notice that BeiBei is no longer howling.

Back in the living room, he clings to Hann sniffling, oh-so-wronged, his head glued to his BaBa's shoulder, and I am momentarily rankled by how our child loves him best of all. Of course, I love Hann best too. He rubs our boy's back and plants smacking kisses on his cheek. The sight of Hann's regal carriage and his handsome, silvery air never fails to make my heart race, yet it is the unrelenting beam in his kind eyes that I fall for again and again. Fear that he will die one day and leave me alone with XX and BeiBei seizes me.

"We're just fine now," Hann says, an ever soothing presence. The baby hiccups.

"You walked in the door right after I put him on the rug," I say. "He was fighting so hard I nearly dropped him."

"I know," Hann singsongs his reply, and sways. "BeiBei has the best MaMa in the whole wide world."

His compliment is sincere, yet I feel like an undeserving fraud. I give BeiBei and Hann pecks on the cheeks and tell them I'm going to start dinner.

XX peeks out his door, sheepish. "I'm sorry."

I say, "He's all done crying. You don't have to hide anymore."

He gauges his brother's reaction before staring at the floor. "I tried to tell BeiBei that it wasn't for him, but he wouldn't listen."

"Who is it for, then?" Hann says with too much enthusiasm. "Come. Tell us."

XX stays out of BeiBei's sightline and whispers, "Shouldn't I wait until after dinner?"

I brace myself for another bedroom surprise.

"Don't know about anyone else, but I can never wait to open my presents," Hann replies, still in singsong mode.

XX crosses his arms. His eyes go vacant as he wrestles with the change in plans. He likes everything just-so. Finally, he says he has a gift for me.

"How nice." I must be ovulating soon. It's sad Hann knows my cycle better than I do. He's always trying to maximize XX's appeal during my fertile window.

XX says, "I picked it out all by myself."

"Yes, you did," his brother says.

Looking tremendously pleased, XX trots back with his gift. "It wasn't wrapped when I came home," he explains. "BeiBei was trying to ruin the surprise." Corners square, the plaid pattern matched up, and tape squarely applied across every seam—his wrapping job is, as always, perfect.

BeiBei reaches for the package. XX is again stumped when Hann asks if the baby can open the present. We all sit down, BeiBei on the couch next to Hann. We watch BeiBei drum on the gift.

"Mine," he says, face gleaming. He turns the package again and again.

"Yes, it's yours," Hann replies.

The two of them banter like that, back and forth, and all is right again with the world. These moments seem so easy, and yet so hard to come by. I put my feet up and my head on Hann's shoulder, relishing the momentary peace.

Seated across from me, XX stares at the present, blinking. I tell him it's okay. I like BeiBei playing with it.

"Isn't he going to open it?"

Hann encourages XX to show him how. It is not easy for XX to lower his girth to the floor, and I feel for him when his hand is instantly repelled. BeiBei begins to cry "mine" all over again.

"Let's open the present," Hann says. "Little BaBa is going to help you." He tells XX to expose the gift with a little tear.

BeiBei stops crying when he discovers new colors beneath the paper. Still on his knees, XX tears a little more, and BeiBei is clued in to the fun. The two alternate: XX starts the rips, and BeiBei shreds. Strips of blue and gold flutter over the couch and onto the floor, and I am able to breathe again. Hann puts an arm around me and kisses my forehead. Finally, everyone is content. We too have our own particular brand of familial bliss. I should go start dinner, but I cannot pull myself away.

Our little moment fills me again with uncertainty about pushing Hann into going the max. If only he would love me from time to time, meet me even part of the way, this could be enough for me. I am asking so little of him that he makes me angry all over again.

When the present is exposed, XX asks if I like it. *The Pursuit of Happiness* is printed across the box. If only I had the luxury of such selfish, Western preoccupations.

"Sure," I say.

"It's a virtual game."

"Oh." I despise virtual games. The controls confound me. I don't see the point. Why would I want to immerse myself in a perplexing and violent world?

"I can teach you how to play."

"Great."

"*GuhGuh* says that," he glances at his brother and receives a re-assuring nod, "you want a new husband because you're not happy. This game is developed by therapists to help people figure out what makes them happy. And then it'll show you what sort of husband to look for."

"That's really nice of you," I say.

He nods in agreement. The huge smile on his face pains me. It's hard to say no to someone so cluelessly selfless.

"Why don't you two go play right now?" Hann says.

"It's okay." I stand to go to the kitchen. "I can wait."

"No, no." Hann rises to stop me and says that he is cooking dinner tonight. The baby reaches for him, and Hann picks him up.

I remind him that he hates frozen dumplings. Hann can't do much more than boil water in the kitchen.

"No such thing," he says. "We love dumplings, don't we? Yes, we do!" He waltzes away with BeiBei.

XX stares at me. "Don't worry. It's really easy. Even you can play this game."

"Even me," I say. XX considers me a technoboob and treats me accordingly.

Packed with computers and three giant screens, there is little room to maneuver around XX's bed. The air is stiflingly warm. I sink into his desk chair. Molded to his heft, it smells like it's been through one too many virtual battles. XX leans over me to clack at his control panel, adding to my claustrophobia. What I can only describe as barnyard stink wafts from him. If I didn't know better, I'd say that he rolls himself in an animal pen at work. I pick up his spider-shaped controller and back away on casters. Buttons and knobs blink and buzz in my hands. I feel a headache coming on.

XX meticulously peels the sealing tape from the game box and, as if handling a newborn babe, delivers from it a contraption resembling a motorcycle helmet. There are already four sitting on various shelves in his room. Not eager to hear the excruciating details of why this particular device is necessary, I stifle the impulse to question the new headgear. He presses buttons on its side. The thing starts to hum.

He tells me to stand in front of his biggest screen. "This new invention is a mind reader. An emotion thermometer."

"I don't want my mind read."

XX freezes and blinks. "We can't play then." Shoulders slumped, he stares down, crestfallen and pathetic.

"Oh, all right." I sigh. He immediately perks back up. I let him lower the thing onto my head. He takes the spider controls from me.

For all its bulk, the helmet is surprisingly light. Still, I can't see out, and it's suffocating inside. The facial shield lights up. An emerald ocean ripples before me. "What do I do? Tell me what to do."

"Relax. Don't get all wound up." He says the computer is mapping my face and calculating my emotional baseline.

"Why is it mapping my face?" Something next to my ears begins to buzz.

"So you can play the game."

I try to project cool—Hann teases that just handing me a remote control raises my blood pressure—but my pulse races on. How am I supposed to know anything about technology when they make us girls focus on communication and the domestic arts at school? I can't breathe. I decide to give this stupid game another ten seconds—

A little waif of a girl materializes before me.

"XX, what's going on?" I wave my arms, but he is out of reach. I cannot keep the tremor from my voice. "Is that me? How did you get that old picture of me?"

He tells me it's computer mapping. "It's just an approximation of a little you."

How did the computer know I wore a pasted-on smile and hand-me-down rags? The too-eager forward lean is also spot-on. I can feel my little girl anxiety. "What am I supposed to do?"

My younger self splits and becomes two. She hovers before a doll and a clutch of girls of varying height. He tells me to choose the scene I like best and stare at it.

I close my eyes, afraid to make a mistake. "What do you mean?"

"Pick which one you like better."

"But who are those girls?" I cry.

"They're who you want them to be. Just choose. It's not a big deal. Pick the scene that you'd rather be in."

I take a breath and peek out of one eye. The vibrations next to my ears have tunneled to the pit of my stomach, cramping it. I bounce from one image to the other, afraid to make an accidental choice.

"Can you make this thing stop shaking?" I say. "I can't think."

"The vibrations are supposed to help you access buried emotions."

I tug off the helmet and rake my fingers across my damp scalp. The open air is a tremendous relief. Hovering anxiously close, XX makes me claustrophobic all over again.

"Are you quitting?"

I sigh. I hate that he thinks I have no staying power with anything technological. "I'm just taking a breath."

Relief washes over him. "This is an easy game. There's no wrong answer. The computer approaches each topic from multiple angles. You won't be able to fool it." He presses buttons on the helmet again. "I'm going to reprogram it from the beginning." Restarting everything from the very beginning—half-consumed movies, music albums, BeiBei's picture books, the list goes on—is one of XX's more annoying tics.

I tie back my hair this time before pulling on the helmet. Knowing ahead of time that my little girl self will appear helps. I wait for her to double and feel ready when the doll and girls come on screen.

There are five. They look like variations of me. Sisters. I ask XX if he told the computer that I have five of them. I want to throttle him when he tells me again that I see what I want to see.

I recognize the rag doll. I slept with it every night when I was little. This was the doll Big Sister grabbed out of my hands to comfort our baby sister when she dropped her. I can still hear *Mei-Mei* screaming on the ground, clinging to my precious doll while her lip dripped blood. Polka-dotted red before turning the color of dung, my doll became unrecognizable. I matched *MeiMei* howl for howl, trying to wrench it back—both stiff and wet, its comforting softness was forever lost—and was pinched and shoved away for my efforts. The injustice I suffered under Big Sister, and under *MeiMei* too, seized me.

The doll was never again mine. For what felt like hours, blood sprayed from *MeiMei* with each of her cries. We were all covered in it by the time a neighbor took her for stitches. After I had soaped and sloshed my doll through basins of water, MaMa warned me that a girl's face is her greatest asset. She made me give my doll to *Mei-Mei* as punishment. I too was blamed for that split lip.

I stare at the doll, now forever brown-skinned, and it flies into my little-girl arms. I rub my face against it, my thumb finding the strip of satin around its middle. Stroking that ribbon was how I tuned out the clack of mahjongg tiles and the angry booming voices that so often woke me. Its reassuring smoothness was how I lulled myself back to sleep in the black night.

A feast appears next to my sisters. I see all my old favorites—shrimp toast, lotus seed buns, egg tarts, malt candy. My parents plied me with these treats the two months leading to my engagement and wedding. *MeiMei* and I were the only two still left in the household. She connived behind her saccharine facade, but even she could not derail my auction. I smile, remembering my record-setting dowry. Landing two husbands in one fell swoop, I had fulfilled my parents' greatest wish for me, and I basked under the full beam of my mother's attention.

When *MeiMei* expressed doubt over her top-bidder—genital herpes showed up in his STD panels—I ate and gloated over her portions. My parents extracted additional dowry to compensate for his less-than-stellar health. She eventually married that man.

On the screen now, though, the assortment of greasy, five-jiao trifles makes me queasy. Why did I think *MeiMei*, scheming and hateful as she was, deserved that man? Why did it not matter to my parents—to me—that she would contract the disease, that her son would almost lose his sight because of it?

Were these leftovers no one wanted from mahjongg nights, these cheap eats what my sister and I bickered over? Why have the five of them mattered so little to me? That is not the kind of relationship I would want or foster between my own children.

Did my parents know that Hann was Willfully Sterile and XX emotionally stunted? Why would they pay for background checks and then ignore the information? How could my sisters and I have equated the size of our dowry with our worth—with our parents' love and esteem—when the high price we commanded landed us husbands few women would have voluntarily married? My sisters and I were valuable resources all right, sold off to the highest bidder, no better than livestock destined for the slaughterhouse.

I look at *MeiMei* and am flooded with regret. My parents assigned her to me, but I did not take care of her. Still the most beautiful of the six of us, her smile zooms large before me. Her sweetness feels genuine for the first time as she comes to hold my hand.

"I'm so sorry," I say to her. Tears tickle my cheeks. When I try to wipe them away, my hand bumps into the face shield.

"Are you okay?" XX says.

I've almost forgotten about him. I pull the helmet over my head and draw in a deep, ragged breath. "I'm sorry. I don't know why I'm—" XX's eyes are kind and full of concern. Beyond his meals, he rarely expects anything from me.

He explains that I've unearthed painful memories. "The instructions say that part of learning what makes you happy is learning what's making you sad."

I ask if we can pause the game for dinner. Feeling wobbly, I drop into the chair behind me.

"We must stop. The directions call for short sessions and discussion afterwards to process what you've uncovered." He peers at me shyly. "You have to tell me why you're sad."

I sniff and try to stop my flow of tears. It mattered a great deal to my mother what I did, how I acted, how I presented myself in public, but rarely did she concern herself with how I felt.

XX asks if the girls were my sisters. "Did you choose them over the doll?"

I shake my head.

His eyes fill with angry disbelief. "Why not?"

I shake my head again, too ashamed to answer. Loved and cherished by his parents and brother despite his profound short-comings, XX will not understand. He and Hann would be shocked and disgusted by the hateful wretch that I am. XX examines me, hovering uncomfortably close. I tell him that I lost the doll when I was four.

"I was so happy to see it that I stared too long." I hiccup. "You told me I couldn't fool the computer even if I tried."

"No, you can't." He asks what came next.

I'm glad to report that on the following round, I had the presence of mind to pick my sisters over food.

"Why are you still crying?"

"I'm not." I brush away my tears.

"What did you remember about your sisters?"

I shake my head and shrug. "Nothing."

"Is it the food that's making you sad?"

The more questions XX asks, the faster my tears fall. Meanwhile, his eyes cannot stop blinking.

"I'm going to get Hann," he says. "Hann will know what to do."

I grab XX's arm.

He says, "The instructions say that if you do not process your feelings, you'll become depressed."

I tighten my grasp of his squirming arm. "I'm ready to play some more."

"That's too dangerous."

"Come on."

He crosses his arms, puts his feet together, and shakes his head three times. When his mind is set, there's always hell to pay if we do not go along.

I smile through my tears, desperate. "I feel like having sex. Do you want to have sex?" I don't know what's come over me.

He scowls. "Now?"

"You feel like it, don't you? It's been three weeks."

XX turns crimson. "Before dinner?" I would not have to spend the night in his bed if we do it before dinner.

Sweat beads above his lip. His eyes blink vacantly. He stands rooted, paralyzed by my unusual proposition.

I tell him to take off his pants. I slip under the sheets and strip from the waist down. After I urge him again, XX turns away and unbuckles. He looks over his shoulder at me, reconfirms my interest before letting his khakis fall. I am grateful he comes to bed in his boxers. Hands at his sides and eyes trained on the ceiling, he lies down rail straight, careful not to impose any part of his body on mine.

I tell him to pull down his shorts and climb atop me.

"I, uh—" His eyelids flutter madly as he struggles for words.

"It's okay," I say. "I'll help you."

He lifts his hips uncertainly and does as he's told.

"C'mon," I say. He struggles to his side and bridges himself above me, still too polite to make contact. His barnyard stink chokes me, and I pull the covers across my nose and stopper it against his chest. I'm grateful for once that he looms above me, that he does not make eye contact with ease. He stays propped on his elbows. Hann has warned him not to smother me with his weight.

I open my legs. "Move. You can rub yourself against me."

"But you're crying."

I push against his groin to make him start. There's no hardness down there. He humps me for a while. His T-shirt grows damp, but I feel no improvement. Soon, XX forgets about not smothering me, and his blubbery heft pins me to the mattress. I rock my hips. It's hard to breathe, but I open my mouth and do it loudly to try to excite him.

I come out of hiding and peer up. XX's hair is clumped with sweat, and his blinking has taken on tic-like proportions. He's hyperventilating too. I've scared him witless. I want to be nice, but the doltish sight of him inevitably makes me mean. I can't help it. I should rub him with my hands, but can't work myself up to it.

"Get off," I say.

He scoots away and plops onto his stomach, arms covering his head. "I'm sorry," he mumbles into the pillow.

I should stop, but XX is quite upset. The thought of having to explain it all to Hann makes me ill.

"Touch me," I tell him.

He pulls the pillow over his head and wheezes. I take his hand and put it on my breast. This is a rare event, but his hand sits there, dead, and I have to coax and move it in circles. After a few seconds, I feel a squeeze. Just one.

"C'mon." I nudge him with my knee. "Turn over."

When I finally get him on his back, he can barely meet my eyes. "The instructions say we have to figure out why you are still crying," he says beneath his breath.

"Forget the directions." I scrub my cheeks with my knuckles. "I'm not crying."

He cringes, a turtle shrinking into its shell. I have a mind to hurl the shell to the moon. Pulling a sheet across my lap, I straddle and ride him. On the rare occasion when Hann allows me to touch him in the groggy hours of the night, when he is sufficiently aroused as to permit me sex with BeiBei asleep in our bed, this is what I work up to, what I want to do with him. Bumping against his nub feels like heaven. I close my eyes and move. I become mildly aroused.

Biting his lip, XX stares at the ceiling. I've been at him awhile, and his inability to get hard makes me frantic. I don't want Hann to know that I am also worthless with his brother, that I am the source of all our bedroom problems. Nor do I want to deal with the shadow of this misfortune in XX's eyes every time we interact. I take both his hands and apply them to my breasts. He gasps, and when I move my hands away, his remain, stiff and viselike.

"Move," I tell him. I continue to grind my hips and his two claws politely squeeze. Soon, we both breathe a little heavier. It's slippery and wet between my legs, and I detect a change in him. I keep moving and bend sideways for the bedside drawer and the pen box in which I hide the condoms. Even though he accepted my bribe, the doctor who switched off my fertility last time threatened to speak to my husbands, and I've been afraid to try again. I told XX that there would no longer be a reason for us to have sex if we had a baby, and he promised not to tell.

"Put this on." I leave the condom on his chest and roll off.

He curls on his side away from me and fiddles with the plastic.

"Ready?" It takes forever for him to unwrap anything.

He is quiet for a long moment. "Why don't you want to talk about it?"

"Turn over."

"On my back?" We've only ever done it one way, but we're not going to get anywhere with him on top today.

Plus, all that grinding and rubbing have loosened something in me. I tug on XX's shoulder and try not to look at his nether regions as he flips around. I rub against him and try to work his penis inside me without touching it with my hands, but our exchange of words has been counterproductive. Never presumptive, XX's arms lie rigid at his sides.

I continue moving against XX, against the ridge of the condom. He begins to work his own cause with his hips. The euphoria between my legs floods my center. I've craved this mutual pleasuring with Hann, with someone other than XX, so I close my eyes to his clammy body and ungainly ways. It is Hann making love to me. I reach beneath my shirt and pull my breasts out of the cups of my brassiere. I place hands on my shirt atop them. I shimmy my shoulders and slide my nipples across palms. That is Hann's mouth kissing my breasts, his tongue caressing my nipples. I let go a moan. I work at the pleasure between my legs. Somewhere along the way, Hann's penis wakes and finds its home inside me.

When I next open my eyes, the sight of XX staring at my face, mouth slack, feels like a gross violation. I glare back, and he cringes, crossing his fat arms over his eyes. He looks so pathetic, the quivering blob of him, that I do us both a favor, lean down, and pull the bottom of my shirt over his head. The bliss between my legs urges me on, and I push a nipple at his lips and rub against them. I tell the lifeless mouth beneath to lick. A tongue flicks across me. Once.

"Don't stop," I yell.

There is a knock on the door before it is opened. Hann enters, telling us that dinner is ready. I yelp and jerk up, my shirt dragging XX's head with me.

Hann backs away and apologizes, both hands up. "Please. Please don't let me interrupt."

XX pops out of my shirt. "She's crying."

Hann closes the door, his smile a punch to my gut. I roll off XX and curl into a ball. I cover my face and give in to sobs.

The mattress bounces as he jumps out of bed and thumps out of the room with the urgency of a tortured animal.

Hann comes into the room, folds XX's pants over his arm, and passes them to him in the hallway. Hann then spends an inordinate amount of time fluffing and rearranging the bedding before sitting down, his back to mine. I cover my mouth to muffle my crying.

When he finally speaks, his voice is slow and measured. "How long have you two been using birth control?"

I remember the condom and try not to panic. It was only a matter of time before XX spilled our secrets. It occurs to me that our peaceful coexistence requires too many secrets.

"I think we should ask Hero to arrange a Compatibility Test." My own request to have a trial run in the bedroom with Wei-guo stuns me. I'm not at all certain I want to marry again, let alone to sleep with a man I hardly know. Hann doesn't react—it's as if he accepts my shocking suggestion as the logical next step—and I am hurt beyond words.

"Why don't you want to get pregnant?"

I sit up and face him. "Why did you marry me when you had no intention of loving me?" I keep my voice quiet and scary like his.

"What's gotten into you?"

"I never would have knowingly married a Willfully Sterile man."

"That decision was not yours to make. Or mine. I've never lied to you."

"Had they known, my parents would never have allowed me to enter this sham of a marriage." I scour the tears from my cheeks.

Hann's mouth opens, but nothing comes out. His Adam's apple bobs as he walks to the table and picks up *The Pursuit of Happiness*.

"You're making no sense. What is this game? You're aggravating Xiong-xin carrying on like this. And he's going to upset BeiBei."

"Will you call Hero?"

He thumps the box on the table. "Your outrageous demands can't brush aside the fact that you're making Xiong-xin wear condoms."

"I like Wei-guo." I can't believe the words coming out of my mouth. "Before I invest any more of myself, of BeiBei, I want to know that we're physically compatible."

"Xiong-xin tells me how often you two have sex, and I've let it slide. But you can't keep taking advantage of him. It's not fair."

I nod, agreeing with him. "And it's not fair that you want no part of me."

"Stop it."

"Would you prefer I call Wei-guo directly?"

"We're not doing anything until you have Xiong-xin's child."

His dictatorial tone riles me. "You didn't really want to go the max. You couldn't have acted snottier at that matchmaking lunch."

"Somebody has to play hard to get in this family."

Heat floods my face as I remember my unforgivably flirtatious behavior with Wei-guo, and I glare back at Hann. I *do* like Wei-guo. He seems like a fundamentally good man, a handsome someone I could have been interested in if I weren't already twice married. I did not lie when I told him he gave me a ticklish feeling of happiness, and that thought makes me feel even guiltier. It was wrong of me to have toyed with him.

Hann throws up his hands. "You can't keep violating your marital contract."

"There's more than one person in violation around here." Hann has no business invoking the marital contract, and he knows it.

He narrows his eyes. "A wife serves at the pleasure of her husband, not the other way around."

I am truly angry now. After Hann confessed his Willful Sterility, he vowed to love and cherish me as an equal, to forge a union where bullying husbands like his father have no place. I remember how grateful I felt when he diplomatically left my father out of that category.

I say, "I've fulfilled my obligation, giving both of you BeiBei. I will not risk bringing a sterile child, emotional or otherwise, into the world again."

"How could you believe that crap put out by the government?" Hann grits his teeth, his brows dark and mean. "You know what I am is not heritable."

I stare back. He can talk himself hoarse, but it is me who will have to raise a difficult child, one who could be shunned, neutered, even taken away.

He continues, "BeiBei has turned out fine."

I do not say that our aggressive and hyperactive son may not be fine. "I don't want to chance a ruined child. Our life is hard enough as it is."

"You think I'm ruined?" The desolation in his voice pains me.

I scramble out of bed toward him, but he recoils and averts his eyes. Pained again that my body causes him such discomfort, I tug on pants. "I love you. It's *you* who do not feel the same way about me."

He sinks down into XX's chair, and I kneel in front of him. I put my head in his lap.

He lets me stay there. "What are they going to think of us, asking for a Compatibility Test?" No one ever asks for a Compatibility Test, especially not the bride. It is more urban myth than reality.

His question stuns me anew. "What a sensible girl, is what they are going to think. She's learned from her mistakes. She didn't test out her first two husbands, and look what happened." I feel him wince.

"What if he's a terrible lover?"

I shrug. "I'm sure I've had worse."

He does not react. "I don't want us to do this because you're mad at me." He reminds me that I still have to fulfill my obligation to XX.

It's clear from the droop in his shoulders, the resignation in his eyes that I've lost. He will not fight for me.

4

XX

At 11:59:45, Guo XX saves his computations and signs out of his workstation. When the lunch bell rattles the noon hour, he is in position to tear off his smock, pull on his coat, and bolt in the direction of the company cafeteria. His stomach has been rumbling the last hour, and he can never understand why people mill around their departments, poking one another and braying, when in just minutes, the lines become pythons.

Every few weeks when he can no longer put off Hann's badgering to make friends, XX will stand next to one of his desk neighbors and wait. It takes the six men in his department on average three excruciating minutes to wrap up what they are doing, rouse themselves, and locate their personal effects. Another three minutes can drag by as they speculate on the cafeteria's offerings of the day and debate whether to eat in or out. Heaven help XX if there should be a news item or office nonsense to discuss too.

Try as he might, the result is invariably the same. They spend half their lunch time smooshed into lines where attending to so many conversations makes him want to crouch and cover his ears. When he finally squeezes a thoughtful contribution into their torrent of words, no one says anything of import back to him. He can't think of a bigger waste of his precious lunch break.

XX pumps his arms and legs—running is forbidden inside the building—and threads his way between lumbering groups. He's super fast and all-powerful when he flies solo and operates well above the fray. He is most effective at his job when his security designs are undetectable and unknowable. In real life too, so much more can be accomplished with a certain kind of invisibility. There is little he cannot accomplish when no one is watching, judging, getting in his way, and weighing him down. He likes that his nickname captures his elusive and unknowable quality, his aura of mystery. He scurries the last few steps, cutting in front of another speed walker. He tries to be one of the first, if not *the* first, in line so that the cafeteria does not run out of his favorites.

The cook begins packing meat buns into bags the second he spies XX. "Same old, same old, comrade?" he says. "How are you today?"

"Yes, and I am fine." XX thanks him and confirms that he wants a dozen. "And how are you?" He always returns the greeting. The cook is his good friend, and XX counts on the man every day for a satisfying exchange.

"Well and fine and good now that you're here. How's the missus?"

"She's a most excellent mother and wife." XX grins devilishly. Contrary to what Hann thinks, he is capable of double-speak. The spareribs smell deliciously garlicky. He places a double order.

"Hold the cabbage?"

"You know me well." He awards himself another point for small talk.

He stuffs the buns into his various coat pockets and carries the bagged spareribs and rice in his hands. He appreciates that the cook is happy to sell him as much as he has the money to buy and never questions his choices. Another good reason to be first in line: There are fewer people around. Despite his explanations that the food isn't all for himself, they continue to titter over his large orders.

He cannot tell them why, of course; feeding stray dogs is illegal. He checks the location of MaMa Dog on his watch and is relieved that she and hopefully the rest of his loyal friends are waiting for him at their usual spot. By violating the one-dog-per-household rule and the oversized-dog ban and by falsifying birth, spaying and neutering, vaccination, and license certificates, he has broken six laws twenty-seven times for his pets. The forms and information are easy enough for him to fake, but a good criminologist could trace a locational tracking chip back to him. For that reason, XX dared place it on just one animal.

XX exits the building's south entrance. Keeping his head down, he flattens the buns against his body with his elbows and hurries past the cluster of smokers gathered around the planters.

"Hey, old man, what are they serving today?"

XX replies as he walks, "Wuxi spareribs, kung pao chicken, five-spiced tofu, cabbage, fried rice, white rice, rice gruel, pot stickers, meat buns, vegetable buns, and hot tea." At the mention of white rice, the guys break out laughing. They always laugh, though XX is just reciting the menu. Hann claims that they are being friendly, but XX knows otherwise. He scowls and ignores them. After all, they are none too bright. Who else but idiots would still be smoking when every kind of smoking has long been proven to cause cancer?

Crossing the plaza to his right is a family of five toting an aluminum kettle and three unusual looking buckets. One of the buckets—a dozen staves held by two metal hoops—swings back and forth from the kid's arm beyond the horizontal line, centripetal force the only thing preventing its cloth-covered contents from spilling out. It is the sort of behavior BeiBei specializes in to annoy and drive May-ling to tears. What looks from a distance like a green bucket turns out to be a tightly woven three-tiered basket, a food carrier of old that XX once saw at a folk museum. He drifts toward them. Three crisscrossing splints fanned at three-degree angles make up the handle. Raised Archimedean spirals emanating from a common pole decorate the lid in dark green. He recalls the polar equation $r = a\,\theta^{1/n}$ and squints, imprinting in his mind's eye the tightness of the spirals, the radial distance, the polar angle. He will investigate basket weaving that evening at home. He must figure out how this basket is constructed.

A wide torso enters his field of vision and stops, hands on hips, blocking XX's view of the basket. "What're you ogling at, you old goat?"

XX flinches and finds two furious men before him. A wall of rage. "I'm sorry." He steps back. "I was just examining the Archimedean spirals."

"*What* did you say?" the taller of the two men says, his voice a thunder boom. He advances even as XX retreats.

The shorter man pulls the hood of the mother's coat over her head and ushers her, a little girl, and the well-crafted basket away. Behind them, the boy kid spins in place, the steady up-and-down motion of his arms and bucket a sine wave.

"Hey." XX finds the big man's hand in front of his face, cutting off his view again. He points at XX and says, "Do you need a whupping to keep your eyes to yourself?" The man lurches after him, pecking his chin like a rooster.

XX yelps and stomps off as fast as his legs will carry him, his bags of spareribs and rice flapping at his sides. "No, I don't," he cries. "I'm looking at the basket, not your women folk." The man calls him an old goat again—a lewd one this time—along with a string of expletives. Though he does not come in chase, XX keeps running. People are unpredictable and always misinterpreting, strangers especially, and that is another reason he stays away from them.

His heart pommeling, XX finally stops in an alley. The man is now a mean dot in the distance. When XX doubles over to breathe, the blood explodes into his head, and nausea grips him. Cold sweat breaks out, and XX has to consciously slow his breathing, to count to nearly a hundred before the sensation that he's about to die eases. He checks on MaMa Dog again. His smart dog, thankfully, has not moved.

Before traversing the alley, XX plugs his ears with his two bags of food. The whine of the heating equipment housed there feels like a buzz saw inside his ears. He has tried to explain the sensation, but no one cares except, of course, his mother and Hann.

XX whistles twice before stepping onto the strip of green bordering the canal toward the large bush, which hides a bench on its other side. It's a perfect location. No one sitting in his work cafeteria can spy them there. Tails flying, his dog friends come running, exhaling white plumes. XX calms when he accounts for all five.

He puts out his hands and stays the dogs even though he has trained them not to rush or jump at him. Dog training sites like Animal Pals for Life and Be the Pack Leader have taught XX that continual domination is necessary for eliciting desired behavior.

"Good girl," he says, approaching MaMa Dog. She is the best behaved, if not the sweetest creature in the whole wide world. XX knows that dogs cannot smile, but he often finds this understanding expression on this ginger-coated mutt. He pats her head twice before giving her a meat bun. XX has never taught her this, but MaMa Dog knows to wait for him to inspect her tag before delving into her meal.

XX hears a rustle behind him and says, "Bad BeiBei." He doesn't need to turn around to know that the dog is about to pounce on MaMa Dog's food. He tells the dumb mutt to sit and raps it on the nose. It's no wonder it's got itself a lame leg. The scraggly thing whines and eventually obeys.

XX feeds BaBa Dog next. The largest of the bunch—there's German shepherd blood in him—this dog is bossy and insistent in the way that he keeps the pack in check. XX's own dad liked to make everyone do as he said, so XX named the dog after him. XX knows his family would be insulted by the names, but he intends to keep the dogs his private friends. His brother is sure to forbid them if he finds out.

XX gives BaBa Dog his two pats and his bun and moves on to Hann. There is an ugly gash on his ear.

"What happened, Hann? You got into another fight!" It is rude to address an older sibling by his given name, but no such rules apply out here. XX holds the whining creature by the collar, but cannot find its license tag. "You bad, bad boy. You are in deep trouble with me."

Ears perked, MaMa and BaBa Dog rise.

"Dammit, Hann," XX says. "How am I supposed to keep you safe if you can't do your part?"

MaMa and BaBa Dog rub against him and circle his legs as he continues to scold. Their wagging tails nearly knock the spareribs from his hands. XX orders the two dogs to sit, but they bark sharply and back him butt first into the bench. MaMa Dog jumps onto the seat next to him.

She will not stop licking XX's face. He pushes aside her snout and yells, "You know you're a dead dog if you get caught now, don't you, Hann?" The creature slinks behind BaBa Dog. It took XX five months to save up for the five collars and licenses. Between the daily doggy meals and May-ling's unpredictable demands for cash, XX is flying through the allowance his brother gives him.

He flails at MaMa Dog. "How am I to pay for antiseptic and ointments too?" He blinks in rapid succession at the thought of having to explain his spending to Hann. After the condom incident, XX has apologized repeatedly, promising never to lie again, but Hann is on to him. It won't be long before his brother tricks all the secrets out of XX and forces him to give up everything that matters.

MaMa Dog will not get out of his face. The more XX yelps and struggles, the more MaMa licks and nudges him. Just as he pulls away to rise, BaBa Dog anchors himself across XX's lap. MaMa takes the opportunity and plants her forelegs on his chest. He thrashes at their combined weight, and his two bags of food clunk to his feet.

"Oh no!" He manages no more than a missed kick at BeiBei as the bad dog pounces. BaBa Dog barks, but to no avail. Jaws sunk into the plastic bags, it doesn't take more than a couple shakes of BeiBei's head before spareribs and rice are dotted across the ankle-high grass. XX attempts to get up, but MaMa and BaBa Dog have him pinned.

XX yells at Hann and May-ling to stay put. May-ling circles the food, whimpers for a moment, tail between her legs, but the temptation is too great.

"You are a bad dog, BeiBei. The worst," XX yells. "I'm never going to feed you again."

He covers his face with his arms and fights off MaMa Dog's licking with his elbows.

"Bad, bad, May-ling," he cries. "I'm not going to feed you either." If he could rid the pack of those two, he would.

"MaMa!" he yells but she won't stop. Her licking tickles more than anything. Her ministrations become more insistent the more XX pushes her away. With BaBa Dog a dead weight across his middle, XX can scarcely move. Finally, he roars, covers his head, and gives up fighting. MaMa Dog lowers herself across his chest and rests her head in the crook of his neck. XX closes his eyes, and the steady huff of her breath and the drumming of her heart become his own. XX's mother used to hold him like this when he became fists and kicks. He hums her song.

After a while, he peeks out at MaMa Dog, her tongue jaunty and her eyes full of understanding. Her smile makes him want to smile. Her licking is so ticklish he laughs, and he reaches into his pocket for buns to lure the two dogs off him.

Eyes trained on his watch, XX plots as he travels his route, adjusting his pace so as to arrive at Lee Wei-guo's studio five minutes before their appointed hour. Never wishing to offend or—heaven forbid—detonate bad tempers, he always arrives exactly five minutes before meetings and appointments. Counting down the seconds, he sets foot into the studio at eight A.M. on the dot.

A client is on his back on a low padded table with Wei-guo's shoulder braced against his leg, forcing it toward vertical. The man grimaces and shakes. XX cannot take his eyes off the three long hairs waving from the reddish-black mole on his chin.

"Good morning, XX. Welcome." Wei-guo twists his head toward a corridor. "Your clothes and valuables will be safe in there."

"No, thanks." XX isn't here to exercise. He approaches the two men.

"We'll be done in a second." Wei-guo introduces XX to his client. "Comrade Wung works at China Central Television."

XX wrinkles his nose. Hann doesn't think much of Chinese

news and television people, whom he says are little more than propagandists of the State. XX supposes he agrees. Media is censored and CCTV, the country's only national network, especially so.

"Hello there," the man says, red-faced. Droplets of sweat surround his mole. He sticks out his hand.

"Hello." XX shakes it and sniffs the air before stepping back. Something smells like sour laundry, and XX is relieved it's not Wei-guo.

Wei-guo says Wung is the executive producer of "Model Citizens." "He was telling me he's doing a segment on Handsome Lee. China Film Group just fired him."

XX is disappointed Wei-guo thinks he would be interested in actors, another mouthpiece of the State, or in "Model Citizens," the last segment of the evening news that either praises an exemplary citizen or condemns a fallen one. Hann despises that propaganda show masquerading as news, so XX does too. He says nothing, though—just widens his eyes and tries hard to ignore Wung's curiously ugly mole. He must be polite and look engaged.

"You know Handsome Lee, don't you? The highest-grossing actor of this last decade?" Wei-guo says.

"Of course I do," XX replies, insulted. "I'm into popular culture."

Wei-guo eases off his client's leg, bends it at the knee, and pushes it toward his chest as Mr. Wung moans. XX hugs himself to keep his impatience at bay. It is now three minutes after eight.

Wei-guo tells him, "Handsome Lee was discovered to have mistresses in Macau, Hong Kong, and Taiwan. Babies in every corner of the globe." He seems in no hurry to wrap things up. "What do you suppose they'll do to him?"

"A man with his kind of profile—they're going to make an example of him, for sure," Wung says. "He'll be kept under custody for a while, fined to kingdom come, his passport confiscated. He won't be allowed to see his children ever again. They've already booked a slot for him on our show—part of his reeducation. His career is over. It's sad. He played a very believable Confucius. I studied Confucius's Analects because of Handsome Lee."

"If you like him so much, why help end his career?" XX cannot help asking. He can never understand people who want one thing but do something completely opposite.

"If it were up to me, I wouldn't," Wung says. "But I don't decide who to feature. My job is to produce the segments."

XX covers his nose with a hand; the smell in here is hard to take. "I could never do a job like yours." Tactfully, he does not ask why Wung chooses to compromise himself when there are so many other jobs out there.

"You're welcome to sit down." Wei-guo's voice takes on a serrated edge. He puts his client into a third torturous position.

"No, thank you. I prefer to stand," XX says.

Wung moans. His eyes make XX uncomfortable, and XX's gaze drifts down to the man's chin. His mole looks like a shiny black cauliflower floret.

"I may not have a say in the people featured." Why is Wung's voice suddenly so mean? "But I control the tone and texture of the pieces. I edit the interviews. I shape the questions and answers we air. I try to be merciful when it is right."

Hot faced and tongue-tied, XX steps back. Wei-guo continues to torture his client, but no one says a word.

XX squints hard and tries to discern what May-ling likes about Wei-guo. She and Hann say he's handsome. XX sees two narrow eyes, two caterpillar eyebrows, a bulbous nose with protruding hairs, and a yap-yap-yap mouth like all the others. His parents' friends used to call XX handsome, cherubic even when he was younger, but his good looks did not help him acquire friends. Hann claims that friendship is a matter of give and take, of asking questions, really listening to the answers, and then asking deeper questions.

XX widens his eyes and steadies his gaze, doing his best to look engaged and interested. Determined to stay on a good footing, he decides to make small talk. "How many stretches will you do altogether?"

"We're almost done here," Wei-guo says, his voice gruff and dangerous.

XX hugs himself tighter and stares at his feet. Wei-guo did not answer his question. It is important they become friends. Despite his best instincts, he decides to hold fast to Hann's prescription. "Is it good to hurt him like that?"

"I'm not hurting him."

XX retreats again, certain from the sharpness in Wei-guo's voice that he is angry.

"Actually," Mr. Wung says, "I wouldn't mind if you eased off a bit." He suggests that they finish up. He needs to take his mother grocery shopping.

Wei-guo complies. He walks Mr. Wung out, reminding him to devote time every day to stretch his injured hamstring. He returns to XX, plants his feet, and crosses his arms.

"You're not going to change?"

XX does not like the knife in Wei-guo's voice. He holds himself tighter. "No."

"Do you want to work out?"

"No."

"Why are you here then?"

"I want to make friends with you."

"You want to make friends. With me."

"Yes."

Wei-guo stares. XX would not call his aura friendly.

"You didn't answer my two questions," XX says.

"Two questions?"

"Yes. How many stretches you do on Mr. Wung and why."

Wei-guo opens his mouth, but nothing comes out. XX cowers as a lump goes up and down Wei-guo's throat like a pumping fist.

"Comrade," Wei-guo finally says, "I can understand that you do not want to Advance your family. That you do not like me. But this is my business. My family's livelihood."

It takes XX a second to realize that Wei-guo thinks he is not going to pay for his session. He pulls out the neat stack of bills he has saved up for the occasion and offers them up.

"What're you doing?" Wei-guo's voice rumbles, a slap of thunder.

"I'm paying you."

Wei-guo holds up his hand and backs up. "Just say what you've come to say."

"I'm here to make friends." XX remembers he brought a gift and takes it out of his coat pocket. Hann says you should always bring a small gift on social visits.

"What's this?"

"A present."

Wei-guo flips the wrapped box. XX hopes he is noticing how well the seams are concealed. It would be nice if they have a love of order in common along with their fondness for war games. XX urges him to open it.

"What's it for?"

"It's a friendship gift."

"A friendship gift?"

"I made it for you."

"You made this?"

"Yes." Short on cash, XX had to resort to something handmade.

Wei-guo stares at the box some more. "Did your brother send you? Or was it May-ling?"

"No and no. I sent myself." XX observes that May-ling and Wei-guo have something in common, which Hann says helps build friendships: they both dislike gifts.

"You can stop worrying," Wei-guo says. "They're not interested in me. They haven't returned my calls."

"You're wrong."

"I'm wrong?"

"Yes, you are," XX says emphatically. "Please open my gift."

Wei-guo finally loosens a piece of tape. It's as if he's afraid the gift will jump out and hurt him. The care with which he slides it out of the wrapping paper, preserving the handiwork, gives XX hope.

"Do you like the box?"

He stares again at XX.

"I made the box."

"You *made* the box?" Wei-guo seems to have a habit of repeating people's words.

He lifts the lid. Short tubes of the same purple, blue, and yellow plaid wrapping paper appear, glued around an old photo of May-ling.

"That's her favorite picture. She's fifteen there. She stares at it when she is sad, and it makes her happy again." In the photo, her face is half-buried in the balding neck of her chow chow. Its milky eyes are half-blind.

"I thought that if she could love that stinky dog, she could love me." XX does not say that he was wrong and awards himself one point for discretion. When Wei-guo does not respond, XX asks if he likes it.

"Yes." The attack finally leaves Wei-guo's voice. A moment later, he says thanks.

XX tells him to flip the picture over. Hann, May-ling, and BeiBei appear on the other side framed by a mosaic border pieced from the same wrapping paper.

"It's a picture of your new family."

Wei-guo looks angry. "You're not in it."

Hann teases that XX gives away secrets with his face. He widens his eyes and relaxes his jaw, so that it is not apparent that he no longer wants to be in a family. He yearns for the quiet of his college years away, when no one told him what to do, whom to talk to, what to say.

XX tells Wei-guo that he snapped the picture. "I'm there. This picture would not exist if I weren't there."

"All right," Wei-guo says. "So what do you want to do for the rest of the hour?"

"I want to become friends with you," XX says. "Have a back-and-forth conversation."

"What do you want to talk about?"

"Will you promise me something?" XX asks. "Will you promise that you will take care of not just May-ling, but of my brother and BeiBei too?"

"If you are right and the three of you should choose me, I know I am marrying your whole family. And I would hope that the consideration is mutual. That you will care for me as much as I hope to care for you."

XX is unsure if there was a certifiable promise in the torrent of words. "Say I promise."

Wei-guo sighs. "If I marry your family, I promise to watch out for Hann and BeiBei," Wei-guo says. "And for you too."

XX sits on his hands and taps his foot, waiting to be called on by his manager. In two months, their company—a private enterprise founded by a high Party official—will be proposing to the Ministry of Finance a comprehensive security plan for its new headquarters. Besides work in the private sector, they've designed security for Beijing's Planning Commission and Bureau of Public Security. If they win the account, the Ministry of Finance will be their highest-clearance project to date. Their company president has ordered Software Design, along with three other departments, to incorporate revolutionary thinking into a visionary approach.

Jei-sun has been speaking for the last eight minutes, alternately tugging on his Escher ascending-and-descending-stairs tie and flashing blueprint after blueprint of the building. He and XX are the most senior members in their department. There was talk that Jei-sun was after Manager Fung's job, but never wanting to get into trouble for repeating or believing what may not be true, XX ignores rumors. He does not speculate on how Jei-sun feels about their new manager, but he does know that Manager Fung shows Jei-sun great respect, asking him to present the overview.

Fung has disallowed questions and comments during presentations. XX already has nine modifications to propose, but he must wait. XX likes Fung, a formidably sized man like himself with a gentle, consensus-seeking voice. Though twenty years XX's junior, Fung is fair, the best of XX's many managers to date. He details what he wants, and he explains his reasoning. In meetings like today's, for example, he says it's important that he understands how his people puzzle through problems.

It takes another nine minutes for Jei-sun to finish. With so many ideas to share, XX can hardly sit still. Brainstorming sessions are the best. It's as if they are designing their own virtual game today.

XX joins in the clapping. He likes to show his enthusiasm by being the loudest of all. He claps ten more times after everyone stops. Their manager thanks Jei-sun and says he has given them a great starting point for their work. A jolt of excitement runs through XX when Fung finally looks at him.

"And thank you all for letting Jei-sun present his vision for this project without interruption."

Fung projects the master slide onto the big screen. The words "site," "interior," and "perimeter" appear, and XX smiles. Fung has made a rule that only one item can be discussed at a time, and XX has a modification that falls under both site and interior. Just like Fung, he does not want to confuse or be counterproductive jumping ahead of the topic at hand. Manager Fung asks if anyone has comments about the overall approach. His gaze comes to rest on XX.

XX's arm shoots up. He waits for a nod before he speaks. "We are not monitoring water pipes, gas lines, cables, electric wires, sewage lines, mole tunnels, ant hills, termite mounds—"

The four junior staffers titter. "Isn't Beijing a tad cold for termites?"

"No it's not," says XX. "The Temple of Heaven is infested with—"

Manager Fung puts up a hand. "I like XX's approach. Let's be unorthodox. Let's be revolutionary in our attack." He scribbles "land," "water," and "air" on the board, draws lines to separate the three categories, and writes "utilities" and "underground animal/insect habitat." He asks for more threats from land sources.

XX's hand goes up again. "You need to add people. Workers, visitors, security guards, deliverymen, neighbors within a three-kilometer sphere of the building, neighbors within missile range. And don't forget about the things people bring in: briefcases, computers, coats, lunch—"

Manager Fung stops him again. "Noted." He adds "people" and "transported objects" under "land." "Let's save the specifics for when we establish entrance procedures."

"Phone lines," XX says. "And data cables too."

Manager Fung taps the word "utilities" on the board.

"But we should be thorough and identify all the utilities. So nothing is missed."

Someone laughs, and XX freezes. Hann has repeatedly warned him not to dominate the conversation, and he does not want to be fired. He covers his mouth, forces himself to shut up. He says he will take notes, covers his mouth again, and meticulously documents everyone's ideas along with his own, aired or not.

They move on to infiltration from the air. In his presentation, Jei-sun was quite exhaustive, identifying satellites, drones, air-space threats, Wi-Fi, cameras, legal and illegal radio frequencies, computers and smart devices, the ever-expanding list of hacker tricks. The ministry already loads monitoring software onto the computers of all guests and business partners by requiring sign-in through its portal. The hardware of all citizens performing web searches involving key words are also tagged and scrutinized. The room is momentarily quiet.

"Birds," someone calls out. "How could we have missed the birds?"

Everyone laughs but XX, who diligently jots down the idea.

"How about mosquitoes? Flies. The wind!"

"That's enough," Manager Fung says.

XX records the ideas. The issue of privacy is super important to him. He hates it when people nose into his business. But does a criminal trying to break into the Ministry of Finance servers deserve such consideration? Unable to resist a chance to show off to his manager, XX pokes two fingers in the air.

He says, "People are the root of all threats. Not their computers and gadgets. The ministry should monitor people."

"Go on," Manager Fung says.

"Scan all brains and faces on their premises, of course." XX has been obsessed with *The Pursuit of Happiness* and its algorithms ever since he saw how well the game worked on May-ling. "They can take emotional temperatures at entry checkpoints, in elevators and bathrooms, at lunch checkouts, vending machines. Anyplace people stop and pause for ten seconds. It'll be apparent who's incubating harmful ideas." The expertise is out there. With some time and hard work, XX is near certain they could stop everyone in the building with malicious intent.

Manager Fung nods, and XX beams with satisfaction as he imagines himself hailed a hero for foiling a major bomb threat.

Manager Fung clears his throat. "The ministry already monitors their partners and adversaries. Their current controls are effective. If I may play devil's advocate, aren't brain scans unnecessarily invasive?"

XX realizes that he agrees with Fung. Even more than disappointing his manager, XX should not have introduced this devil of an idea for a moment of glory.

Jei-sun holds up both his hands. "Let's keep ideological debates out of this. We're just brainstorming right now, dreaming up as many unconventional defenses as possible."

"Of course you are right," Manager Fung replies. "But we should also be sensible. We wouldn't, for example, propose embedding a monitoring chip into every citizen or installing spy cameras in every home. None of us wants that."

"No," XX says. "You are right. I withdraw my idea." He makes a big show of crossing it off his notes.

Jei-sun shakes his head, though. "Don't you see? This is the kind of idea that reaches for the stars. Do you know what it'll mean for our country if we perfect this technology? We would be unpatriotic if we did not try."

What has he done? XX feels sick. Manager Fung looks as white as a ghost.

Jei-sun continues, "And think what it'll mean for our company: we'll win every single government contract for the next fifty years! Just imagine our bonuses."

XX wants to yell out no, privacy is worth more than money, but he is afraid he'll sound like a traitor.

Manager Fung nods again and again. Finally, he says, "XX, you proposed this, and I think among our men here, your expertise is also most suited to it. You and I will work on this mind-reading project together."

All the air rushes from his lungs, so relieved is XX. In the next second, he realizes what a vote of confidence Fung has shown him. XX flies high with the knowledge that they both agree that this technology would be dangerous in hands other than their very own.

5

WEI-GUO

Hero nudges the brim of his gray fedora with a pair of silver tongs and asks if I'd like some Scotch. An impressive collection of crystal decanters line the mirrored shelves of his bar. I don't know why he's wearing a hat inside his own office, but clad in a charcoal double-breasted suit and his hair ironed into a quiet ponytail, he looks more businesslike today than I've ever seen him. I say sure. It's more than nice to get a bit of our sizable fees back in refreshments.

"Wonderful. I like nothing better than savoring a fine drink with a fellow connoisseur."

I smile and look away. His devouring, full-on attention gives me the willies.

Seated across from me, Dad says, "Wei-guo's no connoisseur. He hardly knows his beer from his Scotch. And besides, it's two in the afternoon."

Balancing a gleaming cut-crystal glass between the fingertips of his two hands, Hero presents it to Big Dad. Big Dad waves no and says he cannot drink, doctor's orders. Dad thanks Hero and says that he too should no longer consume alcohol.

Hero sets the glass before me and summons his assistant, another unmistakable Willful Sterile, to get Hero's key and personal stash of Da Hong Pao and brew us a pot of tea.

"You are too kind." Dad beams. This famous oolong is near impossible to find, not to mention prohibitively expensive. I sit up taller just to think that Hero considers us worthy of such largesse.

He slides next to me on the couch and raises his glass. "Here's to a lover for Wei-guo, a family, and progeny. The first beautiful, the second loyal, and the last ever-capable."

Our heavy glasses chime when we clink. He tips back and swallows his entire drink. To be polite, I do the same.

"Hear, hear," Dad says, toasting with empty cupped hands, while Big Dad glares at me, less than pleased by my indulgence.

The Scotch warms my throat, but falls just short of the liquid diesel feel of the *er guo tou* that I can afford. It tastes like a smoggy day in Beijing. Like dirt too. "Very nice," I say.

Big Dad has not stopped frowning since he sat down. "Is the Wu May-ling match dead?"

"It is most certainly *not* dead." Hero's fingers dance on my wrist. "I don't know what you did on your date, but you really impressed them. They adore Wei-guo."

"What date?" my dads say in near unison, and the blood drains from my face.

Hero's eyes ping-pong between us before he slaps my hand and tells me I'm a naughty boy. He informs my dads that I invited May-ling to my studio for a private tour with a leering emphasis on the word "private."

I wish I did not choose to sit opposite my two dads. With their matching silver hair and shabby sweaters, I can't help seeing them as the left and right foot of a pair of shoes eager to kick my butt.

"There was nothing private about it," I say. "Husband One was there, along with the son."

"You kept it private from *us*," Big Dad says.

Dad adds, "Why didn't you tell us?"

I don't know what to say. Truth is I planned to, but May-ling never returned my calls after her bait-and-switch of a date, and I was embarrassed to confess to my dads that I'd been duped and dumped. Besides, I'm forty-four years old—a middle-aged man, for crying out loud. I'm tired of having to tell my dads every time I go to the bathroom. I thought it was behind me anyway, and that Hero had assembled us today to introduce a new candidate.

Big Dad grits his teeth. It is clear that later, in the privacy of our home, he will tell me exactly what he thinks of my idiocy, but right now, he is not about to lose more face. He pastes on a rigid smile and suggests that I start from the beginning and tell them exactly what happened.

Hero pours me more Scotch, and I take a grateful sip. "Wu May-ling wanted me to call her, so I did."

"What do you mean, she 'wanted you to call her'?" Being that he's my biological parent, Dad takes it upon himself to act the bad guy, to ask the tough questions.

"She gave me her contact information," I say, as if it were obvious.

"When was that?" Dad says.

At the lunch, I tell them, and Big Dad shoots Dad an accusatory glare. At moments like this, he readily disowns me and lays the blame at the feet of my true origin.

"I love it," Hero says. "Money can buy you a wife, but all the money in the world cannot buy you chemistry."

Big Dad shakes his head at me, thoroughly disgusted. Dad directs me back to the date.

I shrug. "I showed them my gym, and they taught me to dance."

Dad's jaw comes unhinged.

"Talk about dancing," Hero says, an eyebrow-arched grin plastered to his face. "The Guo family—pardon me, I just can't seem to get with the times—the Wu family really likes Wei-guo. I'm not supposed to tell you this yet, but you must be prepared." He opens his arms as if conferring upon us a special favor. "They're going to ask for a Compatibility Test." He says that Husband One will be here shortly to discuss logistics.

I'm stunned by the request and thrilled I was not wrong about that date. There was indeed excellent chemistry, and not just between May-ling and me.

"This is all very sudden," Big Dad says, his eyes ablaze with insult. "We're not ready to talk about taking any next step."

The groom's side is in no position to make such outright displays of displeasure, and I can't help but feel that Big Dad is being difficult just to punish me. Unpleasant as it is, I make myself stand up and formally apologize. He will not consider the Compatibility Test until I kowtow to him and acknowledge his importance. I apologize next to Dad and hang my head. "I should have been more forthcoming. I thought I had the opportunity to meet May-ling one-on-one, to get to know her without so many people around. I wanted to make sure I liked her before I troubled you." Big Dad would shit a brick if he knew what I'd do to avoid supervised dating. To refocus our discussion, I say, "I like her."

Big Dad scowls. "I've been asking around about the Guos, the Wus, whoever they are, and I am more than concerned."

Hero perches his chin on a fist and tilts his head. "Please, tell me."

"I heard this from more than one source," Big Dad says. Dad nods vigorously. "We've heard that Hann is Willfully Sterile. And we've had more confirmation that XX is a two-percenter, a Lost Boy. His name is evidence enough, I'd think."

Hero yelps, covering his mouth. I'm just as startled.

He says, "Those are very grave accusations. I absolutely understand why you're so concerned."

If the charge of Willful Sterility offends Hero, he does not show it. It takes everything I have not to squirm and look away as his man-eater eyes latch onto mine and burrow in.

"Have they given you that impression?"

I know better than to contradict Big Dad. I say that I hardly know the Wus, though Hann is one of the most gentlemanly men I've met. I note that Big Dad has been as unforthcoming as me, and store away that little piece of ammunition for future use.

Hero reminds us that we can pose our questions directly to Husband One shortly, and I down more Scotch in anticipation of that delightful scenario.

"I'm not saying the rumors are true, but let's say they are," Hero continues. "Think what that means in the bedroom. Can you dream up a better situation for Wei-guo?"

I'd just had the very same thought.

"Wei-guo could be reeducated and severely fined for closeting a Willful Sterile," Big Dad says. "And on top of that, who wants to live with the mentally ill?"

"Guo Xiong-xin has a highly coveted job and a respectable income. And his coworkers affectionately call him XX, so the name has stuck," Hero says. "He is a fully functioning and contributing member of that family, not to mention of society."

Big Dad laughs. "One lunch with him, and it is clear that he's not right in the head."

Brow furrowed, Hero is silent for a long while. "Should I call Hann and tell him not to come?"

"No," I say, and Big Dad shoots me his dirtiest look yet. I would do XX a disservice not sharing the details of his visit. "XX gave me an old photo of May-ling and one of the whole family as well. Hann and May-ling didn't know about it, but he kind of proposed to me. XX is thoughtful in his own offbeat way. He's all right."

"This is as it should be." Hero squeezes my arm. "We should all step back, and let the young people work things out for themselves."

Big Dad shakes his head at Hero. "We're being ambushed. Set up to make a rash decision."

I smile apologetically at Hero and wish I could make Big Dad drink some Scotch and chill. The promised tea has still not been served.

There's a quiet knock on Hero's open office door.

"You're here!" Hero glides to the door in a shoulder-swaying slither. It's an awful and painful sight to witness in a stocky, middle-aged man.

Hann visibly stiffens when Hero snuggles up to him and claims an elbow. The two nearly stumble as Hann shrinks from the insistent Hero, who holds on to him all the way to the couch. Discombobulated, Hann bows and greets my fathers, who stay seated and say hello with cold politeness. I rise and clap Hann on the back and shake his hand and smile through the general discomfort. Try as I might, I cannot find any signs of Willful Sterility in the man. But then again, few dare to cross the line like Hero, not when you could get swept off the street by the police for lewd behavior.

Without asking, Hero sets a glass of iced Scotch before Hann and snuggles up again next to him. This time, Hann unlatches himself gruffly.

Hero smiles triumphantly at Big Dad. "I am delighted to tell you that Guo Hann is here to propose a Compatibility Test. We can structure it any way you like, but thirty years in this business tells me that these trials are most successful when conducted overnight in a third-party location, a five-star hotel preferably." Hann shakes his head and puts up a hand, but our matchmaker does not stop. I'm starting to see how he bulldozes his way to success. "Bride and groom only. An Advanced honeymoon."

Hann says, "We want to assure ourselves that Wei-guo is compatible with our entire family, not just with May-ling. What we are proposing is dinner in our home and then an hour afterwards for Wei-guo and May-ling. No overnight."

"If I may interject," Hero says, "the five of you have already spent time together. You like Wei-guo. Wei-guo likes all of you. He's good with BeiBei. Even XX has proposed." He winks at me.

Hann says, "What are you talking about?"

Steamrolling past that, Hero says, "The heart of the issue is the physical compatibility between May-ling and Wei-guo. Let's address that, and not confuse what is already clear." I've got to hand it to Hero again. The way he drops his bombs and then forges right on ahead is downright masterful.

Hann looks like he could throttle Hero. So do my dads.

"Are you Willfully Sterile?" Big Dad says.

Hero and I reach for our drinks at the same time.

Hann frowns with disbelief. "I'm a married man. With a child," he roars. He pops to his feet but is boxed in by Hero, me, and the coffee table. He jerks his arm away from Hero.

"The Lee family has heard rumors," Hero says. "And of course, they must ask you this question. It is better that they ask you directly, don't you think?" He coaxes Hann to sit.

Hann buttons up his suit coat. "You can destroy my family with accusations like that."

It is so awkward that I stand too to keep him company. Big Dad glares at us both.

"We are honorable, good-hearted people. Get to know us, and you can make up your own mind as to who we are." Hann turns to address me, and for an instant, his eyes soften. "If you decide that we are right for you, then know that we are a very tightly knit, a very close and private family. Cherish us, and we will cherish you. Marrying us is not a decision you will regret."

I like what I hear, but Big Dad stands to put on his jacket, no doubt offended that Hann dares to bypass his authority and address me directly. I'm sick of him trying to sink my chances. Dad scrambles to his feet and follows Big Dad's lead. Despite my dads' brusqueness, Hann is gracious with his farewell.

Hero throws an arm over my shoulder as he escorts us out. "I am grateful you brought your concerns into the open. Family dissolution and forced sterilization are at stake, and I know you will exercise extreme caution with these rumors."

Big Dad does not react.

Hero loops his free hand around my elbow and squeezes it. "I'm glad you are going to take the time to think things over. But do go through with the Compatibility Test." He winks at me. "You have nothing to lose."

Big Dad turns to him, his face ugly with fury. Enunciating every word, he says, "This is Wei-guo's very first match. He is naïve and vulnerable. If we go through with the test, I am very much afraid that he will lose his heart."

I know Big Dad is speaking from a place of love, but that does not make his concern any less smothering. "I'm finally getting a turn, Dad. Please let me have my chance, come what may." I'll gladly face his ire later, but Hero must not leave here thinking this match is dead.

The brush gradually thins as the GPS in my watch guides me up the mountain. It is a tiring climb—one made more difficult by the unseasonal autumn heat wave and the embedded radios, sensors, firing mechanisms, and demobilizing devices in my fight suit—but I cannot stop marveling at the improvements made to our latest night-vision goggles. Color has been introduced to the night scene. The world is a slightly fuzzy, almost impressionistic, painting, made even more spectacular by the full moon and the cloaks of green, orange, red, and gold on the trees. Mopping my face and neck, I fight the urge to rip off my drenched uniform. Not many people get to enjoy the natural world from this lovely vantage. Of the dozen open spaces the city has allotted for our monthly Strategic Games, Snake Mountain Parkland boasts the most scenic terrain.

At the location specified by my logistics officer, I take a minute to catch my breath and survey the treetops for our command post. When I spy our decoy platform a story aboveground with its telltale droop of rope, I turn sixty degrees to the east and walk forty paces. Looking up, I see the shadowy dance of mahogany branches and their pinnate leaves, but no command post. My crew has camouflaged it well.

I toot on my magpie whistle. I've chosen the magpie, the symbol for familial bliss, as our calling signal. The rate of depression and suicide is inordinately high among us single men as we save for a dowry and the hope of a mate. That wait is a long one, even when we are lucky enough to be allowed such a journey, and my aim for Middle Kingdom, our Strategic Games team, is to create a brotherhood, a support structure, a way of thinking that will sustain us. The hope for family must stay front and center in my men's consciousness. In mine too. It is a matter of choosing life over darkness and death.

My call is returned, and I blow out two more warbles five seconds apart. A rope ladder is lowered from the sky. I cannot see Chao, my major and current second in command, but I hear his heels thump in salute.

I peel my damp jumpsuit away from my torso and blow some

air down my front before hoisting myself up the swinging ropes. Chao does not make space for me on the small platform, nor does he mind his elbows retrieving the long ladder. I remind myself yet again that his behavior is an inability to intuit personal space rather than outright disrespect, even though this twenty-three-year-old is an ambitious knucklehead. Middle Kingdom won its division last year. We have a waiting list of more than a hundred guys, yet Chao was forced upon us, military rank intact, through a well-placed call from his city-treasurer uncle.

It has been a week since our Safety Council meeting, and I've been dreading the day I have to offer up five men for psychological evaluation. I consider identifying Chao as one of my five: let's see how good his connections are under these circumstances. Upon second thought, though, I doubt even Chao would fare so well after such a report. Very few would.

He has been here for some time setting up and has stripped to his tank undershirt, the top of his jumpsuit dragging from his hips. His stick arms are slick with sweat, and he smells of armpit. I ask for an update while eyeing pointedly the dirty footprint on the sleeve of his uniform where the firing mechanisms are embedded. He reports that all four of our battalions are at starting position.

I keep staring. Chao is great at enforcing rules upon others, but not so good at following them himself. He finally gets my message and pulls up the top half of his uniform. His night goggles are nowhere to be seen.

"A soldier should always be prepared," I say.

"Yes, sir," he replies. His eyes, however, go blank, unwilling to back up his verbal assent.

"Not only were you not prepared just now, you were also compromising the integrity and performance of your equipment, not to mention endangering the success of our entire mission."

Chao yes sirs me again. "The heat is giving me hives, sir."

I notice the red scratches running up his neck, and I itch to tear off my own suit. "The battle is about to start. Get dressed. Put on your gear."

I stare at the thermos next.

"It's hot. I didn't think you'd want tea."

"I always want tea." I know he resents kowtowing to me, a former lieutenant major. It is equally irritating that he forces me to continually assert my authority, but do it, I must. Obedience is the soldier's number-one virtue, and it is vital to our mission that I have his.

I order him to perform an equipment check on his uniform before squeezing around him and leaving him to manage my tea brewer. My command post appears proficiently constructed. Camouflaging branches form a believable canopy below us. I'll have to make sure to praise my construction team. I tug on my zip line; my escape cable feels taut and secure. The computer booth takes up two-thirds of our roughly one-by-two-meter platform. I nudge aside the overlapping curtains, and Chao follows me inside, fidgeting with his sleeve. I slide my goggles onto my forehead. Our cameras are well positioned. The monitors piece together a near panoramic view of the battleground and also of three strategic crossing areas.

I sit on my stool. The positions of the hundred men in my five battalions glow on the screens, the scouts in yellow and the remaining in green. Five patches of red indicate the locations each battalion will attack first or defend. We have fifteen minutes until the start of battle.

Chao edges forward and leans until he is nearly on top of me. It's all I can do not to plug my nose. "Sir, may I have a word?"

"What is it?"

"I hear that congratulations are in order."

"What're you talking about?"

"Your engagement, sir. I want to congratulate you on your upcoming nuptials."

"I'm nowhere close to getting married." Irritation washes over me, and I stand to reclaim my air space. Hero is also Chao's matchmaker, and jumping the gun like this must be another one of Hero's tactics. The water in the brewer rumbles.

"Go turn that off before it alerts the entire enemy camp," I say.

Chao salutes and exits. I poke my head out of the curtains, the heavy humid air outside a slight improvement on the stink Chao leaves behind. He clunks around the mess kit and returns, proffering a cup with outstretched hands. I accept it and thank him.

"If I may, sir. You have not filled Colonel Wang's position since he married and retired, and I—"

"And you thought you'd inherit the whole shebang, marrying me off as well?" Strategic Games is played only by unmarried men, but this subordinate's desire to push me out when my next move isn't yet certain annoys me to no end. Not a day goes by without someone wanting what is rightfully mine, someone telling me what I can or cannot do.

"Major Chao, as the founding general, I would very much like to know: where in our declarations does it stipulate that married men cannot fight?"

He looks at me in confusion. "I never imagined you'd be interested in playing games once you have a wife." He does not know that I, as founder of Middle Kingdom, sneakily modified our charter. I had wanted to control my fate when the time came.

I shake my head, disgusted. I should not have alluded to my secret in a fit of anger. My charter modification is wishful thinking; it is never going to hold up if challenged. But what really bothers me is, why is he wasting my time on this nonsense minutes before the start of battle? "I do not promote just because there is an opening." I wave his attention toward the screens. "If promotion is what you have in mind, why don't you start by proving your worth?"

As if proximity to the screen produces answers, Chao leans over me yet again. "I'm not a fan of our current positions." It is astonishing how little tact he possesses. "Battalion One is surrounded by rocky hills, trapped and vulnerable to attack on the eastern side. And Battalion Two is exposed at the top of those steep rocks. By the time they hike down to a more advantageous position, the battle will be over."

"The positions are givens. Criticizing your positions will not help us win. With these set pieces, how are you going to command your men?"

I tip back on my stool, but there is no relief from Chao's stink. I drum my fingers. Sweat sprouts from his forehead, catches in his eyebrows, and slithers down his nose. He will not amount to much, not with that sweaty disposition. I almost feel sorry for him.

Chao scratches his scalp next and rakes his hands through his damp hair. "I'd move Battalion One out of that trap immediately. I would put them in a flying wedge formation and order them to come at the enemy shooting, to not stop shooting until they are dead or out of ammunition."

Moments like this, I really miss Colonel Wang. Wang would have intuited right away that Battalion One, with its meager size and glaringly vulnerable eastern side, is a decoy. With one glimpse of the battle terrain, he would have known that I've positioned our best sharpshooters atop the rock faces surrounding Battalion One. Once all our troops are in position, he would have cued the decoy to incite attack.

Chao continues, "Battalion One is grossly outnumbered, but using surprise, our men could take down more than their share of opponents." He ventures a self-congratulatory smirk. "They could divide the enemy troop, and Battalion Three and Four can surround and attack it from behind."

"No," I say.

Chao's head jerks back, and he scowls before remembering to yessir me. Moments later, he cannot resist saying, "But surely there is more than one correct approach in this situation."

"No." A smaller man would have called him on insubordination. "Would you like to know why you are wrong?"

"Yes, sir." I can feel his entire body clenching.

"It is foolhardy of you to assume that my battle plan was of no merit."

"Yes, sir," he barks.

The sarcasm in his voice riles me, but against all my instincts, I force myself to be a good superior, to do for him what I've sworn to do for all my men. I know what it's like to be Chao. I've twenty years on him, and I'm still waiting for my turn at comfort, at opportunities that reflect my worth, at finally receiving my due. Compared to his, my consternation with my government, my bosses, and my elders is exponentially greater.

In that moment, I realize that I don't have it in me to turn him or any of my men in for mental-health tests. What am I going to do? I cannot do them harm.

I take a deep breath and try to concentrate on the task before me. I point to the patch of red near our command post. "Who's left to guard your general if you move Battalion Three?"

"Yes, sir." Chao fidgets in place. He has no good answer.

I ask him what he knows about the soldiers in Battalion Two. He studies the personnel list for today, but arrives at little. The way Chao enlisted and catapulted in rank has not endeared him to many, and he has not made many friends in the five months he's been with Middle Kingdom.

I say, "A commander must know the strengths and weaknesses of his men as well as he knows his own family."

"Yes, sir."

"Tell me: how can you hope for a promotion when you haven't mastered the basics?"

Chao keeps his mouth shut, but irritation leaks from his every pore. Scolded often, I've felt that same annoyance. And I know how well harsh words worked on me.

"What if I tell you that Battalion Two is made up of our best sharpshooters?" Now that Chao has declared his intention, I make myself give him the consideration I myself crave. "What would be the correct course of action in that case?" I've always wanted Middle Kingdom to be a meritocracy, a true oasis where neither pettiness nor favoritism has a place.

It takes him a few stabs before arriving at my opening strategy.

Skirmishes are living and breathing organisms. Tactical moves during the progression and pressure of battle are complex and ever evolving, and I guide Chao through possible scenarios and help him reason his way to the best tactical responses. Throughout our exchange, he sweats, his attention flitting from my gaze to the buzz of cicadas outside our booth, to the monitors, and back to me. His ideas fall short more often than not, but I don't give up on him. I tell myself that even more than winning, my job as the general is to lead, to foster community, to teach.

When we finally arrive at the victory I planned, I say, "It takes more than one kind of intelligence to win a war."

"Yes, sir." He holds himself rail straight, his face sour.

I rise to stand just as tall. "Do you have the kind of flexible thinking, the patience, and commitment to devote to each and every one of our operations and to each and every one of your teammates?"

"Middle Kingdom has all my attention." Chao bites his lips. A smirk creeps into the corners of his lips. "With all due respect, sir, your strategy assumes that we are always the aggressor."

"The best defense is always a good offense." I follow Chao's gaze to the screen and swear at myself for not paying attention to the start clock. I order Chao to hurry down the tree and run to his position. He stomps off like a teenager who has been grounded.

I clear the table of Chao's litter of half-eaten snacks and wrappers, my mind of his greedy ambition, and take a restorative sip of tea. Breathing deeply, I watch the clock tick down the last two minutes.

The numbers blink and freeze a second before the start of the game. I shake my head. The server must be down again. Major Jung and his cohorts like to make it as hard as possible for us to play. I jab at some random keys.

A login box pops up on the screen. Cursing, I type in my name and password. The last time this happened, the names of our hundred players had to be re-entered by hand. My men waited over an hour out on the field for the action to begin.

Large, bold-printed words scroll up the monitor like the end credits of a movie: IDENTIFY FIVE OR MORE MEN ON YOUR TEAM WHO COULD BENEFIT FROM PSYCHOLOGICAL EVALUATION. The instruction ends with a display of everyone in Middle Kingdom, grouped by rank. There is a box next to each name and more instructions to check off a minimum of five. Jung, that sneaky bastard! The deadline for this is still three weeks away. He, meanwhile, has been stonewalling Doc and our request for a meeting.

I have no intention of giving anyone up if I can help it, let alone sending them in before deadline. I hit the Escape button to exit the message. It does not clear. I hover my cursor around the edges of my screen and uncover the Close button. I hit it, and the message shrinks away.

A second later, the big scrolling demand starts all over again.

That devil Jung is going to hold up play until he gets what he wants. My heart pounds in my ears as I await the slate of names. I would sooner not play today than give up my men and subject them to god knows what. I thumb through the contact list on my watch and call the general of the opposing team.

"Don't give them any names," I say before I even identify myself. I close the message on the screen again. "The Safety Council is renegotiating this item. We're going to fight this." The scrolling instructions begin again.

"I just did," the opposing general says. "I couldn't get out of the form—"

My stomach drops. I've got to message Doc and get the word out before we sacrifice any more men to a game.

I hit the Close button on the slate of names a third time. A new message flashes in red. It specifies a deadline for filing and a warning: TEAMS THAT FAIL TO FILE ON TIME WILL NOT BE ALLOWED TO COMPETE.

I close the warning, and thankfully, my master control board finally reappears. It looks like we will get to play today after all, but my heart is no longer in it. This game no longer feels like a game.

You going to buy something?" the tobacco man barks. He's been watching me watch the entrance to Hann's building while I hide in his kiosk fingering his extensive selection of smokeless flavors.

I have no use for tobacco in any form, so I ask if he carries magazines, code word for the dissident periodicals available only on street corners in non-digital form.

"Nothing illegal sold here." He looks me over. "Are you a cop?"

I say no. A few minutes later, he demands to see my resident ID and studies me some more. Finally, he holds his hands out for ten yuan—one can buy three mags for that price—and tosses me one from beneath his shelves.

On its cover, a striking woman, finger pointing and eyes scrunched and furious, exclaims in bold print: "I Am Not for Beating! I Am Not Chattel!"

While I have a hard time understanding why a husband lucky enough to have a wife, let alone such a beautiful one, would treat her badly, Big Dad would say that this story is more proof that not being married is far superior to living in a bad marriage. My dads have forbidden my match with May-ling, but I'm not convinced I'm wrong about Hann. I have been rearranging my work schedule in order to follow him. One day May-ling and I are going to have a good laugh over the lengths I've gone to in trying to become her husband.

So far, I've discovered that Hann takes walks and does not eat lunch unless he meets clients or XX. Seeing him spend time outside his home with his strange brother persuades me further that this is a bighearted family that will take good care of me.

And yet, something still keeps me following. Still has me wondering.

The automatic door of Hann's building glides open again, and a column of white emerges amidst a crush of dark suits. It takes me a second to recognize Hann in the white running jacket and pants. In his hand is a small sports bag with the protruding handle of a racquet. I smile. Finally, he's up to something different.

Once outside, he dons a straw fedora. The hat is stylish, but strictly utilitarian, no indoor prop like Hero's. Every time I see Hann, I am freshly struck by his class and easy elegance. He seems to glide above the fray.

I try to keep half a city block between us as I follow him around the corner and down three flights of stairs to the subway. On the platform, I stand behind a pole a distance away. I open my magazine and hide further behind the pointed finger of the cover woman before I remember that the periodical is illegal.

A train finally rumbles into the station. I jump onto the car next to his and clamber to the connecting door for a view of Hann. He opts to stand, his gaze settling upon the darkness whizzing past the windows. A young man sitting in front of Hann examines him again and again. A head taller than most and his silvery hair thick, Hann is eye-catching and ever more noticeable in white. I am gratified that he seems neither aware of nor interested in the man's attention.

Hann gets off at the Temple of Heaven Station, and I'm relieved that Dongdan Park, a notorious pick-up spot for the Willful Sterile, is not his destination. I trail Hann to the East Gate, where he enters, flashing a pass.

Inside the park, he scoots through a gingko-lined boulevard, dodging the flying feet and bouncing feathers of the *jian-zi* circles and the twirling ballroom dancers. There are just two women today among the dozen waltzing couples. Homely looking and dressed in drab, loose-fitting sweats, the two are neither eye-catching nor graceful. That distinction belongs to two elderly men in green sweatsuits. Nimble, elegant, and ever so masculine in their confident postures, they look as if they've been dancing together for decades. Again, if he notices them, Hann makes no indication. Intent on his destination, he hurries ahead.

He finally stops next to an avenue of sycamores and adds his bag to a pile on the ground. Beneath the dancing shadows of these leggy, high-canopied trees, a dozen or so men in various whites bounce shuttlecocks back and forth. Hann joins the shorter of two lines and shakes the hand of his neighbor.

I stake out a bench a distance away and pull my cap down further. To blend in, I unearth a bag of peanuts from my pocket.

His team appears to be warming up, but there is no method to their process, no nets, and just two shuttlecocks. The birdies travel long, lazy arcs, and the men seem more intent on chatting, on keeping the random-flying birdies afloat, than anything productive. From time to time, their guffaws reach my ears.

The men vary in age, with Hann at the upper end of the spectrum. They vary in height and shape as well. Their togs seem to be of designer quality, more expensive and put together than average, but well in keeping with Hann's socioeconomic stratum. Their overall manner appears reserved, of the professional class. One man is a bit effeminate in the way he swooshes his racquet, but it's impossible to tell if he's Willfully Sterile or just uncoordinated. All in all, the group seems like a random slice of the general population and no different from the many engaged in activities at the park. I don't know why, but it makes me proud that even from my remove, Hann stands out in his bearing and athletic grace.

A young man saunters by with an armful of sports gear. "Is this free?"

I wave him toward the other end of the bench. He dumps his things on the ground. I've seldom seen shorts that tight or skimpy on a man. He groans, untangling his jump rope. One by one, he extricates his two badminton racquets, his Ping-Pong paddles, *jian-zi*, shuttlecock, and soccer ball and deposits them on the seat. Bent over, his sculpted ass cheeks are there for all to see. It's clear this kid wants it known that he takes the pains to work out. I hope I was never such a show-off.

The guy has so much stuff that when he sits down, he is half a butt cheek away from me. I give him a sidelong glance and scoot toward my armrest.

Little has changed with Hann and company. Their feet barely move. This is turning out to be one boring outing.

"You look like a very good badminton player," the young man says. "One heck of an athlete."

"Sure," I say, and make a point of turning back to the badminton rallies.

He rests an arm on the seatback behind me and leans in. "Where do you work out?"

"You looking for a trainer?"

"Perhaps." He laughs, his generously lashed eyes fixed upon mine. "Perhaps I just want to know your secrets."

My breath catches in my chest. I steal another look at the man. With his heavy brows, strong forehead, and wide shoulders, he is as masculine as they come, yet I could not be more uneasy.

"Do you want to play with me?" I must have started again because he smiles crookedly and adds, "At badminton."

I frown and glare and gruff up my voice. "Why don't you go play with them?"

He looks at Hann and his team and turns up his nose. "You like them?"

I ignore him.

"They're brothers, you know."

"They're not brothers," I say, supremely irritated now.

His eyes twinkle with great amusement. "They are comrades who're into BL." He winks. "Boy love."

I don't know why his accusation makes me so angry. "How do you know?"

He smiles again as if in possession of a great secret.

"Are you a, uh"—I take a gulp and force myself to say it—"a brother?"

He scoots until his thighs are right up against mine. "Would you like me to be?"

My heart clambers up my throat. His breath smells like a distillery.

I say, "Why don't you go pick up one of those guys?"

"They're short, fat, and ugly," he says. "I'd rather be with you."

I pretend to study the players. "The tall one there."

"You like that type, huh? I saw you watching him."

"I don't have a type."

"Good, 'cause I'm much better-looking than that old coot."

I suddenly realize that I will not be able to get rid of this guy. "Go pick up Gramps, so I know you're not a cop."

He thinks for a moment and shrugs. "Those are what you call 'elite' brothers. They play with no one without a secret-police-level background check."

"You're making up shit."

"See that fatass on the right and the bald one next to him?" He lifts his eyebrows. "We can go into the woods later and watch them fuck like dogs."

I get up to leave.

He looks into the distance and breaks into a creepy grin. "What have we here?"

I hear jogging steps.

"Lee Wei-guo, is that you?"

My heart sinks to my knees. I turn around and, feigning surprise, clutch and shake Hann's hand.

"I thought that was you." He asks what I'm doing at the Temple of Heaven.

"Just clearing my head." I hold up my bag of peanuts. "And eating lunch."

"Come. I want to introduce you to my teammates."

I follow him, feeling as if I'm walking from one tiger's den into another. Just when I think I'm safely out of reach, the hustler trills out a "yoooo-hoooo!" I keep walking and am thankful Hann does too.

"See you next time, Lee Wei-guo!"

His use of my full name sets my heart pounding even faster.

Back at the badminton game, Hann addresses his group, "This is Lee Wei-guo, our fiancé."

I pull up my dropped jaw—I've no such official status—and cannot help but grin at him for his vote of confidence. The fellows take turns shaking my hand and congratulating me.

Hann hands me his racquet and tells me to step in for him. "Wei-guo is a very famous trainer."

I cannot help smiling again. I say that I am happy just to watch and try to give back the racquet. Someone sends a birdie my way, and instinctively, I return it. Before I know it, I am sending lobs, drives, and smashes at each of them in succession, assessing their individual abilities and offering tips.

"Do you fellows play in a league?" I say, bouncing from foot to foot to model the readiness and energy I want to see in each of them.

"Nah," someone replies. "We're too lazy. Too slow."

"I was watching you from the bench," I say. "You've got game." It occurs to me a second too late that I've just given myself away.

Hann does not seem to notice. "Why don't you put the guys through the paces? Show us what it'll take to play in a league."

"Really?" I reply, more delighted than I can say.

"Sure," Hann says. "Us old dogs like to learn some new tricks from time to time."

With each swing of the racquet, I feel more at ease with Hann and his friends. They seem no better or worse than the guys I hang out with, even if they are Willfully Sterile. They enjoy one another's company, they like to poke fun and tell jokes, and when it counts, these are most likely the people who will have Hann's back. They want no more and no less out of life than the rest of us, and I am struck by the unfairness of the limitations our government has placed on them.

After a while, the hustler gathers his equipment and takes off after another victim, and I relax even more. Hann sports a big smile, and I'm surprised how much it pleases me to please him. These are good men—not good badminton players, but good people—and I'd like nothing better than to call them my friends.

After forty minutes in a queue with phlegm-spewing and irritated patients, it is finally my turn at the clinic's registration desk. I lean on the counter in front of a gum-popping young man with spiky hair and buckteeth and say hello. He stares at his work screen and alternately types and chuckles. After a while, I suspect he's messaging his pals and tell him I'm here to update my Groom Health Certificate. His eyes flick up, and he looks me over as if to assess the likelihood of my nabbing a wife. I say that I also need an intelligence test. His eyebrows rise with something bordering on respect. One does not incur the expense of an IQ test unless there is real interest from the bride.

My marrying May-ling is not yet a certainty, but he doesn't have to know that. I tell him I have an appointment.

He inclines his head toward the adjoining waiting area. "So do they." There must be close to a hundred people coughing and sneezing at one another over there.

I don't know why we bother making appointments when it only adds to the hospital's spin on efficient patient processing. I touch my watch to the sensor to identify myself. I hate people who cut lines, but I can't afford to waste an entire day in a germ incubator and risk catching something. I tell the clerk I'm here to see Doc, my uncle. At Doc's suggestion, a ridiculous number of his Strategic Games colleagues check in as his nephew or brother. My heart skips a beat as I wait for the clerk to challenge me.

He perks up, his horse teeth flashing. "Of course." He sifts through a few slips of paper in a small dish on his desk and passes one to me, telling me to use it rather than the registration number on my watch. That Doc is much respected and loved by his coworkers is confirmed yet again. I've always received better treatment after I mention him.

I take off my watch and hide it deep in my pocket. A pug-nosed guard is on duty in the waiting area, and I lurk at the periphery to his far side. On long benches, men seated elbow to elbow check me out before returning to glare at a screen on the wall that flashes and calls out numbers. They honk and hack, their combined discomfort a music concussive with impatience and mounting rage.

I count half a dozen professional queuers; they're not hard to spot with their face masks and comfortable, portable chairs. It is against the rules of course to pay others to line up for you, but the guard is not eager to pick fights with representatives of the influential and the wealthy and their deep Party connections.

My number is called minutes later. I hurry across the room, my eyes down. People shake their heads and tsk in disgust. A bold one points out that I just got here. I wave my number at him. The guard stops me and asks why I have a paper number.

I puff out my chest and claim that I forgot my watch at home this morning. "Four hours I've been out there on my feet in the hallway so I don't catch anything in this hellhole." I scowl and continue on to Doc's office, the back of my neck tingling. I don't know what I'll do if the guard demands to search my pockets. Our system makes the business of daily living excruciating, yet I am consumed with guilt.

A line of five desks cuts across the workspace Doc shares with four other doctors. I locate him at his station, thread my way between patients, and get in line behind five people. It's a relief to be away from the stifling misery of the main waiting pool.

I try to catch Doc's eye to say hello, but his attention is wholly focused on the man before him. Three of the doctors are at the exam tables behind their desks, and I look away from the moaning man curled on his side, the half-naked one getting a hernia exam. I page through the messages on my watch and try not to listen in on the complaints about chest coughs and constipation. I hate other people nosing in on my visits, so I answer a client request to change an appointment and read a few off-color jokes posted to Middle Kingdom's group chat.

Everyone gets his three minutes, and soon I'm second in line. Seated beside Doc's desk, the man in front of me whispers urgently about an occasional inability to sustain an erection. He looks about my age, and I cannot help check his hand even though most men do not like to wear rings. There is a wedding band. Doc asks some questions about his heart, blood pressure, and drinking habits. He counsels the man to cut back on alcohol. "Good luck," Doc says as he sends him away clutching a prescription for male enhancement medication. Prematurely gray, Doc looks and acts like everyone's favorite grandfather.

I'm surprised he didn't ask if the man has fathered a child. Male enhancement drugs are not supposed to be prescribed to anyone who has reproduced. Our government does not believe in further sexing up our already testosterone-infused society.

But why shouldn't Doc give the man some hope? His patient would need luck and money—lots of both—finding the medication anyway. So little of it is produced that the Party elite are most likely the only people who can get their hands on it.

I slide into the chair. "Uncle," I say for the benefit of the men in line behind me. "You look well. How is Auntie?"

Doc brings my chart up on his screen and brightens. "I see you have good news."

"I am hopeful." I smile. "I can only afford to be a maximum husband, but I feel a strong affinity with this woman. It's a good situation. She only has one child." I can feel the guys behind me press forward.

"What does that matter?" Doc stares up at my eavesdroppers, but they do not back away. "You'll have a woman to hold and a chance at a child and a full life."

"I appreciate you saying that." I've always liked Doc. Status and false airs mean little to him.

"Good, good," he says. "Did you get your checkup this year at the PLA Hospital?"

I say yes. Doc is required to ask the question even though annual screening for sexually transmitted diseases at the People's Liberation Army Hospital is mandatory for all unmarried men.

"Then you are fine." He taps the screen a few times and prints out my certificate. As he signs it and applies his seal, I ask if the document also certifies that I have no detrimental genetic markers.

He frowns. "You understand there is no such thing as a perfect child. Perfect children cannot be engineered. Neither can a perfect spouse." He looks up at our assembled audience. I hate that the lack of privacy makes every patient's time with their doctors public service messages. "And boys are not better than girls. Our current problem is as much about an excess of men as the millions of girls who were killed and never born. Civilized people do not murder their own."

He pauses to collect himself. "You make a spouse and a child right for you and your family through the hard work of loving them and of sharing and living by your values."

"You tell him."

I turn around and glare at the elderly man who presumes to speak during my appointment.

"The doctor is so very wise," he tells me.

"Yes." I have to admit Doc's perspective is refreshing for one in the depths of the matchmaking race. I remind Doc I also need an IQ-test referral. "How much does that cost?"

"You agreed to an IQ test?"

I nod, sheepish. Doc is always telling us, his Strategic Games comrades, to hold on to our dignity and assert our rights, but I'm not in a position to refuse anything.

He shakes his head. "It's absolutely demeaning to be a man these days. A few words with you and it's obvious you are bright and lovable. A good family man. All they need do is pay attention. And they don't even know what they should be looking for. There are many kinds of intelligence: the most important in this day and age, in an Advanced family especially, is emotional intelligence. But no one ever tests for that."

He sighs and gathers himself. "Gentlemen," he addresses the five behind me. "Would you mind giving my nephew a moment to get his head together? Please kindly wait on the other side of that door."

The men shuffle out grudgingly, but shuffle they do, and it occurs to me that this communal spying is the reason our government will never make patient privacy a working reality.

Doc rolls and scoots his chair in front of me and reaches up to palpate my neck. "A farmer has seventeen sheep. All but nine die. How many are left?" he says quietly.

"What?"

Doc looks in my ear with a scope and repeats his question. I don't know what he's up to. I was not a good math student at school, but it's clear that his question is a riddle.

"Nine," I say.

"Good." Doc returns to his desk, taps and taps at his screen and pulls up a mountain-shaped graph. He bends close and explains that it's an intelligence-quotient distribution curve. He points to 115 and swipes his finger between the areas just right of center marked "Above Average" and "High Intelligence." "Your correct answer puts you about here. Agree?"

No one has ever tried to categorize me as high average. Doc taps at his screen some more. He rips up my first Groom Health Certificate as a new one rolls out of his printer. He has given me an IQ of 119.

"That's the test?" I whisper.

"Sixty percent of the population can't answer the question you just did." When I still appear less than convinced, Doc says, "Unreasonable requests deserve special treatment." He tells me that paying for the test will make it official.

I look right and left, making sure no one is eavesdropping, before leaning in and asking Doc if Major Jung has agreed to a meeting yet.

Doc shakes his head. He places a stethoscope to my chest and whispers that eight generals had sent in names before he could notify everyone that we will fight Jung's four point nine percent edict. All forty of the men identified have been picked up and taken away for two-week evaluations. "God knows how many are going to be able to come back."

My breath catches, and I stare at him, big-eyed. "What are we going to do?" I've lost sleep all week trying to come up with a solution.

Doc moves in closer and palpates the glands behind my ears again. "It's done. I've hired a hacker. A white hat. He was the one who notified all our generals of a plan to negotiate. Unless we hear from Jung, our remaining 492 generals will receive another anonymous message with procedures to boycott the submission of names. Our only hope is for everyone to stand united on this, to deny him as a group."

"Yes." I'm ecstatic and grateful Doc has put into motion what I dared not. It is foolhardy, not to mention dangerous, to defy Jung, yet what choice has he left us? The more I think about it, the more I like the anonymity of Doc's plan. It will not jeopardize my immediate or future family. My involvement may even make Mayling proud. "What can they do if we all refuse to cooperate?"

"That's my hope. I have your support?"

"Absolutely."

"I've spoken to Little Sung, and he has agreed to speak to three other council members. Could you do the same? It would save me a lot of time."

I readily agree.

6

HANN

Hann takes the short walk from his office to the seafood restaurant where he likes to lunch with his clients. From time to time, he stops and pretends to check his watch while looking surreptitiously behind him. Wei-guo has been following him recently. How fitting that on the one day Hann wishes to be followed, Wei-guo is nowhere to be seen. It was Wei-guo, of course, who gave him this counterinvestigation idea, and he would pay money to witness the man's panic when his Helpmate sits down to dine with Hann. He laughs, recalling Wei-guo's hide-and-seek tactics. Hann was relieved that Wei-guo had brains enough to confirm the rumors himself rather than endanger his potential family with an outsider. When Hann passed by the tobacco stand two weeks ago—he buys his dissident mags there—the owner alerted him to the surveillance and tailing. After that, it was not hard to spot Wei-guo with his chiseled body and his friendly disposition toward strangers. It took much convincing before the old man would believe that Wei-guo was not some sinister, smiling version of the secret police.

Hann has been putting the guy through his paces ever since and must admit that he likes the enthusiastic fellow Wei-guo presented to the badminton group. Hann led him to the Temple of Heaven to meet his clan; he wanted to see how Wei-guo handled himself in that situation. They had a collective chuckle watching him turn green as Jimmy, the notorious park hustler, pounced. Although competitive play was the last thing they wanted—badminton was their cover, not their reason to meet—they allowed Wei-guo to do his thing. It was good to see how eagerly and naturally he jumped in and led the play, how suited he is for his chosen profession. Equal parts cheerleader and techniques coach, Wei-guo effortlessly elevated their play. With energy and optimism to spare, he would bring a welcome dose of sunshine to any household. After he left, more than one of Hann's buddies volunteered to teach him to switch-hit. They couldn't stop talking about his delicious ass.

Hann looks around one last time for signs of Wei-guo before entering the restaurant. The owner seats him at his preferred table, the one in the back screened by a fake maple bonsai. He orders a pot of flowering jasmine tea and waits for Min Ahn-na. Finding Wei-guo's Helpmate required no more than two well-placed calls. That she agreed to the lunch without asking for compensation was a nice surprise, a move that Hann hopes bodes well for Wei-guo.

At twelve o'clock on the dot—Helpmates are time-conscious creatures—the restaurant owner leads a large, dark-haired Eurasian woman—a White Russian, most likely—toward his table. She is wearing the gray dress, white nurse's cap, and apron uniform required by law, a law many would gladly disregard in this situation, himself included.

Hann rises to say hello. Big-shouldered, heavy-breasted, the same height as Hann, and ungainly, she carries herself with the air of a man in drag. The sadistic recruiters at the Bountiful Love Council no doubt hired her on the spot when she applied. Compared to her, May-ling seems of a different species.

Min Ahn-na nods in greeting. Her face, though plain and slightly pockmarked, is not unattractive, but she wears it like a death mask. A good many Helpmates come from other countries, and Hann wonders if this one came by choice or circumstance. She looks to be in her early forties.

Hann thanks her for coming. She sits rail straight. Her eyes find the tied leaves in the glass teapot and stay there as if the plumped and unfurling chrysanthemum form could relieve her from the conversation to come. Hann asks if the Supreme Seafood Supper, one of the restaurant's four-dish combinations for two, suits her.

"How can I be of service?" she says, her tone and expression discouragingly bland. Her accent is quite good.

There is no point beating around the bush. The State has sanctified and privileged the Helpmate relationship, and the sooner he understands the looseness of her lips, the better. He leans forward and explains again that his family is considering Advancing with Lee Wei-guo, that with a child involved they must be sure they are making a good decision, that his family would be immensely grateful for her assistance. To confirm her proficiency with the language, he asks her to repeat back what he has said.

Her eyes flash. "You want to know if Lee Wei-guo is a good man."

Hann senses in her a formidable presence. "Where did you learn to speak such good Chinese?" He hikes up the corners of his mouth.

Min Ahn-na does not reciprocate. "I was born in Harbin."

Hann waits, but she does not volunteer more information. Her terse answers make for great strategy if their purpose is to make him cough up money quickly. "We want to make sure that Lee Wei-guo is right for us. And also that we are the right family for him." Hann pauses to let the thoughtful reciprocity in his intention sink in. "I hope you will help."

"He is a decent man," she says, her voice neutral and conclusive. There is no encouragement, no impatience, no suggestion of hidden intent in her demeanor.

He says, "Can you elaborate a little on what you mean by that?"

"What do you want to know?"

If she is as unforthcoming in bed, she must be the State's idea of the model Helpmate. "How long has Wei-guo been your lover?"

"Twelve years."

Hann's eyes grow big. Bachelors are allowed to petition for new Helpmates every two years, and women who look and act like Min Ahn-na do not keep longtime clients. Wei-guo is either very loyal or too set in his ways. Her appearance makes Hann question Wei-guo's taste in women and his compatibility with May-ling.

"Were you an assignment or a choice?"

"Choice." She seems to take no offense at the question.

Hann tries not to show his surprise. He asks how Wei-guo found her.

"His last Helpmate introduced us."

"Why did he terminate their love affair?"

"She retired." Helpmates receive their pension after fifteen years of service.

"Was he with her for a long time too?"

"I don't know."

Min Ahn-na seems as loyal to Wei-guo as he is to her. Hann examines her again, but cannot discover what Wei-guo sees in her cold disposition or her grandmotherly, rice-sack chest.

The waitress delivers their first dish. With heads intact, tails fanned, and cilantro patterned like scales beneath crisp pastry, the two fried shrimp rolls resemble dragons in flight above a minimalist bed of radish clouds. Hann serves her a portion. Her two hands remain on the table's edge, clutching it as if to brace herself for his next question. Eating seems to interest her as little as it does Hann.

For the next twenty minutes, Hann painstakingly formulates his questions, and she continues to answer them in the fewest words possible. He learns that Wei-guo is a fair man; that he is not prone to physical aggression; that he has never forced her to commit acts against her will; that he visits regularly each week; that he has no physical deformities; that his hygiene is acceptable; that he has no unnatural sexual predilections; that he seems neither more or less sexually charged than the next man. She has not refused any questions, yet Hann has never felt less satisfied.

He finally pulls the envelope from his inner jacket pocket and wedges it under her plate. "You are very generous to come today. Here's a little taxi fare."

"That's not necessary," she replies. "Lee Wei-guo is already paying me for my time." Her expression is bored as can be.

Hann almost smiles as his estimation of Wei-guo jumps a notch. His exasperation that the information he has painstakingly extracted is tainted, that he has to start all over trying to outsmart her is quickly tempered by the fact that Min Ahn-na has not returned his envelope. She must be here for the money after all, making that confession.

Hann tries again. "Tell me more about Lee Wei-guo."

"What do you want to know?"

His stare produces no reply. "Help me out here. Please."

"He's a decent man."

He wants to snap her thick neck. The money on the table sparks an idea. "Does he tip you?"

"Sometimes."

"How much?"

"Twenty-five, usually." Helpmates receive a salary and are only required to provide missionary or doggy-style sex and lower-body nudity during weekly appointments. Services outside of that are extra, and their fees, payable to the State. Most men are saving toward a dowry, and only the most generous tip. He asks about Wei-guo's preferred extras.

She glares at him. "The occasional touching, oral sex."

"Does he like anal sex?" he asks. "Bondage?"

She shakes her head, brows furrowed.

"Have you arranged any black-market transactions for him?" Procuring the services of Helpmates other than one's own is a frequent, though illegal, practice.

She shakes her head again.

"Set him up with another man?" The question sends a twinge of electricity through Hann.

Her eyes turn hard as she spits out a no. Hann finds it difficult to believe Wei-guo could be so boring. He retrieves another envelope of cash and holds it out to her. After a moment, she takes it from him and deposits it on top of his first offering.

"There's nothing to tell," she says. "It is good, isn't it, that there's nothing to tell?"

That is ultimately what Hann hopes for, but he doesn't quite know how to read this woman who operates in lukewarm. "You have nothing bad to say about him?"

"He's a man. No better, no worse than any other."

"Would you be sorry to lose him?"

She thinks for a moment. "I cannot lose what isn't mine."

Watching her carefully, Hann thinks he senses regret. Wei-guo must be a pretty good guy if she is adamant to speak no evil of him. Hann counts on human nature to rear its ugly head if Wei-guo has done her wrong.

"Has he ever brought you to orgasm?"

She blinks and glares again at Hann. He takes out his last envelope and places it atop her stack.

"I'd like to pay you to teach him how to please a woman," Hann says. "Will you do it without letting on that I'm involved?"

She looks into the envelope this time and hands it back. She tells him he's underestimated the cost for that service. "You pay the Bountiful Love office for that."

Hann did not realize that lessons on the ways of love are now part of the menu of charges. He pushes the money back toward her. "I'd like this to be strictly between you and me."

"I won't lie to him just as I don't lie to you."

Hann combs his fingers through his hair and considers her joyless demeanor. "Do you swear that everything you've told me is true?"

"Yes."

A thought suddenly occurs to him. "Is he in love with you?"

Her reply is swift. "That is not possible."

There is a definite tinge of bitterness in her voice.

Hann squeezes his fists, swallows his yawn, and brightens his expression. Twice a year, the dozen senior managers in his accounting firm are shoehorned into a small, frigid conference room and stripped of their digital devices for hours at a time in order to evaluate their clients' half-year financials. Despite decades of reform and anticorruption measures, their firm's accounting practices still pay heed to factions as varied as Party officials, highly placed investors, hidden nominee shareholders, and the occasional conscientious objector.

In the name of national harmony, Chang, their firm's Party liaison and one of their managing triumvirate, has so far managed to push through positive growth rates for three underperforming State-subsidized businesses and bestow upon a dying one another six months of life. Hann cringes to think this is only the first of a handful more of such meetings.

Zhen, the last of the day's presenters and head of their matchmaker sector, adjusts his big, square apparatchik glasses and drones on, ". . . twenty-nine percent margin for this quarter is an unusual accomplishment. I've examined LoveBridge's books, and I can give you my solemn guarantee that this is no exaggeration."

Zhen's purported 29 percent profit margin is nearly ten points above their firm's internal guidelines for the industry, and Chang's low, stingy forehead and close-set eyes wrinkle in disapproval. Even if accurate, Zhen's numbers will not be justifiable, and not because the industry is saturated and fiercely competitive. No company is to grossly outperform its peers, not since the economic boom twenty years ago when their nation's top 1 percent took control of over 50 percent of the country's wealth, and the elevation of the working class has become a necessary rallying cry once again for their government. Selected teachings of Mao have become popular again, and many Party officials like their own Chang have taken to wearing the old Mao suit, popularizing it as a symbol of solidarity with the workingman. It's laughable, really. Chang's lavish lifestyle—not to mention that of many Party officials—is as far from the workingman's as Earth is from the Sun.

Hann flips through the pages and pages of financial statements from Zhen, the abundance no doubt intended to inundate and confound rather than to clarify. Hann despises these meetings, hates even more that the practice of accounting runs completely counter to everything he learned in school, to all the professional principles he once swore to uphold. Truth, accuracy, predictability—none of these matters when the good of the nation as prescribed by the Party supersedes all. In recent years, it has become inadvisable for companies to stand out, to deviate from the norm; one could just as well be singled out for not performing as well as for outperforming.

In a universe where numbers should not be allowed to lie, our leaders defy the truth that is mathematics.

"To summarize," Zhen says, and Hann perks up at the hint that an end is near. He refocuses on Zhen's bug-eyed glasses and resolves not to wander off again. "Matchmaking is a basic need, as necessary as food, water, and shelter. With the recent legalization of the third husband, the growth for this sector will be limitless for the near future. A twenty-nine percent margin for LoveBridge is not only sustainable, it is conservative."

Chang punctuates Zhen's statement with a rather forceful clearing of his throat. Despite the reforms, little wealth has shifted from the hands of the political elite. Hann wonders if Chang finds his life and duties confining. Because of Chang, Zhen's current charade along with everyone else's has become a nonnegotiable part of the landscape. These tedious meetings allow Chang and the Party to claim group consensus and transparency as working realities. And for his efforts, he not only shot up the ranks to their firm's executive committee at age thirty-five, he was also allowed to be the sole custodian of his wife's affection in addition to the affections of two mistresses—a beauty from Vietnam and a coarse-looking Latina he brought back from a youthful stint in America. Rumor has it that Chang Ming-ze, one of their new hires, is the eldest of his two bastards. And if that is true, Chang fathered that child at age seventeen. Hann shakes his head, and a dry laugh escapes at the fact he worried about Chang's well-being.

The most difficult part of being Chang is not blurting out the name of a mistress while in bed with another.

"In conclusion," Zhen says, and Hann sits up, readies himself for the finish, "supporting LoveBridge's remarkable rate of growth will not only be right for the company, it will show our support for

Family Advancement and our commitment to securing a spouse for each and every member of our deserving Bounty."

Dunn's fingers begin a quiet, drumming roll, stopping when he catches Hann watching him. Another member of the triumvirate and the tallest man in their firm, Dunn carries himself with the gravity and grace of a jungle cat. The handsomest, the most substantive, and presentable of their three leaders, Dunn scrambled up the ranks through hard work, real ability, and astute politicking. If there is anyone at the firm whom Hann would like for a friend—not that he dares have a confidant here—Dunn would be it. Though Dunn has kept his distance, Hann has always had the feeling that amidst the noise, the lies, and the pretense, Dunn sees him. They see each other.

Finally, Chang holds up two circling fingers, and Zhen knows to utter his last words. Chang's scowl appears more irritated than usual. Hann has heard that the vice premier's mother-in-law owns a sizeable block of LoveBridge's preferred stock and is looking to make a killing. The pressure from above must be formidable.

Chang tosses the LoveBridge statements on the table. "Let's vote. LoveBridge wants twenty-nine percent. I say we keep them at eighteen." So that there is no question as to the Party's position, Chang always votes first. "Dunn?"

"I propose that we limit LoveBridge to twenty-four percent," Dunn says, his facial expression and his voice as bright as if he is agreeing with Chang. Dunn votes with the merits of the case and knows that the truth probably lies somewhere south of Zhen's claim.

Loo, the third member of the triumvirate, sides with Chang. More often than not, the executive committee ends up at two to one with Chang. The senior managers vote next, though their opinions will only be taken under advisement.

Ever mindful that a single accusation of homosexuality could turn his world upside down, Hann tries to make allies and build goodwill in subtle ways. He agrees with Dunn on this case and is glad to support him. After the vote count, he is not surprised only one other manager has sided with Dunn.

To appear less of a suck-up, Hann grins and says, "Matchmaking is a good business. I should know: my family has decided to make the sacrifice and go the max." The big-eyed silence around the table unnerves him. His is a patriotic move, and Hann expected at the very least some gratuitous show of support. Instead, there's just quiet.

Finally, Chang says, "We're done for this morning. Everyone back here in an hour."

The men do not waste time pushing back their chairs and rising. Hann's entire body aches as he transfers his weight onto his creaky knees, eager for the dozen steps needed to work the stiffness out of his joints. Chang stops him at the door. As the others file out, Hann tilts his head to stretch the sides of his neck and wonders what Chang wants with him.

Dunn tilts back in his chair, his hands bracing his neck. "Come. Sit with us."

Chang glares across an empty chair at Dunn.

Hann would do just about anything not to have to sit down again, but he takes the chair between them. Chang brushes a piece of lint from his Mao jacket. His eyes consider Hann's tweed coat, his vest, and his linen pocket square for so long Hann begins to feel like a subversive.

Finally, the man says, "The firm would like to clarify its position on Family Advancement, specifically on the matter of our people going the max."

Hann straightens up.

"We are men with important reputations to uphold. As such, we think it right to require that our accounting personnel hold our families at two male spouses. Anything more would look unprofessional."

Hann can scarcely believe he is hearing this from their Party representative. Chang thinks he is above the law. A quip pops to mind: Fight corruption too little, and you'll ruin the country. Fight corruption too much, you'll destroy the Party.

Dunn's eyes twinkle as if amused by Chang's declaration. Unsure how to react, Hann does not speak. He is in no position to make waves, not when he has so much to hide. Chang's little edict cannot, of course, be legally enforced, nor can it be defied, if Hann knows what's good for him.

Dunn scoots his chair closer toward Chang. "Manager Chou's family added a third spouse two months ago. How should we address that situation?"

"This rule, of course, cannot apply retroactively," Chang says, his voice generous with reason. "We can hardly undo a marriage after the fact."

"You are so right. You know Lin, the latest hire in auditing? I just received his wedding invitation. He will be a maximum husband," Dunn says. "How should we handle that?"

"Isn't he a clerk? We place no restrictions on clerks."

Dunn leans closer, his musky aftershave filling Hann's nose. "I heard that they could not pay for the second husband's liver cancer operation without the dowry." His confidential manner sends tingles up Hann's spine.

Chang says, "We all agree that it is in all of our best interest to uphold our firm's pristine reputation, to maintain for our clients' sake the best possible perception of our people."

One would have thought Dunn and Chang best friends, the polite way they address and smile at each other.

One also would have thought that Hann need not be here for this.

"Perhaps Hann too has a hardship." Dunn beams at Hann and asks if he wouldn't mind sharing the reason his family is considering a third spouse.

"We need more space," Hann says, recounting the most innocuous of their many considerations. "With the baby and two bedrooms for four people, no one sleeps. For an old man like me, it does not matter. But a young thing like my wife—" He shrugs the nonchalant he-man shrug of the harried male. "She can barely function, let alone take care of the baby and the apartment and two husbands."

"She won't be getting more sleep with another man to service. And more children," Chang says.

Hann stretches out his arms and shrugs again as if to say who can argue with a woman who's made up her mind.

"We are in agreement then," Chang says.

They certainly are not, but Hann keeps his mouth shut.

Dunn asks how long Hann's been with the firm. Hann's admission that it'll be thirty-four years in September fills him with both bitterness and pride.

Dunn says to Chang, "I think we can both agree that Hann has been an exemplary and dedicated employee. A true revolutionary soldier, especially in the way he shepherded the airplane families last year toward the greatest good."

This is not a pleasant memory. Assigned the job of witness, Hann accompanied a Chongqing Airlines executive to the homes of all two hundred and five crash victims. Details had emerged that the newly hired pilot, along with another fifty, had padded their flying record with the help of the airline's parent company. At every visit, the families alternately bawled and railed at them, lectured and scolded while the executive and Hann kowtowed on their knees and begged forgiveness and promised to recertify all their pilots and mechanics. More than one father tried to exact justice with his fists, but they could not leave, not without first convincing the families to accept the insultingly meager 60,000 RMB compensation. The average visit was two hours. Many cases required multiple visits. Hann barely slept for two months.

Dunn continues, "To help mitigate his hardship, I propose that we put Hann on our housing list. For his outstanding service, we should move him to the very top."

"I'm touched," Hann says, adopting the grateful smile of someone about to be fucked over, "and so very unworthy of your high regard." Every few years, their company is allotted a government housing spot. Just to be on the list requires the glowing recommendation of one's manager and every manager on up the line. The recognition is nothing more than a verbal commendation. Chang is the most recent and one of only three people in thirty-plus years who have actually received this subsidized housing.

Chang's smile tightens, though Hann would have thought he would be more pleased at Dunn's tidy solution.

"I heard that a flat has just been allotted to us because of your tremendous efforts," Dunn says to Chang. "Isn't it strange that we've not received anything for over a decade from the housing authority?"

Suddenly, Hann realizes that Chang is the one Dunn intends to fuck over. This housing benefit came under Chang's purview as Party representative about ten years ago. Dunn must be implying that Chang has been flipping the housing on the black market and pocketing the proceeds.

Chang's smile is now broader than ever. "Hann is tremendously deserving of the award. Before we make promises, however, we must examine our list to make certain that our most deserving employees are not being neglected."

"I heartily agree," Dunn says, rising to his feet.

Hann stands too.

"Don't you worry," Dunn says, clapping him on the shoulder.

"Chang and I will fight hard for you. You have our full support." He ushers Hann out of the conference room and shakes his hand again in the hallway.

"I appreciate your commendation," Hann says, holding on to Dunn for an extra beat to show his gratitude.

"Nothing to it." Dunn extracts his hand. "Nothing to it at all."

"It's final then, Chang's ban on going the max?"

"You are one of our best managers," Dunn says. The warmth in his eyes changes into something guarded and polite. "Be assured that we will always do everything to keep our best managers happy and at their working best."

Hann scoots to the left side of his fold-up lounge chair to find a spot of support for his back. He tucks his jacket tight around himself. He should cart out the stained mattress and broken shelf left behind by the last tenant, clear the floor of papers and debris, scrub the layer of scum and mold from the bathroom tiles, but his bones ache. His eyes feel as if they've been glued shut.

He did not expect to be the recipient of this three-bedroom flat ten minutes from work, nor did he anticipate that this award would make him a pawn in the office tug of war between Dunn and Chang. In order not to show favoritism, Dunn stuck Hann with a newly bankrupt client from his portfolio, a manufacturer of gasoline-powered vehicles that claimed a phantom inventory of cars to keep their books afloat. Hann oversees transportation clients—airlines, bus, rail, and subways—and Dunn decided that this automobile manufacturer fell under Hann's umbrella.

Chang did not bother inventing excuses. He installed his idiot nephew in Hann's department along with the insolent princeling of some Party stalwart. Hann tries to empty his mind of the two troublemakers. Neither has the requisite experience for their positions. From all the dunderheaded mistakes Hann had to clean up and the calls he fielded from pissed-off clients, he would not be surprised if the nephew's glowing, top-of-the-class *dang-an* records were stolen, a purchased identity. What can Hann do but endure his tripled workload and this workplace replete with spies and minefields? The most innocuous of his actions now harbors unpredictable consequences.

Something rustles beneath a pile of scattered papers, and Hann reaches for the plastic bat next to his chair and swats at the floor. A mouse scuttles across the living room and under the torn sofa. He really should buy some mousetraps, but a mouse is no big deal, really. Tenants in government housing have been known to leave behind gouged-out walls, trails of paint, rabid dogs, and the occasional Lost Boy. If Hann could hold on for four more years until he's sixty and retirement eligible, his family would be able to live in this apartment at below-market rents until all three spouses die. No sane person declines such an award.

Which is why Hann has allowed himself one uncomfortable piece of furniture in the flat and one week to come to terms with his windfall before telling May-ling and Xiong-xin. He did not mean to drag it out, but suddenly, two weeks have flown by. The thought that he would be obligated to have scheduled sex with May-ling for the rest of his days, that he would have to diplomatically push her away again and again, that the same unresolvable argument would rule them forever turns Hann's limbs leaden. He just wants to sleep when he comes here, to sleep and dream about a time not so very long ago when he possessed only one big—but manageable—lie.

He squeezes his eyes tighter and orders his mind to go blank, and if not blank, then to at the very least move on to sunnier thoughts. May-ling would be pleased by this big apartment. The recognition too would make her proud, and he very much wants to make her proud. Although, at the same time it occurs to Hann that with BeiBei in a bedroom of his own, there would no longer be a physical buffer in bed. May-ling would be right up against him six out of seven nights every week, a suffocating second skin. But really, what is the big deal? An orgasm is an orgasm, whomever it is with. The act is over in minutes.

Right?

But Hann knows that it will not be that simple. The last time May-ling cornered him, he lost his erection while inside her. Try as she might, he could not get hard again. More important, he did not want to. He told her that age could do that to a man, but she knew the truth. Days afterward, he did not know if he would come upon her concerned, hurt, humiliated, or angry.

Hann considers taking an aggressive stance and using the apartment—its spaciousness, its financial peace of mind, the status it confers—as a bargaining chip. Take it or leave it, he'll say. Nothing else is on the table. Could he bring himself to say that? Is she fed up enough to turn him down? Would she forgive him the ultimatum? He is certain though that either way—more sex or no sex—the apartment would bring death to the relative peace of their current arrangement.

He sighs and tells himself to stop wallowing in end-of-the-world doom and gloom. May-ling loves him, and she loves BeiBei. She has no interest in breaking up their family. She has said so herself.

What he wouldn't give for some quietude, some momentary freedom from this ceaseless noise in his brain. Desperate for the release of sleep, he counts: one, two, three, four, five—

All Hann has ever wanted was for his brother and himself not to stand out, to have lives like every other man. The responsibility of having to spend the rest of his life micromanaging someone who wants no managing fills him with more weariness. Xiong-xin is never going to want or appreciate the feelings of support and belonging Hann tries to engineer for him. It dawns on Hann that May-ling too has been trying to change someone incapable of changing. Does she hate her predicament as much as Hann hates his?

And what if Hann lets Xiong-xin go, returns him the way one returns an impossible and unhappy pet, a pet that refuses to be housebroken no matter how you love it, back to the nature to which it belongs? But where does Xiong-xin belong?

Bang. Bang. Bang.

It takes Hann a second to recognize the apartment. He had dozed off. He gulps in a breath. Someone is at the door. He wipes the drool from his mouth. He struggles to his feet and nearly slips on a waxy piece of trash. The knocking grows impatient. He lurches for the door and jerks it open.

Wei-guo starts, gawks at Hann and the mess behind him. "What are you doing here?"

Hann wants to ask him the same question. "Why are you following me?" He cannot help note that Wei-guo looks unusually handsome in a gray suit, that such a suit looks formidable beneath substantial shoulders and a muscular chest. Hann has a mind to undo the lumpy knot of Wei-guo's tie and fashion him a smart Windsor.

Wei-guo says, "You're all sweaty. Are you all right? You look pale."

There's touching concern in his expression. "You woke me from a nap." Hann wipes his forehead, and his hand does come away damp. "Why are you spying on me?"

Wei-guo looks him in the eye. "Just as you are checking up on me. We'd both be stupid not to find out everything we can about the other."

Hann appreciates Wei-guo's simple honesty, his easy embrace

of what's right. He nods and allows him into the apartment. "What were you hoping to find, beating down the door?"

"I'm not hoping to find anything. You've been spending your lunch hour here for many days. What would you think if you were me?" His eyes dart though he pretends he's not looking around for signs of a tryst. "What are you doing here?"

"Show yourself around if you want."

"Why are you napping here?" Wei-guo presses. He stares at the exposed sponge stuffing in the couch and can't quite suppress his distaste.

Hann says that his company awarded him the flat.

Wei-guo's eyes widen. "This is *yours*?" He paces around the living room before disappearing toward the bedrooms. Hann imagines hope leaking out of Wei-guo as the vigor in his footsteps dissipates. He returns to Hann with a sober expression. "This place is huge. You pay government rates?"

Hann nods.

"You have no need of a third spouse then."

Hann smiles apologetically. "I had to agree not to go the max."

"They can do that?"

Hann says yes, and Wei-guo's face falls. Hann's own disappointment rivals Wei-guo's.

"I'm sorry to hear that." Wei-guo sighs. "I should go. I'm sorry I—I won't bother you anymore." His shoulders round and slump as he stuffs his hands into his suit jacket and drags himself to the door.

Hann too feels inexplicably sorry. "Those pockets, they're not meant for warming your hands."

Wei-guo removes his hands and frowns. He turns around and studies the mess in the living room again. "Why haven't you cleaned this place?"

Hann says nothing. Something clicks for Wei-guo.

"You haven't told May-ling and XX about this apartment." Wei-guo's face brightens when Hann again does not answer. "This place is perfect for your family. You would be crazy not to live here."

Hann does not dare move.

"It's true, then?"

Hann discovers that he does not want to look away. He does not want to deny his most essential self. His heart gallops. Is he foolhardy to trust a man he hardly knows, a man still under the thumb of two opinionated fathers? "It'll be career and personal suicide if we don't live here."

Wei-guo nods. Hann stares into his eyes, waiting for shock, judgment, and disgust to cut him down. He finds instead warmth, acceptance, a sense of safe harbor.

Hann says, "Why have you been with Min Ahn-na for so many years? I find her very hard on the eyes. Ugly, to be honest."

Wei-guo's brows furrow, and he steps back toward the door. "I don't judge people by their looks, by what's beyond their control. I didn't think you did either." Shaking his head, he turns the lock.

His indignation is everything Hann hopes for. "Are you in love with Min Ahn-na?"

"I'd be a monster if I didn't have feelings for her. But no, I don't love her the way I would love my wife. I know the difference."

"Why have you been with her for so long?"

"Respect and loyalty are important to me. My parents taught me to treat people—friends, clients, lovers—the way I want to be treated."

"Loyalty has limits. It's not my experience that twelve years of sexual attraction and chemistry can be willed."

Wei-guo shrugs. "It can be if you're afraid of STDs, of being sent away to god-knows-where for treatment that lasts god only knows how long."

If he is capable of such self-control, he's a better man than Hann.

Wei-guo continues, "It's true that I desired and could have easily had a dozen more women. It's also out of loyalty to both Min Ahn-na and my future wife that I've limited myself. I don't want to come into my marriage with dozens of points of comparison, nor do I want to expose myself, my wife, and future child to disease."

"What if you never get a chance to marry?"

"I won't think like that. I can't."

Hann nods. "Do you want to come to dinner tomorrow night? Just the five of us, to see if we get along."

"Are you suggesting a Compatibility Test?"

"Will you promise not to bring up this apartment until—" Hann stops, unsure what exactly he is proposing. "Until May-ling makes up her mind about you? Are you willing to do that?"

"You want me to lie to her? I can't do that."

"No," Hann says. "I just don't want the apartment and monetary considerations to cloud her decision. You'd be doing her a kindness."

Wei-guo thinks about it for a moment. "That I can do."

7

MAY-LING

It is Wednesday night, my appointed night of the week with XX. BeiBei is asleep, the kitchen is wiped down, and the toys are finally all picked up. I long to curl up on the loveseat next to Hann. Instead, I drop onto the couch and prop my aching feet on the table. He tells me dinner was tasty, but doesn't take his eyes off the late news. I stare at him, daring him to send me to XX's room. Things have been strained ever since he made it clear that he will not fight for me, and I am not about to make the first move toward reconciliation.

The news is wrapping up with a five-minute segment on a non-model citizen, a dejected and tearful man who has collapsed to his knees to apologize and beg our forgiveness. Hann usually switches away at this point. He absolutely cannot stand this feature, which he calls the manipulation of the masses through intimidation. He doesn't this time though—he doesn't want to talk to me—and that further ratchets up my anger.

The interviewer offscreen says, "Do you want to rejoin our democratic life and start down the road toward rehabilitation?"

The man bows. "Yes, I do."

"If that is your intention, then repentance is not enough. You must also confess your wrongs and lay out a plan for rectification."

Still on his knees, the man bows and collapses, his shoulders shaking as his head meets the ground. "It was wrong of me to create and hide behind fake identities on the web." Sobs punctuate his words. He raises his head and bows again. "It was wrong of me to spread lies and to incite others to act on those lies."

I cannot bear to watch this poor man. Though we see not a scratch on him, it's not hard to imagine the threats and the mental torture that moved him to this state. The apologies are coached, sometimes even scripted by the producers, and then tightly edited. There is no truth here. They are simply putting on a show. We understand by the broadly painted apology, nevertheless, that the man has criticized the government and organized a protest of some kind, but we are never privy to the specifics of his action. It is abundantly clear, though, the danger in following his example.

I feel bad for the man, but like Hann, I too have little interest in participating in this charade. Sometimes, though, I worry that we have a hard time watching because it could easily be Hann and me featured on the show for closeting a Willful Sterile and corrupting the next generation. I sigh and shake off the thought—we're long past the point of no return—and tell the SmartGuide to recommend a program. Asia DanceSport Games appears on the top of the list. I choose it. Hann stares at the screen and does not object. The guide puts us at the start of Gi-gi and Fran-ko's dance in the American rhythm portion of the competition. It knows Hann likes these two competitors from Beijing. After years of pressure and major sponsorship from China, Asia DanceSport Games finally changed the rules and allowed same-sex teams to compete.

We watch the men transition from a rumba to a mambo. I wonder if Hann sees the same beauty and athleticism that I see, or if these gyrating men ignite his loins and fuel his fantasies. After a minute of this, I again cannot bear to watch. I turn off the entertainment screen.

"Have you come to a decision on divorcing XX?" I say.

Hann regards me with a look of infinite patience. After a moment, he calls out to XX.

"I'm not going to his room," I say.

He calls again for his brother—louder this time. Hann claims I have no case and has ignored all my attempts lately to further the discussion.

I hush and warn him about waking BeiBei.

"Why don't you make us all some tea?" Hann says. He usually just marches me to XX's room when he decides it's time, and I brace myself. When he wants to speak to both of us, it means he knows I've been neglecting my bedroom duties. It's hard to say which is worse—participating in Hann's detailed, instructional sex talks or actually having sex with XX.

In the kitchen, I brew a full pot of buckwheat tea. Hann thinks it controls obesity and cholesterol. I like that this tea will not keep XX awake. I bring out the dragon-and-phoenix cake one of Hann's subordinates sent us to announce his nuptials. Hann won't like it, but serving dessert will buy me another quarter of an hour.

Back in the living room, the two of them watch me from opposite ends of the couch. I deposit the tray and pour the first cup, slow as can be. I stick my nose over the steam and make a show of inhaling the sweet, almost coffeelike scent. My two husbands stare at me, Hann more impatiently than XX.

XX studies the cake box. "What is that?" The happy family has opted for a modern pink plaid, rather than the traditional red-and-gold wrapping.

"It's buckwheat tea," I say helpfully.

Hann says, "We don't need anything but tea after that large dinner." He is forever trying to manage what XX puts in his mouth.

"Would you care for some?" I say to Hann.

He cuts short my nonsense by leaning over and picking up the poured cup. "I need to talk to the two of you," Hann says.

I groan inwardly. Looking at XX, I say, "Shall I open the box?"

"What's in there?" he asks a second time.

"I didn't eat that much dinner," I say. "I'm still a little hungry. How about you?"

XX looks at his feet with a sly smile. "Me too." He likes to be offered snacks.

We both pretend not to hear Hann tsk. I start an ugly little tear. XX winces as if on cue.

"Oh, I'm a mess at this," I say. "Would you like to do the honors?" XX takes forever performing these inconsequential tasks.

As he works at the tape with his fingernails, I sneak a peek at Hann, expecting great annoyance. Even I'm sick of my stupid Wednesday-night maneuverings. The droop in his brows takes me aback. He looks utterly defeated.

"What's wrong?" Suddenly, I too feel at my wits' end, exhausted by the thought of trying to maneuver XX out of the act, of convincing him that he can lie to his brother, and should I fail, of having to do the deed and bully him into withdrawing now that Hann has banned condoms. Marriage should not be ruled by so much deceit and scheming.

"Nothing's wrong." Hann flashes a smile.

I sit on the couch and keep my eyes on him.

Hann sips his tea and clears his throat. He sips his tea again. "Actually, I have some great news." He smiles a little brighter. "Lee

Wei-guo is coming to dinner tomorrow. And afterwards, he and May-ling can have some time alone."

"Alone?" I say. "You invited him?"

"We did," Hann says.

I say, "I didn't."

XX lifts the first piece of tape from the wrapping paper, intently lines up its edges, and folds it in half. I doubt he heard a thing Hann said.

"You tell me every other day that this is what you want," says Hann.

My eyes well. I pushed for a Compatibility Test because I wanted to make him feel what it would be to lose me. Little did I know he was so eager to give me away. "You promised me that our marriage would be a partnership, that we would make all important decisions together."

XX's fingernail scrapes and scrapes and scrapes at the tape.

Hann says, "Should I tell Wei-guo not to come?"

I narrow my eyes at him.

XX finally frees the box. The wrapping paper rustles and grates as he folds it into an increasingly smaller rectangle. He steals a glance at Hann before lifting the lid and exposing four pastries, each stamped with an intertwined dragon and phoenix.

Hann waves away XX's offering. "What do you want to do then?"

"I want a unit dissolution." Saying the words makes my stomach convulse. "I want to be with someone who loves me back. All three of us deserve that."

"Stop being naïve," Hann says. "We already have that and more."

I shake my head at him and his dismissive tone.

Hann tells me, "The three of us love and support one another. We get along. We matter to each other. Do you know how rare that is? How many wives out there have it much, much worse?"

"Why should other women's unhappiness justify mine?" It is not lost on me that I could not have come up with this argument prior to our marriage. I love Hann because he valued me and taught me to value and stand up for myself.

XX says, "I—"

"It's all right, XX," Hann says. "This doesn't concern you."

XX puts down his cake. "It does too."

Hann sighs and turns his attention to his brother. "What is it?"

"I want a dissolution too. I don't want to live here or do sex anymore with—" XX's eyes drift toward my feet. "Sorry, Mayling." Hann insists that he must always be considerate of my feelings, and right now, I couldn't have loved him more.

"No apologies needed," I say, glad he acknowledges that he is as uncomfortable with me as I am with him.

"Absolutely not. XX mustn't be alone." Hann scowls at me as if I am the source of all the evil in the world. "We all three promised my parents that we'd stay together through good times and bad, that we'd watch over and protect each other always."

"I have dogs. I won't be alone."

"You don't have dogs," Hann says, greatly exasperated.

"I do too."

Hann puts up a hand. "Look: no one is dissolving anything. If you don't like Wei-guo, I'll get rid of him." Neither XX nor I say a word. "He's far from a sure thing. Why don't we eat dinner together and see if we still like him. Sleep with him. Don't sleep with him. I don't care. That's your choice. But we can't make an informed decision without giving him a test run. Right?"

"Wrong," I say, glaring. His *I don't care* rings in my ears.

Hann says, "I don't know what it is that you want."

"I want you. I want you to love me. To choose me."

"You already have me." The fury with which he spits out those words both frightens and infuriates me.

I get up and ask XX if he is ready for bed. He peeks at his brother before agreeing.

Hann stands too and glowers at me. "It's not as simple as you think," he says in a measured hiss. He turns his back to XX and lowers his voice further. "Hero won't do. I prefer variety."

It takes me a second to understand.

He steals another glance at XX. "They don't matter, though. None of them matters because my heart is here. With you and with XX and BeiBei."

His admission slams into me like a full body blow: Hann has *never* desired me. He will never want me. I've been immensely stupid. I so wanted a real marriage I accepted his lie of a nonexistent sex drive. I made myself believe that his preference for men belonged to his past. I let his loving ways with BeiBei, his predictable comings and goings, lull away my apprehensions.

"How could you—" My voice breaks, my eyes pool, and I cannot continue. How could I have been such a willing dupe? How could he lie to me? Cheat on me? I feel ill remembering how vulnerable I felt always making the first move, how persistently I laid myself open to him. How could he let me do that when I never had a chance?

Hann's expression remains an impenetrable wall. "I told you I was Willfully Sterile. I've never lied about it."

I can barely stand to look at him. "Yes, you have," I say. "And you've encouraged me to lie to myself."

His putting it into words makes real his betrayal—the years and years of it. A man who truly loved the three of us more than himself would not have done something so unforgivable. I am stunned to think he would expose me, expose his son, expose this family he claims to adore to untold dangers. The innumerable risks he has surely taken courses through me in cold, shivering waves.

Heartsick, I stuff XX's abandoned cake plus one more into his bear-sized paws. I tow him by the elbow out of the room before Hann can talk him out of dissolving our sham of a marriage.

I will never be enough for Hann.

I close XX's bedroom door before giving into tears. I was idiotic to hope that if I gave more of myself to XX, if I kept a more loving home, if I pushed Hann to realize his innermost feelings and to fight for me, our physical and emotional compasses would eventually align.

I've been deluding myself. A panicked drumbeat pounds against my temple, relentless and inescapable. I realize that by refusing to see, I've also endangered myself. What would they do to me if Hann is found out? Would they take BeiBei away? Hann will never want me. I cannot stake my happiness—or even my safety—on him, yet being without Hann feels like the end of the world. I pace the narrow corridor between the bed and monitors. I cover my mouth to muffle my sobbing.

I notice XX cringing in the corner, eyes blinking furiously and the cakes crumbling in his hand.

"I'm sorry," he says. "I didn't mean to make you cry."

I can't stop bawling. I shake my head and drag him into his cushy desk chair. The last thing I want is to deal with a frightened XX too. "I'm sorry I'm upsetting you," I say. "I'm sorry too that I asked for a dissolution. I like you. I really do."

In a small voice, he says, "Do you want to play the game?"

"No," I wail. He doesn't seem to understand how dire our situation is. "I don't want to play a game right now."

He dumps the cakes on his desk and picks up the mind-reading helmet. He says he's been reprogramming *The Pursuit of Happiness*, that it will help me. "I gave Wei-guo surveillance bugs. They've gathered enough data for you to interact with his avatar. He and I've become great friends."

"Why would he accept surveillance bugs from you?" I ask, despite myself.

"I embedded them in a gift," he says, "a picture."

"That's very wrong," I say. There isn't a trace of cunning or guilt in his expression.

"But it's important that we know him."

"Did Hann put you up to this?"

"No! I have my own good ideas," he bellows, insulted. "Hann can't program."

His deceitfulness astonishes me. I ask what he has found out.

"He has promised to take care of you, of *GuhGuh*, BeiBei, and me too." XX flashes a self-satisfied smile. "And he didn't even know that he won't have to take care of me, because I'll be living somewhere else."

I hardly know what to say.

XX continues, "I know you like to dance. I've programmed Wei-guo to do the tango." He pries his whale of a body out of his chair and pushes the helmet into my hands. He crowds me as if that would make me put it on.

I stare at the contraption and remember how awful the game made me feel, the out-of-the-blue crying jag. I sniffle and shake my head. "Not tonight. I can't handle that thing tonight."

Hovering centimeters from my face, he says, "Are you going to do sex with Wei-guo?"

"No!" I shrink back. But then I remember that Hann will never want me. I have so much on my mind that I admit that I have no idea what I want.

"The game will help, you know."

"No game's going to do that."

"This one will," he says.

"Please, XX? I just want some peace and quiet before I go to sleep."

He does the crisp, one-two-three shake of his head, the one that precedes his fight-to-the-death stare and tantrum.

I beg again.

He grips his body tighter between his crossed arms. "You're not fair. You guys never listen to me. I have to do everything you say, and you never do anything I say."

I hang my head.

"You guys always make me try new things before forming a judgment."

"All right," I say. I'll be able to cry in peace inside the helmet and not have to worry about upsetting XX any further. I plop down into his ratty old chair. Worse comes to worst, I will close my eyes and tune everything out.

XX wastes no time slipping the device over my head. His particular brand of greasy, barnyard stink chokes me. He's been using this helmet. Between the smell, the all-consuming green screen, and XX's hovering presence, my claustrophobia is profound.

"Go to bed," I tell him. "I don't want you watching me."

"I have to make sure you play correctly."

"I know how to play."

"No, you don't."

"Start it already, then."

"I did. It's reading your mind."

I groan when my ears begin to vibrate.

"Don't pick the dogs," XX says. "That part is not for you."

Dogs? Two Lee Wei-guos materialize. The first one smiles beguilingly at me. An arm crosses his middle as he bends over and bows. He extends a hand to me. The second Lee Wei-guo is down on his knees with his arms around two pony-sized dogs. Three more animals circle, vying for his attention.

"Does he have dogs?" I say. "We can't be considering someone with that many dogs."

XX says, "I told you to ignore the dogs."

"All right," I say, suddenly understanding that virtual dog outings must be how XX plays with Lee Wei-guo. Asserting that we have neither the space nor the excess energy, Hann has repeatedly shot down XX's pet requests. Inside my helmet, I stare at the man with the extended hand.

He says, "I've been waiting for another chance to dance with you."

The comforting timbre of his voice jolts me. I am shocked how much the fake Lee Wei-guo sounds like him, shocked too that I believe his words. I've forgotten how engaging his smile can be. "La Cumparsita" strikes up in the background.

"XX," I yell over the music, "did you program his speech? How does this work?"

"My bug has read his mind," XX replies. "My avatar can predict his thoughts to ninety-five percent certainty."

I tug off my helmet.

"What are you doing?" XX hates when I interrupt anything mid-stream.

"Are you saying that I can ask him anything I want, and he'll tell me what he's thinking?"

"Of course. That's what mind reading means."

"Why only ninety-five percent certainty?"

"Under duress, Wei-guo's unpredictable five percent of the time." XX pushes a series of buttons on the helmet and lowers it back over my head.

"Is that like his liar rate?"

"No. He doesn't mean to lie when he is forced into it."

I almost smile to hear XX dissect the finer points on lying. "Is five percent high?"

"No," he snaps. I've posed too many questions.

As I wait for Wei-guo to appear again, I consider what I want to ask him. Some ideas come to me, and I feel uncomfortable. "Can I have some privacy?"

"Not possible."

It's a waste of time beating around the bush with XX. I admit that my questions may be too embarrassing to say out loud.

"It's a mind reader. Read his mind."

"Oh," I say, feeling like a technoboob yet again. The moment I stare at Lee Wei-guo's outstretched hand, he zooms large on the screen until he is head, shoulders, and chest, smack in front of me. His dark eyes smolder and zero in as he wraps one arm around my back and holds the other shoulder height as if clasping mine. The green screen around us transforms into a chartreuse meadow filled with pink, scarlet, and white cosmos. My heart aches at the sight of these wildflowers, at XX's steady efforts to please me. I am in a chair, my fingers interlaced in my lap. I cannot physically sense Wei-guo's touch, but the way the background advances and retreats, pans, dips, and spins, it indeed feels as if he is leading me through the steps of the tango.

"This is amazing, XX," I tell him. "Absolute genius."

"I know."

His carriage strong and open, Lee Wei-guo steers me around the meadow with a confidence that was noticeably absent during our merengue encounter. I am freshly reminded of his formidable chest and shoulders, of his easy charisma, of my urge to run my fingertips across the sculpted strength beneath his shirt.

Hann contends that a person's inner nature is often revealed in the intimate space between dancing partners, in the sense of adventure, challenge, or surprise he creates within it, and I try to focus on the message Wei-guo sends through his movements. There's heat behind his eyes. His attention makes my entire being sing. It's thrilling how desired and coveted he makes me feel. I let myself sink into his arms and glide among the breeze-tossed flowers. After a dozen turns around the meadow, I notice that his intensity has not wavered. He continues to seduce me with those same ravenous eyes, that same hungry smile. That same heat I felt before now grows cold. His gaze begins to feel monotonous and nerve-wracking. I ask XX why Wei-guo keeps looking at me like that.

"He's programmed to express his primary emotion toward you."

"I feel like he wants to eat me alive."

"No. He—"

I hear the hesitation, and it's not hard to figure out what XX is too embarrassed to say. Despite my yearning for that connection with Hann, Wei-guo's blatant desire makes me uneasy. Your face is your rice bowl, MaMa never tired of telling my sisters and me. Without your beauty, you are nothing. I have little illusion that my looks will be enough when Wei-guo discovers that I'm incapable of capturing my first husband's heart, too hard-hearted to love my second husband, and at a loss when it comes to my child.

XX suggests I get started reading Wei-guo's mind. "Think your questions."

And that's not even taking into account Hann's horrendous secrets. I screw up my eyes, and as if any of my questions matter, I ask Wei-guo his opinion of me. He leans forward to dip me, and the words "beautiful," "sexy," and "dangerous" fill my consciousness.

—Dangerous?

—You tricked me into our first date. And you never returned my calls.

I am ashamed to be reminded of my especially flirtatious self on that video chat. I ask if I made him angry.

His gaze snaps away from me before flicking back, fiery as ever.

—I didn't like it, but I understand your motivations, your need to vet me, to proceed with caution. I know this decision isn't yours alone to make.

His answer feels truthful and mature. Generous, even. I move on to his impressions of BeiBei and am comforted that he finds my boy to be a typical, high-energy child.

—Can you love him as much as your own?

—I think so. I want to.

I ask about XX.

—He's kind of sweet, but somewhat lost.

My heart hammers. I have to tell myself Wei-guo did not actually accuse XX of being a Lost Boy. I ask if he could live and get along with him.

—I hope so. I'll certainly try.

—Do you like Hann?

—Very, very much.

His enthusiasm takes me aback. Suddenly he seems to be smiling seductively as much at the thought of Hann as at me.

—Are you attracted to him?

—No.

—Do you want to sleep with him?

—Of course not.

The incongruity between the leer on his face and his denial jars me. I ask him to tell me more about Hann.

—I feel cared for in his presence. Protected and important. He likes me for who I am.

I'm taken aback by his admission: Hann has that same effect on me. He is the only person who has ever made me feel unconditionally loved, and I see that I've tolerated his Willful Sterility so that I would have a permanent place in his heart. I start to wonder if I'd be able to give that up.

—Would you still like him if he were Willfully Sterile?

—I know he is, and I don't think less of him.

Wei-guo's equanimity astonishes me. Is he so desperate to marry that he would willingly break the law? He spins me away and devours me with his gaze for a full second before pulling me back into his arms. I shut my eyes to rid myself of his disturbing heat and ask how he knows.

—My fathers heard, and Hann as good as admits it.

I did not imagine Hann's secret to be so easily discovered, and the perilousness of my situation is hammered home. Hann—or I, for that matter—would not even need to make enemies: any stranger could turn us in. My pulse begins to race again. What am I going to do? If it's no secret that Hann is Willfully Sterile, my divorcing him would admit as much and possibly focus more attention on our situation. I could get in trouble as much for divorcing as for not divorcing him. The only way to secure my own faultlessness would be to turn him in.

And that, I realize, I could never do.

The fact that Hann hid from me this momentous and possibly life-altering admission to another wounds me anew. I had thought I was Hann's closest confidante. A wave of grief seizes me.

I take a deep breath and make myself refocus on the image of Wei-guo before me. I ask if we're in danger of his fathers ratting us out.

—My fathers despise informants more than anything.

—Did they make a deal: time in the bedroom for Hann's safety?

—Oh no. My fathers are against the match. I haven't told them everything.

I sink back into the chair. Is Hann still testing Wei-guo? Thinking that a rebel nature boded well for a family hiding a Willful Sterile, not to mention a Lost Boy, we set up our first date as a way of gauging Wei-guo's willingness to stand up to his parents. Suddenly, though, I no longer care for Hann's deceitful ways.

Or Wei-guo's. Or XX's, for that matter.

—Why should I sleep with you? Your fathers will never approve of us.

—If I truly want it, I can talk my dads into the match. My choices aren't exactly bountiful.

I already have two men adept at deception and am quite certain I have no need of another. I ask who else knows about our secrets.

—I wouldn't worry. I'm sure rumors have been around for years.

Every word out of Wei-guo's mouth frightens me. —Why would you risk marrying my family?

—If Hann has stayed out of trouble this long, he's discreet enough to keep staying out of trouble. Plus, you trust him.

I can't say I do. —Will you do everything in your power to protect him and keep our secret?

He nods, still leering. —Absolutely.

Do I dare stake my family's safety on his 5 percent liar rate? —Why do you want to marry me?

—With Hann uninterested and XX the way he is, I can be number one in your heart. You'll really just have one and a half husbands.

Did he just call XX half a husband and cut Hann entirely out of the spousal equation? I ask how he envisions our life together.

—I see us all living harmoniously together with another boy and a girl, both mine.

—Both yours?

—XX is sterile.

I shake my head, annoyed by his presumption.

—I see my business continuing to prosper and me bringing in my share of the income. I will teach our children to be strong and confident through play and sports. I see myself becoming a good brother and friend to Hann and XX, the way my fathers have grown to be lifelong companions. I will join Hann's badminton team and coach them to league victories. I'd like to recruit XX to Strategic Games—he'll really like fighting in real battlefields—and I plan on clinching many, many more titles with my men.

My eyes pop open for a glance of this man who isn't about to give up his bachelorhood. The meadow spins dizzily behind his come-hither look, and I quickly shut him out again and remind him that only unmarried men are allowed to play Strategic Games.

—I founded Middle Kingdom and established our charter differently.

—You have a plan to conquer the sports arena with Hann, a plan for extending your bachelorhood with XX, a plan for bonding with every member of the family except me.

—You, I plan to love.

It hits me: Wei-guo thinks a marriage is something that occurs only in the bedroom.

The holograms of two Pekingese puppies cavort up and down the aisle of the Mommy-and-Me bus. A perky singer accompanies the adorable, tail-wagging balls of fluff, urging the children again and again to learn from Chairman Mao, to always go forward and not fall behind. Unlike the other kids who watch in dazed wonder, BeiBei pushes off me ready to play every time the puppies frolic by. He adores dogs. Swiping my arm through their images in demonstration whenever they pass, I tell him these pups are only for watching, that they cannot be hugged, but there is a stubbornness in him that cannot be reasoned with. I hold on tight while BeiBei hangs over the aisle, crying for them and fighting my confinement. We've already spent two hours on every available apparatus in the park, and he still has energy to burn.

I suppose not having any quiet before Lee Wei-guo arrives is a blessing. Reeling from Hann's admission, I wavered all night about the dinner and the test afterward. I do feel a connection with Wei-guo. My head tells me I should try to move on, get to know him better, but exposing our secrets to him, his fathers, and who knows who else terrifies me. I fear I'm putting all of us in direct danger. I worry I'm being selfish and petty, punishing Hann for rejecting me. In the morning, when he still refused to soften, I told him in a pique—acted in a way I promised myself I would not—that I intended to go through with the Compatibility Test. His collapsed face was what I hoped to see. I was tempted to call off the evening, but then he suggested that I wear my lavender dress.

I place BeiBei in my lap and wrap my arms around his middle. I remind him of the rule that everyone must sit when the bus is moving. I jostle him from side to side like a roller coaster going around turns, his round-the-clock amusement park ride. Distracting BeiBei is a tightrope act. Too much stimulation could trigger a full-scale tantrum and meltdown. A nap would be impossible after that, and I'd be lucky to have dinner on the table before eight thirty. Too little, though, and he's impossible to control.

The damn puppies wrestle and tumble past us again. As Bei-Bei struggles back to his feet, I curse the State's need to stuff our children's minds with revolutionary ideas at every opportunity. He steps onto my backpack, finds purchase on the armrest, and attempts to scoot his belly over the back of the seat. Fortunately, there is no one behind us. BeiBei has pushed, mowed over, and grabbed toys out of the hands of enough kids that mothers give us a wide berth. His peers, though not yet two, also know to keep their distance. Even the bus drivers have stopped lecturing me on safety, casting no more than a weary glance these days in our direction.

I tell myself to stop fretting. The question of marriage will most likely become moot once Lee Wei-guo spends any extended period of time in public with us. No one likes to feel like a leper. No, that's not fair to lepers. They at least garner some sympathy. As BeiBei's parent, however, Wei-guo would just be charged with our boy's misbehavior and eventually shunned.

I turn BeiBei's feet away from my stomach and bounce him.

One glance at my scabbed shins, my black-and-blue stomach and thighs will send Wei-guo running.

I wanted to go to a restaurant tonight, but Hann said no. Neither am I to make any extraordinary effort cooking or cleaning up. He reasoned that Lee Wei-guo ought to know that I have not the ability or the time to make the traditional three-dishes-plus-a-soup suppers. Our day-to-day life revolves around BeiBei. If Wei-guo cannot adapt to our family realities, then he is not the spouse for us. You'd think this Compatibility Test was my idea, the indifferent way Hann wants to go about it. I guess he doesn't want to get anyone's hopes up; he of all people knows how difficult our family is, how unlovable I can be.

"Up!" BeiBei cries.

"Up you go!" I tilt my body to give him the illusion of movement.

"Sit down," someone in the back of the bus calls out.

I cringe; public misbehavior is humiliating enough without someone trying to discipline my child. A little girl protests, and I let out my breath, relieved that the command was not directed at BeiBei. He continues to bang his hands on my head.

"It's not fair. Wu BeiBei never sits." The verbal precocity of little girls never ceases to amaze me.

I try to coax BeiBei down, but he thrashes harder.

The mother says, "That bad boy deserves a spanking. Do you want a spanking too?"

I rub a hand across BeiBei's ear, hoping he did not hear the remark. He does not mean to be bad. With sterilization a possibility if diagnosed a Lost Boy, I dare not ask the pediatrician too pointedly about BeiBei's oppositional and hyperactive tendencies. But the doctor is not blind. At heart a kind and helpful man, he tells me nevertheless that high excitability is common among boys, that movement is an immature brain's attempt to self-regulate. He advises that we give BeiBei plenty of physical exercise and outlets for play. Without sufficient stimulation, BeiBei will create his own and misbehave.

Not wanting him to be the bad example, I tilt him sideways in my arms. "BeiBei wants to be a good boy," I whisper into his ears even as he howls. I hug him tight, providing the sensory feedback that the doctor says his little body craves, and rock him. "BeiBei is MaMa's best little boy."

He screeches, arches his back, and bucks in my arms as I fight to keep him horizontal. I fear telling the doctor the truth, fear too that his claim that BeiBei's outbursts fall within the scope of normality is part of the State's attempt to disclaim the exploding problem of Lost Boys. I can only pray that BeiBei's single-mindedness will serve him well as an adult. His shrieks make me want to scream. I count just four more blocks until our stop and vow not to lose my cool. Not here. I grit my teeth and squeeze him in my arms. We're almost home, I tell him. You can play to your heart's content when we're home.

The bus finally rolls into our stop. I struggle to my feet, shrug on my backpack—I must always have two free hands—and hoist BeiBei onto my hip. Time to go, I say. No one steps into the aisle; the other mothers know to let us exit first so as to maintain a margin of safety. I cast my eyes down, tighten my grip on my flailing child, and disembark. It breaks my heart that the two of us stand out wherever we go.

Once on the ground, I put BeiBei down, hold fast to his hand never mind the whining—now that he is free to run, he wants none of it, of course—and pull him along as fast as his legs are willing to go. For safety and modesty reasons, women and children are supposed to caravan on foot from the bus stop to home, but BeiBei's antics rarely allow this.

"C'mon. Let's race," I say, exaggerating my stride. He is too heavy for me to carry the distance.

Footsteps clatter behind us. "Comrade Wu!"

Comrade Yang, the wife of one of Hann's coworkers, approaches with her little boy in tow, both smartly dressed in navy blazers and pressed shirts. The little one even tolerates a bow tie. "You walk so fast."

Not fast enough.

I cannot remember when I last fixed my ponytail, let alone ran a brush through my hair. I smooth back my mop and tuck escaped strands behind my ears. I nudge the sagging rear of my sweatpants upward and resist the urge to wipe the streaks of dirt from BeiBei's face. He, meanwhile, has not stopped screeching or tugging on my arm. What could this woman want? Except to point out BeiBei's transgressions and my failures as a mother, no one willingly speaks to us, let alone chases us down in the middle of an outburst.

She smiles as if BeiBei is the most angelic child in the world. "My son would like to give BeiBei a lollipop. Is it all right for Bei-Bei to have a lollipop?"

"Of course," I say, trying not to let my jaw drop. Certain candies are liable to turn BeiBei into a human Super Ball, but I don't want to deny my son this rare gesture of friendship.

Yang kneels, produces the candy from her purse, and hands it to her attentive child. BeiBei howls all the while. "Remember how we practiced, darling?"

Her little one nods sweetly. The sight of the purple treat halts BeiBei's crying. The boy barely holds out the lollipop before Bei-Bei snatches it from his hand. Seeing the gob of snot hanging from his nose, I quickly kneel and wipe it away.

I stop BeiBei from licking the wrapper. "Say thank you." I am hugely relieved when he manages that. I remove the plastic and stuff the lollipop into his mouth.

"Thank you," I say to the little boy, and ruffle his hair. "You are such a precious child."

He snuggles against his mother. "I chose grape."

"Yes, you did," his mother says, kissing his cheek.

The reciprocity of their affection pains me. I wrap my arm around BeiBei while he slurps his treat.

The woman stands. "I want to congratulate you."

I rise too and smile though I'm not sure for what, and I'm suddenly suspicious of sarcasm. Taking on a third husband is not usually cause for celebration among women. Hann is so sensitive about his image at work that I doubt he has told many colleagues about going the max. But then I remember I've never been privy to his innermost thoughts.

I do not really know Hann.

She says, "My husband has long been an admirer of Hann's, and he says Hann so deserves this housing award." Yang reaches over to squeeze my hand. "We are so happy for you."

I force a thank-you from my lips.

A crooked grin appears on the woman's face. "Is it true that the company rescued you from having to go the max just in the nick of time?"

Scarcely able to control my face, I eke forth a smile. "We are so fortunate our husbands work for such a fine firm."

"Go!" BeiBei leans backward to budge me with the weight of his entire body. Purple stains his lips and drips from his chin.

I've never been happier to have him act up. "I'm afraid BeiBei is getting tired." I ask him to say good-bye.

The woman leans down toward BeiBei. "Would you like to come over someday and play with a little friend?"

"Go, MaMa." BeiBei won't stop pulling at my arm.

"That is very kind of you. I'm sure he would like it very much," I say, though I am certain kindness is not the reason for the invitation. As my mother often says: there is a selfish motive behind every act.

What is Hann's motive for keeping this award from me?

8

XX

XX's stomach twinges. He tries to concentrate on his work but finds it impossible not to spy on his manager's every move. Personal business must be conducted on personal time, and unfortunately, Manager Fung arrived eight minutes after the start of work today as is allowed for someone of his status. As the noon hour nears and none of the half dozen men in his department approaches Fung's desk at the front of their bull pen, the chokehold around his gut finally begins to relent.

At 11:59:45, XX saves his work and logs off his computer as usual. Instead of bolting toward the cafeteria at the rattle of the lunch bell, he shuffles quickly toward his manager's desk.

"No lunch today, XX?" says a junior programmer.

"Is the sky falling?" someone else quips.

XX ignores the lot and asks Fung if they could speak about a private matter.

"Of course." Fung leans back, his large frame eliciting a mighty groan from his swivel chair, and invites XX to sit. XX has always found his manager reassuring, his fatherly girth well suited to an important man.

XX settles himself next to the desk with his back to the busybodies, folds his hands in his lap, and alternately squints and frowns so as to convey the seriousness of his intent. "I would like to begin the proceedings for divorce." The municipal website indicates that he must first notify his work unit of his intention.

"The sky has indeed fallen," says another wiseass coworker from the back of the office. "Forty million men out there fighting for a wife, and you are throwing yours away?"

"I'll be happy to take care of her for you."

"Fellows," Manager Fung says. "Kindly show us the courtesy of going to lunch."

Here's another reason XX appreciates Fung: He gets the best out of his men without a fuss. A simple admonition from Fung to XX's hecklers is enough to keep them in line.

After the guys file out, Fung leans forward and focuses his eye beams on XX. "Those idiots are not wrong, you know."

His concern is a fuzzy warmth. XX says, "My wife also wants to divorce me. Ours can be fast-tracked, rubber-stamped on the spot at the registration office."

"Let's back up a little," Fung says. "I'd like to hear *why* you want out of your marriage."

XX's jaw slackens. He thought all he had to do was put his company on notice. The website did not say that a reason for divorce had to be provided. He wonders if there is a wrong answer. He remembers too that he must not accidentally expose Hann.

"Are you all right?"

XX starts. "We are wrong for each other. Always have been." He watches carefully. Fung's face pinches. The reply was incorrect.

"What's changed? Why now? What happened?"

XX wrinkles his nose, unsure if his plan to set Wei-guo up as his replacement helps or hurts his cause.

"You haven't mentioned your brother. Is he in favor of you divorcing?"

"Yes," XX says, certain that his answer will soon not be a lie. When it matters, he knows how to get his way with Hann.

Manager Fung leans uncomfortably close. "Is there someone else you wish to marry?"

"Oh no." XX shakes his head vigorously. "I am not a cheater."

"It's okay, XX. I'm not accusing you of anything. I am asking only because I want to help you. You are one of my best workers, and I am concerned about you."

"The website says that all I have to do is register my intent with you and my neighborhood committee, and then I can have a divorce at the marriage registry."

"Nothing is quick or easy when it comes to government bureaucracy."

XX blinks. "But that's not what the website says—"

"Well, yours is my first ever divorce request," Fung says. "I've heard of women wanting out, but rarely men, not after shelling out their life savings in dowry." He tells XX that they will consult his manager's manual together and mutters to himself as he swipes at his computer screen.

He locates the page. "They want your name. Are you sure you want me to input your name?"

"Yes," XX says, relieved he's finally getting somewhere.

Fung enters XX's name and up pops a questionnaire. "Has the union resulted in a child or children?" He taps on the Yes button.

"No," XX says, "BeiBei is not mine."

Fung reminds him that fathers are responsible for all the children in the family regardless of biological origin.

"BeiBei does not even like me."

"You're better than that."

XX flinches at his manager's scolding tone and looks up. His eyes widen at the hostility on Fung's face.

Fung swipes and taps his screen. He asks how they hold title on their apartment, and XX informs him that he and his brother both inherited the apartment from their parents. In answer to the question about their financial arrangement, XX says that Hann is in charge of the money, of budgeting and paying all their bills. Fung slaps at his screen. XX cannot figure out why his replies make Fung increasingly irate.

"We shouldn't have entered your name," Fung scolds again, turning the display fully toward XX. He switches back and forth between the company manual and a site with "China First" scrawled across the banner. "I am directed to this site after every question. And it doesn't matter if I answer yes or no. And listen to this: 'Divorce leads to the disintegration of society, to the depreciation of Confucian values, to lawlessness and violence. Divorce is an antecedent to crime, and all measures must be employed toward its prevention.' It says here that I am required by law to refer you to marriage counseling."

Fung pages through the site and says it looks like a highly coordinated campaign against divorce. "Do you understand what this means?"

"I have to go to counseling with May-ling?" XX rocks back and forth to force air down his lungs.

"Look at me." Manager Fung steadies XX by the shoulder. "It means that every effort will be expended to make divorce near impossible. You'll be doing yourself a huge favor if you figure out a way to reconcile with your family and not go down this path."

"But I don't want to live with them anymore!" XX says, pulling his shoulder free. "They can't make me."

Fung grips XX's wrist. "You've been hesitant to answer my questions, and I fully understand your reserve. I wouldn't want people in my business either. But a counselor is going to require that you talk, so he can fix your marriage. And it won't be just you and your wife. Your brother will have to attend. Your son too, most likely. Nothing will be too delicate for discussion. He will delve into your sex life or your lack of one, your sleeping arrangements, your childrearing methods, your finances, your bathroom schedule. You'll have to justify yourself and be accountable to making changes. Can you stomach that?"

"But the website says it's fast and easy as long as May-ling and I agree."

"It's a trap. A way to identify potential trouble and to lure you in for intervention," says Manager Fung.

"That's not right," XX growls, crossing his arms. His lower lip juts out.

"I didn't say it was," Fung says gently. "There's something else I want you to think about. If you divorce, your chances of remarrying—the way things are now—are almost nil."

"I don't want to re—"

Fung puts up a hand to cut him off. "Who's going to take care of you when you're old? When you're sick? Only family stays with you through tough times."

"I don't care," XX says. "Hann will still be my brother. He'll take care of me."

"I don't doubt that." Fung asks their age difference.

XX says six years.

"Chances are good he'll die before you."

XX's brows scrunch. "Age is not the sole predictor of longevity."

"You must rethink this. Talk to your brother. Talk to your wife. If you decide not to proceed, then as far as I'm concerned, we've never had this conversation."

"I will never change my mind." XX hugs himself tight. It has taken him years to work up the courage and opening to ask for a divorce, and now that he has voiced his wish, the thought of living any other way feels utterly unacceptable.

With a determined forward lean, XX alternately jogs and fast walks all the way home from the subway station. Hann likes to say that a journey of a thousand *li* begins with one small step, and XX cannot hope to get out of the family without setting in motion the first steps, never mind the mountains ahead. He has neutralized zombies, moles, black holes, viruses, and firewalls—not to mention the jokers and jackasses at work and BeiBei at home. If he has to deal with marriage counselors in order to get what he wants, then so be it. Hann has always said that XX should never be ruled by fear.

A complete unit dissolution is out of the question; Hann could not be without May-ling and BeiBei. And May-ling could not be happy without emotional and sexual love. Replacing XX with a more suitable husband is the best solution, and XX knows that Wei-guo is a good guy in the way that Manager Fung is a good guy. Like May-ling and her tummy itch, he too can tell good people from bad.

XX is drenched in sweat and breathless upon reaching his apartment, but no matter, a little coughing is a small price for getting him one step closer to living in peace. May-ling asked to go out to dinner, but Hann said to treat tonight like any other night, that no extra cleaning and cooking was necessary. Otherwise, she would be lying about their reality. As always, what Hann says is law, but XX sees a problem. Hann's rule is to always give his best effort, and a messy apartment and a boiled, one-pot dinner do not equal best effort. For that reason, XX is rushing home to help and to make certain that nothing goes wrong. He is excited to increase his friendship with Wei-guo and help his own dream come true.

Their front door is jammed. A plastic barn screeches across the floor as XX forces it open. Matchbox cars, trains, airplanes, balls, puzzle pieces—every toy that BeiBei owns, it seems—cover the living room floor. He is jumping illegally on the couch and shrieking, his mouth smeared purple and awful like a clown, and May-ling sits next to him doing nothing about it. And she's crying again. What he wouldn't do to never hear BeiBei's shrieks or her wails again. Both burn like acid in his gut and propel him to curl up in a corner, hands tight over his ears. He stops himself, however, from crying out. If he doesn't intervene, another fight will break out when Hann returns. He will reprimand May-ling for her muddy playground sweats and her beggar hair, and May-ling will not like the criticism. She may very well get Wei-guo's visit canceled. And that can't happen.

XX plugs his ears and yells to drown out mother and child. "What happened here? Get down, BeiBei, and be quiet. You're going to be in huge trouble when Big BaBa comes home."

BeiBei sticks out a purple tongue and, legs squat, bounces like a little devil.

May-ling scrubs the tears from her cheeks. "I'm sorry, XX."

"Wei-guo is going to be here in forty-six minutes. Get up, and go change."

May-ling does not do as he asks. Surely out to undo XX, BeiBei continues his maniacal trampolining and squeaking of the sofa.

"Stop it!" XX roars, to little effect. There is a toy everywhere he steps. "Come clean up." He opens up the toy barn and begins collecting pigs, goats, and chickens. He shuffles his feet next toward the 72-car carrying case and, lowering himself to his hands and knees, begins to jam in Matchbox vehicles by type and horsepower.

After a minute, BeiBei scrambles off the couch and, kicking

aside the toys in his path, approaches. "Ride," he says, stepping onto XX's calf to climb up his back.

"No," XX shouts before remembering Hann's advice that with BeiBei, honey catches more flies. With sweetened voice, he adds, "Clean up first, and then you can ride. We must not have a mess like this today."

He straightens up to dislodge BeiBei and is immediately sorry when the brat lands on his butt, his mouth a big, quivering black hole. XX's eyes round with terror. BeiBei catches his breath and begins to bawl. XX plugs his ears again and retreats into a corner of the living room. The child is beyond all reasoning.

"I didn't mean to hurt him," XX says.

"Of course you didn't." May-ling sniffs.

"I want r-i-i-i-i-i-de," BeiBei howls.

May-ling sighs and drops to the floor. She scoots toward him on all fours. "MaMa give you ride."

"No," he screams.

Why does BeiBei cry harder when given his wish? May-ling scoops him up, and he flails senselessly. XX curls inward and inhales hard. He hums "Little Fat Boy," the affectionate nursery rhyme his mother used to sing to him, to try to drown out the beastly howling.

Gray slacks and black street shoes enter his field of vision. "What's going on?" Hann has come into the apartment amidst the commotion.

"BaBa!" BeiBei lurches out of May-ling's arms and leaps at him with hiccupping cries, a line of snot running into his mouth.

Hann lifts and kisses him, wipes his nose with a handkerchief despite the boy's protestations. "What's wrong?"

"BaBa bad," BeiBei wails again and again, his arms tight around Hann's neck. His shoulders shake as if XX has hit him.

XX comes out of his corner, hands tight over his ears and elbows stuck wide. "BeiBei won't help clean up his mess. He's ruining Compatibility Night on purpose."

Hann rubs circles on BeiBei's back and quiets him with shushes. He asks May-ling what's going on.

"You tell me," May-ling says, her eyes red and scary angry. Even though she has stopped crying, XX does not think it is a good development.

When Hann tries to speak, BeiBei cries harder and bats at his mouth. Hann gives into the child with tickles and kisses and spoils him with all his attention. May-ling is shooting arrows at him with her eyes. A fight is coming.

When BeiBei finally lays his head on Hann's shoulder, Hann stops in front of May-ling. He looks as calm as she is angry. "I understand if you want to change your mind about tonight. You are allowed to change your mind. We don't have to go through with this. Do you want me to call Wei-guo and cancel?"

"We can't cancel," XX says. "It's too late. He's already on his way here."

"What are you playing at?" May-ling asks him. "I wish you'd tell me."

"What do you mean?"

"If you don't want me anymore, say it, and I'll get out of your way. Just please stop lying to me."

"Why are you always doubting me?"

"Wei-guo is going to be here in nineteen minutes. We have to clean up." As usual, they ignore XX.

"You really have nothing to say?" May-ling asks Hann.

"What do you want to hear?"

She wipes hard at her eyes.

"It's your idea to go the max. Not mine." Hann enunciates each word, his soothing voice not soothing at all. "You are the reason we are going down this path."

May-ling bites her lips and shakes her head. Hann's reasonable demeanor seems to make her angrier. XX alone will not be able to clear the floor before their guest arrives. He retrieves the tub for blocks and places it in May-ling's lap.

"Not now, XX." She sets the tub aside. "Think hard," she says to Hann. "What haven't you told me?"

"Yes, now," XX says with force. "You help me pick up." XX holds on to the coffee table and lowers himself to his knees. He retrieves a ZTZ-99 tank and a Tiger 4×4 armored vehicle and, as a concession to time, blinks back his discomfort and slots them into the military section of the carrying case without additional sorting.

"Well?" May-ling says to Hann, but does not gather any blocks.

Hann says, "I wish you would just tell me what's bothering you."

May-ling crosses her arms with a look that makes XX afraid. "I was congratulated by one of the company wives today. It appears you've won the award of the year."

"We must clean up before it's too late," XX says.

Again, the two of them square up as if he does not exist. Hann and May-ling always argue in a quiet hiss, though it's no less upsetting than outright yelling. They can't stop having the same fight. Hann likes men, and it kills May-ling that he's as interested in doing sex with her as she is with XX. They can't see that their argument goes around and around. They need to just get over it.

May-ling says, "Do you know how it feels to learn that you've been secretly plotting a future without me? That you've been maneuvering me with lies?"

"I promise I'm not plotting anything without the three of you."

May-ling covers her mouth with a hand and howls. Tears spout. "Then why did you set up the Compatibility Test without telling me?"

The doorbell chimes.

"You've ruined everything." XX throws down the Matchbox car in his hand and pouts. "I'm never going to get out of here."

BeiBei runs to the front door and hangs from the lever. "Open."

Hann tells May-ling that he can still send Wei-guo away.

She wipes at her eyes. "I don't want to see him."

"All right," Hann says. He opens the door a crack and greets Wei-guo. "I'm sorry. A minor emergency has come up—"

BeiBei squeezes between Hann and the door, flinging it open. "Present!" he says, grabbing a lumpily wrapped tube in Wei-guo's hand. Wei-guo's sweater is so red it pulses like a valentine heart from the doorway.

"How did you know this was for you?" Grinning ear to ear and not at all bothered by BeiBei's rudeness, Wei-guo kneels and holds out his palm. The child slaps it with both hands. Wei-guo laughs and holds his hand higher, and BeiBei jumps and slaps it again.

Hann tries to pull the door behind him, but BeiBei calls out to his mama and runs back into the apartment to show her his gift.

Wei-guo stands, the mess on the living-room floor before him, and sees the sniffling, red-eyed May-ling. "What's wrong?"

XX says, "You're thirteen minutes early."

"XX," says Hann.

BeiBei tears open one end of the wrapping and exposes a black handle. With May-ling holding on to the package, he teases it out and backs away with a seemingly unending length of blue and yellow rope.

"I apologize," says Wei-guo. "The subway ran fast today, and I got tired of circling your neighborhood. I should have—"

"No, no." Hann steadies BeiBei as he trips backward over the barn. "We're sorry. I think it would be best if we—"

"Snake!" BeiBei says.

He flails the rope, and Hann yelps and recoils as it whips him across the face.

"Stop it, BeiBei!" XX storms over, grabs the flying midsection of the rope, and tries to take the handle from BeiBei. "Stop ruining everything."

"I'm so sorry," Wei-guo says, too upset. "I didn't realize a jump rope was so dangerous."

XX says, "It's not your fault!"

Hann holds his nose with both hands. "I'm all right, XX." A drop of blood plops onto his white dress shirt.

"Mine," BeiBei bawls.

"It's okay, BeiBei." May-ling wedges herself between XX and the child and pries the rope out of XX's hands.

May-ling looks at Hann and yelps. "You're bleeding." Dragging the rope and BeiBei crying behind her, she cups a hand under Hann's nose. "Does it hurt?"

"I'm fine," Hann says.

She dabs at his nose with a smeared handkerchief from her pocket. "You better lie down."

He brings out his own and nudges her hand away. "I'm *fine*."

"Lie down, and put pressure on your nose."

Wei-guo is on his knees again, beckoning to BeiBei. "Do you want to play snake?"

Snot running down his nose and four fingers in his purple mouth, BeiBei clutches the rope handles to his chest.

"I'm going to clear a playground for us, okay?"

The more BeiBei pulls back, the nicer Wei-guo becomes. It's totally unfair that BeiBei is receiving all this attention for being bad.

Wei-guo holds up a bus. "Where does this go? Where is its home?"

BeiBei sniffs. Wei-guo jams it into the barn.

"No!" BeiBei says, pointing. "There."

Wei-guo spins his head this way and that. "Where?"

Dragging the jump rope, BeiBei brings the car carrying case to Wei-guo. "Here."

"Go take care of Hann," Wei-guo says quietly to May-ling. He tries to wedge the bus into one of the smaller sedan slots. "It doesn't fit," he exclaims to XX. "Do you know where this goes?"

XX loves to be consulted. "The public transportation section is at the bottom. The second to the last row."

"Your baba says it goes here." Wei-guo points to the slot. "You want to do it?"

BeiBei puts the bus in.

Wei-guo wiggles in place and reaches beneath his bottom to pull out a block. "Ouch," he says, generating a laugh from BeiBei. Grunting hard, he pushes and pushes it into a too-small slot in the carrying case.

"That's no car!" BeiBei says.

"It's not?"

"No!"

"No?" Wei-guo tosses the block over a shoulder. "Bring me some cars then!"

BeiBei, still dragging the jump rope behind him, scoops one vehicle after another into his arms and drops them on the floor in front of Wei-guo.

Wei-guo picks up a jeep. "Where does this go, BaBa?"

"Fourth row."

"You heard the boss," Wei-guo says, handing the toy to BeiBei. "Fourth row."

"Fourth row," BeiBei says, placing the toy in the slot indicated by Wei-guo.

Wei-guo continues to check with XX and guide BeiBei through the process. After stowing three vehicles, the child climbs into Wei-guo's lap.

XX has never seen BeiBei tidy up before. They've never been able to get him to do it. XX brings him half a dozen more cars.

The child holds up a VW Beetle. "Where, BaBa?"

XX points at the fifth row, fourth slot from the left, and cannot help patting the kid's head when he files it away. "Good boy, BeiBei."

"Yes," Wei-guo says, "BeiBei is a very helpful boy."

A few minutes later, XX notices Hann and May-ling watching them from the hallway. May-ling shrugs Hann's arm off her shoulder—they are still fighting—but both manage to smile at Wei-guo. Hann's nose has stopped bleeding. He has changed into his after-work sweats and May-ling into a pretty green dress.

Hann says, "MaMa promises to cook us a nice dinner if we men clean up this room."

XX clenches his fist and pumps it in victory. He is right: Wei-guo is great for their family.

When XX begins to gather up the blocks, Hann shakes his head and quietly takes the tub from him. He must be more curious than XX to see BeiBei work. It is indeed a spectacle the way the kid giggles at Wei-guo's ridiculous questions and then runs around to show him the correct answer. He doesn't even know he's being tricked into cleaning up. After a few minutes, XX becomes bored and wanders off to his room.

He checks his standing in *Metagalactic Domination*. Wei-guo will like this strategy game. XX has only dropped eighty spots while at work. His artillery power of 8,324,135 krps puts him currently at number 238 out of 2,994,345 players. He logs in and returns to the living room.

He calls out to Wei-guo and invites him to his room. "I have something you'll like."

Hann puts up a finger to his lips.

Wei-guo asks if he could have a few minutes to finish cleaning up. Holding open a sack, he lunges to catch the ball that BeiBei hurls.

XX agrees. He considers the size of the mess still on the floor and commands his watch to set a fourteen-minute alarm. Back in his room, an insurgence on Centaurus A, one of the six galaxies he currently rules, sets his heart racing. A faction that calls itself the Space Cowboys—a ragtag group led by one of his lesser ministers— is challenging his Treasury guards, angling to break into the vault and seize the state treasures within. Normally, XX would allow his preprogrammed strategy to play out in real time, intervening and devising new strategy only when necessary. The action could take more than an hour to resolve, but he doesn't want threats of any kind today hanging over his head. He trades in 5,000 krps, plum- meting his ranking by 42 spots, but doing so allows him to sur- round the Space Cowboys with soldiers, drones, and firepower, and wipe them out then and there. He will impress Wei-guo today with his sheer domination.

He checks his alarm. There are eight more minutes before his turn with Wei-guo and time enough to look in on his harem in *One Thousand and One Nights*. He currently owns 37 concubines—20 of them pregnant—5 eunuchs, 8,000 sheep, 40 camels, 12 sheepdogs, 20 tents, and 17 children. Upon his entrance, Kisses, his newest puppy, runs to him, his tail a whirlpool of happiness. His head eu- nuch congratulates him on the overnight births of two more sons. He reports that their current pastureland holds no more than a week of grass, that XX's head concubine has been squabbling with his latest conquest over sheepskins, that four of his concubines are ovu- lating tomorrow, and that his five oldest boys have been stealing out at night with the camels on joyrides. XX informs his head eunuch that his family is to pack up camp in three days and move on to a new pasture in the south that he will soon select. Also, the rule has not changed: each concubine is allotted one sheepskin for her bed and one for the birth of each child. The troublemaker will be denied his affections for a month. He schedules the four ovulators for sex later tonight. And the five delinquents are to be denied meals for a day and begin shepherd training. Though his instinct is to mete out harsher disciplinary measures, success in this game is a balance between material wealth and family satisfaction and obedience.

While one concubine massages his avatar's shoulders and another his feet, and while a golden-haired beauty plies him with ambrosia and another twenty-year-old wine, XX browses the bargain section of the catalogue of brides. He considers a plump, salt-and-pepper-haired widow of fifty-five whose smile resembled his grandmother's and spoke to him of endless patience and understanding.

His alarm beeps.

"Time's up," XX calls out. When Wei-guo fails to materialize, XX goes to retrieve him. The living room is as tidy as it's ever going to be. Wei-guo is holding BeiBei horizontally and flying him with Hann following alongside. "It's my turn now."

"Faster," BeiBei cries.

Wei-guo zooms across the room, making whooshing noises while BeiBei commands him to go even faster.

XX tugs on Wei-guo's arm. "It's my turn."

"Soon," Hann says. "Give them a chance to wind down."

"That's not fair."

Hann yells out toward the kitchen, "Is dinner almost ready?"

May-ling says they can eat in three minutes, and Hann suggests that they go to the table.

XX shadows Wei-guo as he zigs and zags across the room before landing BeiBei in his high chair. When Wei-guo acquiesces to the kid's demand to sit next to him, XX quickly slides into the seat on Wei-guo's other side.

"Promise to come see my room after dinner?" he asks Wei-guo.

"Of course."

BeiBei's books and drawings are scattered all over the table. Anxious to move the meal along so he can have time alone with Wei-guo, XX gathers them into a neat stack before Wei-guo could make a game of it. Before BeiBei gets bent out of shape, he tells the boy that his precious "artwork" will be kept safe and clean in the hanging storage pocket behind his chair.

May-ling enters with a handful of utensils, looks the men over, but does not chatter on and on about nothing. She must be feeling nervous about doing sex with Wei-guo. XX asks what's for dinner. She says braised noodles.

"Oh." XX had bookmarked some appropriate recipes for this special occasion in the Northern cuisine cookbook he had bought her. He sees on the corner table that it lies forgotten atop a yet-to-be-used pressure cooker, tap shoes, a mushroom log—a growing heap of his thoughtful gifts.

"I love braised noodles," Wei-guo says.

Hann says, "We're true Northerners—can't live without our noodles around here."

XX jumps as May-ling clanks the chopsticks and spoons down rather brusquely before Hann and then him. She really is acting strange. He widens his eyes to impart a look of enthusiasm for her one-pot meal. A considerate husband would not speak his mind right now. Wei-guo will experience her bad cooking soon enough.

She returns with a steaming bowl for Wei-guo. The noodles are piled to the brim and covered with bits of chicken, shrimp, and cabbage in a dark, egg-drop sauce, the shrimp her special-occasion addition. She serves Hann, XX, and then finally herself and Bei-Bei. She gives Wei-guo the largest portion because he is the guest. She pauses behind the one empty chair next to BeiBei, looks at

Hann and then XX before screeching it very impolitely across the floor tiles to sit down.

Hann asks if she has noticed BeiBei's remarkable cleanup job. "We truly have Wei-guo to thank. Shall we toast him?"

May-ling does not stand right away to get the beer. She bangs around in the kitchen awhile before returning with a tall bottle and glasses. When Hann reminds her not to forget the bottle opener, she flashes him a scary look, the one that he likes to say is started by a fire in her belly.

"Allow me," Wei-guo says, when she returns with the opener. Surely trying to get on her good side, he offers the first pour to her, rather than to the head of the household as is correct.

May-ling knows to pass the first drink on to Hann.

"No, no. After you." When everyone has a glass, Hann says, "To Wei-guo. To his long and prosperous life."

Wei-guo says, "We must toast our lovely cook first for preparing us this delicious and nutritious meal. To May-ling!"

"Hear, hear," XX says, and takes a sip to hurry the toasting along. The smell of dinner has set his stomach growling. While the table argues over whom to toast next, he dips a chopstick into the sauce, licks it, and then tries a tidbit of noodle. May-ling must have overdone the cornstarch, because the egg-drop sauce is both clotty and mucousy. Furthermore, it is underseasoned, lending the noodles zero taste. With three rapid shovels, XX empties half his bowl into his mouth and swallows quickly to minimize the gagging.

"Good, huh?" Wei-guo says to XX, setting down his beer.

XX forces a diplomatic smile. May-ling chops up BeiBei's noodles, her spoon clinking against the side of the bowl, and begins to feed him.

Hann rests his chin on a hand, his all-encompassing signal for XX to eat more slowly, to not dominate the conversation, to stop whatever it is that he is doing wrong. "XX is May-ling's biggest fan."

Partially chewed goop falls out of BeiBei's mouth.

"Ai ya! Don't you do that." May-ling scoops the mess out of BeiBei's lap, half smearing it. She tells him she's giving him a smaller bite and feeds him again. BeiBei tongues the food and promptly pushes it out of his mouth.

XX suppresses a laugh. BeiBei does not have to lie tactfully about the food.

"How can you not be hungry after running around nonstop all day?" May-ling offers BeiBei a piece of shrimp and turns visibly red when he refuses to open his mouth. She looks at Hann.

Hann doesn't much like her cooking either. He hasn't even picked up his chopsticks. He suggests that BeiBei feed himself.

"He'll just mush the noodles around and make a horrible mess."

XX finishes off the rest of his bowl with a few quick shovels. He never gets any credit for always finishing her bad cooking.

BeiBei pulls a foot up onto his seat and twists to standing.

"Whoa." Wei-guo steadies him. The kid is incapable of a quiet moment. "Do you want to play another game?"

BeiBei shouts yes, grinning. Wei-guo bids him to sit back down, and surprisingly, the brat obeys. Wei-guo lifts BeiBei's bowl to his nose, sniffs, and sticks out his tongue with a bleh, setting off a ringing fit of giggles from the boy. May-ling must like Wei-guo cause she does not appear the least bit offended. Wei-guo sniffs his own bowl next and says mmmm, his eyebrows dancing indecently. He lifts a clump of noodles to his mouth and chews. His eyebrows shoot up, and he quickly devours another mouthful. BeiBei cannot stop watching him. Wei-guo samples some cabbage and declares to May-ling that it's the tastiest vegetable ever.

He eats a few more bites with great concentration before he jerks up. His head swivels between his noodles and BeiBei. "You're still here?"

BeiBei leans back, laughing yes.

Wei-guo wraps his arms around his bowl. "I don't share."

"Share!"

Wei-guo rubs his chin again and again. "Are you going to say please?"

"Please!"

"Oh, all right." Wei-guo combs through the noodles with his chopstick, saying no to each strand and pushing it aside. Oh yes, he says to the clean chopsticks that Hann passes to him. Finally, he sighs loudly and lifts up the teeniest piece of chicken. His entire face droops. "Good bye, my precious," he says to the speck of meat. He holds it toward BeiBei and covers his eyes.

BeiBei doesn't hesitate to close his mouth around the chicken and giggle. Wei-guo declares that he's all done sharing.

"More!"

Wei-guo shakes his head most seriously. "No more."

"Yes more!"

Wei-guo lets out a guttural sigh. He picks through his bowl again and unearths a piece of cabbage. His gaze bounces back and forth between the green and the boy. "Mine!" he declares before gulping it down.

XX laughs, loud like BeiBei.

Hann orders May-ling to bring their guest more noodles and some extra chopsticks.

Wei-guo begins another painstaking excavation of his bowl. Dinner could take all night, the rate he's going. Hann still has not touched his food. Intent on watching Wei-guo and BeiBei, neither has May-ling made much progress on her dinner.

XX stares into his empty bowl. "When can I show Wei-guo my room?"

"Let's give our guest a chance to finish his meal and digest a little." Hann asks if XX is full.

"Yes."

"Tell us a little about your day, then." Hann wants him to recite the highlights they drafted earlier in the afternoon.

XX asks Wei-guo to promise to come to his room right after dinner.

"I promise."

With both hands, BeiBei turns Wei-guo's head away from XX.

XX wrinkles his nose. "Manager Fung has put me in charge of a classified billion-yuan assignment."

"Wow," says Hann.

Wei-guo congratulates XX, but appeases the little attention hog by uttering the words in his direction. May-ling wants to know more about the assignment.

XX does his utmost to keep a straight face. "I can tell you, but then I'll have to kill you," he says, repeating the joke he and Hann worked out. He cannot stifle his laugh. "Suffice it to say that few thoughts are safe from me."

May-ling asks if he's working on mind reading, adapting technology similar to *The Pursuit of Happiness* game.

XX shushes her. "I said I can't talk about it."

May-ling smiles and tells Wei-guo that XX is an excellent software designer. "He works on very high-level security projects."

"Don't talk about it, May-ling!" says XX.

"I don't know any of your secrets, so how can I possibly give anything away?" May-ling smiles as if it's all a joke.

"Stop it."

Hann says, "What else is new with you today?"

XX blows out a stream of air and for Wei-guo's sake, forces himself to move on to the next subject. "Manager Fung says he's recommending me for one of the bigger bonuses in our department." This was last week's news, but he and Hann both agreed that it is an impressive fact for their guest.

"Outstanding," Hann says.

Still facing BeiBei, Wei-guo congratulates XX again.

Hann asks if XX has plans for the windfall.

XX says he will buy *World War Three*, a political war game. "But BeiBei will be in school soon, and we must save for his tuition." Hann wanted to make their family priorities clear to Wei-guo.

Hann says, "Our little guy is growing up so fast."

XX states that he has one last piece of news.

"Oh?" Hann says, no doubt surprised.

Certain that Hann would be mad and would do everything to boss him out of it, XX decided to make this announcement before this more receptive audience. He tells everyone that he spoke to his manager earlier that day. "I registered my intent to start the proceedings for my divorce from the family."

"That's out of the question." Hann swipes a hand across his middle. "We agreed."

XX looks away, pretends he does not see Hann's unmistakable signal for him to shut up.

"Did we?" May-ling says in a small voice.

Hann looks monstrously angry. "This is not the time or place for this. And why are you discussing it with Fung? It's none of his business."

"It is too." XX explains the instructions on the marriage registry website.

Hann shakes his head furiously, and XX is glad that he is not facing his brother's wrath alone.

"There is a reason whenever something is structured in a way that does not make sense," Hann says. "Did you consider that?"

"I know why it doesn't make sense," XX replies.

"Yeah?"

"Yeah," XX says. "They want to stop divorces by sending people to marriage counseling."

Hann says, "And knowing that, you still plowed right on ahead?"

"Yes." XX crosses his arms. "This is what I want." He turns to Wei-guo and gives him a reassuring nod.

Wei-guo nods back hesitantly. XX can tell that Wei-guo agrees with him, but is afraid to cross Hann. XX can read his signals the way one reads a best buddy.

9

WEI-GUO

XX crosses his arms. "My mind is made up."

"Then unmake it," Hann says with quiet but fierce authority, even though authority seems to be exactly what he lacks. After he barged in on May-ling's and my date at my studio, I thought he was in control of this household. The awful state of their living room and May-ling's bristly disposition suggest otherwise. I'm stunned that not even his brother toes his line.

"You won't have to give up the housing award if XX divorces us," May-ling says, her tone measured and strong. Unlike MaMa, who relied on silent treatments and pouting, she confronts issues with refreshing directness. It feels like she has already decided on me and wants me to be part of this discussion. I wonder if nerves explain her prickly behavior all evening. I glance at Hann, and he confirms with a resigned nod that his housing secret is out.

He says, "I guarantee you that my company will like divorce even less than a third spouse."

"You don't know that," May-ling replies.

"I know that, and I also made a promise to my parents—we both did—that we would take care of XX." He frowns at his brother. "That he would take care of us too."

She says, "What XX wants should also matter."

"Our family's well-being is all that matters to me. I've bent over backward, risking everything trying to give you good choices."

"You—bend over?"

Her tone sounds more amused than sarcastic. I don't think she intended it; nevertheless, the image of Hann satisfying another man pops into my head.

"One does not have to live with someone to look out for him," May-ling continues. "I choose for you to stop acting as if you know what's best for all of us. I choose that we respect that XX knows his own mind and understands what's best for himself."

XX's face lights up. "I vote for that too."

I am heartened by the equal footing May-ling and XX appear to possess relative to Hann. It bodes well for me.

"Your choice is a subsidized apartment or a third husband," Hann says to her. "And for your own good, for the good of this family, divorce will never, ever be an option."

May-ling glares at Hann, clearly unhappy. She doesn't know that I know about the housing.

Feeling awkward and excluded, I try to inject myself back into the conversation. "You were awarded housing?"

May-ling waves a hand at Hann, deferring to him. He lifts his chin and relinquishes the query right back to her. XX smiles triumphantly. BeiBei shakes my arm, and I dig through my noodles for a piece of chicken for him.

May-ling frowns. "I can't eat." She turns to me, and her eyes soften. "Are you hungry? Would you like to spend some time together right now?"

Her candor stuns me anew. Hann's smile freezes into a rigid line. Even though I've dreamed all day about being alone with her, I feel used, a mouse trapped between two quietly warring cats. Not in a position to turn her down, I look at XX, the family czar of fairness. "Is it all right if I visit with May-ling first?"

"Yes," he says. "May-ling can have my turn." I was counting on less maturity.

She pushes back her chair without a glance at Hann and comes to me. I place my hand into her upturned palm, her grip slender and determined. I remember the electricity when she pressed her number into my hand at the end of our matchmaking lunch, her sneaky arrangement of our first date. I can understand and forgive the way they tested me, but I'm not sure about this. I squeeze her hand and try to forge a connection, anxious for her to put aside her grudge and see me. To acknowledge me.

"Me go too." BeiBei twists and stands on his seat.

May-ling yelps as we almost miss catching him.

She grabs BeiBei's elbow while he wraps his legs and arms around me. "Don't you ever leap like that again."

"You're faster than a monkey." I laugh to defuse May-ling's fright and anger.

XX jumps to his feet, red-faced. "It's not your turn anymore." His attempt to pull BeiBei off me starts the boy whining and clinging tighter.

I bounce and shush BeiBei and tell XX it's all right.

May-ling interposes herself between the two.

"I won't let him ruin tonight," XX declares.

"He won't," I say, and look to Hann for help. Chopsticks and bowl in his hands, he is finally eating.

"Will you please?" May-ling says.

Hann wipes his mouth methodically before pushing back his chair. He stretches out his arms, but BeiBei will not go to him. When Hann takes him, he scissors his legs tighter around my waist and reaches toward me, crying.

Murmuring and bouncing, Hann says, "Oh, you like me. Don't you want your baba?"

"Go to your room," XX tells May-ling and me.

"I want Uncle." BeiBei's urgent cries root me to the spot.

May-ling too, seems hesitant to leave him. Elbows out, XX plugs his ears. BeiBei continues his heartbroken cries, his little mouth quivering and downturned. Sex in the next room feels impossible, selfish, and cruel even under the circumstances. When XX urges us again to attend to our Compatibility Night, I open my arms to the sobbing child. He lands on me like a basketball.

"My fickle, fickle boy." Hann ruffles BeiBei's cowlick. "How quickly our allegiances shift."

"Stop crying, you." XX pokes at BeiBei's back, and he wails louder. "You already got what you want."

"It's all right." I move BeiBei away from XX. "I don't mind."

"I'm sorry we are all so amped up by your visit," Hann says, looking not terribly sorry. "I have to admit, though, this is life with a two-year-old."

"Compatibility Night is never going to happen." XX crosses his arms and pouts. "I'm going to be stuck here forever."

"XX!" Hann says.

I realize that BeiBei may be just the buffer I need. "I hope May-ling is still willing to join me for some time alone," I say, trailing off. Carrying BeiBei, I walk in the direction of the bedrooms. Despite May-ling's hesitation, I keep on going, more determined now for a private moment with her.

"They can't have Compatibility Night with the baby!" XX tells Hann.

Hann hushes him. BeiBei clings to me, sniffling. I stop in front of a closed bedroom door. May-ling stares at Hann for a long moment. He doesn't say anything as she marches past me, her posture regal and resolute.

Inside the bedroom, a double bed is pushed up against the wall, and three chair backs form a makeshift railing next to the bed. I squeeze myself into the corridor between the chairs and the rolling clothes rack. My hopes sink. It's apparent from the hastily made bed and scatter of clothing and toys that no preparation has been made for Compatibility Night.

May-ling closes the door and squeezes past me to click on the bedside table lamp. We dodge each other as she moves clothes from the chairs and piles them atop the rolling rack. Her hair and shoulders brush against me, releasing a scent of sweet almonds. We are so close an accidental snag of her sash could undo her green wrap dress. She apologizes again and again—for what, I'm not sure—but not once does she look at me. Nudging a stuffed dog aside with her toes—BeiBei owns quite a collection of dog toys—she turns a chair around and invites me to sit. Still keeping her back to me, she picks up toys next—her heart-shaped bottom canting beguilingly each time she bends over—and I do my best not to stare, not to be entranced.

I do not sit. "I really like you. I hope you know how much I like you, how important tonight is to me."

My appeal finally stops her. She picks up a wrinkly faced bulldog and hugs it tight to her stomach. The *V* of her dress gapes, the inner curves of her breasts luscious atop the lace of her white bra.

I say, "There's obviously something that's upsetting you, something you need to work out with Hann."

"Gimme." Still in my arms, BeiBei leans toward her and takes the dog.

May-ling flushes from her cheeks to her chest. "I cringe to

imagine what you must think of us. Of me. I'd understand—we'd understand—if you want nothing more to do with our family."

Alarmed, I clutch BeiBei tight, his sweet baby breath rushing in and out of my ear. "Is that what you want? Are you opposed to Compatibility Night?" If May-ling is going to reject me after all this, I'm at least going to get an explanation.

"I can't exactly be opposed, can I, if I wasn't consulted about it. Just as I wasn't told about the housing award." May-ling hugs herself tight. "I'm sorry. I shouldn't have said that. You must think we are the most mixed-up family. We have a life-altering decision to make, and I'm sorry we are going about it so badly."

I tell her I'm relieved. "I thought you forgot I was coming, or worse yet, didn't care. But truthfully, I don't know how I could possibly compete with subsidized housing."

She stares at her feet. "We wanted to call you off, but we ran out of time. I'm sorry to waste your evening." She is pushing me away again.

"Do you *want* me to try to compete with the housing?"

"I'm not worth the trouble." She shakes her head again and again. I sense more than politeness in her self-negation. "And I haven't the right to ask."

"Of course you have the right," I say. "I grant you the right to take as much time as you need to make up your mind about me. You can say no, though I sincerely hope that you won't. Will you give me a chance?"

Her head tilts. I approach until there is just BeiBei wedged between us. The brooding black of her eyes lightens, becoming almost transparent and soulful the longer I look into them. Her hesitancy melts into a sort of wonderment. After a moment, she nods. I feel seen by her for the first time today.

BeiBei pushes May-ling away with his toy dog. "Move, MaMa!" Smiling at her, I ask to meet BeiBei's stuffed friends and set him down. I pick up a German shepherd and a Pekingese, line up the three chairs once again, and seat them on one to get him started.

I return to May-ling, reclaiming my position half a pace away. I consider how best to convey my intentions in light of her history with Hann and XX. "If you'll have me, I promise you my whole heart, a true union of our souls, minds, and bodies." BeiBei patters about us, and I bite my lip and take both her hands. She does not resist. They feel shaky and chapped, the hands of a hardworking wife and mother.

"I do have one condition." I wait for her to look at me, to acknowledge that to continue, I require her participation. Finally our eyes meet. "If you will have me, I ask that you too promise me your heart, that we hide nothing from each other, that we resolve all our doubts and reservations. I will not be a compromise, a consolation, or a forced situation for you."

The mattress squeaks.

"I'd like that. Very much." She tells BeiBei the bed is not for jumping on. "But what do you see in my family? In me? We're—" She glances at her trampolining child and shakes her head with incomprehension.

"You have your questions backward." I squeeze her hands. "You are first and foremost in this equation. The only piece of the puzzle that matters."

"All right then," she says. I am heartened to see the beginnings of a small, suppressed smile. "Why me?"

"I am drawn to you. I feel an affinity, a deep attraction. You are so beautiful. You're the first person I notice entering a room, the one I yearn to return to again and again."

"Looks don't last. And attraction—" She pauses and straightens her carriage. "Forgive my bluntness, but our physical relationship will be a small part of our overall time together. Looks and attraction solve nothing. The reality is you will be living from day one with my entire family, and my family as you've already seen is far from easy."

"Everything you say is true. But I like and respect your family, every single one of them."

BeiBei slides off the bed and comes over to tug on my elbow. "Play with me."

With him hanging off my arm, I say, "I'm no expert, but it seems plain to me that physical attraction is a necessary first step. A good marriage cannot exist without it. True intimacy and connection is hard to achieve without satisfactory physical relations."

I am nearly certain mutual attraction is missing with both her husbands. Not wanting to say something I'll regret, I let BeiBei drag me away. He has only retrieved two more dogs, so I lift a corner of the bedcovers, wondering aloud if any little friends are hiding there. He tunnels under giggling, and I return to Mayling.

There is a wet glimmer in her eyes. I've struck a nerve. I tuck a loose strand of hair behind her ears and draw her to me by her narrow waist.

I say, "These last weeks, whenever I encounter something new, something funny or interesting, you are the one I want to tell. I go into stores and things that you might like or use jump out at me. I eat a tasty dish, and I want to share it with you. I walk down the street, saving up stories I must tell you later. I can't go anywhere or do anything anymore without considering your response to it, without considering how I could shape my actions to make you proud."

She blinks away her tears.

"May I ask you a question?" I wait for her to give me permission, which comes as a small nod. "Are you attracted to me?"

She breathes in deeply and whispers yes. I bring her hands to my lips and acknowledge her resolve with a sustained kiss. When

I let go, her rough fingertips find their way back to my lips. Her face opens, a morning glory heralding the start of a new day. She leans into my hand, and I stroke her petal-soft cheeks. I nuzzle her forehead, her eyes, the ridge of her nose. I find my way to her mouth, and her hands are on my chest when our lips finally meet. Her mouth nudges mine and retreats, but returns again and again, searching, questioning, testing. I did not know so much could be conveyed through a kiss. I peek and realize she has been observing me, taking my measure. I've saved myself for this first real kiss, but wonder now if I should have paid for one and practiced.

I tighten my arms and fit the lovely length of May-ling against me. The scent of sweet almond, the warm powdered milk of my childhood winter mornings, overpowers me. I kiss May-ling more fervently now, tasting her lips millimeter by millimeter, cherishing every lovely speck of her. An urge to both devour and protect her rushes over me. Her hands wander up and off my chest until the entirety of her soft bosom presses against me. I feel her heart beating in synchrony with mine, the two of us united against whatever may come.

"MaMa! Stop it!" I almost forgot about BeiBei. He grips the makeshift chair railing, a quiet horror etched into his expression.

May-ling stifles a laugh against my ear. "He's never seen such a kiss."

Her admission thrills me and confirms everything I want to know about her marriages. Not wanting to traumatize BeiBei, I release his mother. I lift the corner of the bedcover, peek under the bed, and gasp. "Someone needs rescuing down here."

He stomps his feet. "You get it."

Feeling bad about agitating him, I get on all fours and bonk my head against the bed frame to make him laugh. "I'm too big."

Behind me, the door clicks. My heart sinks. May-ling has opened it. Our time together is over, the magic dissipated.

"Get it," he says, bouncing harder and becoming increasingly upset.

"BeiBei, please stop," May-ling says.

"I will rescue your pup!" I say. The best I can do at this point is to win back his affection. I crawl on my stomach and strain for the toy beneath the bed.

The mattress bounces and squeaks above me, stirring up the dust. I drag out a cobweb-smeared dachshund.

BeiBei slides off the bed. "Gimme."

"Hold on," I say, sneezing. "Let me clean it." I keep the dog out of BeiBei's reach and clap it against my hand to remove the dust.

"Let me do that," May-ling says.

"Noooo!" BeiBei wails, his arms outstretched.

"Sshhhh." May-ling kneels next to him and mouths me an apology. "Uncle has to clean off the spider web. Please thank Uncle for rescuing your doggie."

"No spider," BeiBei cries, his uvula trembling in full view.

"Someone is getting tired and cranky," May-ling says. "I think it's time to get ready for bed."

I give the dachshund one last pat and hand it to BeiBei.

He hugs it to his chest and cries harder. "No bed."

"Did you thank your uncle?"

"I don't want bed!"

May-ling places a hand on BeiBei's shoulder. "It is eight o'clock. Your bedtime. And you must say thank you."

He sniffs and mumbles his thanks. An impish smirk flashes across his wet face before he shrugs off his mother's hand and bolts out of the room, banging open the door behind him.

"Should I go after him?" I say.

May-ling touches my arm. "I've never been so glad that BeiBei can be counted on to play chase at bedtime."

I can't believe she has maneuvered BeiBei's exit. We grin at each other.

We hear Hann ask where BeiBei is going in such a hurry. Mayling's eyes never leave mine as she glides to the door and shuts it, dampening BeiBei's trilling giggles. She slides the bolt.

We move toward each other, and she embraces me with an ardor that matches mine. Soft, substantive, and delicate-boned, she fills me with a sense of calm excitement, of communion and well-being. I love the feel of her in my arms, her head in the crook of my neck, the two of us loving and keeping each other safe. I kiss her forehead again and again.

"I've never felt like this before," she says.

Hearing those words means everything to me.

She burrows her face in my chest. "I'm not a great housekeeper, but I promise you that I clean under the bed once a month."

I laugh and hug her tighter. "Do you think I care if you clean under the bed?" I bury my nose in her hair and laugh some more. "If you will have me, I promise to help you. I promise you will never have to clean under another bed for the rest of your life."

She arches back to look at me. "I'm really nervous." She places a hand over her heart. "It's like I have a bird in here fighting to get out."

"I should be the one who's nervous." I clasp the hand on her chest. Much like my own, it's cold, damp, and shaky. I kiss and rub it between both of mine. "Tell me why you're so nervous."

She smiles weakly and hesitates.

I kiss her hand again. "It's all right."

"You must have had a lot of Helpmates—" She stops and peers up at me. "I'm afraid"—she shakes her head—"I'm not going to measure up."

"My darling," I say, relieved and surprised by her answer, "you never, ever have to worry with me. I'm the one who is inexperienced. I've had two Helpmates for my entire life. I've not paid for a kiss, for full nudity, for a lot of the extras."

"Why not?"

Her incredulity stumps me for a moment. "You must know that being with a Helpmate is the coldest, most unsatisfactory, most begrudging of transactions."

She watches me carefully.

I add that I was also afraid. "Afraid of catching something and getting sent away. Afraid of jeopardizing the health of my future spouse and child."

"Not paying for additional services required great self-discipline."

Her recognition of my restraint lights me up. I resolve to start our relationship off right. "Money had something to do with it too. I didn't have any to waste. Saving toward a dowry and a future felt like a more concrete achievement."

She kisses my hands one after the other. "Thank you."

"For what?"

"For your thoughtfulness. Your sacrifice. What you did was difficult, and it means everything to me."

"Still nervous?"

She laughs. "Yes. You?"

I laugh too. "Most definitely."

She cups my face in her hands, the glint in her gaze intense, tender, and possessive. I feel chosen. Cherished. When her lips find mine, they are full of urgency, desire, commitment. She tousles my hair and pulls me ever closer. Our union feels intimate and expansive at the same time. Two have become one, yet everything feels possible. Everything is now within our reach.

I kiss my way to her ear and whisper, "Before I invited you to my studio, I went online and tried to teach myself how to dance." I chuckle. "You saw how well that worked out."

"You were wonderful."

"I was a klutz."

She leans back to look in my eyes, her gaze assuring and sincere. "You moved with athleticism and strength. I found you very dreamy."

I was certain that day that Hann was the one with the dreamy moves. "Ever since we scheduled our Compatibility Night, I've been reading up on the many, many ways to please a woman."

She flushes pink, her smile nervous. "What have you learned?"

"Shall I show you?"

I slide my hand down her side feeling for the trailing sash of her dress and draw out the knot centimeter by centimeter. May-ling does not stop me. She takes a deep breath, and I am surprised and thrilled to see her reach for her waistline to unthread the sash herself. She slides the dress off her shoulders. The silky green wrapping glides downward, settling in a pool around our feet, her body full and virginal in her white bra and panties. We re-entwine our limbs and kiss and kiss and kiss.

I float home in the best of moods and find my two dads in the midst of their nightly *wéiqí* battle. It is a quiet game, perfect for our one-bedroom apartment. They can duke it out into the small hours and not disturb my sleep inside my curtained bed in the living room.

"There's a bowl of beef noodle soup on the table," Dad says, his forehead wrinkled in grim concentration. His head and shoulders hover over the board as if proximity will help him see the way. "Did you work up a new client tonight?"

I want to proclaim at the top of my lungs that I'm in love, that I've experienced a true body-and-soul connection with a woman for the first time. Instead, I study Big Dad's half-reclined posture, the careless tinkling of game pieces falling through his fingers. Dad is in no danger of challenging. I check the board and confirm that black stones dominate the right half. Big Dad rarely loses and is punishing when he does.

"Anything new today?" I ask.

Dad says there were workers out in the hallway for much of the afternoon banging on the walls and installing security cameras. We had a burglary in the building recently. "The hall outlets were not working, so we let them use ours."

"Security cameras?" I say. "What a waste." We live on the nineteenth floor. With the elevator reserved only for emergencies, no one makes the climb unless they live up here.

Big Dad says. "The building will pay our electric bill this month."

I ask if they've had their medications. Dad takes four different pills to control his blood pressure, and Big Dad two for angina. Dad hums yes, his eyes glued to their ridiculously clunky butcher block of a game board. I study the board with him, but this chipped, water- and grease-stained relic only reminds me of my ancient failings and Big Dad's disappointment in me.

"How about here?" I could not resist pointing out Dad's best option. Big Dad bought me this board of Tibetan spruce, had my name etched onto its side, and tried to teach me this game in which he excelled. I had no patience for it, not at age five. I'll never forget his spankings for my inability to sit still and listen, his taunts for me to use my minuscule brain. Our games consisted of Dad chasing me down and securing me to his lap, Dad explaining options that were akin to white noise and moving the pieces in my stead. He was eager for me to live up to Big Dad's hopes for the son he could not father.

I've come to like strategy games and, from the standings of my Middle Kingdom, have proven too that I'm good at it. If Big

Dad waited until I was older and more ready and did not beat and badger me into compliance, I probably would have come to appreciate *wéiqí*. But he'll never know.

Dad bites his lip, still unable to make a move.

Annoyed no doubt by my interference, Big Dad turns his attention to me and does a double take at my red sweater. "Is that new?"

Dad glances at me, but fails to notice that I'm wearing new pants and dress shoes as well. "Aren't you going to go eat?"

I take a deep breath and collect myself before admitting that I've already had dinner at the Wus.

"New friends of yours?" Dad says, still engrossed.

Big Dad frowns and sits up. "You saw Wu May-ling again without telling us."

"May-ling, her husbands, and son." I meet and hold his gaze.

"Why are you always hiding things?" Big Dad says. "What have we ever done to deserve your disrespect?"

"I'm telling you now." I do not say that Big Dad is such a tyrant and sore loser that presenting events after the fact was how I've learned to get my way. "I love May-ling. I love her family. She and I are highly compatible." I pause to let them catch up to what I did not put into words. "I'd like your blessings should they propose marriage."

Big Dad looks eerily calm, as if he has skipped the anger stage and gone straight to plotting revenge. "We've already told you that's out of the question."

Dad looks as shocked as he is chagrined by the misbehavior of his own flesh and blood. "We cannot knowingly allow you to endanger yourself with a Willful Sterile and a Lost Boy."

I tell them that XX wants out of the union. "They're going to divorce him."

"That's never going to happen," says Big Dad.

I say, "You think you know everything." I can feel Dad cringe.

"They're filial children. Children who value and honor their parents' wishes."

"Their parents have long passed," I say, pretending not to catch his drift.

Big Dad shakes his head as if my stupidity is beyond cure. "There is a reason those brothers married the same girl. They are never going to split up."

I hate how he thinks he can peg people after one brief meeting. "What do you have against the Willfully Sterile? Or Lost Boys, for that matter?"

"Nothing if they are not breaking any laws," he says. "But they're not what's under discussion. What concerns us right now is your disrespect, your pigheaded determination to disregard our combined wisdom and our very best intentions for you. You want to throw away a future that took us forty years of work and sacrifice."

I sigh and hang my head. I want to be more forthright, but Big Dad doesn't make it easy. I bring up the fact that it has been over a year since we signed on with the matchmaker. "I've been featured three times, and I've only had this one nibble."

Dad's eyes crinkle with commiseration. He comes to me and squeezes my shoulder. In his brief smile, I can see that he is glad for my sake that I was able to experience meaningful physical love with May-ling. He reminds me that it also took a year for MaMa to pick him out of his matchmaker's stable. "And then she and your big baba took another four months choosing between me and some plumber. You know how many more men there are now. You mustn't despair."

"The matchmaker matched me in three months," Big Dad says, his irritation giving way to gloating. "Of course, I had a college degree, a highly respectable profession, and a good paying job. But your baba is right. Patience is required now more than ever."

"But isn't that naïve too? I think we need to face the possibility that I may not have another match. That I will be one of the twenty percent who will die a bachelor." Big Dad's boasting makes me reckless to throw the worst scenario in his face, pessimism on my part as annoying to him as inept bargaining when we shop.

Dad says, "You cannot think that way. You mustn't."

"Desperation is no reason for stupidity," Big Dad says.

"What I'm doing is far from stupidity. A stupid person would not keep his options open," I say.

Dad's fingers dig into my shoulder.

"I'm not saying you're stupid." Big Dad exhales with great exasperation. "And don't pretend that there's no risk to what you're doing. Treat us like intelligent adults. Act like one, so we can discuss this rationally."

"Don't misunderstand Big Dad." Dad shakes my shoulder. "C'mon."

Just once, I wish that he'd side with me instead of always playing the intermediary. "I'm sorry." I stare dead-eyed at Big Dad, but he is not obliged to apologize to me.

Dad drags me to the couch and makes me sit. "Tell us what you're thinking."

"You've always told me to treat people the way I myself want to be treated. That how we are born, our wealth, our Party affiliation, our marital status do not determine our worth."

"Yes, we do believe that," Dad says, looking at Big Dad, who remains impassive.

"Do you feel that Hann and XX deserve less than us?"

"Of course not," Dad says.

Big Dad adds, "They've chosen to marry, to reproduce, to defy the law. Why must you jump into the muck with them?"

"Why shouldn't I, when the law is inhumane?" I say. "Would you choose anything less for yourself if you were them?"

"It's not your job to defend them."

"Why not?" I say.

"C'mon." Dad's hand is like a vise around my elbow. "This is your future we're talking about. Your personal safety. We don't want you to marry out of desperation or for some principle. That's not good enough for you."

I close and rub my eyes. When I open them again, the animosity has been coaxed out of Big Dad's face. Dad smiles as if we've all come around to his way of thinking.

"Hann is like the brother I've always wanted," I say to Big Dad, suggesting that I feel his disappointment just as keenly. My dad could have fathered a child for him, but Big Dad would not own up to his own inadequacy and allow it. "He makes me feel cared for, protected, and valued."

"Maybe he wants you for himself," Big Dad says.

I narrow my eyes at him.

"You can tell us if you like men. We can handle it."

I turn to Dad, my jaw hanging.

Dad pats my hand. "We don't think you're Willfully Sterile, but you understand that we have to ask. We have to be sure."

"My friendship with Hann reminds me of what I like best about the two of you." I pause to let them digest that little nugget. "He is someone I admire, a trustworthy companion, someone I see myself growing old with."

My two dads frown and eye each other.

"He's nearly sixty," I say. "I wouldn't worry about his discretion, not when he's kept himself out of trouble all his life."

Big Dad says, "You forget how easily we found out that he's Willfully Sterile."

"But rumors aren't *proof.* Shouldn't the evidence of a family and a child count more than rumors?"

"Who's being naïve now?"

"I really like their little boy." I tell Big Dad that BeiBei reminds me of my young, rambunctious self. "I know how to guide him, how to channel his energy. I feel a responsibility to shield him from impatient and unimaginative adults who think there's just one way to learn, one path to success."

Big Dad frowns. He knows I'm needling him.

"In or out of the picture, I like XX. He always tries his very best to be nice to me." I continue, "Hero was right, you know. This is an ideal situation for me: May-ling will be mine and only mine in the bedroom. It's as close as possible to a one-man-one-woman marriage in this day and age. Don't you want that for me?"

Big Dad is shaking his head again. "What happens in the bedroom is the least of it. The number of people packed into your box of an apartment—that's the number of people in your marriage. You're locking yourself away for the rest of your life with a man who has the hots for you, with another with the sensibilities of a five-year-old—"

"Stop exaggerating," I say.

"—and who knows what else. Don't kid yourself that those two are your only challenges. This is nowhere near an ideal marriage or a comfortable situation."

"C'mon." Dad claps my thigh hard, yet another signal for me to back off.

"This is what I'd like to do." I think better of my statement and add, "With your permission." I remind them that it'll take time to divorce XX and to receive a proposal. In the meantime, I'd like to get to know the Wus, date them the old-fashioned way. I promise to keep my dads abreast of everything from here on out. "And if Hero comes up with another candidate, I'll be thrilled to consider her too." It occurs to me that the marriage hinges more on Hann's housing award than XX's divorce, but I decide to say nothing for now. That beast of a complication can only confuse and further frighten away my fathers.

Big Dad continues to frown. "You know that I always want the best for you." He waits for me to acknowledge his assertion, which I do. "You think that what you propose is reasonable. But it's not. Not when what you're toying with and giving away is your heart."

"I'm forty-four. I've never dated." I know he doesn't want to hear this. "I welcome a chance to live, to get hurt if that's what it takes. Maybe that's as much as I'm going to experience."

Big Dad stares blamefully at Dad. To him, I'll always be Dad's mess.

I decide they are worn down enough for my final argument. "We have a chance to use the Wus' situation to our advantage." I mention that money is going to be tight after my dads put up my dowry, that I worry about them growing old without me under the same roof. "If I'm able to establish a true rapport—make myself indispensible to them—then maybe we can negotiate a lower dowry or more parental support so that you can hire someone to cook and clean and look after you."

My dads are both nearing eighty, and how they will negotiate their final years without my daily presence is a subject that's not far from any of our minds. The traditional living arrangement of three generations under one roof is never an option for the second, not to mention the third spouse.

Dad protests—he doesn't want me to worry about them—but Big Dad stays quiet. Judging by his silence, I think I may have budged him.

The Safety Council–led boycott of the mental-health quota proved effective. Doc's hacker reprogrammed Major Jung's mental-health form. Over 80 percent of our generals—416 out of 500 to be exact—joined us on the date it was due and instead of checking five candidates, filed forms without recommendations. The deadline passed, and Major Jung's reminders and noncompliance threats stopped. The high participation rate of our generals must have been a huge loss of face for him. Rumors about his imminent firing pervaded our chat lines. Doc was right. Our combined voices sent a strong message. Our games have since continued without further interference.

Two months later, after I was certain this firestorm had blown over, I decided to invite XX to a game as my special guest. I thought war games would be right up his alley, that I could introduce him to some like-minded friends as he considers life after divorce, but a very hesitant "I don't know" was his response. Hann, on the other hand, leapt at my offer and accepted on behalf of his brother. I imagined that unfamiliar people and situations were difficult for XX, but with Hann's encouragement I pressed on, guaranteeing that I would be XX's personal ambassador. He ought to know I'm extending him a rare privilege. Not only is Middle Kingdom's waiting list long, Strategic Games is technically only for unmarried men. And still he wavered, citing chaos and disappointment among his online friends should he miss his expected hours of play. He seemed to genuinely believe that he mattered to those strangers he has never met.

When the equipment rental place informed us that they didn't carry uniforms his size, a grin broke out on XX's face. I had sweet-talked, cajoled, and wheedled for an entire week, had had to call our friendship on the line and badger to get him to succumb. I wasn't about to give up after putting both of us through that: I got loud in the store, handed them my Strategic Games Council credentials, and demanded that they stock his size from now on. They agreed, but I had to place a sizable deposit. I'm not sure now if I'd done the right thing. Afterward, whenever I speak too loud or with too much animation, XX's first instinct is to cower.

We picked up the uniform this afternoon, three weeks after placing the order and just in time for tonight's game. I was glad this first hurdle was over only to discover that keeping XX in uniform would be no easy feat. With sewn-in controls, sensors, and lasers, the suit is heavy. XX itched and twitched and sweated the second he put it on. He shied away from my gaze, and I could tell he felt too intimidated to complain. He looked so miserable I finally told him he could pull down the top and tie the sleeves around his waist. And that was how we boarded the train for our hour-long ride to the battlefield.

The hundred men in my troop—the ones who like to socialize—pile into the last train car with food and drinks to share. I climb on with XX and usher him into the booth on the far end. I tell him to sit next to the aisle. To discourage seatmates, I do the same. Though it is a comfortable spring day, his face and undershirt are drenched like it's the height of summer.

I slap a few hands and greet the men who sit near us. XX sucks at his water bottle, so disinterested in my interactions that I decide to let him settle in before introducing him to anyone. When Major Chao and his spiky hair comes up the steps in his usual self-satisfied sashay, I turn and stare out the window.

Of course he makes his way down the corridor, throws his knapsack across our table, and asks XX to scoot over. Chao looks him up and down, no doubt noting the dragging and mistreated half of XX's uniform and remembering that I reprimanded him for doing just that.

"Hello, hello," he says.

I flash him a grimace-smile. When I make no move to introduce them, Chao thrusts his hand at XX. "Just call me Major," the pompous ass says after enumerating his full name and rank. I tell myself it's not funny when XX shakes his hand, reaches into his shirt to scratch his back, and then stares out the window. It is alarming that it does not occur to him to introduce himself.

Chao leans toward the shrinking XX, pinning him against the window. "Are you a friend of our general?"

Still staring at the scenery, he mumbles that I'm his family's fiancé, exaggerating the relationship I expressly asked him to keep quiet. My stomach free-falls. XX is sabotaging his own chances, not to mention jeopardizing my reputation as a fair leader.

Chao nods, the wheels in his head churning. He rummages through his pockets and with two hands, presents XX a small packet of smoked scallops with a bow. He must think XX's aloofness a sign of his status, offering him this prized snack. Legend had it that keeping a smoked scallop on the tongue during daylong marches quenched the thirst of many a soldier.

Chao asks if Hero matched us. "I'm Hero's client too."

XX carefully tears the top of the tubed package and slides all three scallops into his mouth in one go. He chomps noisily on this delicacy that should be savored and swallows everything after a few hasty chews. Surely feeling ignored, Chao checks my reaction. I do not say anything.

XX sucks from his canteen next and swipes his chin with the back of a hand. When I think he's forgotten Chao's question, he says, "Yes."

"How excellent," Chao says. His eyes shift, and I can sense him weighing the situation, plotting his advantage. "When will you be inviting us to your wedding banquet?"

"The banquet and guest list are the responsibility of Wei-guo's fathers," XX says.

Chao opens his arms, ignoring the slight. "Let me be the first to offer my congratulations."

"I'm not the groom," XX says. "Don't congratulate me."

Chao bows his head with great ceremony. Amazing that the snottier XX acts, the more respect he inspires in Chao.

I tell Chao that no formal marriage offer has been proposed.

Chao waves away my protest. "Tell me," he says to XX, "who has the honor of employing you?"

Chao's eyes grow big at XX's reply. CSS is the largest security company in the country not owned by the government. It does not hire anyone without Party connections or serious talent in addition to a deep background check. I too must have taken a leap in Chao's estimation, for he digs around the pockets of his knapsack, mumbling that there must be another package, and comes up with some scallops for me. I leave his offering on the table untouched. He asks XX's position at CSS.

"Security designer."

The kiss-ass bows reverently and ogles as if he's found a pirate trove. "I am so very honored to make your acquaintance. Unsung heroes like you keep our country's precious innovations secure, and I for one, thank you for it."

"You are very welcome." Pleasure floods XX's features, and he seems to register Chao as a person for the first time. A prey to flattery, XX's not too different from the rest of us after all.

"Are you the first spouse?"

"No."

"No?" Chao's eyebrows pop up. I must be courting an impressive family if XX is not the first spouse.

I thank the heavens when the train finally begins to roll. Chao asks about husband number one's profession. Before XX gives away all our secrets, I maneuver into the aisle, call out good afternoon to my men, and wave for their attention. The back section continues to guffaw and yell. Someone must have told a dirty joke.

Major Chao digs through his knapsack and brings his antique bullhorn to his mouth. The relic screeches, sending XX's hands to his ears, before Major Chao parrots my greeting. I motion for him to sit down, to put that ridiculous contraption away. His eagerness to assert his rank is another reason he is not liked among the men.

A respectful and orderly bunch, my people don't take long to settle down. I smile and make eye contact down the length of the car. It is important to me that every one of my men feels a personal connection, if not to someone in the troop, then to me.

"It is always the highlight of my month to see each and every one of you. I look forward to witnessing your bravery and brilliance on the battlefield. And—I am eager for Middle Kingdom's seventh victory against the Han Empire."

Those few words are all I plan to say about the night's battle. The majority of my troop has been with Middle Kingdom for over a decade. They have already received written instructions and met with their unit leaders. They are well trained and adept at executing their missions. During these gatherings, I am more interested in community building and in fostering an optimistic mental outlook. Despite what they'll have us believe, we excess men live on the periphery and are scapegoats for much of the ills of our society.

My soldiers hoot and holler and stamp their feet at my remark. Pinkies splayed, XX sticks a middle finger in each ear. Seeing this and seeing his interaction with Chao, I realize I've made a mistake.

I should not have brought him.

Hoping no one notices him, I move on and ask who has good news to share this month.

Someone yells out that Sergeant Major Lin just received a promotion. More cheering ensues. XX's fingers go back into his ears. I did not realize his noise-phobia was so severe. This behavior tips him from strange and maladjusted into actual Lost Boy territory, and I feel really bad for dragging him to an event he is so ill suited to handle.

I put a finger to my lips. "The train conductor asked if we

could be more considerate of the other passengers and keep our celebrations down." No such thing occurred, but my ploy elicits the intended response for the moment from my soldiers and XX.

I invite Lin to stand and share his success. Our rule is that everyone must use and enjoy his moment in the spotlight.

Lin is jostled to his feet by his neighbors. So shy he can barely look up, he runs both hands through the salt-and-pepper hair that circles his balding pate. It worries me that someone in his late forties can still be so unworldly, so unfit for wooing. Lin finally squeaks out that he's the new chief of sanitation for the World Trade Center Tower, the fifth tallest building in Beijing. When he comes up with no more, I pass him an index card. For the more reserved among us, I've outlined talking points for just such moments.

Though a number of us are celebrated in just this manner every month, Lin studies the list with panicked eyes. I keep my hands up, reminding the crowd to support their comrade with some quiet.

Lin stares hard at the card as he speaks. He tells us that this is his eighteenth year working for Beautiful Beijing, that he has gone from lavatory chief to crisis manager to head of dispatch to assistant building manager. These days, grand titles are conferred upon the most undesired jobs. In an industry that's taken over by robots, certain tasks—the occasional scrubbing of a stubborn toilet stain, safe cleanup of spills and broken glass—still require human hands.

Lin says that he is most gratified that after nearly two decades of "fieldwork," he now holds a desk job where he supervises a fleet of robots from monitors. He stares at his feet, but there is a timid smile on his face when he says that it's as if he's paid to play virtual games.

My men are boisterous in their approval. Though not in a sought-after or well-respected field, Lin has nevertheless made the improbable leap to management.

XX stares out the window. I wonder if he is oblivious or just plain disinterested.

Lin does not address the last question on the index card, so I ask what's next for him. It's important to me that my men stay forward-looking and find different ways to define their worth.

"If I'm fifty and still single, me and my dowry fund are visiting Macau. We're going to eat and drink our fill and find our luck at the tables." He glances at me, sheepish, no doubt thinking of my optimism policy.

The car explodes with enthusiasm. Lin sprints down the aisle as is our tradition, slapping hands. I join in the clapping and decide to stay mum. During our long, long wait, who among us has not entertained fanciful notions? I've resolved many times to blow my dowry fund after my dads are gone on a private sports car, a gel bed, a cook, and myriad luxuries that add up to a wife. There is power and satisfaction in such fantasies. And I know for a fact that Lin's mother is still alive and in control of his purse strings.

After Lin returns to his seat, I ask if anyone else has good news to share. No one speaks up. "What about bad news?" I say. Our policy is that we do not sugarcoat around one another. "Anyone experiencing work or health issues? We can't help if we don't know your problem." As tough as it can be, we've proven to be a great resource for one another, finding new jobs, responsive doctors, and caregivers for ailing parents too many times to count.

Chao stands. "We're not done with the good news." He hitches his elbow to my neck—the nerve of him—and shakes me around as if we're peers. "Our fearless leader will soon be a married man!"

I shoot a dirty look his way. My men will not stop hooting and hollering. I raise my arms, but they continue to cheer and drown out my protest. A sharp whistle sends XX's hands again to his ears. Needless to say, he is in no shape to be introduced. I put a finger to my lips and pray that they'll quiet soon.

"Our general is one master apple polisher," Chao says, eyes twinkling like he's one of our well-loved jokesters. "He knows that our Middle Kingdom is the very best and has invited his future spouse to participate in our formidable army." He asks everyone to join him in welcoming XX and begins clapping.

Waved to his feet by Chao, XX comes to a standing crouch beneath the overhead luggage rack. His hands fall away from his ears—there's only a smattering of applause—and there's a disturbing scowl on his face. His wave goes on and on.

Two rows behind me, Lieutenant Bai, an entitled, spoiled brat like Chao, says, "Married men aren't allowed in Strategic Games."

Out to topple me, Chao's congeniality suddenly makes sense.

"They can in Middle Kingdom," XX replies, his voice too loud and his tone lecturing. "Every army is chartered differently."

There is a palpable silence.

"Was Sergeant Chiu told that before he retired?" someone in the back of the car asks. Though popular in the lower ranks, Chiu was a troublemaker I was eager to lose.

I say that he did not petition to stay. "Once married, our soldiers have opted to spend their leisure time with their brides and families." I make it sound like the norm adopted by a large group even though there have only been two marriages in recent memory.

Still half-bent, XX's eyes are locked on the contents of Chao's knapsack. He does not appear to be listening.

"What about Colonel Wong?" someone else adds.

Heat rises in my cheeks. "I too miss our colonel," I manage to say. I did not disclose Middle Kingdom's marriage loophole to my former second-in-command because I wanted to be the first to make use of it. Close scrutiny by the Strategic Games Council would likely invalidate the fine print that I buried in our charter.

Chao says, "Guo XX is a noted defense designer. He will be an excellent leader and addition to our espionage team."

Damn that man. I say, "I want to be clear: Comrade Guo is only observing today as my special guest. We are trying to get to know each other, and no invitation has been extended to him to enlist." Chao's suggestion to leapfrog XX to the head of our surveillance unit will surely piss off more than a few people, not to mention undermine my ability to stay on.

"Married men will ruin our dynamic," Lieutenant Bai says. "I say no to married men."

XX's introduction could not have gone worse, but he breaks into a smile. I wish he would sit down.

"But it's written into our charter," Chao says. "Our general did so when he founded Middle Kingdom."

Bai leans back in his seat and points his finger at me. "Didn't you say that we are all equals here in Middle Kingdom?"

"Absolutely," I reply. "I've said many times that I want Middle Kingdom to be a social, emotional, and political oasis for each and every one of us. I could not be more serious."

XX reaches over his shoulder to scratch his back, exposing a strip of his bulging gut in the process. I tip my head at him, signaling for him to sit down, to stop displaying himself so unflatteringly, but he doesn't get it.

Bai continues, "So you'll change the charter?"

"I'm happy to put it to a vote." I say, "But why are you so against married men? You're going to be one too, one day."

"They run our government, our richest businesses. They've cornered all the women. Hell, they've gotten so fat, they can barely fuck, so why should we let them into the one area that's ours?" The men titter.

"But it's not us against them," I say.

"Married men do not have everything," XX says. I cringe at his uncompromising forcefulness. Bai must have struck a nerve with the fat insult. "We have no freedom, no peace of mind, no quiet."

"Oh, we feel so bad for you," Bai says.

XX seems unfazed by the taunt. "Marriage is warfare," he says even more loudly. "It's like we're sentenced to guerilla warfare for the rest of our lives."

There is a momentary silence before a single cheer erupts from the back of the car. Private Lang cups his mouth and yells, "This one is all right. This one can stay for today." He leads a smattering of applause.

XX's eyes bulge. He waves rather woodenly and picks that moment to sit down.

I exhale, relieved that he is out of the spotlight for now.

"Ho, ho." Chao grabs my shoulder and shakes me. "No one is better at guerilla warfare than our general!"

My legs feel shaky. I'm exhausted, and the games have yet to begin. I am impressed, though, that by being himself and spouting his rather unusual beliefs, XX has drummed up some supporters. They say dumb people—not that he's dumb—have their own dumb luck, and I'm beginning to sense how XX bumbles through. And that thought makes me smile.

With or without Hann's help, he will make his own way.

My men crowd into the aisle as the train approaches the station for Heavenly Lake. They are squirrelly as schoolboys after an hour and a half in these close quarters, but the exit doors will not open. Neither will the windows. When pounding on them brings no results, a few begin to shake the seat backs and howl. It is hard to breathe in here; the central air system has shut down along with the doors. I don't see a soul on the small platform, not even a station employee. That in and of itself is not a surprise. Strategic Games players are most likely the only visitors tonight to this remote station. But in light of our recent boycott, I feel uneasy. Someone hammers the button for the hydraulic door to the next car. It is also out of order. The windows are fogging up.

"People are coming," a voice yells.

The sight of black-uniformed men cutting across the platform sobers us. A dozen of them spread out evenly along the length of our train.

Next to me, XX pants, mouth hanging. I made him pull on the upper portion of his uniform before we rolled into the station, and sweat studs his forehead. I ask if he is all right.

"I'm fine," he says. "What's going on? Who are they?"

"Equipment problem, most likely." I don't want to scare him, especially not on his first outing with us, but I myself am alarmed. Beyond the foggy blur of the windows, the black uniforms resemble Mao suits. They have no patches, name tags, or identifiers, and I can't tell if the men are guards, police, or soldiers. They stand about seemingly unarmed and without the formality of military men, but appear no less sinister.

"Those station guards will get us out soon," I say, trying to believe my own words. "Why don't you sit and relax while we wait?"

I'm relieved XX does as I ask and begins to occupy himself with his watch.

Outside, a uniformed man with a large tablet walks next to the train and talks to his cohorts. Something is afoot.

"We'll be out of here soon," XX says, not looking up from his watch.

"Sure thing," I say.

The doors whoosh open. My men cheer, jostle, and clamber to disembark.

"That wasn't me," XX says.

I'm about to ask what he means when two uniformed men come up the steps in the center of our train car, their arms forming barricades. They demand that we back up as they push their way up the two steps.

"Where is the general of Middle Kingdom? Where is Lee

Wei-guo?" a skinny, red-cheeked man yells, waving his tablet back and forth. His voice is high for a man. Almost squeaky.

"I am the general," I say with matching stridency though my heart is hammering. My men make way for me to come forward. I've been summoned by a boy with cheeks inflamed by acne, a boy whose voice has yet to go through puberty. He couldn't be a day over seventeen, yet he intimidates me all the same. "What is the delay? Our game begins in less than an hour, and we must set up."

"Come." The young man orders me down the steps and onto the platform.

His partner—another lanky and loose-limbed adolescent—holds up a hand and tells my men to remain on the train.

"This is fucked up," someone yells as the door sucks shut behind me.

I scrutinize the line of black uniforms: we're being held hostage by a band of teenagers. A few train cars away, two guards descend the steps with another man. I recognize Doc's cousin, the general of our opposing team. He is led away from me to the opposite end of the platform. A terrible dread seizes me: The two of us have been hand-selected for this confrontation. Major Jung and the powers that be are sending a message to Doc and the Safety Council.

"Who are you?" I demand.

My pimpled handler smirks. "I can be your best friend. Or your worst nightmare. The choice is yours, isn't it?" His partner snorts at the corny line and joins us.

I puff out my chest and try to channel the indignation I usually feel when disrespected by the barely weaned. "I want your name. Your affiliation. Your rank."

The boy laughs. "Unless you two submit the required paperwork, tonight's game will be suspended and the rest of your season cancelled. Drag your heels some more, and we'll haul you in and disband your team."

"What paperwork?" I say, though I know. I was stupid to think that Major Jung would give up easily. "All of Middle Kingdom's paperwork is up-to-date. I personally make certain of it."

"Your Safety Council report is not." His squeaky voice carries an awful sense of menace.

"You are mistaken," I say. "I filed it months ago when it was due, and I have the digital stamp to prove it."

"Just filing a report does not make it acceptable." His ill-mannered eyes rake me up and down. "You do not appear to be the sort who likes to be arrested in front of an audience, the sort who drags his boys on a long and tedious ride just to send them right back."

Inside the train, men are wiping the windows with their hands and elbowing one another to get a view, their pounding peppered with growing fury.

The punk turns on his tablet and hands it to me. "Select five, and apply your thumbprint."

The heading says MIDDLE KINGDOM: CANDIDATES FOR PSY-CHOLOGICAL EVALUATION. Below it is a list of our members, arranged by rank. I look across the platform at my counterpart. Doc's cousin is impossibly far away, but not too far away for me to see that he too has been similarly tasked. My heart pounding, I cast about for a plan. I realize that some kind of delay tactic is the best I can hope for, and such a tactic will work only if neither of us capitulates. When Doc's cousin looks in my direction, I hold up a flexed palm, something resembling a wave and a signal to not give up names. We affectionately call him Doc Number 2. Like Doc, he is prematurely gray, a medical man, and a loyal supporter of Strategic Games. I can only pray now that he possesses convictions as strong as my dear friend's.

"Hey," the partner guard pushes my arm down.

My handler slaps the tablet. "Your attention. Here," he shouts into my ear. "Pick five names now, or the train returns to Beijing without you."

The tablet weighs down my jittery hands. "I do not know of any mentally imbalanced men on my team. It would be wrong to submit an inaccurate report." The idea that I might not see my dads or May-ling again frightens me. That I might worry them leaves me nauseated.

"Now!" he shouts.

I read over the names, every one of them a friend. I don't know what to do. My finger hovers above my own name. The platform echoes and booms as my men begin a rhythmic beat on the train doors and windows.

I notice a large red lever next to the train door—an emergency door opener. Could I run there and release the doors before these two clowns stop me?

The pimpled boy turns to my soldiers. "Him, him, him, him, and him," he says, pointing at men who have climbed onto the seats and tables, a howling man who is beating his chest, men rattling seatbacks. "Put down those animals, and you can go play your game."

I want nothing more at this moment than my men out here with me, the hundred of us united against these hoodlums, but the combined fury of my men also scares me. Right now, Doc's cousin and I are the only ones in danger of arrest. I don't know if these guards possess weapons or if they have additional reinforcement outside. If I am able to let my team out, there is no telling what could happen. Someone will surely get hurt. Someone could die. A mass arrest would be the best possible outcome if the situation escalates.

Desperate, I stare across the platform at Doc Number 2. He too seems frozen in place.

If I choose to forfeit the game, would I still have to submit five names? Would we then be allowed to take the train home? I contemplate how to phrase that question most advantageously when I hear a whoosh, a yelp, and curses as two of my soldiers tumble onto the platform on their hands and knees.

"Close the doors!" my handler shouts.

But now gray-uniformed Strategic Games soldiers spill out of the train cars, as unstoppable as an invasion of ants. They outnumber the black guards within seconds. Major Chao and some of my biggest soldiers rush toward me. They surround my two interrogators and demand explanations.

The pimply boy pushes out his skinny chest. "Lee Wei-guo is just filing a late report." Despite his confident posture, his eyes betray his fear.

"This is bullshit," someone on the platform yells.

My handler gets in my face and hisses quietly, "Finish this up now, and I will let all of you go."

I glance at the two narrow turnstiles, at the throng squeezing its way out.

"What's this report about?" Self-important and nosy as ever, Chao reads the tablet over my shoulder and takes it from me. "You want candidates for psych evals?"

The pimpled boy whisks the device from Chao's hands and tucks it under his skinny arm. "This is for classified personnel only."

"No one is in need of psych evaluations here," booms Sergeant Wen, the big soldier on my left. "We're leaving." His paw-sized hand propels me toward the exit.

A black-clad guard blocks our way, shining the bloody red tip of a pen at my chest. "No one leaves until we say so." Is he trying to stop us with a laser pointer?

His pimpled leader catches up and takes the laughable thing from him. He adds his skinny frame to the blockade. Suddenly this band of teenagers seems ridiculous. With the entire Chinese army at his disposal, this is what Major Jung sends? He really must be on the outs with his superiors.

I cup my hands around my mouth. "Middle Kingdom: time to move."

Even though the black-uniformed guards seem without bite, my spine prickles with every step as I walk away. My soldiers surround me, and I pray that the sea of gray fight suits renders me anonymous. I breathe easier when we finally set foot onto the dirt trail to Heavenly Lake Park.

Chao says, "What was that about?"

I decide to tell him. Perhaps his well-connected uncle could wield some influence. "The Safety Council—"

"Lee Wei-guo!"

I freeze, my shoulders again at my ears. XX waddles up, huffing and grinning most inappropriately. I clutch my chest. I forgot all about him. I glance behind us and all around. The black guards have not followed us out of the station.

"That was me," he says, beaming. "I told you I could do it."

"Do what?" I say.

"I unlocked the doors. I got us out of there."

10

HANN

As if his Mr. Universe physique and his dark, smoldering good looks do not already make him the focus of attention, Jimmy wears—in the confines of a subway car in April, no less—the same ass-cheek-exposing shorts and cropped, six-pack-revealing muscle shirt he favors at the height of summer at the Temple of Heaven Park. Strange that Hann did not notice him back at the station, but he did see the guy board the train after him. Jimmy catwalks up and down the length of the half-empty car. Hann pulls up his collar and turns his head toward the window, hiding as best he can. Jimmy is registered Willfully Sterile, but flaunting oneself like that is never a good idea. The police have been known to start investigations for much less.

Jimmy prances around a pole at the center of the car and pauses from time to time to strike a provocative pose and bat his lustrous lashes in Hann's direction. Hann finally glares back, his groin tingling. Jimmy winks and blows him a kiss. Hann turns away quickly, hoping the exchange went unnoticed by the other passengers.

Just like at the park, this guy is forever trying to win Hann's business, and if not that, to rile and goad him into a reaction. Was he meeting a john in the financial district? His getup makes no sense. No customer would dare to be seen with him dressed like that.

For the rest of the trip, Hann stares out his window at the dark, whooshing tunnel. When his stop arrives, he allows himself a swift glance and is sorry to note that Jimmy is still on the train. Hann hurries out of the bustling station and jostles his way up to the street. He does not escape far before he hears footsteps behind him that match his gait step for step. He stops, and the footfalls quiet as well. Hann turns around.

"Uncle!" Jimmy says, his eyes dancing. The change from his usual "lover boy" to a more respectful form of address offers Hann no comfort. "I was wondering how long before you admit that you know me and stop to say hello."

"Why are you following me?"

Jimmy moves toward Hann, shrinking an already uncomfortable speaking distance. He places his hands on his waist and cocks his hip. "You're not happy to see me?"

Hann steps backward only to have Jimmy follow as if on a tether. "What do you want?"

"I don't want anything," he says, smiling suggestively. "I have a gift for you."

Hann glances at Jimmy's empty hands. That's the oldest proposition in the book.

Jimmy taps Hann on the nose. "You naughty boy."

The subway's escalator spits out an unending stream of people. Hann spots a neighbor and curses. He sticks out a hand this time as he backs up.

"Don't be like that, Uncle." Jimmy advances chest out into Hann's palm and wriggles.

Hann almost trips, jerking backward. "Stop it."

"Don't be angry."

"What do you want?"

Jimmy pouts. "I can't tell you when you're so angry."

Surely his neighbor has noticed the two of them by now. Another neighbor rounds the corner and gawks at them. Hann throws up his hands and begins to walk away.

Jimmy quickly loops an arm through his elbow. "I can't let you walk away from me angry," he says, his flirtatious voice nothing like his deadly grip.

Hann cannot jerk free. Passersby crane their necks to watch. One man stops. Hann and Jimmy look like quarreling lovers. Pulling back his shoulder to recapture some dignity, he stops struggling and orders Jimmy to let him go. His command comes out shriller than he would have liked. Two more busybodies stop to watch.

Hann tells their three spectators that he does not know this man, that this man followed him out of the subway and refuses to let him go. He implores them to get a public security agent. No one moves.

Jimmy snuggles up to Hann. "Don't you go hurting my feelings pretending you don't know me." He reaches two fingers down the front of his pants and slowly, slowly teases out a corner of a waxy, white paper. A photograph. "Are you sure you don't want to see my gift?"

For a split second, the ground beneath Hann's feet tilts. He steadies his breathing, forces himself to quiet his racing thoughts. Saying yes would be an admission that he was somehow entangled with Jimmy. Saying no brings its own kind of trouble. On sleepless nights, Hann has imagined different scenarios. Rival coworkers and, lately, Director Chang accused and outed him rather than people he had nothing to do with. Hann has been exceedingly careful. Except for Hero, he has kept to the same half dozen trustworthy partners for over a decade, has not allowed himself an outdoor tryst in that same amount of time. Hann cannot imagine a situation where an incriminating photo could be taken.

At least his late-night hand wringing led to some strategizing, the understanding that he must go on the offensive to keep his accuser off balance. He says to his spectators, "It's blackmail, whatever that is in his pants." He sneers at Jimmy's outfit. "Who dresses and acts like that unless he's out to mine gold?"

"Oh, Hann," Jimmy says, slapping him on the forearm with a wiggle. "How could you say that when I'm wearing your favorite shorty shorts? Will you good people be my witnesses? I swear to you on my mother's ashes that we are best boyfriends." He flattens a hand against his chest and glides it repulsively down to the picture.

Hann still cannot free his arm. He can think of nothing but to beg for some basic human decency. "Comrades, true or not, this man clearly has something damaging he wants to hang around my neck. Would you please do me the kindness of going away so that he can tell me how he's going to extort me?"

"Yes. We want to be alone," Jimmy says. "Shoo!"

The men shake their heads at one another. They do not disperse until Jimmy switches to his gruff man voice and tells them to get lost.

"Buy me a cocktail," Jimmy says, bumping Hann with his hip.

Hann rips the photograph from the hustler's waistband. In it, Hann is on his knees, bare-shouldered, his profile unmistakable, his cheeks sucked in, giving head. Cut off at the navel and naked, his partner is unidentifiable, though Hann is certain from the bedspread behind them that he is Chu Shin-ren. They usually closed the drapes first thing, and Hann shivers to think how long Jimmy had been tracking them, how long he had lain in wait for that shot. In order not to establish a pattern, Hann rarely met with any of his lovers more than three or four times a year. He tears the picture into smaller and smaller pieces before pocketing it. He asks Jimmy what he wants.

Jimmy finally releases him. "My father was just diagnosed with brain fever. He needs an operation."

Hann shakes his head, certain that Jimmy's father, if he has one, needs nothing of the kind. "What do you want?"

"Oh, Hann." He pouts. "Where's your heart?"

Hann narrows his eyes.

Jimmy flutters his thick lashes before sweeping his eyes down to Hann's groin. "I'd love to see more of you." He teases another, smaller piece of paper—a business card—out of his pants and tucks it behind the pocket square in Hann's suit coat. He blows Hann a kiss before sauntering away.

The card shows a string of numerals separated by dashes. An accountant of nearly forty years, Hann quickly registers that he has been given a bank identifier code and account number. Jimmy is expecting a bank deposit for his silence. Hann realizes he doesn't know Jimmy's real name, let alone how to contact him. After another beat, it also occurs to Hann that a ransom figure was not proposed.

Hann watches his back all the way to the Relaxation Lounge. He hardly slept the previous night, debating whether Jimmy already knew about the lounge and, if not, whether Hann ought to be leading him to this club owned by a straight friend, this highly reputable businessmen's retreat with private libraries, meditation rooms, and hot tubs where Hann had met the majority of his lovers for the last decade. The exclusivity of its membership makes this a relatively safe place to meet Chu, and right now it is vital that Hann find out whether his activities at the Relaxation Lounge were compromised. He needs to warn his partners if that is the case.

At the front desk, Hann studies JJ, the receptionist, for an extra beat. There seems a sinister cast to his big smile. Hann asks for a steam room. Like most club members, Hann visits an hour at a time, once to twice a week to get away from his crowded home and noisy office. He has done his best to check out a variety of spaces here so that his use of the steam room does not stand out.

"Number five, Comrade Guo?" JJ says.

"Is it available?"

"For you, always." JJ knows Hann is a friend of the owner and often assigns him this larger, out-of-the-way steam room.

The years of receiving JJ's special attention suddenly makes Hann afraid. As Hann's watch is swiped and encoded with the room's entry code, Hann cringes to imagine that Jimmy might have been in league with JJ.

Not bothering to visit the locker room to change, Hann winds through the corridors to his assigned room at the far end of the building. The steam is not turned on, but the lingering wet heat grabs him by the throat. He locks the door behind him.

Slowly, he examines every piece of the sky-blue tile on the wall and ceiling. The technology is so good now, for all he knows, cameras could be embedded in a piece of tile. Was he naïve to feel safe here? He had reasoned that with the steam on full blast, he and his partner would be difficult to film—should anyone try— if they remained quiet and in the center of the space. Straining to his creaky knees to examine the azure tiles of the bench and floor, Hann chides himself for believing that distance from the front desk rather than frequent location changes equaled safety. Yet for all that worry, he finds nothing obviously suspicious. Truth be told, he has no idea what to look for.

Xiong-xin would, but bringing his big bumbling brother here on a detective mission would attract attention. Hann decided last night that he would not frighten his family if he doesn't have to. May-ling is sorely disappointed in him, and he cannot handle more turmoil from her, not if he hopes to investigate the situation and work out a solution with a cool head. The humane thing would be for him to solve the problem that he himself has created and leave them in peace.

He struggles to his feet and shakes off the ache in his back and knees. Twice in the last year, sex in this heated chamber had sent his heart racing for long, frightening minutes. Hann has not wanted to admit that he must give this up before he is caught dropping dead of a heart attack here or—worse yet—surviving one.

He checks the time. Chu will be here soon. Hann pulls up a corner of his shirttail and returns to the reception area mopping his brow. JJ immediately asks if Hann is all right.

"I changed out of my clothes and then spent ten minutes fiddling with the controls, trying to get the steam to come on." Hann watches JJ through each of his lies, but detects only mild surprise at the failed equipment.

JJ apologizes and offers to put him in a different room.

Hann says he's feeling a little hot and dizzy after the ordeal and asks for a prayer room instead. "Perhaps I had better spend my hour more restfully."

"Of course." JJ checks his register and directs Hann to swipe his watch. His eyes steeped with concern, he comes around the reception counter. "Let me walk you there."

"That's all right," Hann says. "I'll take the elevator. I'll be fine if you put me in a room close to the bar."

"Of course," JJ says. Again, Hann fails to detect anything other than helpful politeness as JJ makes another room change.

Hann passes the hot tub, sauna, and massage-chair sections and rides the elevator as promised. He has never used a Buddhist prayer room before and has turned down JJ's first assignment, so he figures the new room ought to be safe. Unless JJ has bugged all the rooms. Hann shakes his head at his own paranoia. He cannot go on much longer like this. He messages Chu with his room number and location.

Hann had called Chu yesterday right after his encounter with Jimmy. Afraid of a bug and of leaving recordable evidence, he invoked their emergency code phrase: "I need some work advice." Hann suggested they grab lunch at the Relaxation Lounge.

As usual, there is no one at the self-service bar. People come here to relax and be alone. He often thought it ironic, the sense of freedom and lightness he feels from locking himself into the small, windowless spaces here. He picks up two complimentary sandwiches—a *char-siu* and cucumber, and a ham and potato salad—to complete his cover story.

Hann locates his room just off the bar. Inside, four bowl-shaped lights, one in each corner of the floor, add a buttery glow to the yolk-colored walls. The space is beautiful and serene, yet all Hann can see are the additional hiding places that light fixtures and furniture and their many nooks and crannies afford. He sets his sandwiches down in front of the smiling bronze Buddha on the table. He struggles to his knees again—he really is too old for this—and runs his fingers along the dark table's underside, grateful for its clean lines. Finding nothing, he crawls next to the large pillow on the ground. Is one to sit or kneel here, he wonders. His family stopped visiting temples generations ago when the government declared religions feudal superstitions. He unzips the pillow and nicks his forearm as he stuffs it inside to feel around. He is about to remove the entire outer covering when he realizes that perhaps he has it all wrong. Perhaps the deserted public spaces at the Relaxation Lounge are the safest places. Who would think of discussing secrets out in the open? He struggles to his feet.

The door creaks open. Chu sticks his head in, scouts out the room before barreling inside. "What's going on?" he says, the boom of his voice gruff and commanding. Chu's confidence, outsized personality, and wealth more than make up for his tiny stature.

Hann breathes easier just being in the presence of his accomplished, take-charge friend. Chu runs a food conglomerate, and there isn't a crisis he has not weathered, difficulties he has not overcome. Chu claims that he has a dozen fixes for every problem, and Hann finds his confidence empowering, not to mention seductive.

He puts a finger to his lips before pulling the left half of the taped-together photograph—Hann's nose and mouth glued to the dark fuzz of Chu's lower regions—from his shirt pocket. He retrieves the image of the rest of his head from his suit pocket and puzzles the halves together. He tells Chu that Jimmy followed him out of the subway and accosted him with this picture in front of his neighbors.

"Shit," Chu says, his tone more angry than alarmed.

Chu's outrage gives Hann an unexpected boost, a sense of self-righteousness. He quietly asks if Jimmy has also come after Chu.

"Shit, shit, shit," Chu says with greater vehemence, his eyes stuck to the photo. "What does he want?"

Hann is both relieved for Chu and perturbed. With a much deeper pocket and an outsized reputation to protect, Chu ought to be Jimmy's first choice for blackmail. He pries the picture from Chu's hands, exchanging it for Jimmy's card, and tells him the numbers are the codes for an account at Bank of China.

"There's no amount here," Chu barks.

Hann reminds him again to shush. He peeks his head out the

door and, once certain the halls are empty, waves to Chu to follow him out of the room. "It might be safer to speak at the bar."

"Why?" The suggestion seems to make Chu angrier.

Hann tells him they have no idea the extent of Jimmy's scheme. Bugging might be a possibility.

"Then why are we here at all?" Every one of his questions feels like a challenge.

"This is the quietest, most private spot I could think of," Hann says. Chu seems incapable of lowering his voice. "We can't go to your place." The two of them usually met at the studio apartment Chu keeps for late nights at the office. Like most of the super-wealthy, Chu lives an hour outside town with a wife he does not share and more children than he's allowed to have.

"You've just compromised the Relaxation Lounge and everyone you meet up with here. And I hear there are many."

Hann scowls. "You're delusional if you think Jimmy doesn't already know about this place." And since when does Chu have a right to take issue with Hann's sex life? And who is he to speak to Hann like a subordinate?

Hann shoos him out of the prayer room. He looks up and down the hallway for signs of people and then of security cameras. Seeing none, he says rather loudly, "I'm starved. Let's have a bite while I consult you about my business problems."

Chu stands his ground and shakes his head at Hann as if to say that his bad acting is convincing no one. "You left your sandwiches inside."

"Fuck the sandwiches," Hann says, thoroughly ticked.

There are four small tables in the bar, all unoccupied. Ignoring Chu, Hann wanders to the one in the center of the room and sits. Again, he can identify neither listening devices nor cameras on the surrounding walls and ceiling. Chu spends an inexorably long time picking over the free eats and examining the two different Scotches.

"Hungry, are we?" Hann says when Chu finally sits down with a big assortment of food.

The fight seems to have left Chu. He sets a plate and a drink in front of Hann. This is as good an apology as Hann is going to get. Hann suggests they find out if Jimmy has approached anyone else in their badminton circle.

"I'll talk to Jimmy. I can reason with him."

"You shouldn't get involved until he involves you."

Chu says, "We must band together. Negotiate as a group. Jimmy needs to know that we are united, that there's no playing one against the other."

"I agree, but—"

"He's coming after me sooner or later. He has to," Chu says. "I have the most to lose. I should be the one to handle him."

Hann has been aching for someone to take charge of the situation and make Jimmy magically disappear. He knows there's no such person, but Chu, a natural leader and wily negotiator, comes close. Hann wants to say yes when a thought occurs to him. The members of his badminton group have all agreed to limit their sexual partners to each other. Hann had every intention of abiding by the rule, but he has erred on occasion, however discreetly.

Hann leans toward Chu and lowers his voice, doing his best to keep his tone nonaccusatory. "Is there anyone else Jimmy might be targeting? Someone outside our circle that you've taken to your apartment?"

Chu narrows his eyes at Hann. "Do *you* have people we should include?"

"No," Hann replies. "I don't think so. But I'm not going to lie to you." He explains that since Jimmy started hanging around, Hann has strayed with a registered homosexual, a reputable businessman who would not sell him out. Chu looks pained. Hann's stomach cramps as he fumbles for his words. "I know I shouldn't have done it. I did wrong, and I'm very, very sorry to have jeopardized everybody."

Chu frowns and exhales deeply. Hann cannot tell if his friend is angry or disappointed. Hann sits quietly, taking in the reproach.

Chu says, "I fucked Jimmy."

Hann's eyes grow big.

"He's in love with me, or so he claims, and wants to move into my studio. I told him no, and now he's working you to get at me." Chu sounds matter-of-fact and not particularly sorry.

Hann breathes out with relief even as fury takes hold. He shakes his head at Chu. How dare he go on the attack earlier when he is so clearly in the wrong. And with Jimmy, of all people. Chu has no judgment. And even less taste.

"You better make this right," Hann says, crossing his arms. "You buy that son-of-a-bitch a mansion if you have to, but I'm not going down because of you."

Chu nods, chastened finally.

"How many more have you fucked in that apartment of yours?"

Chu looks away. "You don't want to know."

"I do."

"A lot. I can't—" Chu shrugs.

Hann curses, in no way certain that trouble in the name of Jimmy or something else will not be rising up again to bite them all in the ass.

A message flashes across Hann's workstation: Director Chang would like to see you right now.

Hann wonders what stinky project Chang is going to saddle him with this time. Ever since Director Dunn pried their company's latest housing allotment out of Chang's greedy little hands and coerced him to award it to Hann, Hann has become Chang's lackey extraordinaire.

Outside Chang's office, his secretary—and personal henchman—rises with nary a greeting. As gangly as his boss and just as ugly, he summons Hann with a crook of a finger and struts ahead as if his ass has sprouted a long and perky tail. Hann has always thought that he and Chang connived like a pair of thieving monkeys.

The secretary points at Hann and then the straight-back chair in front of his boss' rosewood desk. "The director will be with you when he is able."

Behind his stately piece of furniture, Chang sits hunched, his low forehead thickly wrinkled, his close-set eyes plodding back and forth across his large work screen. The self-important man does not bother to acknowledge Hann's entrance. He could be playing virtual mahjongg back there, and no one would ever know.

Hann looks away from the small, skinny man to the credenza behind his desk. As usual, there are no family pictures; Chang couldn't very well display his brood of illegal mistresses and children. There is a new photograph, however, of Chang in his self-appointed Mao suit uniform with the mayor and the Party chief of Beijing, both in casual clothing and sunglasses. Taken on some outdoor terrace, Chang balances a beer glass in one hand while jostling the mayor good-naturedly with his elbow. The message is hard to ignore: Chang not only knows the most important folks in town, he is on intimate footing with them.

Something dings, and Hann jerks up. Chang is staring at him rather humorlessly, his gold fountain pen in hand. Did he just strike his cut-crystal glass with it?

Hann bows even though he has been bidden like a dog. "What can I do for you today, Director?"

"There's nothing I hate more than deceit and trickery," Chang says, hurling aside his pen, an expensive bribe no doubt from some client. The fury in his gesture jolts Hann upright. "Am I not a straightforward man? No matter how difficult, do I not always do you the courtesy of telling it like it is? And what do you do but betray me in the sneakiest and most insulting way? And to think, I held you up in front of our entire company as a comrade of the highest order, a model exemplary citizen. You. Make. Me. Sick."

Chang seldom raises his voice. A man who gets everything he desires doesn't have to. His heart at his throat, Hann can scarcely breathe. Did Chu botch it with Jimmy?

Chang's chest heaves. "What do you have to say for yourself?"

"I—" Hann scrambles to his feet and bows. Please, please, please: do not let this morning be the last time he sees his child. "Whatever I've done wrong, I apologize most sincerely. Please tell me what I can do, how I can make up for my offense."

"How dare you," Chang says.

"Please, sir," Hann says, bowing again, "I would be most grateful for your enlightenment and your tutelage."

Chang glares at him, red-faced. "I want an explanation."

"This company is of utmost importance to me. My reputation is of utmost importance to me. I would never do anything to jeopardize—" Hann stammers, fully aware that he must not admit to anything.

Chang looks unappeased.

Hann rubs his face to buy some time. "Whatever's been said, it's not true. None of it is true. I'm being blackmailed."

Chang scoffs, unearths a bright red envelope from beneath his papers and hurls it in disgust at Hann. "You've shamed me. You've shamed every single person who works here. How am I going to explain to our comrades, to our Party, that the man, the family I hand-selected to receive our firm's highest distinction is an undeserving and lying cheat?" True to character, Chang's foremost concern is how the actions of others affect his image.

Hann bows again before bending down to retrieve the envelope that bounced off his chest. "With your guidance, Director, my family and I will leap at the chance to correct our flaws. We want to merit your confidence, to represent our firm and you, especially, in the best possible light."

The red envelope—is it a wedding invitation?—is addressed to Chang. Puzzled, Hann removes its four folded pages, also in red. "China First" is scrawled across the letterhead. Chang, their firm's Party representative, is named again and notified that Guo Xiong-xin, second spouse of Wu May-ling and Guo Hann, is seeking divorce. Chang is officially charged with the task of saving the marriage.

Hann blanches. "I didn't mean to imply that our second spouse—you know he's my brother—he's not blackmailing me. I don't know why I said that."

"Do you think a director of this firm, its Party representative, no less, has time for your nonsense?" Chang cries. "You, sneaky bastard, will not be divorcing one man to marry another, so as to get around my two-spouse limit. Do you understand?"

"I have no intention of the kind," Hann says. Did the blackmail comment not register with Chang? And did Chang just admit that the two-spouse policy is his rather than their company's? Never has Hann felt so grateful for this mental dwarf. "My wife and brother had a silly little fight over the bathroom. You know, seat up or seat down." Hann shakes his head and shrugs. "Too many people in too-close quarters. Many thanks to you, we will be moving as soon as our new apartment is fixed up."

Chang stares at him, dead-eyed.

Hann continues, "I can guarantee that my brother does not want out of the marriage. He certainly has not filed any papers."

Hann relaxes ever so slightly when Chang does not contradict the claim. Hann speculates that Xiong-xin probably looked into divorce during the heat of the argument. "You know how many precautionary tracking measures they put into those websites. May-ling spent last night in his bed. That's hardly the sign of a disintegrating marriage."

Chang says, "Count yourself fortunate that I am not about to lose face retracting your award. Behind your closed doors, you can kill each other for all I care, but you see to it that there is no divorce. Do you understand me?"

"Yes, sir." Hann raises the papers in his hand and asks to keep them. He does not want anything reminding Chang of this disaster. Behind the cover letter is a listing of neighborhood committees and family counselors.

"You will study those pages, and you will get your family in line," Chang says.

Hann keeps his eyes down and nods. What can he do but continue to grovel even as Chang shows his hand and retreats? Artfully splashed with slogans in different sized fonts, the last page of the papers catches his eye: *There is no perfect way to be a spouse, but a million ways to be a good one. Being in a family means you will love and be loved for the rest of your life. Give the gift of love, and advance your family.*

An idea seizes Hann and refuses to let go. He knows that it is never in his interest to goad Chang, but now that the reaming appears to be over, he cannot help but feel a little vengeful. "Did you see this? It's quite interesting," he says. "*The strength of a nation derives from the integrity of the home. A patriotic, peace-promoting citizen chooses to go the max.*"

"What of it?" Chang is furious all over again.

"I'm sorry I did not tell you this before. We suspected, but it's just been confirmed," Hann says. "My brother shoots blanks. He cannot father a child. That's the true reason we contemplated going the max. Our son bugs us every day for a sister. We too yearn for a daughter, both for ourselves but also to help relieve our national crisis."

"So you father one for him."

Hann widens his eyes.

"A child of yours is as close as your brother's going to get to having one of his own."

"But that's illegal," Hann replies most innocently.

"Who's going to know?"

Hann lets his jaw drop, feigning shock and dismay. He wants Chang, their Party representative, to register him a coward, but more important a law-abiding and patriotic coward. He stands rooted, mute and dumb, until Chang orders him out of his office in disgust.

11

MAY-LING

Despite my pleas for him to wait, BeiBei races after Ming to be first in line for the Mommy-and-Me bus. Calling out that they absolutely must stop when they see the guard at the park entrance and not venture out onto the busy street, I follow the boys in an awkward shuffle, stuffing half-eaten snacks, thermos, and jacket into my backpack.

Whereas Ming and most other two-year-olds toddle and windmill their arms for balance, BeiBei runs with an intensity of purpose and coordination beyond his age. He soon catches up to Ming. Watching my boy in motion fills me with joy and glimmers of hope. He knows he is fast and so do the kids and their mothers. It is wonderful for him to begin to learn his own strengths and also to be recognized for something good, rather than always for misbehavior. His hyperactivity could serve him well yet if I learn to help him channel it productively.

At the white-painted border of the soccer field, BeiBei slows and faces Ming. "I'm faster, I'm faster," he sings.

Ming lurches at BeiBei and grabs on to the hood of his sweatshirt. BeiBei takes off again, dragging the boy for a few choking steps. Ming has yet to beat BeiBei to the bus post. Yesterday after he lost, he took out his frustrations by pinching his baby brother.

"Hands to yourselves, boys," I cry as I glance around for Ming's mother. A field away, she is chatting leisurely with the other moms, oblivious. It irks me that she assumes that BeiBei will always be the troublemaker and leaves it up to me to supervise.

Ming hangs meanly onto BeiBei's collar, leaning back with all his might. Before I can separate the two, BeiBei shoves at Ming, and the boy claws him across the face. My heart skips a beat when BeiBei covers his eye, howling.

"Let me see." I kneel before BeiBei and pry his hands off his face. There are the beginnings of two red lines, one fortunately just missing his right eye.

"I know it hurts," I say again and again as I pick him up and hug him to me. I rub my hand up and down his back and let him wail into my ear.

Ming has reached the yellow post by the park gate—the winner's pole—and swings around it, staring at his feet. The blue-uniformed guard—the one mothers here nicknamed "Big Nose"—approaches the boy and tugs him by the ear toward us. He must have witnessed the altercation. Ming's mother finally notices and jogs across the field, a hand braced around her baby's neck.

"What happened?" she barks as she passes me, her tone accusatory and put out.

Ming howls too now, terrified, and stretches his arms toward his running mother, but the guard hangs tight to his ear. The guards are supposed to protect the women and children in the park from unwanted intruders, but Big Nose also thinks he has authority over the mothers, the teachers, and the children inside the park. He takes it upon himself to keep the boys in line and loves little more than to stick his big honker into toddler spats.

Ming deserves a talking-to, but no child deserves to be frightened by Big Nose. I hurry forward, BeiBei still crying in my arms. "It's all right, Comrade. Ming's mother and I will handle it from here." Big Nose has grabbed and reprimanded BeiBei many times in the past. My feisty child keeps a wary eye out for him now, but many of the children bawl at the park gate and refuse to enter when he is on duty.

Big Nose gives Ming's ear another tug. "Stop sniveling and look at me." He glares until Ming quiets to quaking sniffles, the poor kid. "Next time I put you in jail, you hear me?"

"Jail!" Ming's mother cries, incensed. "What are you talking about?"

"Ming's going to be good," I say, nodding vigorously at the child. "Right?"

He nods with me, and Big Nose finally releases him.

"Thank you, Comrade," I say. "We will talk to the boys right now."

Big Nose crosses his arms and does not leave.

Balancing her baby on one arm, Ming's mother wraps her other around her boy while shooting me daggers with her eyes. "What did BeiBei do this time?"

I can't believe the nerve of this woman. Turning my bawling child to exhibit his cheek, I tell her what happened. I'm almost glad to have Big Nose standing next to us, backing me up. This is the first time BeiBei has been on the receiving end of another child's bad behavior, and I hate to admit a perverse part of me liked being a member of the injured party, just another one of the mothers.

Squatting next to her son, she says, "Did he hurt you?"

"Tell the truth," Big Nose says.

Ming kicks the dirt and shakes his head.

"BeiBei should not have taunted him, singing I'm faster, I'm faster," I say, "but Ming laid his hands on BeiBei first. He started it."

Ming's mother gives me a sour look.

Rather than waste my time convincing her, I kneel and set a sniffling BeiBei down in front of Ming. "You two boys need to apologize to each other." I couldn't have put it more diplomatically.

"Yes. Apologize to each other," Big Nose says.

I continue, "Ming, please tell BeiBei you are sorry for pulling on his shirt and for scratching him." My boy has been in enough of these scuffles that I know just how to move these painful little encounters along.

Ming clings to his mother, goggle-eyed. "I'm sorry." He probably has never had adults other than his parents call him to task before.

"Now you, BeiBei. Your turn to say sorry," Ming's mother says.

This woman is something else. "Ming's not done yet." I give Ming a reassuring smile and tell him that forgiveness is the next step. "Sweetie, please ask BeiBei to forgive you."

The mother harrumphs.

"She's right. Your son needs to ask for forgiveness," Big Nose tells the woman.

She harrumphs again, but her son does as he is told.

"Good boy," I tell Ming. I squeeze BeiBei's shoulders. "Ming is asking your forgiveness. What do you say?"

Ming slumps against his mother, his attention already elsewhere.

"You say sorry now," Ming's mother urges again.

BeiBei cries, "That's not fair."

"Sssshhhhhh," I say. No one has ever apologized to him before when he was in the wrong. I wrap my arms around my boy to stop him from running to the winner's pole. "What are you going to say to Ming?"

"He needs to apologize." Ming's mother looks at Big Nose. "Tell him to apologize."

Big Nose's nostrils flare. There's little he hates more than someone telling him what to do. "He will when he is ready."

"That's not fair." BeiBei begins to wail again.

She stands, her baby's head lolling. "Say it. Or you're not going home."

I pick BeiBei up off the ground. This nasty woman does not get to bully my child. "We'll finish this up later when the children are calmer." It's obvious she wants his apology for herself.

I head for the gate, and thankfully Big Nose does not stop us. Ming's mother must have really ticked him off. BeiBei and I will wait for the bus on the street.

"No wonder he's always fighting," Ming's mother mutters. "No class. No upbringing whatsoever."

"True, my son has been in a lot of fights," I stop and tell her, "but I've always acted fairly. He and I have apologized whenever he was in the wrong. You can ask any of the mothers out there. Or our guard here." I turn my back on her and march out of the gate, unwilling to get into it with this woman. Our reputation is bad enough without me also joining the melee.

"It's not fair," BeiBei cries and thrashes. Fairness is big with XX, and now BeiBei too, it seems.

"I know. I know," I say, fuming. The one time BeiBei did not start a fight, this obnoxious mother forces him to apologize. I kiss and examine BeiBei's cheek again. His two scratches look darker red now, raised and swollen. It strikes me again, how dangerously close Ming's fingernails came to his eye. It sickens me too that Bei-Bei is one of those boys destined to learn life's lessons the hard way.

There is a feistiness, a stubborn streak in BeiBei, and our talk about not taunting will have to wait for a calmer moment. I rock and bounce him and take deep, patient breaths as he roars in my ears. He finally cries himself out and lays his head on my shoulder, his chest heaving. I rub my cheeks against his. A little nap on the bus would be the best I could hope for right now.

As BeiBei sniffles, I pace and try to calm down. I remember how beautifully Wei-guo manages him, how much the two have taken to each other. Even XX competes for Wei-guo's attention. He parents with the playfulness and physicality of a younger man. But it's more than that. He gets BeiBei and combative boys like him and draws him out in a way Hann and I do not. That he appreciates my difficult child fills me with wonder and sunshine. I hate to admit it, but he makes me like my own child more.

My entire body aches for Wei-guo. He was my first taste of sweetness, of salt, of everything essential that I had gone without before. I remember his smooth, muscled body against mine, his electrifying hands encircling my waist, cupping my face, my breasts, my hips, his lips exploring my fingertips. I picture his slow and seductive unknotting of my sash, my own impatience to show myself to him, to please him, the euphoric calm and closeness we felt afterward. This is how it should be between a man and a woman. I was not wrong to insist on more from Hann. I understand too what Hann could never give me, and that revelation fills me with unexpected peace.

A bus passes, and Wei-guo appears in its doorway as if in fulfillment of my deepest wish. My heart leaps. I smooth my hair and tuck some loose strands behind my ears. How I wish I didn't look and smell like I've spent the morning chasing a child and a soccer ball across a muddy field. I follow the bus the short distance to its stop, and Wei-guo disembarks with utter delight in his eyes and sumptuous pink peonies in his arms.

I hurry toward him only to see not twenty paces away, mothers and sons filing out of the park and the wife of Hann's coworker, the one who clued me in about the housing award, in their midst. I am reminded that it is indiscreet for women to be in public with unmarried men who are not relatives. As happy as I am to see him, Wei-guo should have known better than to meet me here.

"Me first," BeiBei cries when he sees Ming leading the line. He pushes off me and tries to get down. "Not fair."

I turn my struggling child toward the advancing Wei-guo. "Look who's come to see you."

BeiBei's mouth rounds with excitement. "Uncle!"

Every male acquaintance is accorded this term of respect, but I am nevertheless glad that the line of women could confuse Wei-guo for a relative.

Wei-guo tucks the flower stems under an arm and reaches out for BeiBei only to curl his hand around my boy's cheek. "What happened?"

I give him a quick summary of events.

"How about I take you for a special ride? Would you like to ride in a cab?" Wei-guo asks BeiBei.

BeiBei throws his arms around Wei-guo's neck, Ming all but forgotten.

I usher the two of them away from the mothers. Technically, Wei-guo and I have BeiBei as a "chaperone," but it is to both of our advantage for Comrade Yang's wife and the gaggle of magpies in line to observe us together as little as possible.

Wei-guo passes me the peonies. "These are for you."

"They're lovely." I stare at him for a beat to convey my appreciation, but I keep him walking. I sense footsteps approaching from behind.

"Comrade Wu!"

It is Yang's wife and son. I have no choice but to stop and greet her.

She rubs BeiBei's back. "How are you!"

BeiBei arches away from her. "We go!"

"We'll go soon," Wei-guo says with reassuring authority.

Yang withdraws her hand apologetically and says to BeiBei, "I wanted to invite you over to play."

"How nice of you," I say.

She smiles at the gorgeous unfurling of petals in my arms and then at Wei-guo. "BeiBei sure adores you."

"His Uncle Wei-guo is the best," I say, hoping that my observation could pass for an introduction. To divert attention from Wei-guo, I bend and pat her little one's head. He is holding a large piece of paper. Unlike BeiBei, he lives at the crafts table at the park. "Did you draw this?"

Her beautifully assembled child—pristine sailor suit and hat today—nods angelically. I ask him to tell me about the picture.

"It's my family."

I tap on the little boy. "Who's this handsome little man?"

"Me," he says, beaming. He begins pointing. "And this is MaMa and Little BaBa and our building."

"Very nice," I say. "Don't you have a big brother?"

He shakes his head with great conviction. "He can't be in my drawing. He called me monkey butt."

"We go," BeiBei cries.

I chuckle as I stand, sparing Yang the next logical question. Her boy has also left out his Big BaBa—Hann's coworker. Yang pulls her son to her side. She tilts her head, her smile bashful and girly, as she takes in Wei-guo's ripped arms and broad chest. It's clear she wants a full introduction.

I tell Wei-guo that Comrade Yang's husband works with Hann and frown at him for an extra beat, hoping he picks up on my signal to be tactful. "He's one of their best account managers."

Yang waves away my praise. She asks how he knows me and my family.

Wei-guo says, "I'm hoping to become Wu May-ling's third husband."

The blood drains from my face.

BeiBei covers Wei-guo's mouth possessively, but it's too late. Wei-guo smiles as if he has uttered the blandest of statements, and I can't tell if he is naïve or aggressive.

"Is that right?" Yang's smile stretches wide as her eyes twinkle at me and my bouquet.

I don't know which of them I want to hurl the flowers at more. "We'd gotten to know Wei-guo well before Hann received the housing award. As you can see, we've become attached." I tilt my head toward BeiBei. "Wei-guo is coaching Hann's badminton team and working out with XX. BeiBei loves it when he surprises us, dropping by unexpectedly like today." I hope I've made clear Wei-guo's relentless pursuit and my inability to control him.

"So are you going to make this indispensable friend a part of the family?" Yang says.

How I wish BeiBei would fuss right now. "Well," I say in my meekest voice, "that's up to my husbands, isn't it?"

Yang bows, mildly chastened.

Reminded that Wei-guo has his own agenda, that it is up to me to maintain propriety, I pry BeiBei from his arms and return the flowers to him. "Time to go," I say over my child's kicking and tears. "Uncle will come visit when your babas are home."

"BeiBei's hurt," Wei-guo says. "Let me escort you home."

I tell him that's hardly proper in a loud voice. BeiBei bats at the flowers in Wei-guo's hands, and I gesture for him to keep his distance so that BeiBei will not lurch for him. I harden my expression even as Wei-guo mouths his apologies and sags in disappointment.

"Our bus will be here any minute," I tell Yang over BeiBei's howls.

She follows me to the end of the long line. There is no more mention of a playdate.

With BeiBei finally put to bed and asleep, I return to the kitchen to tackle the day's dishes. XX is in his room as usual playing virtual games, interacting—as he calls it—with the world. Hann sits on the couch pretending again to be watching the news, his attention stuck inside a thick file. I want to tell him about my encounter with Wei-guo, but he seems grayer and more stooped as of late—preoccupied and secretive the way he whisks files closed whenever I come near. Even though I know he has our future on his shoulders, that in forbidding us to go the max, Director Chang is violating the law, resentment for my sham marriages seeps through me. I try to be kind and show Hann sympathy, but he invariably bristles and insists I come to a decision about Wei-guo.

I squirt my concoction of rice water and sugar on the greasiest parts of the wok and begin scrubbing. Hann thinks he can wait me out. He wants me to shoulder the responsibility of the decision, but how could I make a career-ending choice for him?

I tell myself that my encounter with Wei-guo has made plain that he will be another man in my household with a mind of his own, another man I will have to get to know, manage, and persuade. It occurs to me that even though I am not enamored with his recent tactics, Wei-guo is fighting hard for me. The realization makes me smile.

The doorbell rings. It is 9:34, rather late and rude for an unplanned visit. Wei-guo has adopted the full-court press recently, dropping in at all hours bearing gifts. While Hann answers the door, I sneak to the bedroom, giving myself the option of pretending to be asleep. Or changing.

"Comrade Tang," Hann exclaims. "Please, do come in."

Dread runs through me as I peek out at our neighborhood committee head. As if a ridiculous red bow tie could refine his thuggish reputation, the short, squat man waddles in bow-legged, snarly as a bulldog. He plops himself into the center of our couch uninvited, uttering not a single apology or nicety. Tang must have heard about XX's divorce inquiry and come to investigate the state of our marriage. In these last decades, this committee has cemented its Mao-era snoop network reputation and taken on the brash authority of the former Red Guards. Subsidized by "dues" from local businesses, it has nosed further into our lives by monopolizing the caregiving industry for children, the elderly, and the disabled. It is clear that divorcing XX is out of the question. Our family secrets will not survive such intervention.

"Let me ask my wife to make some tea," Hann says.

"There's no need," Tang replies. "Gather up your spouses. I will speak to all of you."

"Oh," Hann says. "May I ask what this is about?"

"Telling you all together will waste less time."

Tang's no-nonsense tone petrifies me. I undo my ponytail and run a brush through my hair. As Hann searches for me in the kitchen, I stuff myself into my most uncomfortable bra, the one that digs, smooshes, and lifts, and slip into the green dress I wore for Wei-guo. Tang is notoriously partial to pretty women and to his stomach.

"I'm afraid my wife has gone to bed," Hann announces from the kitchen. I hear him fill the kettle. "Let me go wake her."

Hann enters the bedroom to find me knotting my dress.

"You look nice," he whispers. "Thank you for changing."

I signal to him to shut the door. "I'll be out in a second. You go and talk some sense into XX."

He nods, looking as scared as I feel. I wrap my arms around him, and we hold on to each other for a moment. Hann apologizes for putting me through this. I assure him that everything will be all right as long as XX puts a halt to his notions about divorce.

"We haven't much time. Go talk to him." I push him out the door.

I slip on my highest heels, the ones I wore to matchmaking lunches, and teeter out. "Comrade Tang," I say with a flirtatious smile, "Welcome!" I strut like Miss China and clasp both his hands in mine. He rises, but sits down quickly. I'm sure it kills him that I'm half a head taller. I perch myself next to him. "It's been a long time. How's your missus? And your young lords?" I try to recall his biological child's name and fail, but I do remember Tang likes to brag about his boy's academics. "Your son must be in college now." By the sour expression on his face, one would never guess that he is stroking my hand, copping a feel.

"He's at Peking University." He nods as if the accomplishment is just as it ought to be. "He was born brainy."

"He has a big future ahead of him," I say as Tang fondles the meaty part of my palm. I ask what his son is studying.

"Computer science."

"How perfect," I say. "CSS is always looking to recruit the most outstanding graduates from Peking University. We must put XX in touch with your son when the time comes."

Tang nods noncommittally as if his boy is a much-coveted prospect, as if my exceedingly generous offer is an imposition.

The kettle whistle begins to shriek. "Perhaps you'd prefer something stronger? We might have some Maotai. Maybe some Johnnie Walker too." I clap, remembering that we also have some chestnut cake.

"Hmm," he says.

And that's how you get the most expensive liquor in the house without asking for it. Feeling his eyes on my backside, I sway on my heels, determined to do what I can to help our cause.

In the kitchen, I grab the Scotch and just three glasses (Tang is surely one of those chauvinists who believes that only men should drink) and arrange the little cakes on a plate. I return to Tang just as my two men emerge from XX's room.

Though Hann has not changed out of his sweats, he has made certain that XX looks more than presentable. His dark dress shirt flatters his girth, and the expensive sheen of the fabric gives XX an air of importance. He approaches Tang with a purposeful stride and a confident handshake. I stand next to him and, in the manner of an affectionate wife, incline my entire body in his direction.

Tang orders us all to sit. And that's when I realize that by picking the center spot on the long couch, Tang has essentially divided us and done away with whatever strength and moral support we might have derived from sitting next to another family member. So that XX would not have to, I choose the spot next to Tang and urge him toward the loveseat on my other side. Hann is left with the armchair on the opposite end.

XX jumps right in. "Let me save everyone some time by saying that it's all a big misunderstanding. May-ling and I had a stupid fight over the bathroom, and I was so mad afterward, I told my manager I wanted to file for divorce. I didn't mean it."

"What?" I stop pouring the Scotch, drop my jaw, and widen my eyes in shock. Hann must have really scared him. I did not expect such cooperation. Or good acting.

XX starts at my tone of voice. "I'm sorry."

"You thought about divorcing me?" I say, milking the moment.

"Only for a day," XX says, staring me in the eye. "I was furious." Boy has Hann coached him.

I smile sheepishly. "I was furious too. It really was a stupid fight." I gasp as if an idea has just occurred to me. I look at Tang.

"Is this the reason you're here? Did we ruin your evening because of our silly fight?"

"Guo Xiong-xin," Tang says, "will you be petitioning for divorce?"

"No."

"Are you positive?"

"Yes."

Tang asks me the same question. I reply, relieved that he seems to take our words at face value. He turns last to Hann.

"No one in this family wants a divorce," Hann says.

"All right," Tang says. "Let's move on then to the next item, the one that actually concerns me more. Guo Hann, what is your relationship to the male prostitute who goes by the name Jimmy?"

Hann springs to his feet, his face instantly red. "I have nothing to do with Jimmy," he says with great vehemence. "He hustles at the park where I play badminton. Everyone knows him there because he pesters all the regulars. Two days ago he followed me home, making a ridiculous scene in front of the subway station, demanding that I give him money because his father has brain fever, whatever the hell that is. I don't know him. We're hardly wealthy. I don't know why he thinks he should squeeze me for money."

He shakes his head at me. The desperation in his plea feels like an admission of guilt. The understanding that this Jimmy represents the sort of "variety" that Hann prefers wounds me anew. The glass clinks, and I realize my hand is trembling. I put down the Scotch bottle and set the drink before Tang. The speed and ease at which Hann rouses himself to anger shocks me. I had no idea he is such a good liar.

Tang says, "It is my experience that when you smell smoke, there is usually fire."

"You're going to take the words of a prostitute against mine?" Hann asks. "Prostitution is illegal, not to mention extortion. You should arrest and reeducate him rather than accuse me because I have the misfortune of being his victim."

"Jimmy will be dealt with," Tang says. "My job is to make certain your immoral behavior does not harm your spouses and your children."

"Immoral behavior!" Hann exclaims. "What immoral behavior are you referring to? Playing badminton? Him accosting me on the street for no good reason?"

"Hann," I say, afraid that his fury will come back to bite us. Surely the guilty are not entitled to so much outrage.

"I am here to inform your family that you are under investigation."

"Investigation?" Hann throws up his arms. "I'll give you something to investigate." He dives into the thick file on the table. His secretive behavior suddenly makes sense. I hug myself to stop shaking. I've never seen him so out of control. He finally comes up with a business card and jabs it at Tang. "Here's the account number that Jimmy ordered me to wire funds to. Why don't you do the right thing and investigate that?"

XX walks over to his brother, takes the card, and looks it over before passing it to Tang.

Pocketing it without a glance, Tang says to XX and me, his voice cold and officious, "While the investigation is ongoing, Guo Hann's presence in this household is not permitted. He is to have no contact whatsoever with the children. Enforcement is up to the two of you. Should Guo Hann attempt to contact your children—"

"We have just one son," XX says.

Tang scowls. "Should Guo Hann attempt to contact your one son, he will be incarcerated. Do you understand?"

"Yes," XX replies.

Tang turns to me, and a peep escapes my mouth.

"Should you and Wu May-ling so wish, it is within your rights to also bar Guo Hann from contacting you during the period of the investigation." He asks if we care to take formal measures to ensure his separation.

XX says no. I shake my head. Hann has stopped pacing. He looks ashen, his chest sunken.

"A room will be provided for Guo Hann at the Sex Corrections Institute," Tang says. "He can continue to go to work."

Tang turns to Hann. "I advise that you own up to your wrong-doings sooner rather than later, confess, and show true repentance. Make the future easier on both you and your loved ones."

"You assume I've done something wrong," Hann says, but the fight is gone from his voice.

Tang cocks his head at him.

"I have nothing to hide, nothing to admit to," Hann says.

"Then you are ready to go to your new quarters," says Tang.

"Now?" I say, my voice quaking.

Tang says, "You can bring him some clothes and necessities—"

Hann bolts toward the back of the apartment, his footsteps thumping.

"Stop right there!" Tang tosses back his Scotch before jumping to his feet and chasing Hann to our bedroom door. He clamps a hand over Hann's mouth, the other around his chest, and yanks him backward. "You will not wake the boy."

"Please don't hurt him," I say, tugging on Tang's arm. "He won't wake BeiBei."

Hann hangs on to the doorjamb, his eyes drinking in the sight of our sleeping child. How I wish this memory of our boy is not of a gouged cheek and playground scuffle.

Tang orders XX to shut the bedroom door and wrenches Hann's elbow behind his back. "Shall I call for backup?"

"Let me get him a coat, at least," I say. "A toothbrush."

"We have toothbrushes," says Tang, propelling Hann forward with a twist of his elbow. He barks at me to open the front door.

"I'll be quiet," Hann says, but Tang does not ease up.

I grab the blanket off the couch and stuff it into Hann's free hand.

He pulls me to him and kisses my forehead. "I'm sorry, sweet pea," he says. "I swear I have nothing to do with Jimmy. I would never endanger you like that."

I burrow my head into his chest, desperate to believe him.

"Open the door," Tang yells again. "Now."

XX peels me off his brother and passes him the watch he has taken off his own wrist.

Hann squeezes XX's shoulder. "You're in charge now. Take good care of our family."

As Hann disappears step by step down the staircase, I realize this is the beginning of the end. Now that it has happened, this event feels as if it has always been inevitable, and I wonder how I could have deluded myself for so long. I'm far from surprised that Hann has erred with Jimmy. What surprises me is that despite my fury, my feelings for Hann have not changed. I do not love him any less, even as I cannot imagine Wei-guo would want anything more to do with me or my family. What sane person would? I'm further surprised by how indignant I feel. Hann is a good father. His instincts and love for his son are as good, if not stronger, than those of the average man, and a good man should not be taken away from his child just because he desires someone of the same sex. Our government has no right to harm our child and destroy our family for the larger good.

It occurs to me then that I do not understand what good our government is striving to achieve.

I grab on to XX's arm and steady my shaky self, overwhelmed

by the knowledge that for BeiBei's and our own sake, the two of us must now stand together.

Hann usually roughhouses with BeiBei in the morning while I cook breakfast, and not surprisingly, BeiBei wakes looking for his baba. I tell him that Hann is going to be gone for a while on a long business trip.

"He didn't say good-bye." BeiBei's lower lip trembles, his eyes fill, and I am reminded that he loves Hann best of all.

"Oh, but he did," I say, hugging him. "He hated, hated, hated to leave you. He stood there by the door and blew you a hundred kisses." I proceed to kiss my boy until he giggles and shrieks. I pretend to pin him down before giving him the upper hand. Last night, as I packed a suitcase for Hann, I realize that I am all that BeiBei has. I resolved to steel myself, to do what I must to protect him and myself. I am lucky he is two and still highly distractible.

XX left an hour ago to deliver the suitcase to Hann. I am grateful that he had the presence of mind to slip his brother his watch. "I know *GuhGuh*'s location twenty-four seven," XX informed me afterward. The ability to follow a little blue dot across the city map last night to a destination forty-five minutes away, the same destination Tang had indicated, was immensely comforting. Hann's curfew and roommates prohibited a voice call, but he was able to message us his safe arrival. He encouraged us to go about as usual, to not act guilty when we have nothing to be guilty about.

I'm not at all sure about his claim, but going about our business is what I must do. As much as I'd rather hide out at home, BeiBei cannot tolerate being cooped up. We are not much liked on the playground as it is. Rumors will hardly make our situation worse.

Just as I zip BeiBei into his last layer of clothing, all of the devices in the apartment ding in unison. XX has sent me a message.

Hann thanks you for suitcase. He is in ankle monitor that tracks conversation, digital activity, location, vital signs, and more. Messaging of any kind from home or within 75m of BeiBei is prohibited. DO NOT ATTEMPT.

I sense that Hann's supposed freedom is an ingenious trap. The government could learn more about Hann out in the open than if he were fully locked up.

I punch XX's icon on the computer screen, but a glance at Bei-Bei changes my mind. I cannot discuss Hann without upsetting myself and in turn, BeiBei. He understands so much more these days.

I type my message instead. **How is he feeling?**

Okay.

Does he need anything?

No.

I remember why I seldom call or message XX. BeiBei tugs on my arm, anxious to leave for the park. **Please, please, please tell me something to ease my mind.**

I endure more whining and tugging as XX formulates a reply.

Don't worry about Jimmy.

I sigh, not at all comforted. **Why not?**

Later.

Meet me for lunch.

I'm having lunch with Hann.

Good. I'm glad. Message me right afterwards. I want FULL report.

When I realize that he's signed off without a good-bye, I let BeiBei drag me out the door. One flight down, we encounter Granny Feng, our kind, eighty-year-old neighbor, on her landing ready to clunk down the stairs with her grocery cart. The son who doesn't live with her—a grandpa himself—meets her downstairs every morning and escorts her to do her shopping.

"Good morning," she says, patting BeiBei on the head.

I wish her a good day as well and nudge my boy to do the same. I take the cart from her. She often lets BeiBei wheel it on the street, and he clamors to help.

She asks if everything is all right. "There was quite a commotion last night."

As much as I'd like to confide in someone sympathetic and grandmotherly, I could not begin to tell her the depth of our troubles. I hide my face and start down the stairs, mumbling that everything's fine. I say that we are late for our bus and that I'll leave her cart at the building's entrance.

In the small concrete square in front of our building, between chatting mothers, scampering toddlers, and seniors practicing *qigong*, I see Wei-guo. A lonely blue balloon floats above his head, and I can't help but wonder about his sanity, meeting me again in the absence of my husbands, advertising our doomed courtship before my neighbors. A huge grin lights up his face when he sees us, and BeiBei runs to him with matching fervor. Wei-guo tosses him in the air before kneeling and securing the balloon string to his wrist. That he thought to construct an expandable loop of string so BeiBei would not lose the balloon, that BeiBei's own father will not be able to do these small things for him anymore bring tears to my eyes. It doesn't help that in the next breath I think how easy it would be for me to throw over Hann, how much I want to give myself to this lovely man.

I feel like a traitor.

He picks up BeiBei and stands to face me. I remind myself that Wei-guo will soon be backing away from me and my criminal family.

"Don't you ever work?"

His eyes soften at the hostility in my voice. "I'm sorry. I haven't been able to sleep, knowing I've angered you. I cancelled an appointment this morning to come and apologize."

His candor catches me off guard. Hann seldom apologizes without my making a case for it. Granny Feng comes out of our building and waves at me. I wave back and, not wanting her to see me with Wei-guo, cross the street.

"I am deeply sorry," Wei-guo says, following with BeiBei. "I shouldn't have tried to make a stand. It's just that I sensed you pulling away, and I couldn't do a thing about it."

When I neither confirm nor deny his observation, he continues, "I know I'm not in a position to make demands, but I know you are the one for me. I want to spend my life with you." BeiBei stretches upward for his balloon, and Wei-guo closes his arms around my child. "With all four of you. I'm more than willing to wait if I have a chance. But if I don't, please tell me."

His quiet vulnerability fills me with guilt. Even though I avoided being alone with him and exchanging private words, I've lived for his impromptu visits. I know in my heart I've led him on.

I see too that I've been a fool. Hann could never love me the way I want to be loved. And here is a man who adores me, whom—I'm ready to admit—I also adore.

I take BeiBei from Wei-guo and set him on the ground. He immediately grabs Wei-guo's hand. Keeping BeiBei on the far side and Wei-guo next to me, I keep walking as I quietly tell him that the neighborhood committee has taken Hann.

"They saw some prostitute named Jimmy hassle Hann on the street and accused them of immoral behavior. Hann swears it's not true."

"Jimmy!" Wei-guo says.

"You know him?"

"Yes, if it's the same Jimmy who harasses everybody at the

Temple of Heaven Park," he says. "Hann can't stand him. The Hann I know would not be stupid enough to do anything with him."

Wei-guo's vote of confidence is an unexpected shot of strength. I tell him that until the completion of a thorough investigation, Hann is not allowed contact with BeiBei. The unwavering sympathy in his demeanor eases me into my next question.

"Do you still want to marry me?"

He makes me stop walking and look him in the eye. "Of course I want to marry you. This doesn't change my feelings for you. Does Hann still want this?"

Relief washes over me. It isn't until this moment that I realize how much his answer matters to me. I decide that my future can no longer be entirely up to Hann. "If your fathers agree."

He beams. "They will."

I'm not at all sure, but his confidence is empowering. I start again, "If your fathers agree, then get in touch with XX. Don't drop in on me anymore like this. Too many people are watching. If I don't see you again, I understand. I wish you every happiness. I thank you for making me feel loved."

"You'll see me again," he says. "And I promise we're going to bring Hann home."

I bathe in the warmth of his smile one more time—in the honest crinkle of emotion in his eyes—and pray he is right. It dawns on me that I would be lucky to have Wei-guo and not the other way around.

12

XX

His pockets and briefcase loaded with meat buns, XX walks along the canal bank in the diminishing light, whistling for his dogs. Because of his unscheduled lunch with Hann, he did not get a chance to feed them today. The timing was especially bad. On occasion, a dog will miss the noontime feeding, but never have the same two dogs (BaBa and BeiBei Dog) not shown up for two days in a row. XX had planned to scour the area if needed during lunch.

Unfortunately, he only dared add GPS capabilities to MaMa Dog's tag. She is up ahead along the canal bank, and he prays that the other dogs are with her. Now that Hann has reviewed the family budget with XX at lunch and entrusted him with the bankbooks, XX wonders if he could risk chipping all his dogs.

He resists the impulse to shout out their names. Dogs can hear four times the distance of humans and a dog like BaBa has two hundred million more scent receptors than people. If his dogs are in the vicinity, they know he is looking for them. If they are near and not coming to him, it is up to XX to be the detective.

Dotted by the occasional willow tree, this stretch of the artificial river offers few places to hide. Now a storm channel and drain, this northern starting point of the ancient Beijing-Hangzhou Grand Canal is concrete from its banks to the sidewalk.

The timing really cannot be any worse. Hann must take priority over his missing dogs. XX's insides twist: he must find out everything about Jimmy as soon as possible. He would have preferred to have taken today off from work, but Hann insisted that they all go about as usual so as to demonstrate their confidence in his innocence. Furthermore, XX will likely be the family's sole breadwinner soon, and he must not neglect his job. If XX did not have six coworkers seated behind him staring into his monitor, he could have investigated Jimmy at work. He could have hidden his digital trails too.

XX checks his watch again. It is 5:23. The streetlamps have already come on, and the sun will set in another seven minutes. He is usually home by 5:45. He whistles louder and picks up his pace. May-ling will be in tears and hysterics if he is not on time today. All afternoon, she kept pinging him with questions even when he replied *not now* and *later* and *tell you when I'm home.* Even though he reminded her they were being monitored, she still could not behave correctly. XX spent nearly two hours at work surreptitiously composing and hand-copying behavioral instructions: a simple and detailed version for May-ling and another with possible consequences for every kind of violation for Hann. Handwritten notes are the safest way to transmit information in this day and age if the reader destroys them upon reading.

Tall bushes border the strip of green up ahead, offering the first real hiding places. XX hurries forward, his lips parched from whistling. Heavy with long seedpods, the branches droop to the ground, obscuring the base of the plants. In case the missing dogs are not with MaMa Dog, he swats at the bottom of the bushes from time to time and whistles.

A small, shadowy object darts out. XX takes an involuntary step back, his heart racing. The rat remains on its haunches, strangely bold. XX stomps his foot. When it fails to scurry, Hann's warning about rabies flashes to mind. XX backs away, afraid to take his eyes off the vermin.

He hurries to the next bushes, but no longer dares to disturb them. His watch indicates that MaMa Dog is within five meters. Still whistling, he bends and peeks beneath whenever he spots an opening, but it has become too dark to see.

A low, rumbling growl sends a shudder through him. XX freezes and hears the sound again. He turns on his watch's flashlight and sweeps it across the base of the shrubs. A green pair of eyes shines back, unblinking and ghostly. Resisting his urge to flee, XX backs up and whistles again, and the creature's growl and accompanying bark confirms that it's a dog.

He does not think it is one of his dogs—a dog of his would have bounded out to greet him—but he must be sure. According to the dog experts, an extended, low-pitched growl is usually a warning, a sign of hostility. Low-pitched growling accompanied by barking signals an attack. The creature could be guarding its supper. XX tosses a meat bun to the edge of the brush and retreats at an angle all the way to the canal railing.

Soon enough, a snout edges out of the shrubbery, snatches the bun, and dashes back under. XX should have set the treat out in the open. Hoping the animal is still hungry, he drops another. It doesn't take long for the ginger-haired mutt to emerge growling and baring its teeth. It looks like MaMa Dog, but MaMa Dog is never mean. She would never act like this with him.

The creature creep-limps toward the food, favoring its left side. A line of metal drags beneath its body. With his light, XX makes out a dogcatcher pole dragging its rusty links of chain. Cinched around the upper portion of the dog's front leg, a twist of wire has opened up a brown, weeping gash. XX recognizes the dog's red collar.

"MaMa Dog!" he cries.

She pounces on the meat bun and consumes it with bared teeth. To prevent her from retreating, XX tosses out another treat two dog lengths away.

"I'm going to help you," he says in his most soothing voice. He edges forward. Her growl sounds higher pitched this time, less threatening. "But first, I have to set my briefcase down and open it." He hopes that the small pair of scissors in his stationery kit can cut wire. He unzips the holder and finds the scissor slot empty. He grunts in frustration: May-ling is always borrowing his things without returning them.

After eating the third bun, MaMa Dog hobbles to her feet. XX hurriedly throws out another, but she shuffles and points herself back toward the bush. XX grunts again, furious at May-ling and her bad habits and anxious that he needs to hurry home to work on Hann's emergency.

Even though MaMa Dog could bite through his arm, XX lunges and snatches up the pole. "Quiet, MaMa," he scolds. Her growls deepen again, a low and frightening rumble, but XX stands his ground. MaMa Dog could die if he lets her go. *Be the alpha*, he tells himself as he stands taller. *Be the Pack Leader* taught him that dogs intuit human emotions. He cannot exhibit any fear or anxiety. When she growls again, he steels himself and gives the pole a small jerk. He is relieved to hear her whimper.

He can release her with an easy flick of the pole's crude wire locking mechanism. She would run off, and her wound would surely become infected. It would be difficult for her to survive the coming cold in that weakened state, let alone elude dogcatchers a second time. XX hopes his other dogs have not been captured.

He must take her home—give her an actual home—and treat her leg. MaMa Dog is the gentlest, the sweetest creature on Earth, and he is certain that with food, medication, and training, she could become a good pet. Remembering that the number-one way to communicate his pack leader status is to walk in the lead, he gives the pole a gentle tug and sets off toward his apartment.

May-ling has been pinging XX every few minutes wanting to know his location, but it is dangerous to be distracted while walking an injured dog. He stops and lets MaMa Dog catch her breath and drink out of a puddle. Now that he is twenty minutes from home, he will answer her next voice call.

It does not take long for May-ling to ring. *Be the Alpha*, he tells himself again. He will not give her the chance to yell at him. "I'm seventeen minutes away. I know you're worried. Hann is okay. I haven't called because there's nothing new since *last night*."

"Why haven't you replied to my messages? Why aren't you home yet?" May-ling says. "You must communicate with me, XX, now more than ever. You and I have to band together, or else Hann's not going to make it. You have to tell me what's going on. We have to come up with a plan together. Do you understand?"

He hates her yelling, her condescending tone, her assumption that he never gets it. With Hann gone, he is legally the man of the house, and the Alpha sets the rules. Alphas do not need to answer questions or explain. That's the only way he's going to be able to bring MaMa Dog and Hann home. "I need you and BeiBei to meet me downstairs in fifteen minutes. Under my bed, in the third bin from the left, you will find a dog leash. Bring that with you."

"How could you be out buying a dog?"

"What do you have against dogs?" XX says, pleased by his own daring.

"You know I like dogs," she says, and XX realizes he's stumbled into a bit of luck. May-ling grew up doting on a stinky, skin-diseased chow chow. "But this is no time for a new dog."

"She's not new. And she is not negotiable," XX says.

Stunned, no doubt, May-ling does not reply immediately. XX uses the opportunity to hang up and establish his dominance.

XX spies May-ling and BeiBei waiting for him under the cone of a lamplight at the small plaza across the street from their apartment. He studies the few people milling in front of their building and the pedestrians rushing home to dinner to make certain no one is demonstrating extra interest. The distance between May-ling and BeiBei shrinks as he and MaMa Dog approach. By the time they are within shouting distance, May-ling has interposed herself between them and the child. XX stops in the middle of the plaza about twenty paces from her and far from trash cans, lamp-posts, and fixtures wired with cameras and monitoring chips. He checks to see that May-ling has brought the leash.

Praying that their hour-long trek has firmly established XX again as the top dog, he commands MaMa Dog to sit, a command they have been working on. She mercifully obeys.

"What is going on?" May-ling looks scary mad.

XX waves the bag containing his last dozen meat buns. "Here's dinner." Alphas determine the topic of conversation.

BeiBei shuffles around his mother. "BeiBei pet dog."

May-ling clamps one hand around BeiBei's wrist and spreads the other wide to keep the boy behind her.

XX removes a bun from the bag and holds the rest out toward May-ling. "Take this and my briefcase too."

"Can't you see that my hands are full?" She throws the leash toward his feet and goes back to corralling BeiBei. "Where did you get that dog?"

XX tosses the bag to her anyway and tells her to guard his briefcase as he sets it down. In need of all his concentration at the moment, he ignores May-ling's question.

He reminds MaMa Dog to stay down. His eyes on the creature the entire time, he slowly slides the dogcatcher pole toward May-ling.

"Hold this."

May-ling says, "I'm taking BeiBei upstairs. This is too dangerous."

XX pokes the pole in BeiBei's direction and asks the boy to take it.

"What are you doing?" May-ling screeches as BeiBei dashes around her and happily does as he is told for once.

"Keep it down," XX says in a powerful voice. "Nothing will happen if you don't frighten the dog. Can't you see she's hurt?"

"Dogs can turn on you when they're hurt," she hisses.

"Doggie has booboo," BeiBei says.

Unable to pry the pole from him without causing a tantrum—XX has finally discovered a use for the boy's bad temper—May-ling wraps her arms around his middle and backs the two of them away as far as the wire will allow.

"Yes," XX says in his most soothing voice. "MaMa Dog has a terrible booboo, but she is a very good girl. She will sit still and let us help her."

"Help her, BaBa," BeiBei says. "She's bleeding." It occurs to XX that if BeiBei likes the dog, he could be the key to keeping her.

Hoping MaMa Dog is still hungry, he places a meat bun in front of her. She sniffs it for a bit before biting into it. Reminding her again and again that she's a good girl, XX edges around her and slowly snaps the leash onto her collar. They've never practiced being on a leash. When MaMa Dog does not turn around to bite him, he sags with relief.

Uttering "good girl" like a mantra, he forces himself to pat her head. He is grateful when she again does not chomp off his fingers.

XX avoids May-ling's livid looks and asks her to very quietly flip the snap mechanism at the end of the pole. Crouching down very slowly behind the dog, he jiggles the wire in the hope of loosening the deep hold it has cut into her flesh. MaMa Dog whines, back rounded and tail droopy.

"You're okay, MaMa Dog," XX says in recognition of the anxious body language. "I'm going to free you." He continues to jiggle the line.

"You're okay," BeiBei echoes.

The wire finally falls from MaMa Dog's leg. She whines some more and limps away, but the leash jerks her back. For an instant, white rims her pupils. May-ling picks up BeiBei and backs a safe distance away, leaving XX's briefcase unattended. XX commands MaMa Dog to sit. The whites flash again before she obeys. XX wraps the leash around his hand until his grip is nearly at her collar. She needs a little time to calm down and get used to the leash.

XX uses this opportunity to speak to May-ling. "Four of my five dogs are missing, kidnapped most likely by dogcatchers. I have no choice but to bring MaMa Dog home. She is the gentlest of all my dogs. I'm going to buy her a cage."

May-ling takes a deep, deep breath. "Please, XX. I don't understand. Can you explain how you can own five dogs?" Her voice has lost its angry needles.

His domination strategy appears to be working. XX decides that he will answer to polite deference. "I paid their registration fees. I bought their collars. I feed them. That is the definition of an owner."

"Do you shelter them?"

"I will after our divorce."

May-ling points excitedly at BeiBei, a warning for XX to watch what he says. It is totally unnecessary. The boy never listens.

"So she is a wild dog?"

"For now."

"Do you think wild dogs can stand being cooped up in an apartment? Inside a cage?"

"She is hurt. I have to take care of her."

"Wild dogs are unpredictable. Injured dogs even more so. What if she attacks one of us?"

"She won't. I'll keep her tied up."

"Do you think she'll be happy with that? What if she barks all day?"

"She won't." There is such power in refusing to answer her questions.

"She's a big dog."

"She's less than thirty-five centimeters at the shoulders," XX says though she has never stayed still enough for him to measure her accurately.

"Do you remember Ling Ling, my old dog? She was not of legal size. We had to bribe our neighbors to keep quiet. We never let her out of our apartment. She could not be walked except in the dead of night when people are asleep. Your MaMa Dog is bigger than Ling Ling."

XX decides to change the subject. "Why did you harass me all day? We are being monitored. When I say I'll tell you when I get home, I mean it is dangerous to discuss Hann's case over public channels."

Her eyes diamond-shaped like a clown's, May-ling jerks her head again and again at BeiBei.

"I won't be quiet now, not when outdoors may be the only safe place for us to talk." XX explains that any device that sends or receives data can be used for surveillance. "Write down on paper your messages to Hann, and I will deliver them in person. We will come outside whenever we have important things to discuss. Do you understand?"

She frowns and points at BeiBei again. "Find anything on Jimmy?"

"I'm working on it."

"What about—" She raises her eyebrows. "How's he handling it?"

"He just has to stay out of trouble until I clear him."

"I mean emotionally."

"Of course he's scared and doesn't like it."

May-ling sighs as if XX is the stupidest person in the world. "Tell me about his rooming situation, his bathroom, the food they serve. Paint me a picture. Please."

"No idea about the food. Five roommates, two-by-four-meter room, one communal bathroom." She is interested in the most trivial things. XX digs the manual he wrote for her from his coat pocket. "Read this. These are your new rules."

"Rules?" Her disrespectful tone is back.

"Study it here while I get MaMa Dog used to the leash. Do you want to walk with us, BeiBei?"

"No way," May-ling says, nearly losing her balance as BeiBei pushes off her stomach and bends sideways to get down.

"BeiBei," XX roars and waits until he has the boy's attention. "Listen to me. Stop fighting if you want to walk the dog. You do everything I say, or I will send you back to your mother. Understand?"

The boy nods.

XX likes his new authority. "You can't touch the dog. And you have to hold my hand. Do you understand? Say you understand."

"I understand."

"Will you please take a test lap first by yourself?" May-ling's tone is pleading. Respectful.

It's a sensible idea, so XX obliges her. He tells BeiBei he is next if both he and the dog behave. He waits for the boy to agree.

"Up." XX tugs on the leash, pulling MaMa Dog to her feet. Thankfully, she rises without further signs of aggression. Keeping the leash short and taut, he leads her in a wide, circling limp around May-ling. As his dog trails him without protest, XX marvels at how this injury may be the best thing to happen to the two of them. When they stop before May-ling, MaMa Dog again obeys his command to sit. XX cannot feel more smug.

"That's not how you walk a dog," May-ling says.

"Do you want to control the dog, or do you want the dog to control you?" XX says. "Send the boy here, and read my manual."

She flashes him a dirty look but gives the boy over.

BeiBei holds XX's free hand, and they begin to lead the dog around the small concrete plaza in front of their building. Staying a few steps behind MaMa Dog, May-ling follows them. XX reminds her that she is supposed to be reading, not exhibiting herself as the lowest-ranking member of the pack.

She sighs. "Walk in a big circle around me then."

BeiBei is probably more unpredictable than MaMa Dog, so XX complies. He doesn't even get a chance to complete one lap when May-ling scurries back to them.

"There's nothing new here: I already know all the ways I'm not allowed to contact Hann, all the ways you prefer I not bother you."

"Then why do you keep breaking the rules? I'd like to start working on Hann's case, but I can't if you keep wasting time arguing. I can't if my dog is not safe."

May-ling places her hands on her hips. "Your dog can stay until her leg heals and not a minute more."

"I'm the man of the house now," XX tells her. "I make the money. I make the decisions."

She cocks her head at him. "Are you planning to take her to work with you every day?"

"Of course not. Dogs aren't allowed at work."

"Then you'd better think twice, throwing your weight around like this."

For once, she says something that makes him think.

XX yawns as he lugs another suitcase for Hann onto the subway along with his own briefcase and two lunch boxes filled with May-ling's tasteless cooking. May-ling would not accept that Hann's small, shared room could not house the contents of another suitcase or store perishables properly. So, here is XX again at six in the morning delivering more unnecessary things. May-ling just does not understand that XX's time would be better utilized investigating Jimmy and masterminding a plan.

The good news: MaMa Dog could be thirty-five centimeters tall, depending on where one decides her shoulder joint starts. XX made sure last night the second May-ling left them alone. And the bad news: Last night was a waste. XX was not able to do any investigating because May-ling would not allow it. She insisted they were not safe unless XX gave MaMa Dog his one hundred percent attention. No one slept much either. MaMa Dog alternately howled and whined until XX allowed her, smelling none too good, into his bed at two A.M. May-ling had plenty of waking hours to compose a tome to Hann. XX unsealed the envelope on the subway ride and confirmed that it was one big grievance about the dog and about XX's ineptitude. May-ling does not understand that XX is their only hope for getting out of this mess. Without XX's investigative and programming powers, they are sunk.

XX yawns again, still trying to shake off dreams of suffocation and of drowning dog baths. He needs time for BeiBei and May-ling to fall in love with MaMa Dog, so he memorizes the three key points from May-ling's memo—she rambles so—and tears it up as per the rules he drew up for all of them. His brother cannot forbid XX from keeping a dog he does not know about.

He decides to pass along BeiBei's drawing even if it is of MaMa Dog. For all Hann knows, it could be a horse, a bear, or any number of four-legged creatures.

At the Sex Corrections Institute, he finds Hann sunk into a ratty couch next to the front door. He looks like he hasn't slept either.

His brother comes to him and grabs his shoulder. "You look awful." He brushes at XX's sweater. XX tenses as Hann picks at it and pulls off a web of ginger-colored fur. "Are you dating a redhead?" he says. "What happened to you?"

XX frowns, petrified. "I'm not dating a redhead." It's like Hann has a degree in criminology when it comes to tricking secrets out of XX.

"I'm sorry." Hann squeezes his shoulder and sighs. "Here I am, giving you a hard time, and I've turned your world upside down." Hann ushers XX toward the guard at the entrance. "This is my brother, the best brother in the world."

XX is in the middle of a wave when Hann sweeps him out the front door. Hann takes the suitcase from him, and they walk down the street. Two buildings to the east, in front of a shoe shop, Hann sets his load down on a wooden bench.

XX says, "We can't talk here."

He finds the manual for Hann and tells him to read the second page. Hann flips through the document before stuffing it into his shirt pocket.

"Read it now," says XX.

Hann promises to read it later. "You don't have much time before work. I'd rather spend it talking with you."

XX grimaces and points at Hann's ankle bracelet, the security camera on the traffic light nearby, and the automated trash can next to the bench. Hann sends him a puzzled look, and XX is forced to retrieve the manual from Hann's pocket and point at item number five: *Your ankle bracelet is capable of triggering and communicating with any municipal device with Internet connectivity. Beware of your activities and conversations in proximity to security cameras, traffic signals, lampposts, flowerpots, garbage cans, etc.*

Hann sags. XX picks up the suitcase and leads his brother toward the open square between two high-rise apartment buildings. He finds a lone concrete bench, one far from in-ground lights and trees. Hann drops heavily into it.

XX sets the lunch boxes between them. "May-ling packed you more clothes. And food." He unzips a side pocket of the suitcase and pulls out BeiBei's drawing.

Hann studies the two figures, a tall dad and a little kid holding hands, for a long time. The dog gets little notice. When he looks up again, his eyes are wet. XX scratches his stomach, not sure how to comfort him. After a while, he asks if Hann has a letter for May-ling.

Hann shakes his head. "I've torn up several. Nothing I write captures how sorry I feel." He says he'll draw something for BeiBei right away and asks how the two are faring.

"They're fine."

Hann sniffles. "I don't want anything to change. I still want to hear from you every day at four. We will continue to work up your daily highlights and conversation starters with May-ling."

"Okay." XX hates that exercise, but anything is preferable to a down and dejected Hann.

"And your Wednesday nights. That's your husbandly right. If

you give that up now, you'll never get it back. Remember: It's our parents' greatest wish for you to have a child. Mine too."

XX agrees again to get Hann off his back. He hates these expectations he has no interest in living up to. He says with lowered voice that May-ling has three areas of questions. He motions for the tear-off pads and pencils in Hann's shirt pocket—a practice XX started him on yesterday. He jots down *Willfully Sterile* before saying, "First, she wants to know how many men are there and if they're—"

Hann glances at XX's pad. "Everyone on my floor is there for the same reason." He writes, *The gov must get its jollies creating a den of temptation. I hear they've hidden fake detainees & prostitutes, to try to entrap us.*

When Hann writes no more, XX asks again how many are housed there.

"Thirty or forty on my floor," Hann whispers. "Another hundred or so—men with STDs, adulterers who got caught, and transvestites—in the rest of the building. You know the actor Handsome Lee? Believe it or not, he's here too."

"I know," XX says. "May-ling also wants to know if you're eating, what they're feeding you."

Hann shrugs. "I have money. I can buy myself whatever I want."

"You have to answer her question."

"What does it matter?"

"She's not going to stop bugging me until you answer."

Hann sighs. "Ma-Po tofu. Cabbage. Rice. Tell her I get two dishes and soup every night."

XX scribbles May-ling's last question on the pad. *She wants to know what Jimmy is blackmailing you for. Should I tell her about the photo?*

Hann closes his eyes and rubs his face. "What do you think?"

XX sits up. Hann rarely asks his opinion. XX suggests that they wait. He has had enough of her hysterics in the last two days, and her knowing about the photo will not help anyone. His brother readily agrees.

Tell me all the evidence out there against you. The complete list of people who could incriminate you. XX passes his pad to Hann.

Hann writes, *Jimmy must have taken more pics at Chu's flat. Not only of me and Chu, but of Chu with others too.*

When Hann offers nothing more, XX writes and asks again for the list of people with whom Hann has had relations.

Hann pulls a sealed envelope from his jacket pocket. It's addressed to Chu and shows an address. *Please deliver this. Tell them you're my brother, and Chu will see you. Destroy the letter after he reads it. Find out if Chu has contained the situation with Jimmy. Chu will start a notification system that is already in place. My friends will know how to band together and keep their mouths shut.*

How is Chu containing Jimmy? Is he being blackmailed too?

Better you not know.

I need all the names.

Hann shakes his head. *Your investigation could lead the gov to them.*

I know how to hide my tracks.

I'm not going to escape this. Hann stares at XX for a long moment. "*I'm not,*" he mouths. *The best we can do is to make sure our family does not get dragged down.*

Chu's in your badminton group, isn't he?

I will handle Chu and Jimmy. You concentrate on Wei-guo. BeiBei needs another father, May-ling a husband, and you a friend. Use all the tricks at your disposal to find out where he and his fathers stand on my arrest, if he is still right for our family. Hann asks if XX will promise to do this for him.

XX agrees. He is not worried. He has already downloaded all the pertinent files and activity history from Hann's watch and computer last night. He has all he needs to investigate Chu.

13

WEI-GUO

Inside the Temple of Heaven Park, I burst into a run toward our badminton practice area in the sycamore alley, dashing around the meandering blocks of family units shielding wives and the occasional daughter at its center. I've been meaning to, but still haven't found the words to tell my two dads about Hann's latest troubles. Or about my own run-in with the black-uniformed guards at the Heavenly Lake Station. Both weigh heavily on me, but I want the time and freedom to make up my own mind. I know my dads will demand that I give up on May-ling and quit Strategic Games and won't stop worrying until I do.

But they really need not worry so much. The Strategic Games situation is settled for the time being. After our altercation with the black guards, word spread that the government was setting a quota on mental-health reporting. Hundreds of Strategic Games chat lines across the country roared with such outrage that government censors had a hard time deleting all the protests and demands for fair and humane treatment. Strategic Games headquarters soon announced that Major Jung would no longer be our overseer. They also said that all players must pass mental-health tests next season in order to continue their participation. It was not an ideal outcome, but a better one than I dared hope for. At the very least, it would not be the generals' responsibility to throw random men to the wolves.

I could have told my fathers about the black guards then, but I knew what Big Dad was going to say. Instead of being impressed by the strength of our fifty thousand voices, he would press me to quit Strategic Games anyway. I'm aware the fight is not over, but for my team's sake, I'd like to finish out the season. It's just one more game.

It occurred to me this morning that until I also obtain Hann's go-ahead on the marriage and not just XX's as May-ling had suggested, there is no sense riling up my parents.

I've been showing up every week to play with Hann's badminton team. It's a thrill to see disinterested players become better athletes and strategists with a little coaching and encouragement. I like being with these people who appreciate my talents and enjoy my company. It feels wholly different from the authority and respect that I command as general of Middle Kingdom. To be a good leader, one can never truly be one of the guys.

The men welcome me each week with boisterous bravado. At one point, they must have agreed that I was in on their secret, and trustworthy. The guys tease me about joining their "team," each boasting in joking and not-so-joking tones of his unparalleled ability to change me for the good.

I turn a corner and stop smack in my tracks. Beneath the leggy, high-canopied sycamores, Jimmy is rallying with the group, sporting a gold-embroidered white tracksuit, one identical to Chu's. It looks like one of Chu's Versace outfits, one too expensive to sweat in. His face etched in concentration, Jimmy chases after the birdie with an athletic grace uncompromised by vamping. Gone are his ass cheek–exposing shorts and his provocative demeanor. A sense of foreboding washes over me. He has made himself into a new person.

Hann has not yet arrived. Wary of this new Jimmy, I sidle toward a ginkgo tree and conceal myself behind its trunk. My seven men form two lines and are back to rallying with just one birdie even though I encouraged them to warm up and practice in pairs.

An action hog, Jimmy poaches shots that belong to his neighbors. A showboat too, he lunges at errant birdies, even those not on his end, succeeding more often than not in keeping them in play. Whenever he claims the turn, he points to a player on the opposite end and calls out the type of stroke before executing it. I root for a miss, just one, but he has yet to foul up. I want more than anything to stomp out the smugness from his every feature with my superior hand-eye coordination and footwork.

Soon, the men drift to one side, and Jimmy becomes the center of the action. He hits to the men from left to right. My friends drag their feet, their expressions dour and wary. They return the birdie to him as if out of obligation. The joy seems missing from their very bones.

A juicy lob comes Jimmy's way, and he dinks it back to Chu. Jimmy is not shy about going for the kill, smashing the birdie once right into Teddy Bear's chest. There's a mean, competitive streak in him, and Teddy is as wide and slow as they come. I watch a little bit more. The shots Jimmy sends Chu's way are all soft setups.

Not only are Chu and Jimmy wearing matching tracksuits, their hats and shoes are identical as well. Chu is the wealthiest of the bunch and the most snobbish too. He would not dress as any-one's twin—let alone a nobody hustler like Jimmy—without a gun pointed to his head.

I jog toward the group and apologize for my late arrival. "Let's get three more birdies in play."

My friends stand stony-faced, and my stomach lurches. Jimmy approaches me, hands on hips.

"Nice outfit," I say.

"What are you doing here?" Jimmy's dark brows and his gener-ously lashed eyes drip with venom. It makes no sense.

I walk past him toward Chu, the unspoken head of the group. "Why is this buffoon talking to me?"

Jimmy throws an arm over Chu's shoulder before butting his nose right up to mine. "You answer me when I speak to you." Being ignored makes him crazy.

I sidestep him again and stare at Chu. He shrugs Jimmy off and tries to lead me a distance away. Jimmy will not stop dogging us. Finally, Chu stops and tells me quietly that he's very sorry that Hann has left their group.

Jimmy gets in my face again. "Not 'left.' He was kicked out."

"Will you kindly give us a moment alone?" Chu says to Jimmy, his tone impossibly polite.

"Of course. I'll be right over there. Call if you need me," Jimmy replies warmly. I wait for a wink, a flirtatious gesture, but none comes. I can't figure what he's playing at.

Under the sycamores, the men are glued to our every move, but I sense a distance, a divide that none will cross. Chu suggests that Jimmy restart practice, and the guy leaves us in a manly swagger.

I say, "You'd better have a very good explanation."

Chu's expression hardens. "We cannot put ourselves in danger associating with a potential criminal."

"You cannot possibly believe that having Hann on your team is riskier than associating with that hustler."

"All of us—we've all agreed to certain terms up front."

"What terms?"

"You were welcomed here as Hann's guest. Now that he is gone, you too must go."

His words feel like a punch in the gut, a mockery of my months of friendship and goodwill. "Hann did not consent to being betrayed."

Chu remains stony. "Is there anything else?"

"What does that hustler want with you?"

"There are no hustlers here."

"You may not consider me your friend, but I considered you mine," I say. "The Chu I've come to know and admire would not dress like that hustler's twin." I urge him to tell me what's going on.

Chu thinks for a long moment. "Dignity, respect, a bright and unlimited future—that's what Jimmy wants, that's what every man on this team wants, and we've sworn an oath to make that a reality for each other."

"And your oath to Hann?"

Chu shakes his head as if I'll never understand. He says he's sorry and walks away.

"Who needs enemies with friends like you?" I wish I could come up with a better putdown.

Chu pauses before turning around. "You haven't seen Hann since his arrest, have you?"

I adopt his stony glare, damned if he's going to see the hurt in my eyes.

Chu says, "Hann and I have been in touch. And should he decide to speak with you, he will tell you that he broke his oath to us and not the other way around."

I take off in the direction of the subway and call up Hann as I run. I tell him I'm on my way to visit him.

"Why?" His voice is barely audible, his tone dejected.

"I'm your friend, and I want to see you."

"Why do you want to be my friend?"

I ask why he is not at badminton practice.

"I quit."

"They forced you out."

He does not reply.

"Those guys are not your friends," I say. "Friends do not kick you when you're down." I tell him again that I'm on my way to his office.

"I don't work there anymore."

"What do you mean?"

"I've been fired."

I ought not be shocked, but I am. I ask where he is. Hann does not reply, and I let the uncomfortable silence simmer. Friendship is a two-way street, and I wait for him to take the next step. Finally he asks if I'd like to meet him in a half hour in front of the PLA General Hospital.

"Are you all right?" I say.

He says yes and hangs up.

I hope and pray that Hann did not try to hurt himself.

For the forty million men like me who make up "The Bounty," the mere mention of the People's Liberation Army General Hospital induces a cold sweat. From age ten to the time we marry, annual "checkups" are required by law, though our public health system is in no way able or willing to provide any such service. What we are subjected to instead are endless lines, stinking facilities, and half-day waits for underpaid orderlies who in the quest to root out sexually transmitted diseases fondle, poke, and jab us in our most private and tender places. And until our results come back acceptable—which can take another half day—we are barred from leaving the premises. A good visit lasts ten hours. Men who test positive are taken away for treatment, which could take months. Sometimes, for those without family and connections, residency is "reassigned," and that could be the last we see of those men.

Modern, imposing, and ugly, the hospital is the tallest building between two subway stops, and I wonder every year when I make the ten-minute trek why I willingly deliver myself into its torturous unknown. Two army men with rifles guard the entrance, and I find Hann sagging on a bench outside next to one of them. A white crisscross of medical tape holds a wad of bloody bandage over his right ear.

I break into a run. "What happened?"

"Your boy toy is here," the guard says to Hann, an ugly smirk pasted on his sun-darkened face.

"I don't have any boy toys," Hann says. His words take great effort as does the act of staggering to his feet.

"Tell that to the chip in your ear, you pervert."

"Ten-hut," I say, and my commanding tone snaps the two of them to attention. Few things rankle me more than soldiers who abuse their power. My army days are long past, but they don't know that. I clasp my hands behind my back and make a show of pacing between their confused faces, memorizing their badges. When they are finally good and scared, I demand their job titles here at the PLA General Hospital.

"We're guards, sir," the two say in sloppy unison.

"Is that all?" I ask.

The young men eye each other. The dark one elects himself the spokesman. "We verify checkup release papers, sir. Make sure they are properly stamped."

"And?"

After a moment, the other soldier volunteers, "We help lost people?"

"And is harassing your patrons how you help them?"

They stare blankly ahead.

"Apologize to the gentleman." I order the dark one to go first.

He exchanges hesitant looks with his partner. "May I see some identification, sir?" There is a self-satisfied sneer on his face.

Out of the corner of my eye, I sense Hann moving, a twitch of his head urging me to leave. But I cannot let this idiot slide. "You'd rather I report you?"

He grimaces into the distance. "I apologize."

"Say it to the gentleman, and mean it."

"I apologize to you, sir."

Unsatisfied, I turn to Hann and curse at myself. In my efforts to teach the soldiers a lesson, I failed to notice the dark scrunch in my friend's brow, the scream of pain in his bent carriage. I rush to support his elbow while barking at the second soldier.

"I am sorry," he says, his tone also unconvincing.

Hann quietly tells me to let him go, but alarmed by his infirmity, I hold on tighter. He removes my hand and clutches his middle as he drags himself away from the soldiers. "Did they kick you?"

"It's just a stomachache." We round the corner. "They made me pick out a chip from a dirty ashtray," he says, pausing between phrases to catch his breath. "They injected it into my earlobe. Without anesthesia."

The exposed portion of his ear above the stiffening brown bandage is angry red. I ask about the pain.

"It's bad."

I stare at the thick cuff around his ankle, the scrunch of pant leg that will not fit around the device. I ask what added benefit the chip provides on top of that monitor.

Hann shakes his head. "It's temporary. It'll be removed when I'm exonerated."

His optimism surprises me. As soon as we turn the corner, he lurches toward the first windowsill and doubles over, hands on his stomach.

I help turn his body and guide his bottom onto the ledge. His brow is covered with sweat. I notice fresh dots of blood on the shoulder of his gray suit coat. I kneel down to get a look at his face and tell him we need to go to a real doctor. I ask where it hurts, how I can help, and his whole face pinches as if just my speaking causes him pain.

I give him a minute, which stretches into two and then three. I've never felt so helpless. He finally takes a deep breath and sits up a little. He tells me again he has a bad stomachache. "Talk first," he says, handing me a pen and a pad of paper from his suit pocket. On it, he has already written a message: *Everything I say and do is being monitored. Write down anything of import.*

He scribbles on a second pad. *The ear chip is a way to mark me and tease out more accusers. The gov is looking to pay for evidence.*

I suck in my breath. His badminton group's betrayal seems the least of our concerns.

I am not allowed to see BeiBei, to speak or message with anyone within 75m of him. He stares at me with pained eyes. *You could be investigated for just talking to me.*

"Don't worry about me," I say.

He breathes heavily. Every character he etches out seems to cause him pain. *Most people have something problematic in their past.*

My stomach twinges as I think of my involvement with the mental-health boycott, the black guards that XX thwarted, the unconventional bylaws I drew up for Middle Kingdom. I understand that my love for May-ling is born of desperation. And a small measure of opportunism too.

"Why are you here?" Hann asks in a near whisper.

"You need a friend, and I'd like to be that friend." These words also feel true.

He cocks his head and grimaces at me.

My face flushes with heat. "And I want your blessing to go ahead with May-ling."

"Why do you want our kind of trouble?"

Hann is right that theirs is a perilous situation, one that will, on top of a heavy emotional toll, involve public denunciations and shaming, hefty fines, and god knows what else. If the family is found to be intentionally harboring a Willful Sterile, it could be broken up.

And none of that matters to me.

I say, "I love May-ling. I've come to love your son too. I couldn't forgive myself if anything bad happened to them."

His expression remains skeptical. The inadequacy of words overwhelms me. I take a deep breath, struggling to convey the roil of emotions within.

I ask Hann to think back to the day he and May-ling taught me the merengue. "You described family life as a group dance. A joyous and intimate collaboration with a built-in safety net. I feel cared for, important, and at home every time I'm with all of you. I treasure that sense of belonging. I love that I matter to you."

He does not react.

I continue, "I want to do everything in my power to keep Bei-Bei and May-ling together."

He squeezes his eyes shut, pained, I'm sure, by my allusion to this most dreaded possibility.

I perch myself on the ledge beside him. "It surely won't come to that, but if BeiBei also has me as a father, if they understand that this is a real family, that someone is anxious to join it, then chances are better that we can stay together."

Hann points at the paper pad, reminding me to use it, and says, "XX is part of this family too."

I tell him that I understand. "May-ling is frantic with worry. I would be happy to watch BeiBei so that XX can bring her to visit you."

My offer quiets him, and I decide this marriage will be possible only if I am brutally honest. My pulse hammering in my ears, I write down what I need to know in order to proceed. I ask what Jimmy has on him.

Hann considers his answer. "Nothing anymore." He shakes his head when I press further.

Jimmy's changed appearance begins to make sense. I write, *Has Chu bought his silence?*

Hann frowns. I stare back hard, and he eventually nods. Again, he declines to provide details.

"There's no easy way to put this, so I'm just going to say it straight. I hope you know how much I admire the family you've created, how sincere my intentions." My hands shake as I write: *Your savings could be in jeopardy. Adding funds, esp. one as sizeable as a dowry, to your family account at this juncture is unwise.*

Something hard flashes in his eyes.

I'd like to propose a true love marriage. A union of like souls and true hearts.

"You claim to be our friend," Hann says, his face contorted in fury, "but friends do not take advantage. Like you said, friends do not kick you when you are down."

I do my best to ignore the pounding in my chest. "I bring with me a deep affection for your family, my earning power, a second income. I don't want to hide from you that my fathers need convincing, that this proposal may be my best hope for securing their approval. They own their apartment. They've always been frugal. Whatever they don't use in their lifetime is mine, and what's mine belongs to my family."

"It's not the place of 'The Bounty' to propose marriage."

"Forgive me," I say. In my calculations, they need me as much as I want them, and I believe he knows that.

Hann grabs on to the metal cage protecting the window and pushes himself up. I allow him the dignity to rise on his own.

"May-ling will be greatly insulted," he says.

I tell him that I understand. "I want us to be a family that tells each other the truth," I say. "I will not lie to you."

"I'm fine now." He walks away in a careful shuffle. "You're free to go."

I follow along an arm's length away in case I need to steady him. He says, "Don't you have to work?"

I say, "I'll cancel my next appointments if I have to, but I'm taking you to see my friend Doc, and then safely home."

I'm sorry the moment the word "home" leaves my tongue. We stagger along in silence, him still clutching his middle, and I take comfort in the fact that he doesn't shoo me away again.

I drape a blanket over my head and tell myself that I am not cold. I have the luxury of a mountaintop cave while my men face a December nighttime battlefield with just their fight suits. I urge myself to appreciate all the moments tonight—the ass freezing as well as the thrills of battle. This is likely my last Strategic Game.

Our fight with our governing board will continue on. They would love nothing more than to shut us down. As much as I love this game and the people in it, I don't know if I have the stomach to go through more ordeals. I was more than lucky to escape Heavenly Lake Station unscathed. I know my reticence plays right into their hands, but if I am to marry May-ling, I cannot put her or myself at risk. For my team's sake, though, I'd like to finish out the season tonight with a memorable win.

The weather bureau's same-day predictions are always so precise, and I can't get over how cold it is, how wrong this morning's forecast. I walk to the cave entrance, lift up the tent flaps, and am surprised again by the swirl of fat snowflakes that hit my face. The air is flecked with white, the ground covered. The computer is supposed to call off the game the moment the temperature reaches freezing. I check the weather module—four degrees Celsius. I didn't realize that snow is possible above freezing.

At my command station, I click on Little Sung, our opposing army's second-in-command and my Safety Council's most outspoken member. Aware of my feelings for Chao, he bet me peanut shelling services during our next Safety Council meeting that he would outkill and outlast my second-in-command. We have yet to meet Major Jung's replacement, but none of us harbors great hope. So far, Little Sung is leading in kill count.

It is 9:15. The first soldier has been down for nearly ninety minutes, and I decide not to override the program or contact the opposing general. Once laser guns strike the chest sensor, the fight suit's built-in weaponry and field communication capabilities shut down, and the suit becomes rigid, forcing soldiers to lie on the ground in simulation of death. The heat crystals in the suits activate and can keep the downed men warm for only two hours. If no general is captured, this game will be called when that heat runs out in half an hour. This being our last game of the season, my men will want this last chance to move us up to a third-place finish for the year.

I check the fatality count—Middle Kingdom, 79; and the People's Republic, 82—and am stunned again. How did a low-ranked army in our league kill forty of my men in the last three minutes?

The monitors show my third battalion, the one guarding the area around my mountaintop cave, to be the only one still intact and capable of carrying out any meaningful mission. With no scouts remaining and no assessment as to enemy positions, I decide to leave them in place. I hate to be passive, but on a night like this, not putting my remaining troop into harm's way may be what's needed to win the war.

The screen flashes: one of the guards stationed below my command post has been eliminated. A second later, X's appear over the green icons of two more guards. The People's Republic's soldiers seem to have a sixth sense as to our locations. I hurriedly strap the field monitor around my waist, don my night-vision goggles, and climb up the zip-line platform and onto the plastic disc of a seat. Expecting the enemy to be on the move, I clip myself onto the line in the direction of the first downed guard and maneuver to the edge of the platform.

I tap the radio in my ear and ask Major Chao what he sees from his vantage point halfway down the mountain.

"I count seven," he whispers back, and I tense with alarm. His post is a ten-minute walk from the downed guards. This is a well-calculated attack. Chao says, "I'm ready to fire. Zip off when I say go."

Keeping my elbows and knees in front of my face and body, I push off without waiting for his self-important cue. Branches scratch, cut, and shower me with snow while the cold bites into my exposed cheeks, and I am reminded how much I hate escape by zip line.

Chao hisses something, but is drowned out by the whizzing air. I cover my earpieces and hear, "—not going down. I've hit three on the chest, and they're not—"

Static fills my ear as I hurl down the mountain bouncing and tossed from side to side. I yell for him to clarify, but Chao does not respond. I tilt my waist monitor screen up toward my eyes, and it confirms his death.

I pull hard on the brake as I approach the landing zone and squeeze the line with my other gloved hand for extra insurance. I hit the ground running and do a quick survey of my surroundings. The thin carpet of snow here has no footprints. My advance team identified a hiding place nearby—a crevice beneath a rocky ledge—for just this scenario, and using my field monitor as a guide, I conceal myself behind one tree after another, hurrying in its direction. The countdown clock shows that I need to stay alive for another eighteen minutes.

My field monitor shows one of my downed guards up ahead. Chao made it sound as if there were zombie soldiers out there, and I slip and slide in the wet muck toward my man for a report. Every once in a while, armies find new ways to cheat. I wouldn't be surprised if that's the case tonight. It would explain our high casualty count and the speed at which my men perished.

The snow is heavy and wet, and every step of my boot is a noisy tussle with mud. I squish my way forward as quietly as I can, my head on a mad, swiveling lookout.

I finally find the guard flat on his back, his helmet askew, and his mouth hanging open. I'm surprised not to hear snoring. It is not uncommon for men to fall asleep during this forced "meditation" time and miss the train home. I crouch and shake him gently, speaking in my quietest voice. When he still doesn't budge, I shake him harder. I undo his helmet and push his goggles to his forehead, my gloved hands clumsy. It is Sergeant Major Lin, our newly promoted Sanitation Chief of the World Trade Center Tower. His eyes are still shut. I lean over his nose to listen for breaths, but hear only the pounding of my own heart.

I tear off my gloves and jab his neck with my fingers, but find no pulse. I unzip his fight suit and swear at his layers upon layers of long underwear. I pull up three shirts, untucking them from his underpants. A greasy, unwashed stench fills my nostrils when I put my ear against his heart. He is warm—his fight suit has made sure of it—but again I hear nothing. There is a strange purple circle on his skin just below his chest sensor, a bruise.

I struggle to recall the CPR ratio of chest pumps to breaths. I remember that I am supposed to call for help first. I press the emergency button on my field monitor. The medic takes so long to reply that I force myself to count aloud while I wait. When I reach thirty, I push the button again. I count another thirty seconds and decide to radio the captain of Battalion Three, to see if his emergency system is working. That's when I notice the mass of *X*'s around my former command post.

My breath stops. How did the People's Republic's soldiers cover the area so quickly? Including me, Middle Kingdom is down to four men.

I push the emergency and the radio buttons at the same time, crying out for help. I see another Middle Kingdom soldier crossed off the screen. Over the radio, I yell out again and again for my two remaining men to send for the medic. I tell them that I suspect that SGM Lin has had a heart attack.

I turn up my radio, tear off my helmet and goggles, and begin pumping Lin's chest. The snow has melted on his exposed skin, and he is cool and slick with moisture. I decide to give him two puffs of air after about twenty depressions, but he remains slack and unresponsive. After three rounds, I stop to check his pulse and his breathing. There is no response from him or from my men. I resume CPR, the snowflakes flying into my mouth and sticking to my lashes.

As I pump his chest, I remember that surrendering is an option, one I've never resorted to, but a good one under the circumstances. Surrendering opens all communication channels and restores mobility to all fight suits. If no one else, my men will surely come to their fallen comrade's rescue.

I locate the menu for surrendering on the monitor and hold down the flag icon. The result that flashes across my screen perplexes me. The final tally of men is Middle Kingdom 3 to the People's Republic 2. If I had held out, we would have won.

I click on the field map to see which of my two men possessed the godlike ability to take out the last eighteen opponents, but nothing makes sense. My closest man is two kilometers from Battalion Three. I bring up the kill count of the two men. Dashes flash where numbers should be.

I push the emergency button again. I dry Lin's face and chest with his shirt and go back to pumping his heart. I listen with all my might, unable to comprehend the silence. I keep working on Lin even though I suspect he is past saving. After another minute and no heartbeat, I take some deep breaths and put my gear back on.

I check my men's positions—the closest one is a kilometer away—and begin running downhill in his direction. The field monitor strapped to my middle bounces with my every step, and I secure it to my body with a hand. The wind has picked up, and the snowflakes stick to my face. Can storms disrupt radio signals? When my feet almost slide out from under me, I force myself to slow down. My cheeks are frozen, but I am hot and swampy beneath my suit. I push a gloved finger inside my goggles to wipe away the fog.

I check my target soldier's position again, afraid that he is outpacing me, afraid that I will spend all night chasing men anxious to leave the cold behind. I can hardly trust my memory when I note that his coordinates appear not to have changed. I wonder if the network is down, and then I remember that my surrender froze the final positions of all the remaining players.

I finally see a soldier on the ground. No one would choose to remain down after a battle is over, not on a freezing night. I approach the man. His nose is pressed into the snow, his helmet awry, his lower body twisted. I know he is dead before I turn him over. I remove the helmet and goggles. It is Old Tao, the dirty-joke master of our group. Jaw slack, he stares into the distance, glassy-eyed. I close his lids, brush the snow off his nose and mouth, and straighten his legs. His face is icy cold. I cannot find a pulse. I look for signs of injury, for bullet holes in his suit, for blood, but there is nothing. I can believe that Lin died of a heart attack, but Old Tao too? He is barely fifty. Or could it be hypothermia? I reach two fingers just beneath the zipper of his fight suit. It is toasty.

I put on his earpiece and increase the volume on both our radios. My own whistling sounds in my ear. There is nothing wrong with the communication channels. Icy needles prickle my spine.

"Lee Wei-guo, is that you?"

I nearly jump out of my skin. The high voice sounds familiar, and I turn to locate its source in the stand of conifers behind me. Between the shadowy trunks and arching boughs, a uniformed player takes shape as he walks hesitantly toward me. I can't identify the person behind the goggles and helmet, but I relax when I see the red Middle Kingdom patch on the man's breast pocket.

"It's me. I think Old Tao is dead," I say. Something glints around my teammate's waist. Is that a master field monitor? "And Sergeant Major Lin too." I'm the only person who is supposed to have a monitor on our team.

His gait does not quicken to my alarming news. "Yes. They are. They are all dead—because of you."

A red light deepens in color near his knees and then disappears. It looks like the tip of a police baton, a billy club the length of an arm. None of us is allowed to carry anything resembling a weapon, not even a stick. I rise slowly to my feet, afraid of making any sudden movements. "Who are you?" The laser pen the black guard from Heavenly Lake Station wielded on me—the sinister red light at its tip—springs to mind.

"I could have been your friend"—he starts to raise the baton— "but you'd rather I—"

That corny line again. Rage and panic course through me. Time seems to slow down as I leap, aiming the weight of my body at the man-child who tried to arrest me at Heavenly Lake. His high squeak of a voice still haunts me in my sleep.

He falls back with a bent knee, blocking me, and a whoosh of white heat from the baton just misses my ear. My chest lands on his kneecap, but I curl my chin at the last second and plow my helmet into his nose. Snow flies all around, and my entire body tingles and zings. He means to kill me. My chest heaves. I can barely catch my breath. I could have died a second ago. The boy groans and curses. His nose spurts blood. His knee pushes me off him, the ground a bed of ice.

The red of the baton arcs as the boy rolls away. It must be some sort of a voltage gun. I scuttle sideways on all fours and lunge. My tender ribs fall against the baton, my helmet and waist monitor crash against his, and I grunt, my chest, head, and neck throbbing. I grab the baton, wrapping my fingers tight around the thick stick at my first opportunity. Whoever controls the baton controls the other's fate. The boy's acned cheeks and nose are streaked with blood. He huffs and puffs as our four hands grapple for purchase, and I have to turn my nose, his breath sour and off-putting.

I push up onto the baton, pressing it hard into his chest. "How many have you killed tonight?"

"We'll have all two hundred as soon as I take care of you," he snickers through bloodstained teeth. "No one can save you this time."

His easy admission stuns and sickens me. "Why?" I cut my eyes at the handle, but the firing mechanism is hidden beneath his hand. "The men have done nothing. Why kill them?"

He sneers, his grip on the baton iron strong. "To punish you and your traitorous friends."

"Who sent you?" I edge the baton toward his collarbone, wanting more than anything to crush this killer's windpipe. He and whoever sent him deserve to die. Helmeted and goggled, he is the face of all the sick and bloodthirsty insects he works for.

"It doesn't matter. There's no one to blame but yourself."

The boy expels his breath with an animal growl. His blood splatters my mouth and my already foggy goggles. While I flinch and spit, he thrusts up his hips and flips me. I cling to the baton as my helmet bangs into the ground. Icy flakes singe my neck and jump under my collar and helmet. My head spins.

The boy slithers up my body, digging his knee viciously into my stomach. This time I'm the one who lifts his hips, bridging up onto my shoulders, forcing him to slide down my torso. Before he can anchor his feet, I roll and throw him off. His legs wrap around my waist and take me with him as he goes, neither of us relinquishing our hold on the baton.

This boy is an experienced street fighter, making up with quickness and grit what he lacks in heft. Despite my fitness and training, I am sorely lacking in hand-to-hand combat experience, the one discipline Strategic Games strictly forbids. So while I outweigh the boy, I flail about with increasing desperation.

It is not a pretty fight. But I suppose there's no such thing.

The ground beneath us is more muck now than snow. We wrestle and roll, our waist monitors catching and clacking, our uniforms slimed with mud.

Centimeter by centimeter, I fight to slide the baton up and across his throat. He struggles to aim the firing end up and at me. My arms shake with fatigue. It feels like he could tussle forever. I've always prided myself on my conditioning. I've made my livelihood as a prime example of male physicality. Supported my fathers with that strength. So the thought of letting exhaustion take me—no. My fathers will not bear losing a son. Just as important, I don't want to die. I have to kill him right now. I have to kill him before I tire and lose my size advantage.

They've fought dirty. I must too. I position my right knee.

"Please." I huff with fatigue even though I have him somewhat pinned beneath me. "I can't anymore. Please. I have a lot of savings. Dowry-size savings. I'll pay you to let me go. I don't want to die."

He sneers, but relaxes momentarily. It's all I need. I slam my helmet as hard as I can into his. My head ringing, I push up onto the baton and knee him ferociously in the groin. As he wheezes and curls into himself, I point the baton at him, rear back, and ram it into the side of his throat. He sputters and chokes, and I push to my knees and do it again. And again. I do it for the men he killed. I do it until his gasping mouth slackens. I do it until his neck and jaw are a pulp of bloody flesh and smashed shards of bone.

Panting, I sink back onto my heels and drop the baton. My hammering heart pounds at my ears. I fight to steady my heaving chest. I'm drenched. Feeling an incredible urge to break free, I throw off my helmet and night-vision goggles. The world becomes pitch-dark, the moon and stars obscured by storm clouds. My head is instantly chilled. Snowflakes blow into my cheeks and nose, their landing ticklish and then cold. I collect a handful of snow from the ground and rub it across my face and neck, cleansing myself of sweat, of grime, of blood, the icy shock of it sobering.

The wind whistles, and a new current of anxiety shoots through me. I struggle to pull on my goggles, my heart galloping again. I hurriedly wipe the lens with snow. Every tree and every boulder seem to harbor shadowy killers. I retrieve the baton. There are surely dozens more black guards out there. The baton handle seems molded to the hand, two trigger buttons beneath the thumb and index fingers. I wonder if both must be pushed at the same time—some sort of safety measure—for it to fire. At its end, a spot of red shines through a mess of coagulating blood and tissue. I wipe the baton on the ground all the while keeping my eye and ear out for more killers. I see my blood-splattered gloves and pull them off, my hands instantaneously cold.

What have I done?

I've got to get out of here.

I take deep breaths and try to think, the drumbeat of my heart unrelenting. It is no coincidence I ran into this particular black guard. He must have been tracking the GPS chip in my fight suit with his field monitor, relishing the opportunity to kill me himself. I realize that the other guards out there will only stop coming after me if they think I'm dead. I point the laser gun in my sleeve at my heart and shoot. My chest sensors buzz and vibrate, but the suit does not go rigid to simulate death. The game is over, after all. I've already surrendered. Still, if nothing else, I've created some misdirection. I power down my suit to stop it from broadcasting my location. I take more breaths and look around again to make sure that no one is coming.

I look down at my monitor. The screen is covered in gore, and I hastily rub it down with snow. Clean, all I see is a jumble of gray pixels. I push a few keys, and the shadows shift to form yet another unreadable puzzle. Was the device broken in the scuffle? It is water resistant, but I wonder if it was a mistake to rub it with so much snow. Then I remember I logged in on this monitor. It is also registered to me and trackable. My icy hands shaking, I unsnap its buckle and toss it at the boy.

I should have turned it off. I crawl over to do that and think: what if they mistake the boy for me?

I stuff the baton under my left armpit. Without looking at his oozing, half-maimed face, I push and coax him to his side—his rail-thin body seems to have acquired both weight and bulk in death—and unbuckle the strap of his monitor. Huffing and puffing, I tip him this way and that and replace it with mine. I power off his fight suit, unzip the blood-splattered top, feel around his inner pockets for his wallet, and pocket it. I consider leaving my ID on him, but no. I need it to get back on the train, plus replacing a lost ID is a nightmare. His gloves are even more blood soaked than mine. I strap on his monitor. Lastly, I have no choice but to crawl back over to my gloves and pull them back on, my icy fingers numb and near useless. My heart pounds in my ears as I push to my feet, half dizzy. A wave of nausea hits me.

I glance around again for more killers. I must start moving. I check the boy's field monitor: The score has not changed since I surrendered. It did not register my self-inflicted "death." I switch to the map function, identify the nearest border of our battleground and the closest town, and orient myself.

I survey my surroundings one last time to make certain I've not been discovered. I get ready to leave, but realize I need to do one last thing. I need to know how this weapon works. I aim the baton at the boy's middle and push the triggers with my thumbs. A streak of light shoots forth, not much different from the feel of the laser leaving my sleeve. And then there's nothing, no sense of heat, not even a small kickback. It's a weapon without consequence for its user. A weapon for cowards.

I take off running. I move as quickly and stealthily as I can through the dark night. I am less than two kilometers from the edge of our battleground—the edge, I hope and I pray, of direct danger. In a small clearing in the far distance, I notice three logs on the ground. Or are they soldiers beneath that dusting of snow? I know I should keep moving, escape while I still have the chance, but I cannot stop myself from witnessing what I must. I see the waffle tread of combat boots first. I bend over the men, one after another, strain to turn them over when needed. I dust off the snow to expose the faces of Min Wen-chien, of Liao Bann, and Jiang Ren-wei, three loyal but unremarkable soldiers, men who will not have family to remember them in ten years. I find no rips or blood on their uniforms. Shaking, I bow and pay my respect to each in turn. A wave of grief and outrage overwhelms me.

Do unmarried men like us matter so little that two hundred of us could be killed off just to send a message to the Safety Council without fear of consequences?

If I die tonight, if no game player makes it out alive, would anyone know what happened? Would people think that the opposing general and I made a foolhardy decision proceeding with the battle despite the storm? He and I would be blamed for two hundred deaths. It pains me to think of the sadness and burden such an unfolding of events would place upon my dads. I wish I had given them a chance to talk me out of tonight. I was most certainly foolhardy to come, preoccupied like a child intent on getting his thrills. I touch my watch to call them, but the thought of leaving them frantic and sick with fear stops me. They are everyday folks who get along by following the rules. They have no friends in high places, no special privileges. What could my seventy-year-old dads do?

What would they do when they learn that I've killed a man?

Hyperventilating again, I shake off that thought and force myself to dig through my mental file of friends, of friends of friends, of acquaintances near and far, and can only come up with XX. I don't want to trouble him right now, not when Hann is in crisis, but I am desperate. My realization that watches also have built-in locational capabilities sends a new surge of panic through me. Besides the battle equipment, did the government think to track the pocket computers, watches, and implanted body chips in the field? I quickly scroll through XX's contact options and select his voice line at work. XX is most likely not at the office at night, but CSS specializes in security. Surely it has built-in measures against government monitoring. XX's voice recording invites me to leave a message.

I'm in trouble, I say as I jog. I provide the awful details. I can barely get the words out to admit that I've killed the black guard from the Heavenly Lake Station, and I'm almost glad XX is not on the line. I tell him where I am, where I'm headed. If he is willing to help, I will have my watch turned on every quarter hour. I remind him to contact me from a secure device. Lastly, I ask that should I not make it, if May-ling would gently break the news to my fathers before allowing them to hear this message.

I power down my watch and realize I did not look at the time. Tom-toms in my ears again, I remember that the field monitor shows time. I note it and pick up the pace, running.

I run and run and run.

It feels like I've been on the run forever. The snow is coming down faster now, the wind whipping it into my cheeks. The air stings with every inhalation. The entire forest seems to resound with my gasping, the shush-shush-shush of my feet. I slap away the branches forever scratching and grabbing at my face. I am grateful for their cover even if the trees are barren of leaves, but each second within this maze deepens my sense of oppression, my claustrophobia. I want to hack open a clearing, rip myself free of my anvil-like suit, and throw off my stifling helmet and foggy goggles.

I run for an eternity and then an eternity more, leaning into the gusty wind. It seems the howling air is the only thing holding me up even as it threatens to topple me. When I am near certain that fifteen minutes have lapsed, I check my monitor. It has only been seven. I keep going, my lungs on the verge of collapse.

Finally, fifteen minutes pass, and I switch on my watch. It comes to life vibrating and buzzing. XX's jowly Buddha face materializes on my small screen, exuding the calm of that holy man. I thank him again and again for calling me back.

I grit my teeth and ask if he's willing to help me.

"You're one of my best friends," he says. "Of course I will help you."

My legs almost give out under me to hear his answer. I ask if his line is secure.

"Of course." He sounds insulted. "All my lines are. Hann's are too, but I don't tell him. He's not careful enough." He says to hold on, and the screen goes dark.

I curse, but give him a moment. What could be so important at a time like this? After a long minute, I call him back, but my watch is as dead as a brick. I curse some more as I touch the screen, push buttons in succession, and shake my arm. My lungs begin to wheeze when I realize that without my digital address book, I cannot get back in touch with XX.

I force myself to breathe, to settle down, to keep on moving. Not getting caught should be my only concern right now. I know where XX works. It'll be easy enough to contact him once I'm safe. I've almost talked myself back from the brink of hysteria when my watch begins to vibrate. I stare at the screen, afraid to believe in miracles, and there again is XX.

He says, "I contacted twenty-two people from your Middle Kingdom roster, and not a single person responded."

I speak in the most polite voice I can muster. "You put me on hold to make calls?"

"No," he replies. "I was wiping your watch clean. It's not safe for us to talk without assigning you a new signature."

"Oh." I am reminded again of the joy and exasperation that is XX. "Thank you."

"I've loaded your new address book with phony contacts. Cartoon and movie characters. I am Cujo. You are Lassie. Can you remember that?"

"Sure."

"Take off your uniform right now. You can't be identified with Strategic Games."

"Okay," I say, removing the field monitor before slipping the fight suit off my shoulders. I'm stunned XX doesn't question my story, that he has already checked it out. It takes just a few seconds for my damp undershirts to chill me to the core, but it is a relief to cede control for a moment, to have someone capable helping me.

XX reminds me to remove all identifying features. "Keep the goggles to see, but nothing else." He tells me to power down my suit and hide everything. I roll my helmet inside my uniform and stuff them inside a rotting log.

XX asks if I can photograph the baton from various angles with my watch, zoom in on model numbers if there are any, and send him the pictures right away. I do as I'm told and remind him of the dead boy's wallet and field monitor. He quizzes me on the monitor's capabilities and guides me through the process of uploading its data to his Cujo address.

"Leave the monitor turned on, and find a hiding place for it high up."

I tuck it into a tree hole.

"Open the wallet. Tell me the boy's name. I need to check him out."

Shivering with cold, I swallow and push down the rising bile. I tell XX the boy is—was—Lee Gwang. We share the same family name. I do the math and am flooded with a horrible sense of waste and alarm. How does a mere child, a sixteen-year-old, go so wrong? I find a State meal card, the sort issued to soldiers and orphans, people entitled to three government-paid meals a day. The boy is most likely both. A government adopted and trained killer.

XX tells me next to find or break off a dense tree branch, an evergreen if I can manage it, one long enough to touch the ground. I look around for something that fits the bill.

"Got it?" he says.

I tell him not yet. "There aren't any evergreens nearby."

"Find one yet?" XX asks again.

"Give me a second."

"You're announcing your location with the field monitor."

"Got it!" I grab the first dead branch on the ground and begin running, my heart again in my throat.

"Drag it behind to obscure your footprints."

I imagine my escape route spread out behind me, a glowing trail, and chide myself for not guarding against that. Running half turned while sweeping the branch madly over my tracks proves exhausting and slow. I do it for a few minutes before I give up and drag it in an all-out run. The wind bites and singes, and having lost the most protective layer of clothing, my entire body chatters with cold. I'm grateful to be on the move.

XX tells me to bring up the map in my watch. "I've programmed a flight plan for you. It'll guide you to a temple 1.7 kilometers away where I'll arrange for you to be picked up by a self-driving car."

I am flooded with gratitude. And awe.

He continues, "I want you to keep the baton for now for protection, but before you get into the car, you have to hide it somewhere. It could have a tracking chip on it. You must mark and send me its location, so we can go back for it later. Can you remember to do that?"

I tell him yes.

"I'll prepay the car from an untraceable source. It will be under Lee Gwang's name, so you must swipe his ID when you get in."

I thank him again and again and promise to pay him back.

XX says, "You can't go home tonight."

I had not thought beyond my immediate safety, and the gravity of my situation sinks in. I am a wanted criminal. A killer. I've never felt more isolated and lonely. XX asks if I have a place to hide for the next few days.

"I want to go home," I say. There is comfort in just saying the word "home."

"No," he says.

As I tick through my list of friends who live alone, the evening's losses become real. "I have no one," I say, forcing my legs to churn a little faster. I put May-ling out of my mind. How could I ask her to love a murderer?

XX absorbs my statement for a moment. "I'll meet you at Mao Memorial Hall."

14

HANN

A rough hand shakes Hann, rousing him from a restless sleep.

"Counselor Zhou wants to see you."

Hann finds the guard for his floor, a lanky giant of a man hovering over him praying mantis–like, his eyes bulgy and unmoving. Hann glances at the watch on his wrist—another manacle that cannot be unshackled at the end of the day unless he wants it stolen—before pulling his arm across his eyes to block out the overhead light. It is 8:49, and he has slept at best two hours. With five others in the same room snoring, farting, and getting up to pee, sleep is only possible in the hours after the bulk of them leave for work in the morning, so he sees no reason to get excited by the news that Confessor Zhou, as the men here call him, is ready to manhandle him.

"Get up." The guard thumps the frame of the bed with his foot. "He's waiting."

Hann pulls himself to sitting, and a dull ache grabs his ear. The room swirls, and he is momentarily nauseated. The guard seems behind a layer of opaque glass. Hann rubs his eyes and pats the pile of clothes at the foot of his bed for his pants. "I'll be out momentarily."

"Forget changing. Zhou's gonna make you pay for every second you make him wait," the guard says, his threat delivered as advice. The man backs up a few paces, his menacing form framed by the doorway, the crook of his lips suggestive and dangerous.

Frowning, Hann takes his time peeling off the sweats he lives in these days and stuffing himself into his least wrinkled shirt and pants. He's not going to be put at further disadvantage looking like a hobo. The guard runs his eyes down the length of him as he changes, and Hann wonders if creating sexually charged encounters is part of his duties. Hann says that he needs to void his bladder.

Still leering, the man gestures at the piss pot that Hann and his roommates are relegated to after the nightly lockdown. The bowl is nearly full, its cloudy contents and stink adding to Hann's queasiness. He spreads his legs wide and bends his knees to close the distance and minimize the splatter. This indignity is a mind game, yet another way to break him, and Hann ignores the eyes fastened to his penis. This idiot seems to believe that he can trick an erection out of Hann, that he is such an animal any male attention will ignite his loins. Hann stops just before the pot overflows, his urge to pee still tickling.

When Hann indicates that he is ready, the guard winks and holds his gaze seconds beyond what's comfortable. Edging ever closer even as Hann retreats, he leers out of the corner of an eye at Hann down the narrow staircase and all along the dim, serpentine corridors in the basement. Hann is dying to smooth his cowlick, to clean the corner of his eyes of crud, to make himself presentable for his meeting, but fears sending the wrong message.

Outside a closed door at the end of the hallway, the man stops. "Wait here." He backs away slowly, sex unmistakable in his eyes. "You know where to find me."

"Shouldn't we tell him that I'm here?"

"A closed door means he's not to be disturbed."

"Didn't you say he was waiting for me?"

"He's busy now," he says, lifting his eyebrows like a cartoon sex maniac. "Don't knock. He hates interruptions." He winks before sauntering away.

Hann sighs, straightens his shirt, and tucks it more carefully into his pants. His ear aches every time he moves his head. He needs to take his antibiotic after this meeting and change the bandage.

Just thinking about the upcoming session in this dank and hopeless space tightens his neck and shoulders. He shrugs, shakes his arms, and paces. He presses his ear to Zhou's office door but hears nothing. The next door down the hallway is metal and pad-locked. A furnace roars on the other side. Hann notes that he is not shivering. It must be ten degrees warmer in the basement.

He listens at the next door. A voice inside drones deep and sonorous, its cadence increasingly urgent and punishing. A wham jolts Hann upright. Hann checks Confessor Zhou's office before returning his ear to the door. A different voice, higher pitched and jagged, pleads. Its desperation pierces Hann's core and grates, and he steps back, afraid of losing the bravado he needs for his own session.

A loud snort comes from Zhou's direction. Hann edges closer, and machine gun–like snoring pommels his ear. He shakes his head and raps at the door. He bangs on it three times before it opens.

Hann's jaw drops, stunned by the angelic face in the doorway so contrary to the sloppy, old man he envisioned. Zhou—if this is indeed Zhou—possesses a delicate and fine beauty. He could put on a simple sack dress and turn heads as a woman.

"I'm sorry to disturb you," Hann says. The office behind the man is empty. "I've been out here for ten minutes."

"Why didn't you knock? I've been waiting for you." He cannot sound nicer.

Hann almost tells on the guard, but what's the point? He asks the man if he is Counselor Zhou.

"Yes, I am your counselor. I am your front-line advocate here." Zhou grasps Hann's hand warmly between his two.

Hann moves from the radiant compassion in the man's eyes to the gently lifted corners of his plump lips. The faint stubble on his chiseled jaw adds a mesmerizing yang to his yin. What kind of game are they playing here?

Inside Zhou's office, two red leather couch chairs lend the windowless space a comfortable and sophisticated feel. Black-and-white prints of majestic oaks and shapely pines grace the walls. Sinking into the plush chair almost eases away the sores in Hann's bony protrusions caused by his plywood bed. The unlikely room seems an oasis in this shit hole, and Hann reminds himself again to be wary.

Counselor Zhou drops tea leaves into the insert of a glass tea-pot and fills it from a sleek, stainless-steel hot water dispenser. He arranges the teapot and two glass mugs on a cloisonné tray, his every gesture as magnetic as his physical beauty. There's not a file or piece of paper in sight. This is more a living room than an office, every object here as beautiful and as well-made as its inhabitant.

"We'll let that steep a moment," Zhou says, setting the tray on the black leather footrest that doubles as a coffee table. He opens a drawer in the black credenza along the back wall and brings back a black leather box, one thickly stitched along its edges. He flips it open to reveal first-aid supplies. He stands in front of Hann and gestures at his ear. "May I?"

Hann nods, unsure what the man is playing at. He can't help flinching when Zhou touches his ear.

"Ssshhhh," Zhou says. "It's all right." With a gentle but sure touch, he peels away the bandage and gauze. The compassion and horror in his quiet gasp bring a rush of hot tears to Hann's eyes.

Zhou tips iodine tincture onto a cotton ball. "How are you holding up?"

Though he yearns to trust and confide in this man, Hann says nothing. He flinches again at the sting of the iodine and hisses.

"Barbarians," Zhou says under his breath. "I hate that you're letting them do this to you."

Hann hardens his expression, disappointed how quickly Zhou turns on him.

"There's no need for you to suffer."

"I've been wrongly accused," Hann says. It's time to begin his defense. "I'm heterosexual."

Zhou looks deep into his eyes, stares as if he possesses knowledge that can wrestle forth truth. "I want you to know that you and I are the same. I used to believe that being Willfully Sterile meant that I was a lesser person. Someone worthless and shameful." He squeezes ointment onto a finger and coats Hann's injured lobe front and back. "But that is not true. Our people add immeasurable value. What would the world be without psychologists like myself, without nurses, fashion designers, and executive assistants? And look at how successfully you've managed to cross over into finance. I've found peace and freedom in choosing not to hide, in embracing my true self. And in doing my work well, I've earned meaning and respect. I want the very same for you."

"I'm happy for you," Hann says. "But I like women. I have a wife. I've fathered a child. I am superb in my hetero profession because I am hetero." He would never see BeiBei again if he admitted to his sexual orientation.

Zhou secures a bandage to Hann's ear. "You should know that Chu Shin-ren was separated from his wife and children yesterday. He's told us about you. He's confessed to everything."

Hann's stomach twists, and to buy time, he asks for some tea. "I don't understand. What did he do?" He makes himself blow on the tea and sip it. His badminton group's most sacred rule is to never admit to their sexual orientation if caught, to never ever implicate one another.

"I can't help you if you won't help yourself." There's something about Zhou that makes Hann eager to please him. But that would be akin to a moth throwing itself into a flame.

"I haven't any dealings with Chu beyond our badminton club."

Zhou's forehead crinkles as if regarding a foolish child.

Hann says, "I know Chu as a worthy teammate, a prominent and successful businessman. That's all."

"Prominent and successful businessmen can be Willfully Sterile too," Zhou says.

"When was he detained?" Gossip travels faster than lightning in this building, and Hann has heard nothing about Chu.

Zhou tilts his head, a portrait of patience and understanding. "You can put all your suffering behind you right now."

"If you want to help me, to be my 'front-line advocate,' then help me convince them of the truth. I've already lost my job because of these false accusations. Don't make me lose my family too." Hann does not know how to interpret Zhou's congenial nodding. "Why isn't Chu here?"

"Men who have examined and taken responsibility for their actions have no need to spend time here."

Hann always knew that if caught, he would be alone in his fight, but he didn't think Chu would betray him and so quickly. But does one really know anybody? Chu, after all, slept with Jimmy and carried on with a string of men outside their group.

Zhou leans in, his smile quiet and supportive. "You know I'm not allowed to divulge details from Chu's case, but just between you and me, I would not trust that man. He's not like us."

Hann pulls back and frowns.

"Don't get me wrong: Chu is Willfully Sterile. But he doesn't care about anyone but himself. The first thing he did after confessing was to kick his lover boy to the curb. His kind of wealth buys him a set of rules you and I cannot begin to imagine."

Hann could scarcely breathe. "Chu is a badminton teammate and friend. Nothing more."

Zhou will not stop smiling, and Hann sees in him a cartoon cat just before it swallows a bird. "You need to think of yours as a criminal case, of me as your defense attorney. I may be paid by the State, but your welfare is my only concern. Chu has provided enough evidence for the government to prosecute you. Your confession will not be necessary. If you choose to come clean right now and repent, however, I may be able to convince them to lighten your sentence. I cannot urge you more strongly to take advantage of this opportunity. I would like to see you move on to the next phase of your life on your own terms."

Only an idiot and a highly desperate one would believe that self-determination is still possible, but Zhou tells his lie with beautiful concern and conviction. If Chu had in fact sacrificed Hann for his own benefit, then Hann's confession would be the bullet that finishes him off.

He inhales the jasmine tea deliberately, swallows a mouthful, and stands. "You've been kind, and I thank you for that and for this tea."

Zhou rises too, his brow crinkled with worry. Hann almost regrets disappointing him. "Think this over, but do it quickly. You haven't much time left."

Hann forces his face into a semblance of a smile. "I have nothing to confess."

"I've come on too strong." Zhou grabs Hann's elbow. "Please forgive me. Please don't go yet. Let's sit, relax, and do something else. Let's play a game together. You have another twenty minutes before my next appointment."

All Hann has done since he arrived is to scheme and play their deadly games.

Zhou blocks the door, his grasp urgent and unrelenting. "I have the perfect one. It's called *The Pursuit of Happiness*. It's designed to help you discover your personal version of happiness."

The mention of the mind-reading game Xiong-xin brought home recently—the game that reached into the most vulnerable part of May-ling's mind and left her sobbing and erratic—knocks the breath out of Hann. His earlier nausea returns. For decades he has kept his secret from all but a few, but he will not be able to defend himself against this.

"My ear is throbbing." Hann groans and dry heaves. "I feel really queasy. Would you mind if we played the game another time?" He cradles his bandaged ear for effect.

Zhou says, "I wish you'd talk to me. I so very much want to help you."

"You know how to help me." Hann pushes the door gently against Zhou to force a way out.

Zhou's hand moves to Hann's chest. "Promise me that you'll let me help you next time. You won't be alone. I will personally shepherd you to the other side. And beyond."

Barely able to control his quivering self, Hann turns sideways and squeezes through the door opening, eager to be free of Zhou, of his agitating touch and his beatific smile. In Zhou, the government has unleashed a formidable and treacherous weapon. The cruelty and intimidation of ear-chipping are child's play compared to this psychological warfare, this fake seduction, this betrayal disguised as concern from one of his own kind.

Hann stumbles up the basement stairs and out the building's door. He gulps the fresh air and takes in the open but smoggy sky as he hurries away. Yet the sense of expansiveness and ease will not come, not with that monitoring manacle clamped onto his ankle. His urge to contact Chu is immense. The knowledge that the government has more to gain by allowing Hann to roam free and incriminate himself adds to his claustrophobia.

He forces himself to move, to put one foot in front of the other, but the truth is he has nowhere to go—no home, no job, no emotional shelter. Regret permeates his entire being. He regrets shocking and disappointing May-ling, not being the honest, upstanding man she had believed him to be for so long. He regrets forcing so much responsibility onto XX, regrets subjecting his family to this ordeal, regrets even more the effect his absence will have on Bei-Bei. He regrets getting involved with Chu, placing trust in a man not to be trusted. But most of all, he realizes he regrets getting caught.

There was a time long ago when he regretted his sexual orientation, but no more. He has met too many like himself in his six decades on this Earth. Like Hann, they were born the way they were born, and there is nothing wrong with any of them—even Zhou pointed that out. So many of them contributed so much to society. What's wrong is the government that refuses to treat them as full-fledged human beings.

Yet Hann can't put aside the suspicion that Zhou is right about one thing: short of a miracle, Hann's conviction is an inevitability. The longer he insists upon his innocence, the longer he endures this limbo. If he is still here at the thirty-day mark, the government begins to charge rent. Should he still be unemployed, a job will be assigned regardless of his ability to pay the rent. All of Hann's five roommates—an architect, a doctor, a schoolteacher, and two businessmen—wake every morning at six and spend the next ten hours cleaning the city's parks and latrines. The idea of giving up family and fatherhood, five years of income, and whatever else the government deems fit for his crime is near unthinkable.

Hann turns onto Fucheng Road, the boulevard that leads to Xiong-xin's office. Hann has been making the hour-plus trek daily to meet his brother for lunch. It is a tremendous relief to keep moving, to have a purpose to his day.

Hann's watch buzzes. May-ling appears. The sadness that defines her every feature wrenches his heart. It is just after ten—park time for BeiBei. Because of Hann's curfew, the impossible babysitting logistics at home, and the mandatory seventy-five-meter communication buffer around BeiBei, he and May-ling have communicated solely through notes hand-carried by Xiong-xin. Assuring himself that May-ling understands the rules, he answers her call.

"Hello, sweet pea," he says. "How have you been? It's such a joy for me to see you."

"Hann." May-ling covers her mouth and cries quietly. Her despair hits him hard.

"I'm so, so sorry. I hope you know how sorry I feel." Hann waits, desperate for her words of forgiveness, but nothing comes. "Where's BeiBei? Who's watching him?"

May-ling wipes her tears and sniffles. "He's running around the track. We have to talk fast."

"How is he? Are you all right?"

Her tears start again. "I don't want to burden you more, but I don't know what to do, where else to turn. I should be asking about you, and here I am crying again. How's your ear?"

"It's fine. Please tell me what's wrong."

"It's Xiong-xin. I think he's gone crazy. He's adopted a wild dog—an injured one—and keeps it in his bedroom. When he's at work, it charges at his door and barks nonstop. And at night too. BeiBei and I are terrified. The neighbors are furious. And he calls the dog MaMa."

"What?" He needs to apologize again more thoroughly.

"And yesterday in the middle of the night, he woke me up saying he's going to rescue a friend. I asked which friend—you know he doesn't have any friends—and he yelled, 'Quiet, woman!' at me. He took the dog, and he hasn't come back. He won't answer my calls. Do you know what's going on?"

Hann says he'll get hold of Xiong-xin right away. "Don't worry, okay? I'll take care of him."

"How're you going to let me know?"

Hann thinks a moment. Without Xiong-xin as middleman, communication between them is near impossible. "Worst case, I'll have Wei-guo message you." He says there's something else May-ling should know.

"Hurry. BeiBei is running in my direction."

"Did Xiong-xin tell you that Wei-guo took me to the doctor and stayed with me until I was all right? That same afternoon, he proposed a true-love union."

May-ling says, "We need his dowry to help pay your fines."

"There aren't going to be any fines. We're going to beat this," Hann says. She needs to have hope, even if he doesn't. "And you're not getting married again to pay my fines."

"I have to hang up. Bye—"

"Love you." The line goes dead. "I'm sorry I ruined your life," Hann murmurs. It is not lost on him that he yearns more than anything to be back in the cocoon of their bed with her and their child, snuggling.

H ann calls and messages Xiong-xin, but he does not answer. He tries his brother's manager next. Fung says that XX has taken the day off to attend to personal business. Hann stiffens: Xiong-xin was scheduled to deliver Hann's letter to Chu later today. Could Chu be the friend Xiong-xin went to rescue last night?

After three more attempts by Hann, Xiong-xin finally messages back. **Can't talk now.**

Hann dictates, **Emergency. Call me right away.**

He leaves the street for a secluded alley and waits. His watch finally buzzes. "Where are you?"

"Later," Xiong-xin says. "What happened?"

"I'll tell you over lunch. Where can we meet?"

"I can't meet today."

"Why not?"

"Later."

"No," Hann says. "We meet, or you tell me now."

Xiong-xin is quiet for a moment. "I can't, but don't worry about your case. I'm working on it." Prior to Hann's arrest, his brother would not have defied him so pointedly.

"My friend is busy this evening. Did you already give him my present?" Hann hopes Xiong-xin understands his cryptic statement.

"Good. I don't have time for that today."

"So you didn't deliver it?" Hann says.

"Why would I?" Being the man of the house seems to have gone to Xiong-xin's head.

Hann decides to move on. "I know you've wanted a dog for a long time. I'm sorry I didn't let you have one, but you can't bring a wild animal into the apartment. It's not safe, and with everything going on right now, it's the worst possible time to be doing something like that."

"I don't have a dog."

Hann has never thought Xiong-xin capable of outright lying. "May-ling called me this morning, beyond frantic."

"I already gave it away."

"Are you telling me the truth?"

"Yes."

"Is that where you went last night? To get rid of the dog?"

"I didn't get rid of the dog. I found it a new owner."

Hann takes a breath. "We're brothers, XX. I may get mad from time to time, but you know you can tell me anything."

"Yes, I know."

"Why do you call the dog MaMa?"

"Because that's her name."

"But why name her that?"

"Because she's nice like a mom."

Hann sighs, cognizant of the part he is playing in his brother's crack-up. "I miss her too."

"How can you miss my dog?"

"No. MaMa." What Hann wouldn't give for his brother to have some sense. He softens his tone. "I wish she were here to help me too. But then again, I'm grateful she never lived to see this week."

"Uh, Hann," Xiong-xin says, "I have to go."

Hann tells his brother to call after he settles the dog. "I'm proud of you for finding it a more suitable home." Xiong-xin has already hung up.

Again, Hann forces himself to place one foot in front of the other. Hann has always placed Xiong-xin's welfare foremost in his heart. He thought he could count on his brother to champion his case, yet less than a week after Hann's forcible separation, a stray dog has usurped his place in Xiong-xin's heart.

Hann wanders the boulevards of his city, hoping that their stately and straightforward beauty will clear his head and help forge a path forward. His eyes return again and again to the meager tremblings of color remaining on the trees, to the gold, orange, and red still clinging to life. It takes little more than a passing bus to jar the leaves loose and send them whirling to a bruised and shattered death beneath spinning wheels and passing feet.

Hann approaches the city's central business district and his former office building. It saddens and angers him that his thirty-five years of exemplary service came to so little. He wishes he had never been awarded company housing. More than anything, it was Dunn's interference that brought on Chang's attention. Desperate to confirm Chu's betrayal, Hann wonders if Dunn would be willing to get his hands dirty again on Hann's behalf. The ablest of his firm's three leaders, Dunn has often felt like an ally, someone who has looked out for Hann's interests from a safe remove. Hann possesses no evidence to the fact, but more than once, he has had the intimation that he and Dunn are alike in ways neither cares to acknowledge.

The noon hour approaches, and Hann joins the growing throng of office workers on the street. Calling or messaging Dunn for an appointment would give the man a chance to turn him down. Hann pats his shirt pocket, feeling for his notepad, and quickens his steps. He will compose his request while he waits for Dunn to go to lunch.

He perches on a planter a distance away with an oblique view of the front entrance. On paper, he lays down the facts for Dunn: a street hustler is rumored to have implicated him and Chu, and Hann needs help confirming if Chu has in turn betrayed Hann. He poses his request without drippy emotions. If there is indeed rapport between him and Dunn, it was built over the last two decades. Either the man is willing to help, or he is not. Hann has too much pride to force the issue.

The building's revolving glass door spits out men who emerge singly and then form into clusters. He was one of them just a few days ago. Shame overwhelms him whenever Hann spots a familiar face. Wishing he had a hat or even a pair of sunglasses, he turns his back from time to time so as not to be recognized. He brushes the lint from his pants, ashamed again that he left his room this morning in an unwashed hurry. His urge for concealment brings back the memory of Wei-guo lurking at this very corner waiting for him. He never imagined that he would look back upon that spying with fondness.

When Dunn appears, Hann pulls back his shoulder and edges into his path. Dunn's footsteps slow when their eyes meet, and Hann decides to let the man come to him. Or not. He is gratified when his former boss advances without further hesitation. Hann never tires of watching the grace with which Dunn moves, the intelligence behind his eyes. Those same eyes sweep over the bulge of ankle monitor at Hann's feet, his wrinkled shirt, his absent coat, and his bandaged ear before resting on Hann's face.

Dunn reaches out to shake his hand, but his touch is light. Cautious. "I was sorry Chang let you go. I hope you are well."

"I'm all right." Out of politeness, he asks after Dunn. His question brings into focus the sagging web of lines around the man's eyes and the dark pouches beneath. Hann does not remember Dunn looking so old, so downcast. Is time away and distance allowing him to see people anew?

Dunn says, "I'm on my way home."

The reply feels like a brushoff. Hann forces himself to remain polite, to ask if anything was the matter. Dunn will not witness his collapse and be subjected to begging.

"My son didn't come home last night." Dunn explains that his boy played war games. "My wife just learned that his buddy fell asleep on the field and froze to death."

Dunn's handsome features crumble, and Hann quickly reassures him, speculating that his son most likely got held up and forgot to call. He asks if the electrical engineer is the child in question. The son by the second husband is still in school. Dunn confirms that it is indeed his flesh and blood who is missing.

Hann says, "A friend of mine is the general of Middle Kingdom."

"My son's team fought Middle Kingdom last night."

"Perfect." Hann collects the pertinent information from Dunn and calls Wei-guo on the spot. He encourages Dunn not to worry as the line rings and rings, but strangely fails to switch over to voicemail. Hann dictates a text and sends that off instead. He promises Dunn to be in touch the second he receives a reply.

"You'd better get going," Hann says. "Your wife needs you." Dunn appears so haggard that Hann decides to say nothing about his own problems. Dunn has no bandwidth for anything else at the moment. Hann will have another chance at him soon.

Dunn squeezes his hand and thanks him. He turns to leave, but hesitates. "Were you here to see me just now?"

Hann says he can wait and urges the man homeward. If Bei-Bei were lost, he would want nothing to stand in the way of him finding his child.

15

XX

X's toes and fingers are icicles, his teeth and body looped in chattering shivers. Since Chairman Mao Memorial Hall's 08:00:00 opening, he, Wei-guo, and MaMa Dog have waited under the portico near its service entrance, shifting with the meager December rays, for eight hours, thirteen minutes, and twenty-one seconds. 8, 13, 21—the serendipitous appearance of the seventh, eighth, and ninth Fibonacci numbers tickles XX's brain. He rocks in place and wiggles his toes as his mental abacus clicks toward the subsequent figures in the sequence. He reaches the eighteenth—1,597—and feels soothed for the first time since Wei-guo arrived in the hired car with soppy long johns, a bluish face, and a mouth twisted by howling. Waiting for hours in the blindingly white slush-covered landscape with an inconsolable Wei-guo has made XX claustrophobic.

. . . 2,584, 4,181, 6,765. Wei-guo's snores jolt him back to the present. XX examines his best buddy on the ground next to him, his arms around his knees and back against the building's exterior wall, head lolling. Wrapped and hooded in four layers of Hann's clothing, Wei-guo resembles a cartoon Eskimo the way his teeth clatter in his sleep. XX relishes having Wei-guo to himself, but this opportunity to be his hero is not quite working out. Instead of following XX's directions, his friend raves and cries and refuses to listen. Even May-ling at her worst does not act like this. XX hopes he doesn't wake up before their meeting with Madam Mao.

XX pats MaMa Dog on the head. If not for the dog, they could be waiting inside the mausoleum for Madam Mao. That, of course, is not her real name, but a title of respect from her following, one she earned by proclaiming Chairman Mao her personal hero and savior. Representing discarded foreign wives like herself who refused to marry new husbands but have no home to return to overseas, Madam Mao eased the burgeoning unrest some years ago by proposing that they take a pledge to Mao in the manner of nuns and become live-in caretakers of his final resting place. Her good heart and pragmatic approach endeared her to wives foreign and domestic and to many who felt oppressed. Mao's Mausoleum became a sanctuary, one whose protection could only be gained through a personal interview with the woman herself. XX likes that it is predominantly a refuge for women and not a hiding place that comes to mind for a war games soldier.

Just around the corner, five nuns advance toward them in a gray line, their shorn heads in woolen caps, their bodies in padded Mao suits, and their brooms sweeping at nothing. From what XX can tell, they travel in fives, and there are many more of them than work to be done. This is their fourth turn around the exterior since XX arrived.

XX and Wei-guo have already cajoled, pleaded, and even bribed (meat buns) these five gaunt women for an audience with

Madam Mao, but have received only bows in return. XX combed microblogs, hacked into invitation-only confabs and underground forums for hours last night, trying to locate Madam Mao's procedures for seeking asylum. He found precious few details, just reassurances and wonderment at how she always comes to the aid of those who have demonstrated neediness, heart, and faith. XX has interpreted that to mean a willingness to wait and a belief in Mao and his teachings. It was while he was telling Wei-guo everything about the Chairman that Wei-guo nodded off.

XX rolls to his knees and from all fours, pushes and huffs himself to standing. MaMa Dog hobbles after him, and he shortens her leash to maintain control. He faces the alpha, the tall nun with the buckteeth, and bows with hands clasped before his heart in imitation of their greeting. Her darker coloring and large round eyes suggest a Southeast Asian origin, Indonesia perhaps.

"Long live Madam Mao," XX says, hoping to elicit a favorable reaction with this anachronism.

With brooms between their palms, the nuns return his bow in unison.

"Please, will Madam Mao please see us now? Many lives are at stake." Only Wei-guo's life is at stake, and XX's eyes blink as he insists on this falsehood.

The women bow again. The nuns have yet to speak, but none of XX's research indicates that they've taken oaths of silence.

"Sisters," Wei-guo says, awake and struggling to his feet. "We can't wait any longer. The evidence is deteriorating, and two hundred deaths need avenging."

XX's heart claws at his throat. He hisses at Wei-guo to hush, to stop violating their agreement to confide only in Madam Mao. Glancing around, XX is relieved to find no passersby or onlookers within earshot.

Wei-guo elbows XX aside. "My name is Lee Wei-guo. I am

the general of one of the two Strategic Games armies massacred at Cloud Fog Forest Mountain Park last night."

XX tugs on Wei-guo to make him stop. The hatred with which Wei-guo bats and shoves away his hand starts MaMa Dog barking, circling, and cinching the leash around their legs.

XX grabs Wei-guo to stop himself from toppling. He tells the nuns that they must speak directly to Madam Mao. "It is dangerous for you to know this, dangerous for us to tell you."

The tall nun flinches. She angrily waves her companions back to work.

Wei-guo untangles himself and shakes XX off. "We have proof that the government murdered two hundred innocent men."

Brooms whooshing in synchrony, the wall of women glides away.

Wei-guo turns to XX. "Send me the field data. I want it right now."

"What for?"

"Those women don't care. I'm going to give it to my soldiers' families. Plaster it on the web. People need to know. The government must pay for what it did."

"No," XX says. "You'll get yourself killed."

"That data belongs to me."

"No, it doesn't," XX roars, fists clenched.

XX pushes past Wei-guo. He has to bargain and pester these women. Persistent bargaining always worked with dictatorial Hann. "I am a security expert." He trails the women, his impressive, two-paneled business card between his outstretched hands. "For housing and protecting my friend, I will install all the equipment needed to fortify your premises."

The tall nun stops. Her eyes blaze as they scour him up and down. She takes his card by two fingers and studies it. Finally, she tells them to follow her. XX cannot believe it: these do-gooders were waiting for compensation.

She heads down the steps surrounding the building and away from the memorial hall. XX, Wei-guo, and MaMa Dog scurry along behind her. The four remaining nuns bring up the rear. They squish across the slushy plaza toward the boulevard.

They approach a bus stop, and XX panics. "We will not be escorted off the grounds!"

The lead nun widens her stride and marches on. When the other nuns skirt around XX and Wei-guo as easily as a stream around pebbles, they have little choice but to keep up. She stops a distance away from the bus stop and its dozen people. The nuns form a circle around the men.

"Who seeks asylum?" the head nun asks. Her Chinese is remarkably serviceable. Most foreign wives have a hard time reproducing the tones.

"Me," Wei-guo says.

XX grunts with relief. He adds, "The dog too."

"Dog!"

XX says he'd like MaMa Dog to stay with Wei-guo. "She will protect him and your sisters too."

The nun yells at him with her eyes for more uncomfortable seconds. "Why is it limping?"

"She wandered out without her collar and was mistaken for a stray." XX wiggles his itchy nose. "She's of legal size."

The tall nun glowers as if she sees through his lie. She inclines her head toward the bus line. "You leave now."

"Has Madam Mao accepted him?" XX whispers. The whole bus line is looking at them.

"Your friend let you know."

XX is afraid that if he leaves, Wei-guo will admit to the killing and tell her all of their secrets. XX stresses that Wei-guo is not seeking permanent shelter. "I must explain this to Madam Mao myself."

"For safety of everyone here, of everyone coming, entry is secret." She reiterates that XX must leave immediately.

"No." XX crosses his arms and shakes his head.

The head nun too crosses her arms. She starts a staring contest. XX bugs out his eyes and counts in order to maintain eye contact and demonstrate his sincerity. It takes thirteen excruciating seconds before she finally relents and asks them to wait. She pulls up her sleeve and walks a distance away to speak into her watch. XX's estimation of her and of Madam Mao skyrockets when he sees that the nuns rely on the same obscure, high-performance model as he does.

Upon returning, she orders them again to follow her. They enter a hip-high stand of junipers. Within the green, snow-dusted spires are recently swept steps leading into the earth. A covered space the size of a small bus shelter appears at the bottom.

MaMa Dog whines at the top of the narrow steps, and with Wei-guo's help, XX drags her down by the leash. There is a rusted metal door, but the head nun insists that they face a dark corner on the opposite end. XX looks back up the stairs, and the other four women are gone.

The nun tells Wei-guo that Madam Mao is listening. "Make your case."

"She's not going to meet us?" As XX squints to locate the camera in the dim corner of the ceiling, his opinion of Madam Mao rises again though he finds her grossly impolite, even if she is a master-mind. He is never permitted to behave this way.

"We already make special allowance for you."

Wei-guo squeezes his arm painfully. "We appreciate that very much."

The nun urges someone to start talking. Wei-guo introduces himself, stating his name, occupation, and involvement with Strategic Games. He begins well enough with the faulty weather forecast and the unexpected snowfall, but goes into mind-numbing detail recounting his decision not to overrule the computer and continue the games despite the weather. By the time he arrives at the high casualty count, the strange circumstances of the killings, and the reports of zombie soldiers, his voice is shaky and his breath ragged. He is on his way to another awful breakdown. XX begins to pace, the pit of his stomach itchy. Her back hunched and her tail tucked, even MaMa Dog is anxious.

XX is right. Wei-guo is a crying, hiccupping, and angry mess when he tells of finding his men cold and dead on the ground. XX can barely make out his words. Madam Mao cannot possibly understand him.

XX states his name, occupation, and expertise for Madam Mao. "Lee Wei-guo is my best friend, and I will do everything I can to save him." He decides that it is okay not to explain their situation. People always think they know what's best for you, and he does not want to be talked out of Wei-guo's marriage or his divorce.

"Please know three facts. One: Twenty-six hours of weather reports were faked. Reports to the generals before and during the battle underestimated the snowfall. Reports to the public afterwards exaggerated it. I have proof.

"Two: Yesterday's snow was not heavy enough to close down the areas around the battlefield. Power was manually shut down. Highway and railroad cameras all show that little effort was made to clear the snow. I have proof." He hopes that Madam Mao finds this information convincing, because sharing the truly damning field data will jeopardize his larger plans.

"And finally: Our government values its 'Bounty' even less than discarded wives like yourself. It dares to commit murder. The news will confirm the deaths." Proud of building common ground, XX glances away from the camera's unfeeling lens to the leader nun only to shrink from her glare.

He blinks and presses on. "The government is building a scenario for deniability. I guarantee you that by tomorrow, the near two hundred deaths will be blamed on Lee Wei-guo and the opposing general and their bad judgment.

"This was a planned massacre. Lee Wei-guo witnessed it. He will be a dead man if they find him. He needs your protection."

Proud of his concise and fact-supported speech, XX finishes with a deep bow to the camera. It's so nice to hit every point in his argument without interruption. Next to him, Wei-guo sniffles, having thankfully regained some self-control.

The nun stares at her watch. When she looks up, her brow is pinched. Angry. "You telling us Lee Wei-guo be target of government hunt. You want Madam Mao risk good name, risk good everything for you?"

XX nods. "That's your mission."

"We save women with no home. No choice. Not men with job and money who play game."

"But everyone says Madam Mao is a protector of the weak and the oppressed."

"I know no everyone," the nun says, hands on hips, ready to peck at him like a nasty hen. Did XX so grossly misunderstand Madam Mao?

"Two hundred men have been killed for no reason. I'm the only one left who can bear witness. I am the only one left who can find these men justice," Wei-guo growls.

The nun says, "Why they want to kill all of you?"

"I know it makes no human sense," Wei-guo says. "But one of the killers admitted to me with great, great relish that my men were killed as punishment for my actions and the actions of the Safety Council. We were ordered to identify five percent of our players as mentally unstable. We could not do it. We organized a boycott of those orders instead. And like my friend XX just observed, there is no population our government finds more dispensable—or more threatening, as it appears—than excess males."

XX reiterates that Wei-guo's need for asylum is temporary, that he will install the latest security measures in exchange. "My company bills me out at a thousand yuan an hour, and my company only serves China-100 clients."

"More security is not food. Is not clothes."

"Two hundred people are dead, and Madam Mao wants money?" Wei-guo says, loud and mad.

The nun says, "Madam Mao investigating you now. I be practical."

"Does my acceptance depend upon a gift?"

The nun cracks a treacherous smile. "Of course no."

"All right then," Wei-guo says. "I agree to a contribution."

XX wishes she would stop it with the long and mean stares. "So, is he in?"

The nun continues to regard Wei-guo.

"XX will explain the situation to my fathers. Only they can decide how much we are able to give."

She stares at him some more. After consulting her watch, she walks to the door on the far end of the landing and holds it to the lock, unlatching it. Inside, a light clicks on, illuminating rough shelves filled with shovels, dustpans, sacks of sand. As they squeeze into the small maintenance shed, a cot, a chamber pot, and an electric cooking pot come into view.

"Comrade Lee and dog stay here tonight." She fiddles with a metal box on the cement floor. Warm air begins to whoosh and fill the room.

Her polite address floods XX with relief. Lifting the pot lid, he discovers rice gruel simmering. They were going to accept Wei-guo all along. XX's instincts were right. This was the place to bring Wei-guo.

May-ling stops at the ninth-floor stair landing, rests BeiBei's bottom against the windowsill, and shakes out her arms. XX keeps a distance away and watches her out of the corner of an eye. Every step up these stairs seems to make her angrier, and he is afraid she is about to explode any second. Hann's arrest has left her jagged, teary, and tyrannical, so her stern composure in the face of Wei-guo's news surprises him. She must still love Hann more.

May-ling tells XX to go ahead, that she'll catch up. More out of breath than she, he too takes a break and bends over, his hands on his thighs. Blood pounds in his neck and against his forehead. He is drowned in sweat and vaguely nauseated, and the financial circumstances of a family that must inhabit this shabby, elevator-less high-rise sink in. No wonder Wei-guo's fathers cannot hold on to a look of prosperous old age. If each man is sixty kilos and the trip takes fifteen minutes, XX calculates that each trip up these nineteen flights costs nearly one hundred calories.

"BeiBei walk, okay?" May-ling touches one of the boy's feet to the floor. "BeiBei is such a good boy."

"Noooooo!" He immediately begins to cry and claw his way up her legs.

Hann would have helped carry the child, but the thought of the shrieking and snot-snorting brat centimeters from his ears makes XX's insides itch. May-ling hoists BeiBei back onto her hip, sighs, and continues up the stairs. The boy is especially cranky at bedtime, and putting him in XX's arms right now would be like holding a flaming match to gasoline.

He trudges after her. "Don't forget," he says. "Not a word until I check out their entire apartment."

"You told me that already," says May-ling.

"Hann's future is at stake. Wei-guo's too."

"I know."

XX knows that she knows, but May-ling has been so unpredictable as of late. She looks frightful too with her tangled hair, mudstained shirt, and puffy eyes. He would not have brought her, and in turn BeiBei, if Wei-guo did not specifically ask that May-ling be the one to break the news to his fathers.

She is snippy right now and will blow her top if he doesn't think up a way to ease her load. They make it up three more flights before she stops again to rest. He knows from observing Wei-guo that the best way to control the child is to make everything a game.

"BeiBei," he says. When the kid doesn't respond, XX pokes his back and calls his name again. He lays his head on May-ling's shoulder and tightens his arms around her neck. "I bet I can reach the nineteenth floor before you. I bet I run faster than you."

"I run faster."

"No, you don't."

"I run faster," he whines into his mother's ear. His feet drum her stomach. "I run faster."

"You are my fastest little boy," says May-ling, shooting XX a wicked look.

XX says, "Let's race."

May-ling mouths for him to stop it. He whispers back that he's going to let BeiBei win. Again, she tells him to stop.

"Don't you want to see Uncle Wei-guo's home?"

BeiBei turns to XX and stops kicking. His fingers squeak in and out of his mouth as he considers the question.

May-ling gets in BeiBei's face and tells him Uncle Wei-guo is not home right now. Twice.

"But maybe Uncle's daddies will give you a treat for being the fastest," XX says.

The mention of treats sends BeiBei twisting for the ground and May-ling throwing her arms up at XX. You would not have guessed the kid is tired the way he scampers up the stairs.

May-ling sidesteps XX to run after the boy. "What if they have no treats?"

XX holds up the box of cookies they brought as a gift. That's another reason he and she should not stay married: he will never understand her. "Did you want to carry him up seven more floors?"

In front of Wei-guo's apartment, he finds May-ling on her knees. "BeiBei got here first. BeiBei wins." She breaks open a packet of broken crackers from the bottom of her purse and tries to convince him they are a treat.

No dummy, BeiBei pushes out his lip, ready to fuss.

"Do you want to ring the doorbell, BeiBei?" For once, XX makes use of the fact that the kid has the attention span of a gnat.

"Ready?" he asks May-ling while BeiBei pounds on the button.

XX has to plug his ears against the doorbell's screech—the walls here are made of the cheapest materials—and when Wei-guo's big dad opens the door, XX still has not affixed his note to the box of cookies.

The man's scowl feels like a stomach punch. "What are you doing here?" BeiBei will not let up on the doorbell, and he scowls at the kid next.

Wei-guo's other dad peeks out of the door, his smile lifesaving. "You brought your little one!" He gets one good look at May-ling— she insisted that no one cared about her hair or clothes at a time like this—and the smile petrifies. "What's wrong?"

"It's good to see you, Big Uncle and Little Uncle," May-ling says as she maneuvers BeiBei toward the two men. "Come meet Uncle Wei-guo's babas."

BeiBei turns shy at the strangers' attention and clings to his mother. XX takes the opportunity to square up his note to the striped wrapping paper on the box and tape it down with his pocket tape dispenser.

"Why are you here?" The big dad stares rudely at his old-fashioned watch.

"I know it's nine fifty-four." XX pushes the gift at the big dad and taps his note, urging them to read.

After one glance at the first sentences—*Do not say a word. Weiguo is alive and not hurt. We're hiding him at a safe location.*—the frown on the big dad intensifies.

The little dad steadies himself against the doorframe. "What happened? Did he do something wrong?"

XX shushes this man who cannot follow instructions and drags his finger down the length of the note to remind him to continue reading. XX's going to have to watch him.

The big dad swings the door open to let them inside. May-ling stops to remove BeiBei's and her shoes, but XX cannot be bothered, not when there is so much to do. Four steps into the apartment, and his path is stopped by a rectangular table for six, half of which is piled high with wadded trousers, shirts, and boxers. Protected by a mesh dome, a plate of ham-and-egg fried rice—Wei-guo's dinner most likely—occupies the other half. XX surveys the small room and marvels at the overstuffed U-shaped sofa, the curtained canopy bed, the trinkets display shelf, and square coffee table puzzle-fitted into the space. A big screen and a wealth of photographs and paintings of every style cover the soot-tinged walls in the same manner. XX nods, impressed; like him, these folks have not wasted a square centimeter of their horizontal and vertical real estate. A finger to his lips as a reminder, he turns on the screen and proceeds to the keyboard on the coffee table to inspect their system. It is ancient and slow to boot up.

The little dad escorts May-ling and BeiBei around the bed and onto the couch. He ruffles the boy's hair and sits next to them. On the coffee table, there is a *wéiqí* game in progress. Trapped into two corners of the board, whoever is playing white is sunk. Stirring and clacking the bowl of white stones, the little dad smiles at BeiBei. It doesn't take long for the boy to climb off his mother's lap and stuff both hands into the bowl. XX can see the disaster to come. That little dad is none too bright.

The computer beeps and finally comes alive. Its operating system is a couple of generations behind, but password protected. XX enters a string of commands and hacks his way in. He is glad to see it needs no updates. He glances at the big dad hovering bossily over him and confirms that neither he nor his spouse, both of them the increasingly rare technoboob, is objecting. XX checks out the hardware next and hums. This machine is not good for much beyond the consumption of news and entertainment and not even in 3-D. He examines the security settings and is happy again. Their matchmaker really did find them the kind of family XX specified: conservative, old-fashioned folks who guarded their privacy and limited their digital footprint. Every commonsense protection has been activated. XX scans for surveillance bugs and spyware, finds nothing of note, and installs a shield and counterspying software that he himself designed.

He stands up to inspect the apartment.

"Can we talk now?" the little dad whispers.

XX puts a finger to his mouth and whispers back, "I have to make sure your apartment is clean." The man's panicked eyes dart from the paper mess beneath the coffee table to the laundry pile to whatever lies in the rooms beyond. XX must remember to talk simple to him.

He pulls out a second note from his pocket, the one that asks about security cameras and visitors in the last month, and holds it up. The big dad shakes his head no, and the little dad breaks the rule again to say not in the last month. Activating the bug detector in his watch—another proprietary program he created for his company—XX begins his sweep at a corner and waves his arm over the furniture and wall. The big dad tails him like a mosquito.

Something crashes behind them, and May-ling apologizes again and again. As XX knew he would, BeiBei has scattered the bowl of stones everywhere.

Before he ruins the game in progress, XX approaches the *wéiqí* board. "You black?"

The big dad nods. Pointing at the board, XX shows how he can put away his opponent in four swift moves.

"Never mind that," the man hisses.

XX thought he would have appreciated a conclusion to his game. He circles every piece of furniture, sweeping his detector over them. He does the same in the sparsely furnished bedroom to the two beds and furniture; the sink, tub, toilet, and line of wet laundry in the bathroom; the refrigerator, stove, crate of packaged ramen, and sink of dirty dishes in the kitchen; the waist-high store of cabbages on the balcony.

A lone game piece lies on the floor when XX returns to the living room to complete the sweep of the apartment perimeter. Folded towels wall the edges of the coffee table. A half-consumed roll of antacids stands on end as a target, and the little dad is showing BeiBei how to shoot the stones at it with his index finger. The old man pops up suddenly and waves his hands madly for XX's attention. He points at an electrical outlet next to the front door.

XX holds his watch to its plastic cover, and his watch face changes from green to a flashing yellow, indicating audio but no video surveillance. Grinning, he holds up his arm to show everyone the warning. This is his 348th win, and being at the scene of the crime makes it his third most exciting.

"*Repairman*," the little dad mouths, and holds up two fingers. "Months." The timing of the plant corroborates Wei-guo's assertion that the massacre was punishment for his Safety Council's boycotting of the mental-health crackdown.

"How big is your unit? How many bedrooms?" XX asks. "Give us a tour." Unwilling to disturb the bug just yet and tip off anyone, he points to the bedroom. The big dad leads the way, insensitive as a zombie to XX's attempt to keep their action unsuspicious. XX turns to May-ling and grabs his chin. He loves using Hann's cease-and-desist signal on her.

Thank goodness she snaps to. "BeiBei has been so excited all day to visit Uncle Wei-guo's daddies." May-ling helps the shell-shocked little dad up and takes hold of the kid's hand. "Did Wei-guo grow up here?" She chatters on and on about nothing.

The bedroom is quite utilitarian—two sloppily made twin beds with complementary-colored bedding, two lamps (one modern metal, the other blue Tang-style porcelain), and an entertainment screen on the wall. The five of them squeeze into the tight aisles around the beds. XX strips off a blanket and stuffs it under the door. He asks quietly if any strangers had access to the bedroom in the last six months. The dads shake their heads.

"We need background noise." XX taps BeiBei on the head. "I have a job for you. Go jump on the bed." The boy gladly obeys. XX is getting better at this fatherhood thing. BeiBei's feet thump nicely on the mattress.

May-ling yelps, apologizing again and again, and confirms with the dads that it's all right. Of course it is, and XX hates that she is always second-guessing him. She wrestles off the boy's socks and insists that he hold her hand as he jumps.

The little dad says, "Why does Wei-guo have to hide? Who's after him?" He explains that Wei-guo sometimes goes straight from battlefield to work when the games run long. They did not realize anything was amiss.

"Don't you watch the news?" XX asks.

"We usually watch at ten."

XX points at May-ling. "It's time to start. Talk fast. Wei-guo is in danger. We need a decision quick."

Her face scrunches into a painful smile. She insists the dads sit down for the news, so the four of them crowd into the corridor between the two beds. XX sits opposite the men, and they lean in close.

Holding BeiBei's hand behind her, May-ling remains on her feet. "We assure you that Wei-guo is not hurt. He's at a safe location. But something unthinkable happened at war games last night."

XX reaches under his shirt and scratches his back hard. He has already told the dads two of these three things. He needs to get home to work on the case. That he is so little trusted by Hann and May-ling—and now Wei-guo too will not rely on him to tell this simple news—is another reason he cannot remain in this marriage.

May-ling goes into a long-winded narrative next about the fake weather reports—BeiBei is going to get tired of jumping if she doesn't hurry—and repeats again and again Wei-guo's lack of culpability in sending his men into battle. She details how his battalions perished with inexplicable speed, how he became trapped in his command center up in the mountains. XX cannot believe she thinks it necessary to explain in detail why Wei-guo must not be caught by the opponent.

"We understand the rules," the big dad, smart man, finally cuts her off. "What happened next?"

May-ling is quiet for a moment, her feelings surely hurt. The bed frame squeaks, tearing into XX's eardrums with each of BeiBei's hops. XX sits on his hands and rocks, barely able to contain himself.

"Wei-guo zip-lined out of command central and bravely escaped. On the battlefield, he saw that the opponent soldiers were not dying according to the rules. Their uniforms did not freeze up when shot."

XX shakes his head at her erroneous accounting. May-ling's eyes are glued to the little dad. It is quite rude the way she now tells the story only to him.

"Enemy soldiers were everywhere, but Wei-guo hid, he ran when he could, he used every bit of his training and smarts to elude capture. Even as he was running for his own safety, his aim was to reunite with his remaining troop, to lead them to victory. It wasn't long before he encountered one of his downed soldiers. The man was unresponsive. Wei-guo did everything he could to revive him, but the man was dead. Killed somehow by those enemy cheaters."

XX wishes she would not pretend she was personally at the scene.

May-ling's eyes pool with tears, her first breakdown since Wei-guo's mishap, but she stands taller, sniffs, and shakes it off. "Wei-guo discovered one dead soldier after another." She covers the little dad's hand with her own. "And then a killer came after him."

She shakes her head again and again and does not go on.

XX wants to jump out of his skin and scream, the way she is dragging out this news.

"He didn't have a choice," she says, her head still shaking. "He had to do it." She honks her nose and takes her time wiping her eyes. "Thankfully, he called Xiong-xin for help. We're afraid Wei-guo is the only one still alive from Middle Kingdom."

XX can't believe that after the long wait, she skipped over the most important detail. He has fulfilled his promise to Wei-guo to let May-ling break the news and decides he can cut in. "Wei-guo killed his pursuer. I would have done the same under those circumstances."

May-ling holds back XX's hand, but it is his turn. "May-ling is correct in that Wei-guo would not be alive if he had not contacted me." XX addresses the big dad, the Alpha in this household. If they are to get his cooperation, someone has to pay attention to him. "But her sequence of events is wrong. She is especially wrong about the zombie soldiers. We think they were government agents. The opponent army has also been exterminated. Wei-guo believes that Strategic Games is being punished because the Safety Council refused to meet a mental-health quota. A key council member was eliminated last night, and if Wei-guo had been killed, that would have been two."

May-ling pats his knee. "Slow down. Give them a moment, okay?"

The little dad's face sags like a bloodhound's. "Is Wei-guo hurt? Where is he? What's going to happen to him? Please, you have to tell us more."

XX decides to forgive his repetitions. The man is in shock. "I told you right off the top of my note that he is alive and not hurt. For your own good, I can't tell you where he is." The last question is a waste of time, and XX does not bother to answer it.

"But why? How could they do that?" the little dad asks May-ling. "How do they dare?"

XX says, "We don't have time to speculate."

"It doesn't make sense how threatened our government is by a little opposition," May-ling says, talking over XX as if he has nothing of value to say.

"I sent a car to Wei-guo last night," XX tells the big dad. "We spent the day waiting to apply for asylum. For his safety and yours, I cannot tell you where. He's been granted temporary refuge for tonight, but they want money. You have to decide what you're willing to pay."

"Wha—" The big dad holds up his hands, cranking up the

frown that has yet to let up. He specifies a news channel and orders XX to turn it on. As if on cue, the screen shows corpses being carried down hilly slopes, corpses so frozen and stiff they do not sag at the shoulders and hips. The body count scrolling across the bottom of the screen is at forty-eight. The announcer says that the unofficial word is that all two hundred Strategic Games participants are dead.

May-ling wipes the tears from her cheeks. Mouth trembling, the dads gape at the screen like two suffocating fish. Even BeiBei has stopped jumping to watch. XX switches away from the counterproductive footage to a cartoon channel, his babysitter of first resort, and turns up the volume. There won't be any more jumping now.

"You can watch after BeiBei leaves," he tells the protesting dads. He stands up and crosses his arms. "We're telling you the truth. Wei-guo's safety will cost money. You need to figure out how much you're willing to pay. Right now."

"What is this asylum?" the big dad says, each word louder than the next. "How long does he need to be there? And how do we know that after we pay, they're not going to turn around and ask us for more? Or turn him in?"

"Wei-guo can't be seen in his uniform. He needs warm clothes and a thick coat," the little dad cries. "And what's he eating? How is he handling all this?"

"He's fine," XX says. "I don't think these folks are after money, but they are insisting on a donation. Pay what you can afford, but it can't be too little."

"That makes no sense."

"Their operation is not well funded by the government."

"The government? How can you place Wei-guo in a government-funded facility?" the big dad shouts.

XX crosses his arms and shakes his head from side to side. "I already told you I can't tell you more without endangering you."

"Xiong-xin!" May-ling frantically strokes her chin.

The big dad says, "How do we know you're not trying to swindle us?"

"I am not trying to swindle you," XX shouts back at the ingrate.

May-ling says, "I assure you we are not. To secure Wei-guo a spot, XX has promised to personally install a security system for the shelter at our own expense."

"You're not getting paid?"

"I'm paying them with my invaluable time and services."

The big dad screws up his eyes. "What's in it for you?"

XX jiggles his legs to hurry along this terrible waste of his time. "One: Wei-guo is my best friend. I always help my best friend. Two: I want out of my marriage, and I want him to take my place." He ignores May-ling, her mouth agog and eyes round. "Three: Wei-guo sent me battle data that compromises the government." He decides not to mention the baton gun. They will freak out even more. "If we can keep him safe for a few days, I can use it to negotiate both his and my brother's freedom."

"Your brother!"

"Hann has been detained for Willful Sterility." Fair is fair. The two dads are quiet for so long XX fears he should not have mentioned this.

Finally, the big dad clears his throat. "Do you still want to marry our son? Have you thought about what it means to be with a man who has killed?"

XX sucks in his breath.

May-ling's eyes are watery again, but hard. "That's all I've been able to think about, and my first and only reaction is that I very much want to marry him. It was his life or that man's, and I'm glad Wei-guo is strong and clever enough to be the one left standing.

"Advanced families are hard to break into, but Wei-guo has found the key to ours. He fits our family, and each of us has fallen in love with him. He is genuinely kind, thoughtful, bighearted, and courageous. A few days ago, when Hann was in trouble, Wei-guo took half a day off to help him. He stood by Hann when none of his friends would. And the thought of Wei-guo alone, cold, and in danger . . ." She sniffs and wipes away her tears. "I promise you that Xiong-xin and I will do everything we can for him. He is already family to us, and we will not let one more member of our family be taken away without a fight."

The big dad nods. The madness in his brow eases. "Do you agree with Xiong-xin's plan?"

"I do. Absolutely. And helping Wei-guo includes helping you as well when he is away." She turns to the little dad. "Do you have enough food for the next few days? Nineteen floors are a lot to negotiate."

The little dad reaches out and squeezes May-ling's hand. May-ling is demonstrating her fitness as a daughter-in-law, and XX decides not to point out that with their packaged ramen stockpiles, the two men need not leave their apartment for a month. Perhaps Wei-guo was right to insist on her presence.

The big dad says, "If we agree to pay, this payment, big or small, has to come out of Wei-guo's dowry."

"I know you have no money," says XX.

The frown returns to the big dad's brow. "All right then," he says. "If you tell me where you're hiding Wei-guo and let us talk to him, if you promise to involve us in every single decision from here on out, then we will work out a figure."

16

MAY-LING

I could have cooked dinner and cleaned up the kitchen, perhaps the entire apartment, in the time it took BeiBei to settle down and fall asleep after our visit with Wei-guo's fathers. I hurry to XX's room. His door is locked; he had installed some sort of multi-chamber, telescopic-pin lock to keep his dog safe from me. He yells for me to leave him alone. He's working. I ask if he's making progress, but he will not answer. I jiggle his door handle in a rhythm that matches my jittery impatience, and I do not let up. Hann's arrest has been hard on XX, but he seems to have little sense that his brother's and Wei-guo's troubles affect me too.

He finally cracks the door, his air stern and resentful. "Every second I talk to you is a second I'm not working."

"I am Hann's wife. Yours too. Please let me help."

"Are you capable of analyzing 15.7 exabytes of data? Can you manipulate that data so that we will not be exposed?"

"What have you found?"

"Wei-guo will be discovered soon. And you and I along with him. Don't waste my time."

I squeeze between him and the doorjamb. The dog stink inside chokes me. It dawns on me why XX used to smell like an animal pen. His desktop and bedside tables have been cleared of every last object. Those objects in addition to boxes and boxes of game figurines and collectibles from his lower shelves have been piled atop his display cases and stuffed into upper cubbies. Shredded papers, chewed pens, and mangled boxes litter the floor. Beneath the dog cage, pee has dried along the edges of the slide-out tray. I climb over the cage and across the bed to open the window.

"It's minus four outside."

I tell XX it's only for a few minutes. "Fresh oxygen will fire up your brain."

"You mean fresh air. Oxygen can't be fresh or stale."

I force myself to calm down. "You are absolutely correct." My job right now is to support XX in whatever way I can so that he can help Wei-guo.

He eyes me suspiciously. I ask the whereabouts of MaMa Dog.

"You said to get rid of her." He stomps back to his computer and keyboard.

I apologize. "I hope you found her a nice home. A more suitable home than ours."

"She's guarding Wei-guo."

The idea of Wei-guo in his exhausted and frightened state having to restrain an equally frightened animal petrifies me. "Has Wei-guo ever had a dog? A pet of any kind?"

"I taught him how to be her master."

I bite my tongue and try not to imagine the worst. I will be useless to Wei-guo if I do not stay strong. I ask if XX minds me moving the dog crate to the balcony temporarily. He grunts without taking his eyes off the screen. So that he will not lock his door again, I promise him a cola and some cookies. He needs the caffeine and energy and a peace offering. When I return, I ask if I could change his sheets and pick up a bit.

"Fine," he says as if doing me a great favor.

I stand behind him and give him a moment to chew and swallow. "What do you know so far?"

He drains the soda in one gulp. "Three people were monitoring the battle in real time."

My knees go weak, so profound is my relief. I wasn't sure if XX could or would uncover anything. "You did it." I clap his back. "You found them."

He twists away from my touch and types. "MONKeyKing," "QinShiHuang," and "TheBoooda" appear on his computer screen. "These handles are hosted by three different servers. It could take days to break in, identify the men, and reconstruct their activities."

I watch as he types string after string of commands. The blue screen flashes. "What's happening?"

XX sighs and turns around. "Quit bossing me."

I can't afford to start another fight. I change his sheets and sweep the floor too. I return to him when I'm done. "Find anything?"

"Go to bed."

I know he won't be sleeping tonight, so I slip under his sheets. "I promise I'll be quiet." He needs the company, and frankly, so do I. In XX's presence I feel an inkling of hope, the possibility that Wei-guo will be returned to me.

They're on to us."

I shield my eyes from the ceiling light.

XX looms above me, his bloodshot eyes darting. "They suspect he's not dead."

My heart gallops as he plays me a clip from CCTV news. Wei-guo in black workout clothes smiles in a photo I recognize from his website. He is identified as the general of Middle Kingdom and a possible survivor of the snowstorm that killed two Strategic Games armies. I'm deathly afraid as a broodingly handsome Wei-guo from his resident ID picture appears next. His image remains on the screen as the public is persuaded to help find and rescue him.

It is 2:49 in the morning.

"We need to start negotiations," I say. "Now."

"I've just begun to sift through the data."

"We're going to have to bluff." I ask if he's uncovered the identity of our three men.

"We promised Wei-guo's fathers that we'd include them on every decision."

I say, "How do you propose we contact them right now?" He of course cannot name a safe method. I assure him that I will go visit the two dads tomorrow and let them yell at me.

"You can't visit Wei-guo's fathers anymore." XX goes rigid with this realization. "What if they were already watching us last night?"

He stumbles back to his desk, nearly tripping over his chair, and clacks madly at the keyboard. A map of Wei-guo's neighborhood materializes on the screen. XX clicks on his building. After more interminable typing, video feeds crowd his monitor. He locates our appearances in the archive.

"Has the video been viewed?"

He shushes me.

Next, XX pulls up a street map and lights up every other corner around the apartment building. My stomach goes into free fall when I suspect the red dots between the building and the subway stop from which we emerged are all cameras. He opens a family album, and photos of the four of us and of Wei-guo too, in happier times, appear. XX returns to a red dot. He sits back and chews on his thumbnail. He bangs away some more.

I wish XX would explain what he's doing. "Are we going to be okay?"

"Quit crowding me."

"Can't you break into their network?"

"Of course I can," he says with great irritation. "I'm programming the system to recognize and search for all our images from yesterday and to destroy them."

"Oh." I drop into the bed behind me, amazed by his ingenuity. I watch awhile before pulling the covers over my legs. I could help if he would only let me. The scroll of codes across the screen is so mind-numbing I eventually lie back on the pillow.

"Yes!" Something slams.

I jerk awake. XX is still drumming away at his keyboard. There are a lot more empty soda cans around him now. I check the clock; I've zoned out for nearly an hour. I ask what's going on.

"I can trace the messages back to military, administrative, and parliamentary servers."

I sit up, my pulse in my ears.

XX says, "We have to start making demands before they find Wei-guo." He says he's already located personal contact information for the president.

"President!"

He crosses his arms and narrows his eyes. "Yes."

I soften my tone. "You are absolutely right that we must act right away, but is it wise to start with the president?"

"Wei-guo could be found any minute. We too are in danger. It's my decision, and I say we stop wasting time and go to the very top."

Nausea grips me. "If the president or someone very high up ordered the massacre, we will give him face-saving room and de-

niability by negotiating with and accusing his three henchmen."
I can't rid my voice of its shakiness. "But if those three men are
rogue operators, they will not want their superiors finding out.
They will respond to our blackmail."

"If the president is responsible, he does not deserve to save face."

"At whose expense do you plan to obtain this justice?"

XX growls.

I make myself start over in a nicer tone. "Can we agree that
Hann and Wei-guo must come first? That we may never pursue
justice and punishment for those responsible if it compromises our
family's safety?"

"I'm the one who explained that to Wei-guo."

I go to him and kneel to get to his eye level. "You and I—we
have to be on the same team. What chance does Hann or Wei-guo
have if the two of us can't even agree to put our heads together?" I
jostle his arm, trying to nudge some sense into him. "Please? I am
so scared. What if we can't free either of them? What's going to
become of them? Of us?"

"I guarantee you that I'm going to save them."

I don't know where he gets his confidence.

XX crosses his arms. "I will inform the three men of the evidence in our possession. Then I will demand that they release Hann
and leave Wei-guo alone."

"Yes." I force myself to sound agreeable, but my yes trails off
without conviction. "Let's say we link Hann and Wei-guo in the
same sentence. Wouldn't they trace the demands right back to us?"
I shudder with the realization that this business of blackmail is far
from simple. We need a plan nothing short of perfect.

XX hugs himself and stares at his keyboard. He begins to rock,
emitting a low hum. After long minutes, his eyes close, his rocking
slows and then stops. His breathing becomes noisy and even. He
hasn't slept in over twenty-four hours.

I shake him gently. "Wake up."

"I'm thinking." He swivels back to his computer. A few keystrokes later, he tells me that there are thirty-six Willfully Sterile men housed in Hann's building. "I'm going to demand that they pardon and release them all." He types for a few more minutes. A blank message form appears. XX has named us the Truth+JusticeLeague.

"Clever," I say, glad for the chance to compliment him and mean it. "Much more impressive to be a league rather than an individual."

He fills in the addresses for MONKeyKing, QinShiHuang, and TheBoooda and utilizes both their real names and government titles in the salutation.

Our organization possesses one baton voltage gun and a 15.7-EB file of the field data from the December 11th People's Republic vs. Middle Kingdom strategic game. That file proves that you are the leaders of deliberate action that massacred 200 men. We link you to 1) doctored weather reports, 2) soldiers who carried out your order with lethal voltage guns, 3) fake power outages, 4) unnecessary infrastructure closures, and 5) delayed rescue efforts.

We demand justice for the dead. Should anyone survive, and should you attempt to silence him, the above information will be made public. We also demand that you pardon and release the following thirty-six men from the Sex Corrections Institute by 7 A.M. December 13th.

As XX adds on the long list of names, I try to think of the least critical way of telling him that his message makes no sense. "If you're demanding justice, you can't sell your silence in the next paragraph. And seeking justice for dead soldiers has nothing to do with the release of Willfully Sterile men."

He stiffens. "Who says it has to?"

I put up my hands. "What if we change our name to some sort

of equal-rights organization, something that supports sexual deviances?"

"It took me a half hour to make Truth+JusticeLeague untraceable."

"What if—" I bite my lip and jiggle my legs. "What if we claim we obtained the file from a Willfully Sterile citizen? And that every member of our league now possesses a copy of that file. We create some misdirection along with a reasonable story and a threat."

XX makes the change without bothering to acknowledge my good idea—which I guess is his way of acknowledging it.

"Second paragraph," I say, "change it to 'should you attempt to silence *them*.' Make it sound like there could be more than one alive."

XX again does as I suggest.

"Better yet, make it 'should you attempt to silence them or any other witnesses or anyone in our league,'" I say. "That would include you and me."

"Fine."

"I'm not done." I study the letter some more. "Truth and justice should demand that their gunmen be charged with murder." I shove aside my disgust that we are enabling guilty officials to once again escape punishment. I ask if we know how many hit men they employed.

XX says yes, but reminds me that we're already asking for the impossible, demanding the release of so many Willfully Sterile men.

"Put the gunmen in, and demand that they release not just the Willfully Sterile, but every last person in the Sex Corrections Institute," I say. "Let's give ourselves room to negotiate."

Promising to keep a vigilant eye on the Truth+JusticeLeague message box, to wake XX when there is a response, to not do anything on my own, I finally convinced him to sleep for a couple of hours so that he would be of sounder mind and judgment for our seven A.M. deadline. His rocking and humming alarmed me.

I sit in front of XX's computer and stare at the inbox, refreshing it every time I feel anxious. I try to think ahead to happier times, to Hann's homecoming and our family reunion, but my thoughts return in a panic again and again to Wei-guo. What if he has to stay forever in hiding? What if I've lost him for good? I don't want to be without him or Hann, but my yearning for Hann feels selfless, for the good of our family. As good as Wei-guo is for my family, I want him for myself. I remember the feeling of completeness, of invincibility and deep contentment when I was in his arms. I think of his insistent optimism, the thrilling way he wooed me, dropping in uninvited, his hope-filled peonies. Love had come for me, and I was too blind and angry, too stuck on what I could not have, to appreciate it.

A loud rat-tat-tat-tat-tat hauls me upright. It is a second before I realize that the computer screen before me is dark, that the noise originates from the alarm on XX's wrist. I pound the keyboard to rouse the computer. I've drifted off, and it is 6:30. The inbox is still empty. My pulse keeps time with the mad pommeling of the machine-gun alarm.

I go to XX and touch the face of his watch to silence it. He snores lightly, dead to the world despite the racket. I shake him and call his name. He rubs and rubs his eyes.

I place my hands on his shoulders and tell him the three perpetrators are ignoring our demands. "Go call Hann. We need to find out what's happening on his end."

His bleary eyes finally register me. He instructs his watch to contact Hann.

I slap at his watch. "Remember the seventy-five-meter ban?"

"Don't worry about it."

"Of course we have to worry about it."

He sighs and calls again. "I promise you it's safe."

A recording answers, stating that curfew is in effect and voice calls are prohibited between nine P.M. and nine A.M.

"*What's up?*" XX dictates into his watch, and sends off a text message.

"'What's up?'" I say. "That's what you're going to ask him?"

He yawns in my face. Half a minute later, Hann bids XX good morning. He is still in bed. I wrap my hands around my stomach and groan.

"*Please go downstairs and tell me what's for breakfast,*" XX dictates to his watch.

"*Not hungry yet.*"

XX rakes his fingers across his forearm, trying to come up with a next move.

"Tell Hann that BeiBei and I are planning a surprise and need to know," I say.

That appears to do the trick, but Hann takes his sweet time before rice gruel, peanuts, and radish pickles pop onto our screen. XX asks what's new.

"*Just another day of learning here at the Sex Change Institute.*"

XX signs off. I feel the tick of every passing second in the pit of my stomach. Twenty minutes left in our deadline, and our three crooks have yet to get started. XX orders me to quit making him nervous and brew some tea. He goes back to analyzing field data. When I return with large mugs and a box of almond cookies, it is 6:48.

"Anything?" I take a nervous bite.

XX shakes his head and swallows cookie after cookie. My tea will not make the grainy lumps in the back of my throat go down.

"Since when is it safe to contact Hann from here?" I ask.

XX blinks self-consciously and resumes typing. "Let me work."

"Answer me."

"I manipulated my GPS recently."

"So I could have been talking to Hann?" We've only managed two hurried phone calls since his arrest.

"It's not safe."

"You just said it was."

He crosses his arms, and I do the same. We stare each other down.

"All right. I could have told you."

"And?" I say.

"I'm sorry. Okay?" He goes back to his typing. "I'm not apologizing for bringing MaMa Dog here." He sneaks a sideways peek at me. "I'm the Alpha. I'm doing what's best, and I don't need to answer to you."

"Your blackmail demands are better because of me. We'd probably already be in jail if not for my ideas."

As much as I know it's counterproductive to argue right now, I cannot let him treat me like a worthless hindrance. We bicker on. I gasp the next time I glance at the clock. The time we set for our ultimatum has come and gone. We stare at each other, our breaths ragged. After a while, XX goes back to analyzing data, his blinking out of control.

Eighteen minutes after seven, all the devices in our apartment ding at the same time. A reply has come from MONKeyKing.

> Good morning, comrades. Most people do not attend to their mail, let alone possess the power to move heaven and earth in the middle of the night. We are relieved your oversight has shown us you are not the trigger-happy sort.
>
> You are not concerned with all of the inmates at the Sex Corrections Institute. Tell us the man you want released, and we'll see if we can make it happen.

I breathe easier knowing that our opponents are willing to engage. I point at XX and dictate: "Out of courtesy to you, we will restart our clock. We repeat: release all 113 men and place your 30 gunmen under custody by 9:00." I'm surprised XX does as I say without argument.

As we wait, he scrolls through lines and lines of data while tearing at the welts on his forearm.

MONKeyKing's reply comes quickly. **What happened on December 11 was an act of nature. 30 arrests not justifiable to our superiors or the public.**

"While two hundred deaths are." I wave at the keyboard and dictate, "You are right. We prefer monetary compensation to the tune of 100,000 yuan per soldier."

XX refuses to send the message. "You are forgetting Hann and Wei-guo."

"I'm not." I reach over his shoulder and press the Send button myself.

We have no authority to dispense money. 10,000 yuan per man may be possible in tax credits.

I grit my teeth. "Tell them if they send us another insulting counter, we will make them sorry."

MONKeyKing does not answer so promptly this time. **20,000 yuan per and you surrender to us your file, all computers and devices, and the baton.**

"They've left out the Sex Corrections Institute," XX says, scratching hard. "I told you not to forget Hann."

I assure him that we're still negotiating. I say, "80,000 tax credit per soldier and release 113 men at Sex Corrections Institute by 8:30. We are keeping file and baton to ensure you follow through."

Even the president cannot pardon 113 men without cause. We urge you yet again to be specific.

I am surprised and pleased they did not counter my 80,000 figure. I tell XX to send the list of thirty-six Willfully Sterile men.

Their answer takes but a second: **Pardoning sex criminals will necessitate approval from multiple departments outside our purview. Name one man.**

XX's breathing comes hard and fast. I too am having trouble staying calm. I ask him how many men we need pardoned in order to keep us relatively anonymous.

"The more the better," he says. "And I'll need time to fabricate evidence to confuse them." We cut our requests by half.

One pardon from each of us is the most we can manage. Final offer.

XX cannot stop blinking.

I say, "80,000 per in tax credit. Nine Willfully Sterile Men released by 8:30. And no harassment of surviving soldiers, witnesses, and league members." I check the time—8:30 is less than an hour away.

MONKeyKing counters:

20,000 yuan tax credit per soldier with surviving parents. No harassment. Pardon of 3 sex criminals who will be officially registered Willfully Sterile and prohibited from resuming heterosexual privileges. Surrender of your file, computer devices, and baton at 0900 today.

"Those dog turds," I say, furious they are going back on our tax-credit agreement. I reply, increasing the payout per soldier and the number of men pardoned and removing all their conditions. I also take the file, computers, and batons off the table.

XX says he could give them a file, but copying will take time, provided he has a hard drive at home large enough for the task. I tell XX to push the file delivery time to noon.

He does as I say. Hurrying to his closet, he digs around the floor in search of a usable hard drive.

Their next reply does not budge from their previous offer. A chill runs through me. "Tell them our last offer was also final."

"Is that a good idea?" XX will not get up from the floor of his closet. I type the threat myself.

They answer almost instantaneously: **Consider us warned. Who will you cry to first?**

I gasp.

XX scrambles to his feet. "I told you not to do that. Didn't I tell you not to do that?" Breathing hard, he drops into his chair, hugging himself and rocking.

I cross my arms over my stomach and pace. Tears pool in my eyes, and I let them come. These last weeks have been so trying, so awful, so beyond the beyond. I sink into my wretchedness, and XX and I echo each other's animal cries. We go on for so long I start to worry that we'll wake BeiBei, and the thought of having to put on a happy face for him sets me crying anew.

Our computers ding.

Our last offer too is final. Except now we are only willing to pardon 2 sex criminals. Send us those names in the next 60 seconds.

I seize XX's arm.

"Who?" he asks, hyperventilating. "I haven't done any research on anyone."

I think for a second. "He can't be one of Hann's roommates."

I pick out a random man from our list of thirty-six. XX checks to make sure he matches our criteria and sends the name along with Hann's.

8:30 is less than fifteen minutes away. Could Hann really be free in fifteen minutes? I cannot help but worry that he will hate a life without BeiBei just as much as his life at the Sex Corrections Institute.

XX unearths three old hard drives and decides that together they can hold the data. He connects one to his computer and begins to duplicate the file.

Except for BeiBei waking up, 8:30 comes and goes quietly, and we realize we should have made proof of release a condition of our deal.

I park BeiBei on the living-room couch in front of a cartoon show—one that will hopefully amuse him for the next half hour—and return to stare with XX at the small window in his computer screen where a bar showing the percentage of file transferred slowly fills up.

"We can't call Hann, can we?" I say.

XX shakes his head. I put a hand atop his to stop his scratching and ask him how else we're going to verify that MONKeyKing and his cronies fulfilled their end of the bargain.

He blinks. "We should not have called Hann earlier."

I mention that Hann is expecting a surprise from me. "Maybe you can tell him that you can't make it, that you got called into work." I gasp. "What are you going to do about work?"

He says that as of yesterday, he is on a one-week vacation. My heart cartwheels over the long and incriminating trail we've left behind. XX thumps at the front panel of his desk, counting down toward our doom with his foot. In the living room, BeiBei pounds on the couch and joins the insane cackle of some cartoon character.

The computer beeps; the hard drive is full. Only 27 percent of the data has been transferred. XX switches it out. I observe that they haven't made handoff arrangements yet for the file.

He says that giving them a pickup location after we drop off the file would be the safest approach. And he would need to deliver the hard drives in disguise. We pat ourselves on the back for the file duplication time we bought ourselves by waiting for them to raise the issue. We talk over possible drop-off locations, and XX feels fairly certain that he could disable city cameras on the way to a hidden nook.

Nine o'clock comes and goes, and there is still no word from

Hann or MONKeyKing. I give BeiBei a bag of rice crackers and find him a quieter show. More time drags by. Finally it occurs to me that we could still demand proof of release. I have XX send the message.

What sort of proof? I can see the three men stuffing their faces with a sumptuous breakfast while roaring at our ineptitude, waiting for us to self-implode.

"Voice calls from the two men to their families in the next five minutes?" XX says.

I say, "Make it three."

The two of us stare at XX's watch. Three minutes pass, then four, and then five. Nothing happens. Inaction appears to be our opponent's strategy of choice. We ask MONKeyKing why the men have not called.

They have. Surrender the file now, or we will stop processing their release.

Their families have not received calls.

You have one minute to send the file.

I say to XX, "Tell them we will post the file to the web in one minute unless we hear from both men. And that we will drop off a physical file, not send a traceable one like dummies over the Internet." Their insistence on receiving a file seems strange, their methods undisciplined, given the fact that we told them multiple members of the league possess copies.

We have done our part. Your 1-minute countdown starts now.

My heart stops. I don't know how they did it, but a stopwatch appears on our screen and starts ticking away. "We have to talk to Hann."

XX agrees and makes the call.

Hann answers on the first ring. "I'm being released." He says he's called us twice without success. "I'm out of here as soon as I get my ankle monitor removed."

XX doubles over in his chair, panting. "Go get your ear tag out immediately." He hangs up with twenty-five more seconds to go.

In the next instant, his watch rat-tat-tats. No caller ID appears.

"Should we answer?" I say. "Could it be Hann?"

"No." XX extends his arm and the watch on it as far away from himself as possible. The call will not roll over to voicemail.

"QUI-ET!" BeiBei yells from the living room.

XX unfastens his watch. "The icon to ignore the call is gone." He lowers the volume, but the rat-tat-tat goes on and on. It will not stop. He stares helplessly at me before tapping the answer button.

"Wu Xiong-xin." The voice on the other end is reprimanding and supremely irritated.

XX's mouth drops.

I take the watch from him. "Truth and Justice League. There is no Wu Xiong-xin here."

"Where is your lover, Lee Wei-guo?"

I begin to shake. "You will have nothing to fear from our league if you carry out your end of the bargain."

The man laughs drily.

I say, "We will give you a pickup location for the field data as soon as it is dropped off."

The man laughs again. "Did you really think we trust you to dictate the fate of something so vital?"

XX gasps as red washes over his computer screen. A spot of yellow zooms toward us, growing into the hammer and sickle of the Party. He frantically yanks cords from his computer and hard drive and bangs on buttons. The hammer and sickle windmills, and a sucking sound accompanies their disappearance into a vortex. The screen goes black. XX jiggles the power switch and jabs at the keyboard. His system is dead.

The voice in the watch continues, "We will speak with Lee

Wei-guo and hear his reassurances for ourselves. Give us Lee Wei-guo, and you and your family can put all this behind you."

Our doorbell rings, followed by earth-shaking pounding and orders to open up. XX grabs the one hard drive with the successfully downloaded data and circles the room in panic. I dash to the living room for BeiBei. XX is stuffing the drive deep between his mattresses when I return with my bewildered child. I lock the door and gratefully engage XX's fancy new lock. The banging will not stop.

There is fear and fury in equal measure on XX's face. He is fanatically possessive of his computers and his "intellectual property."

He snatches up the watch and yells into it, "Every member of our league has a backup file. And we all know who you are." He spits out the three men's real names with great vehemence. "Make your men go away."

The door battering continues urgent and furious, every thump aimed at the pit of my stomach. BeiBei clings to me, frightened and quiet like never before.

"All of us will be watching you," I yell, my entire body quaking. "We have your baton gun. Stray from our bargain, and we will come after you and your families. You'll be dead before you know what hits you. Call off your men right now, or we go public."

I hear a wood-splintering crash. Gasping, I sidle toward XX. The line goes to a high, drilling whine. XX grabs his ears, and I slap at his watch to shut off the noise. We cower together, not daring to move or make a sound as we listen for the inevitable footsteps and more pounding.

Silence has never felt so terrifying. We wait and wait and wait. No one comes. We wait some more, but our apartment stays quiet.

Finally, XX goes to his closet, to the side shelf where he stores his cache of old computers. I've always thought it a waste that he upgrades his systems every year, but I cannot be happier now. He powers one up and types frantically. He connects his watch to it and clacks away some more. I bounce BeiBei in my arms, his thumb squeaking in and out of his mouth. I pace and pray.

On his computer, XX brings up a picture of our living room. I realize it is a live video feed when the camera pans to the bright red head of an ax lodged on our front door. The door is still closed. It looks like no one has entered our apartment. I sag with relief.

A thought occurs to me. "Does this have sound?"

"Of course," XX says, "but there's no sound out there right now."

I wonder if he has installed cameras in Hann's bedroom, but decide to let it go for now.

XX instructs his watch to call Lee Wei-guo. When he answers, XX says, "You have a client who works for CCTV."

"Whuh?" He was asleep.

"Good morning," I say. "It's May-ling and XX. Are you all right?"

XX snatches his watch from me. "The producer of 'Model Citizens' at China Central Television, the one that I met at your studio. Wung's his name."

"XX, I have something to tell you." He sounds quite stuffed up.

"I'm dialing him right now. You say hello, introduce me, and then let me talk. Remember, I will do all the talking."

"Please forgive me," Wei-guo continues. "I couldn't keep MaMa Dog inside last night. She barked and growled and charged at me. I could not calm her down."

The watch falls out of XX's hand as the line begins to ring. In his chair, XX slumps forward and covers his head, mumbling no again and again.

I put BeiBei down and kneel next to XX, heartsick for him. I retrieve the watch and rub his back and whisper assurances about

MaMa Dog that I myself find difficult to believe. When someone answers the line, I ask for Comrade Wung. I pry XX's hands off his head and wrap them around his watch, reminding him that Hann and Wei-guo are counting on us. I pat his hand and remind him that he has a plan, that he will speak to Wung, that he must convince Wung to help us.

WEI-GUO

With May-ling and BeiBei at my side, my fathers and XX behind me, and all of us dressed in funereal shades, I enter CCTV's lobby. To spread the word and gather as many supporters and witnesses as possible, XX made me message all my clients and voice call a dozen of the most prominent and well-connected among them. Doc was the only one I wished to speak with, but XX thought the risks too high and me, too unstable. It made me ill that Doc should think for a second longer than necessary that both Little Sung and I were dead, that poor judgment on my part caused the deaths, that what happened was anything short of premeditated mass murder. Finally, May-ling sided with me and made XX include Doc in my group message.

XX insisted that I not go into details in my communications, but promise to reveal all on the evening news' "Model Citizens" segment. I'm certain the State considers me a non-model citizen, but XX claimed that is the very reason I need to act the exact opposite on the show. I've been declared missing, and I will not be allowed a life until I provide an acceptable account of my whereabouts. He assured me that all will be fine if I follow his script faithfully. I desperately want to believe XX can mastermind yet another escape for me.

May-ling agreed that I have to speak out and that I will not find a more sympathetic newsperson than Wung, my client and friend of ten-plus years. Minutes before we walked in here, she stopped, took my face in her hands, and reminded me that I know in my heart of hearts that what I did was not just for my own good, but also for the good of my men and ultimately, for the good of our nation. I am to hold fast to this truth.

I still can't believe May-ling would want to be with a man like me. Unlike my fallen compatriots, I am immeasurably lucky and beyond blessed. I did not know to look for more than beauty and amiability in a mate, yet here is May-ling next to me, strength, sensitivity, and smarts all rolled into one.

A handful of my clients were free during their lunch hour, and I see three now waiting for me as agreed, no questions asked.

They come to shake my hand, these still-to-be-married clients who've become my friends and supporters over the years. As they offer a chorus of condolences, bile chokes my throat, my eyes pool, and it's all I can do not to cry out that my men—our brothers— have been slaughtered for our civil disobedience, that their killers are running free.

The lobby door whooshes open, sending in a draft of cold air and Doc in its wake. I didn't know he was coming, and I am overcome by another surge of grief. Coatless, his silvered hair smooshed to one side, and his face gaunt and gray, he looks like he hasn't eaten, slept, or thought of himself for days. I hurry over and clasp him tight. He is icy to my touch.

"It was mass murder," I tell him quietly, hanging on to his shaking shoulders. "I have proof. Battle files. Murder weapon."

"I shouldn't have started the boycott." He stifles a stuttering sob. "I am the reason they're all dead."

XX comes toward us, a massive scowl on his face and BeiBei kicking at the end of his outstretched arms. He thrusts the child at me. "Quiet," he hisses. "Come. Now."

I hug the boy and focus on his squirrelly warmth as I drag myself back to my assembled friends. My voice croaks when I speak, and Big Dad takes over the introductions. He knows I'm not fully on board with XX's plan, that I consider what we're about to do a betrayal of my men. May-ling squeezes my elbow and wraps her other arm around my back.

XX checks in with the guard at CCTV's entrance, and Wung appears within minutes, dwarfed by Tommy Chen, the reporter XX requested. Wung's bosses agreed to interview me, but stipulated that my story would air only if it is deemed of educational value. Wung must have really pled my case and sung my praises for them to send this eye-candy reporter, the one who usually does the model-citizen pieces. Wung's other reporter, the one who drags the confession, tears, and repentance out of citizens to be made examples of, is bad-tempered and difficult.

Wung grasps my free hand. "I'm so relieved you are all right." Seeing the tears in my eyes, he pulls me in for a bear hug. BeiBei squirms and pushes him away, and Wung tugs on his little fingers. "And who are you?"

May-ling coaxes BeiBei to give his regards to Uncle Wung.

"No. No spidey bug," he says, burrowing into my chest and pushing away Wung's intruding chin and the short hairs sprouting from the mole on it.

"Behave," XX says. His tone makes everyone uneasy, and I am

reminded how not so long ago, XX himself could not take his eyes off Wung's mole when they met at my studio.

Thankfully, Wung laughs. "My 'spidey bug' has kept many staffers in line over the years. Isn't that so, Tommy?"

Tommy echoes his boss's laughter in the affable and toweringly handsome way that has charmed us over the airwaves. "I would never dare cross you." He shakes my hand, and I feel the squeeze of his bulky jade ring. He must come from money; he is young to have already saved up for a wife. "I am honored you chose to tell your story to us."

"Can we start?" Afraid of losing control of the interview, XX has warned me again and again not to answer questions or engage in unpredictable pleasantries until we are all seated, camera rolling. We're hardly the ones calling the shots; nevertheless, he sent Wung a set of questions to follow and limited the interview to ten minutes. I don't know what I've ever done to deserve Wung's consideration. I can't imagine the personal price he paid to get this approved by his bosses.

Tommy says they're ready for us in their studio.

"We're going to do the interview over there," XX says, pointing at the ratty horseshoe couch in the corner.

"In the lobby?" Tommy says, just as the front door whooshes open again. Two men enter in animated conversation. They examine our assembled throng, playing into XX's plan to expose ourselves to as many witnesses as possible.

XX tells me to go sit with BeiBei on the right prong of the horseshoe. He orders May-ling to the spot next to me and perches my poor arthritic dad on the sofa arm beside her. He arranges all four of my friends behind me. XX positions himself on my other side and indicates that Big Dad is to be next to him. Finally, he points to the side opposite us and tells Tommy to sit there.

Tommy cocks his head at Wung, and Wung tells the guard to

send for the cameramen and lights. That Wung respects me enough to give into XX's bossy demands chokes me up again.

Tommy sits and studies me. "What happened? How did you not freeze to death with the others?"

"No," XX barks "I was very clear in my instructions that we will only tell our story one time on camera."

I mouth my apologies to Wung. He too scrutinizes me.

"But why? Is something going to happen if you tell it more than once?" The look on Tommy's face is amused, teasing.

"We agreed," XX sputters, pulling out folded papers from his coat pocket. "It's rule number three in our agreement."

"I'm just making chitchat, Comrade. I assure you I take your requests most seriously." His delivery is good-natured and respectful.

Crew shouldering cameras and lights emerge from CCTV. On their heels comes a middle-aged man in a black Mao suit. I freeze. They know I killed Lee Gwang. I wait for him to come and arrest me, but he stands on the periphery, arms crossed, and his snarly, slitted eyes trained on me. Skinny and average in height, the man is shaped like Lee. Neither would have warranted a second glance on the street. He makes clear that I am being watched. That there will be consequences if I do not control my mouth.

Tommy and Wung pop to their feet, their ease gone. They bow effusively at the Mao suit and usher him toward me. "What a nice surprise!"

Wung introduces him as their quality assurance manager. "Tommy and I always do our best work when Comrade Gao graces us with his presence. We call him Quality Gao."

Wung smiles weakly as his pun—*gao* also means "high"—falls flat. Hands clasped behind his back, Quality Gao stares pointedly at me, XX, and May-ling, but does not bother to return our greetings. He looks Doc up and down before positioning his sinister presence next to the camera lens behind Tommy and in my direct line of sight.

Gao seems to recognize Doc. Alarmed, I look over my shoulder at my friend. He appears both irate and defeated, capable of revolt and breakdown both. I want to somehow convey my regrets for what I'm about to do, but XX gets in my face and tells me we're starting.

Tommy addresses the camera. "I am here with Lee Wei-guo, general of Middle Kingdom, one of the two Strategic Games armies that froze to death in the winter storm on the night of December 11." Tommy turns to me, his anime-sized eyes mesmerizing. "Please tell us, General Lee: What happened two nights ago? How did you manage to be the sole survivor of this tragedy?"

His use of my game rank startles and flatters me. I thank him for granting me the interview and launch into XX's script. I start by acknowledging the many people who have come to support me. I introduce my fathers. "As you can see, we wholeheartedly embrace China First and the Advanced family as the means to keep our country strong and prosperous. Next to me is a woman ready to sacrifice and go the max again for the good of our nation, the woman I hope to marry in the very near future. And on my lap is the boy I hope to help father into a man worthy of this great nation of ours." I do my best to portray myself as a model citizen and receive a near imperceptible nod from Quality Gao.

In my lap, BeiBei is curled on his side, his hands shielding his eyes from the spotlights. "You're on camera, little man," I say. "Would you like to say hello?" He uncovers an eye and gives a tentative wave.

"Hello, little brother." Tommy laughs, and everyone laughs with him.

I introduce XX next as the rock of the family, a good friend, and a model big brother to me.

"We're missing someone, are we not?" Tommy says.

My heart skips a beat. Tommy has managed to do his research in the few hours before our interview.

"That's not on our list of questions," XX says.

Tommy turns to XX, "I understand that Guo Hann, who is both your brother and husband, has been accused of Willful Sterility and is housed at a sex corrections facility."

"You are not allowed that question." XX is halfway to his feet before I tug him back onto the couch.

Quality Gao trains a camera on him. The last person to enter the lobby stops to gawk.

"You are correct," May-ling says, her voice shaky.

XX and I turn in unison to gape at her. Talking about Hann, let alone his sexual nature, is strictly forbidden.

She runs her fingers through BeiBei's hair as if to remind everyone that her impressionable child is listening. "My first husband did not understand his own nature when we first married. In our seven years together, he and I have worked very, very hard to overcome it."

I receive another nod from the quality man. XX wheezes quietly at the edge of his seat. I'm not sure May-ling's intentions, but I'm pretty sure she just made it impossible for Hann to ever return to the family.

May-ling continues, "Both Hann and I wanted a good marriage, a real and lasting union. He wooed me earnestly, and we fell in love like a true couple. We lived together like a real family. We all love, admire, and need him—Lee Wei-guo included." She glances at me, and I grasp her hand and XX's too to show our solidarity. "Hann is an indispensable member of our household."

Tommy says, "Is Guo Hann's Willful Sterility the reason you have only one child?"

She rubs BeiBei's ears, covering them, and lowers her eyes

to the floor. "Hann and I have adhered to our weekly bedroom schedule." The idea of her physical intimacy with Hann pains me even as I doubt her claim.

"Who is your child's father?"

May-ling frowns. "My son belongs to both his fathers. Believing otherwise undermines the loving dynamics of our family. Of all Advanced families."

"I apologize. That was most insensitively phrased," Tommy says, head bowed. He is beloved for posing nosy personal questions we cannot politely ask ourselves, for his good-natured humility when called on it. "Would you be willing to share with us the biological father of your child?"

"I thank you for your apology," May-ling says. "It is no secret that XX fathered our son, but that's not what we're here to talk about today."

I'm alarmed by Tommy's tenacity, alarmed even more by the ease with which May-ling tells this lie. I understand now Hann can no longer be her priority. Her priority must be to keep her child safe. The quality man looks bored by the paternity discussion. May-ling nudges me.

I return to XX's script. "I am a certified personal trainer, and I started Lee Wei-guo's Studio nearly a decade ago." XX insisted that I plug my business and say my name repeatedly. "These men behind me are my longtime clients and loyal friends." I present Beijing Electric Power's vice president and the son of Peking University's dean of students, Beijing Capital Group's senior vice president and son of our city bureau director. I continue in this vein, stressing the positions and connections of my supporters. Tommy's eyes twinkle, both impatient and curious. Quality Gao frowns, much irritated.

I save Doc for last. We didn't know he was coming and did not obtain the specifics of his background. "My good friend, Dr. Lu

Shu-ren, is a most respected and beloved physician at Beijing Tiantan Hospital and my personal doctor. I also have the good fortune of serving under him on the Safety Council for Strategic Games."

"Actually—" Doc says. XX moans in frustration. "As of this morning, I've been relieved of my duties. I am to be reassigned to a clinic in Inner Mongolia."

Hands on his hips, Quality Gao takes a warning step toward Doc. A big-eyed silence grips us. We all know what reassignment means, and no one dares to console Doc or ask questions, not in front of Quality Gao and cameras.

I realize that just like me, Doc needs to be known far and wide to try to stay safe. "Listen up: people of Inner Mongolia," I say. "My loss is going to be your gain. The most patient, caring, and capable doctor—Dr. Lu Shu-ren—can soon be yours. You would be wise to ask for Dr. Lu Shu-ren at your local clinic."

XX scowls. He waves at Tommy, urging him to continue.

Tommy says, "Lee Wei-guo: Why did you bring this show of force? Why take so much time getting to your story?"

I begin to deny his statement and abruptly stop, unsure how to play down the obvious. I bounce BeiBei just for something to do and realize I don't need to be convincing. By necessity, we have all become experts at reading between the lines. There will be no justice for my men. Not if I value my life and those of my future family. The best I can do is to hint at the truth and inject doubt into the official story through silence and unresolved inconsistencies.

After a pause, I say, "My men died, and I was not there to help or protect them. I was not at Cloud Fog Forest Mountain Park on December 11. I've been sick at home with the flu these last three days."

Quality Gao draws up a corner of his mouth and gives me a sinister half smile.

Tommy looks me up and down. Two days in the cold fighting for my life have hollowed me out in much the same way as a bout of influenza. "You are on the official list of the missing. Two hundred bodies were recovered, and one of them is wearing your equipment. Your identification swiped in at the Beijing Station and swiped out at the game site."

"I was too feverish to play, but I did go to the station to hand over my command module to Major Chao, my second-in-command. I can't explain the headcount. But with so many bodies"—I pause dramatically—"is it a surprise if they were miscounted?"

Tommy leans in closer. "Who was that extra dead man?"

I close my eyes and cover my mouth as if a thought has just occurred to me. "Major Chao was looking for a last-minute replacement for me. He must have found someone." My last seconds with Lee Gwang—the horrors of those last seconds—flash before me, and I choke up. BeiBei turns and places a hand on my cheek. I squeeze his hand.

I sniffle and shake my head helplessly. I've said all that XX intended for me to say about that night. My orders from this point forward are to claim ignorance, end the interview as quickly as possible, and get us all out of here. May-ling clutches my hand. Half a dozen people have trickled in through the lobby door and lingered to watch me break down.

"What do you suppose happened that night?" asks Tommy.

I shake my head some more. "None of it makes sense."

"There is talk that you and your opposing general underestimated the weather."

"That's not possible." I know I shouldn't, but I can't help but explain that our chances of holding a game grow slim as we approach December. "We're eager to play, and everybody—the People's Republic's general, the men—we all begin studying the weather maps days before. There are firm regulations in place: if the temperature with wind chill is forecasted to dip below freezing, the games are automatically cancelled. There was no forecast of a snowstorm." Quality Gao circles a finger for me to move it along. XX wheezes helplessly next to me.

"No forecasts of a snowstorm?" Tommy says. "Even I knew it was going to snow that night." He questions my weather source.

"Strategic Games uses a proprietary program that provides forecasts and weather specific to game sites."

Tommy cocks his head at me. "Walk us through what should have happened on December 11."

Quality Gao strides to the camera at the opening of our horseshoe couch so that both Tommy and I can see his displeasure. His disdain makes me a little reckless.

I tell Tommy that the men would have checked the weather right up to the moment the train pulled out of the station. No one would have wanted to waste time on a useless trip. "That night, when the temperature dipped below freezing, the master computer should have shut down play. Soldiers should have received an automatic 'Game Over' message. Laser shots should have stopped firing and registering. The fight suits on men taken down in action should have reactivated and allowed them to get back up."

A reporter at his core, Tommy presses on, "Is ending play a computer, rather than a human, decision?"

I tell him that the generals could also agree to end the game prior to the computer ruling. XX exerts a vicious pressure against my elbow.

"Why didn't they then?" he asks.

Quality Gao pulls a black pen from his breast pocket and casually flips his wrist and the red tip of the device in my direction. Icy prickles run down my spine. He is threatening me with the same laser pen the teenage black-uniformed guard used at the Heavenly Lake Station.

I make myself look away. Two hundred men have been murdered, their hopes, dreams, and boundless potential cut short. How dare Gao brandish a weapon in so public a setting and with such nonchalance.

"Do you know what time the temperature touched zero that night?" I want the audience to hear the damning answer.

Tommy says, "Three twenty-five A.M. Well past the end of the game."

I give him my most innocent, wide-eyed look. "How is that possible when five centimeters of snow sat on the ground at nine o'clock?"

Red beams from the tip of Quality Gao's laser pen and from his eyeballs. My breath catches. Even with a room full of witnesses, Gao is ready to kill me right here. Would he stop at just me? I let the wiggling BeiBei climb onto May-ling's lap.

Tommy leans forward. "Why did you surrender?"

"I didn't," I say, putting my hands up. "I wasn't there."

Quality Gao drags his pen repeatedly across his throat.

Tommy doesn't acknowledge him. "Why would Middle Kingdom surrender when it was one man up and minutes away from victory?"

I shake my head. "Without my command module, I can't know of course. It makes no sense. Perhaps someone was trying to signal an emergency?"

There was of course a huge emergency. Tommy asks me to go on, but I break eye contact and drift off. I give the audience a chance to stew over what could have prevented two hundred men from calling for help or emergency rescue teams from responding.

Tommy exhales woefully. "What would you like to say to the parents of the men who died?"

I blink. I was eager for him to speculate, to draw some damning conclusions. But he has already taken on considerable personal risk in continuing to press me for answers. It is his job not to verge into territory that may implicate the government.

I bow my head. "I am so very, very sorry. I've failed my men." Shame that I will let my men down and their killers go unpunished washes over me.

I continue, "My ninety-nine men ranged in age from twenty to sixty-two. They were businessmen, engineers, teachers. We had a doctor, an opera singer. The People's Republic had a man who served with Doc and me on the Safety Council for these games." I lock eyes with Doc and reach back behind me. He wraps his fist ferociously around my hand. I allow my audience a moment to witness the emotion, to imagine what we are afraid to say.

"These men were an optimistic, peace-loving bunch, model citizens in their own right. They never stopped believing in marriage; they worked and saved with a family in mind and children in their future. They were upstanding men, contributors to our society. These good people did not deserve this fate."

"Hear, hear." Tommy bows his head. After a moment of silence, he asks what's next for me.

I swallow, irked. Has he already dismissed my men?

When I do not reply, Tommy turns his gaze upon May-ling. "Your presence here today gives hope to so many of our bachelor audience." He asks how we met.

May-ling says that, just like everyone else, we relied on the expertise of a matchmaker.

"How did Lee Wei-guo win you over?"

May-ling catches my eyes. "Wei-guo invited me to his exercise studio and gave me a complimentary fitness evaluation."

Tommy chuckles. This lightening of topic sickens me. Quality Gao tucks his weapon back into his breast pocket.

"My two husbands and my son were there as well," May-ling says, eyes lowered. She is quite the liar. "Wei-guo wanted to learn to dance, so we taught him the merengue."

"You are giving our audience some very good ideas." Tommy leans toward her. "Have you proposed marriage?"

May-ling smiles demurely and looks across me at XX. "We wouldn't be here today if we weren't ready to make Wei-guo a part of our family."

XX points repeatedly at his watch.

Tommy nods. "Well, I for one wish all of you a lifetime of happy companionship. And I think I speak for my audience when I say that we would love to see that courtship dance. Would you demonstrate for us as we close out our segment?"

"Two hundred men are dead, and you want us to dance?" I say.

Quality Gao flicks two fingers upward, ordering me to my feet.

May-ling squeezes the life out of my hand. "We will be happy to dance in honor of the fallen men."

She sets BeiBei down and coaxes XX and me to our feet. The four of us hold hands, moving as one to the middle of the lobby. May-ling leans down and asks BeiBei if he remembers how to dance. She counts out the one-two beat and demonstrates the step and drag of the merengue, and we begin to circle in place. May-ling is cheerful and lively, but a far cry from the sexy, hip-swinging woman at my studio. I go through the motions, matching her heatless performance. BeiBei settles into a bouncing shuffle, thrilled to be moving. XX follows along flat-footed, the look on his face one of pure relief. I suppose we survived the interview.

As we circle, I feel Hann's absence keenly. I remember the generosity he showed me on that long-ago day in my studio. I try to channel his grace and remember the pride he took in the family he built.

May-ling stretches out a hand and invites my fathers to join us.

They in turn reach out to my four friends, to Tommy and Wung. No one invites the quality man. The cameras and our onlookers back away to make room for us to form a larger circle. I grip Doc's hand.

"The merengue was invented out of necessity," I tell everyone. "It was the only dance possible for ankle-chained slaves in the cane fields of the Caribbean."

Holding on to our neighbors' hands, we step and drag and step and drag, our feet as heavy as our hearts.

Next to me, Doc's face is wild with fury, wet with tears. He slams a foot down. The noise is anarchic and jolting. May-ling answers with a crashing heel of her own. Quality Gao jerks upright, back to full alert. We all join in, protesting with one foot and dragging the other, the sharp clack of our shoes electrifying.

May-ling says, "Long. Live. Middle. Kingdom."

Our feet thunder at the start of each word. We chant with her. We make the dance our own, expressing with our feet what we dare not utter with our mouths. We go around and around for the people who have gathered to gawk. Comrade Gao's face storms, but he stands aside, helpless to intervene, as we mourn for our fallen compatriots and for our country.

The crash of a pot in the kitchen jolts me awake. I check the clock, 4:45, and curse. Big Dad announced yesterday that it was time for me to go back to work. Dad must be preparing to send me off with a hearty breakfast and big box lunch. I pull the covers over my head.

There is no quiet to be had at home, not with my bed in a corner of our living room. All I want is to hibernate, to hide and despise myself for what I dared not do and say. My "Model Citizens" appearance was scrubbed clean of all ambiguities and edited into a propaganda piece I am loath to recognize. XX's plan worked: I am now a household name. We've so far circumvented arrest. I have become the public face for China First, for the Bounty, for Bachelors by Choice, for citizens both for and opposed to Strategic Games. Bachelors vie for me to become their trainer and dating adviser. Grieving parents ring at all hours, begging to understand their sons' final moments. Their crying pleas play night and day in my head, and the shame that I've not called anyone back—that I've chosen myself and the safety of a family I hope to join over their anguish—sits like a boulder on my chest.

Dear Doc, on the other hand, has had no such luck. He never made it to Inner Mongolia. The powers that be clearly saw in him a veritable threat and swept him off the streets the morning after my "Model Citizens" interview for fabricating evidence to overthrow the government. I regret inviting Doc to the interview, regret not recognizing the emotionally explosive state he was in and the fact that he needed to go immediately into hiding. When Doc's wife begged to know where he was taken, she was told that he, who made himself an enemy of the People, is now at the mercy of the People. I despair of ever seeing him again.

Yesterday, the Safety Council, under new leadership, formally declared Doc mentally unstable. I was made the new head and also investigative liaison for the December 11 accident. My appointment makes me want to both laugh and cry. How better to make official their version of events than with both my reputation and my life. They own me now every which way.

The ceiling light clicks on. Dad tells me my first client is at five thirty. I groan and cover my head with my elbows. Dad stands over me and after a moment, peels back my covers to tell me I must get up. I mumble that I never have clients before six.

"You're in high demand now. Big Dad and I filled your schedule."

I open my eyes to glare at him. "I will not cash in on my men's misfortune." He and Big Dad spent an inordinate amount of time the last two days on the computer whispering to each other. I thought they were playing quieter online *wéiqí* for my sake.

"XX says it's important that you maintain your celebrity, keep yourself in the public consciousness."

I never should have let Big Dad manage my billing and scheduling. "You know I don't do half-hour slots."

"One hundred eighty-four men want to give you their business." Dad hands me pieces of paper with names, contact information, and requests for bodybuilding, dating advice, dance lessons, life coaching. "Your big dad and I think you should convert half of your schedule to small-group training. Perhaps even hire someone to help with the load. Your studio has the space for it."

"He does, does he?" I hate that Big Dad thinks he knows everything about everything, hate it even more that Dad would get up in the middle of the night to do his bidding.

"We both think it's a good idea, and it's not about the money. You need to do everything you can right now to stay visible and maintain your innocence."

"Famous people get arrested all the time."

"C'mon." Dad pulls back the covers, exposing my body to the cold apartment.

I say, "Has he sent Madam Mao a donation?"

"He intends to."

I cock my head at him.

"Get up, and go do it yourself then," Dad says. "Go figure out how to send that money to her."

I suppose he's right. It's not as if we could just transfer funds to her foundation. I scowl and slowly sit up. "What did you promise the five-thirty client?"

Dad walks to the dining table to consult another piece of paper.

"Your first client is sixty, married, and looking to get back into shape."

"Sixty and married?" None of my clients are married. "Didn't that sound strange to you?"

"What does it matter? Exercise is exercise."

I snatch the paper from him. Ignoring Dad's plea to have a bite to eat, I pull on my gym clothes and a thick coat and slam the apartment door on my way out. It is barely five o'clock, and the streets are dark and deserted. I do not need to take more than ten steps to know that I'm a changed animal, one who senses danger lurking in every shadowy recess, in the whispers of the wintry wind. I walk faster, every cell in my body vibrating on full alert. The cold sears my lungs, and my breath is short and panicked. I feel alone and cornered, on that endless flight from Cloud Fog Forest Mountain once again. When a car zooms around the corner in my direction, I take off running before its headlamps can expose me.

Needles jab my side, but I can't stop. There is power in speed, release in flight. I skim the pavement with my feet, gulp down the frigid air, and fly. It takes no time at all to get to my studio. I slow down a distance away. Ever since my interview, everyone under the sun has vied for a piece of me. Everyone except the men who masterminded the massacre. What if they were the ones who booked this early slot?

There are twenty more minutes until my appointment, yet I see two darkly clothed and hooded figures milling in front of my building entrance. I tell myself to stay calm, that these men— if they are here to see me—are not the breaking-and-entering type. (The doors are not unlocked before 7:00.) Even with their shoulders hunched against the cold, they look tall and imposing. I remain on the opposite side of the road and creep along the dark edge of the building.

They spot me. One calls out my name, waves, and jogs across

the street, and something snaps in me. I too break into a run when I recognize Hann. We throw our arms around each other and hold on tight. Choked by emotions, I bury my head in his shoulder.

"I'm so glad you are all right," he says again and again.

"What about you?" I peel myself away to examine him. There is still a bandage on his ear.

"I'm fine." He says the chip and his ankle monitor have both been removed. "I haven't had a chance to thank you. I owe you my life."

"We both have XX to thank for that," I say. "But what are you doing here? Where have you been living?"

His eyes well up.

"You're going to be all right." I clasp his hands. "BeiBei will always know he is your son. We will not abandon you."

He wipes away a tear. "There's someone I'd like you to meet." He indicates the man across the street. Hann is tall and charismatic, but his friend is even more so in a more broad-chested and commanding way. I hesitate, uncertain I want to be introduced quite so soon to the flesh-and-blood reality of his paramour.

But then Hann says that the man is Dunn, the most capable managing director from his accounting firm. "I've known him for nearly thirty years. He has watched over my career, promoted me. He was the one who recommended me for the housing award. I want you to know that I trust and admire him."

"All right," I say.

"Mr. Dunn's son was in the People's Republic."

My stomach cramps and seizes. I'm back on the battlefield once more, ambushed this time by friendly fire. "I can't talk to him." I don't know how to make right my actions. "Don't make me talk to him." I turn and walk in the opposite direction.

Hann follows, but does not try to stop me.

"Does XX know what you're up to?" I say. "XX does not want

me to speak to anyone under any circumstance. Parents especially."

"Our family will be under surveillance for a long time to come. I know XX would agree that it will be safer for someone else to be the guardian of the battle data and voltage gun."

"You want me to tell Dunn?"

"I've known Dunn to be level-headed, politically astute, and fair. What I'm asking is for you to work with him in your studio, to get to know him. I want you to decide if he is the one to be entrusted with our evidence, the one who could potentially do something with it."

I stop walking. "I want those murderers to pay."

"I want that too—and much more—but we must be smart about it. There are many kinds of justice, and Dunn could be that smart man."

We walk the half block back to my building. I survey the area to make certain no one is watching. Dunn waits for us to approach. He thanks me for coming back, for agreeing to see him. His voice cracks.

"I'm so sorry." My voice falters too, and I can't find the right words. Up close, the corners of Dunn's eyes droop with sorrow and fatigue, and I clasp his hands tight to impart what little comfort I can. It feels good to be able to start on a plan, to work toward the possibility of redemption.

I unlock the door to my building and invite Dunn out of the cold. I ask his son's name. Dunn brings up a picture on his watch, and I see a younger version of him, a vibrant and promising young man, a life usurped.

I ask Dunn to tell me a story about his child.

BeiBei retrieves his paper airplane from the ground and launches it with the weight of his entire body. He throws the plane a little too hard again, and it swoops nose-down, lifting, thankfully, at the last second to veer a hard right. He sets off after the plane, following its sweeping arc to the edge of the canal. "Oh no," May-ling exclaims as it flutters toward a watery grave. We hurry after him, and May-ling calls out for BeiBei to stop climbing the concrete balustrade. The plane sits on the surface of the water, trembling with the current, and May-ling's hand tightens around mine as we await BeiBei's reaction. He likes to take his frustrations out on his mother.

He climbs down and runs to us, his eyes already welling up. He grabs May-ling's wrist and jerks it side to side. "I want it back."

Thirty paces ahead, XX stops waving the five bulky detection and deactivation devices he now straps to his arms at all times and hugs himself, bracing for the tantrum that's sure to come. XX has become maniacally focused on keeping us and our evidence safe. The government has not stopped trying to break into our computers, and XX is forced into round-the-clock, cat-and-mouse programming. It breaks my heart that to the average man on the street, our fiercely loyal XX appears ever more strange and unapproachable, a vacant, muttering old man who passes his hands over everything and everyone with obsessive-compulsive wackiness.

It does not help matters that someone has stolen a copy of our unedited "Model Citizens" interview. In one leak, my question about the unfathomable five centimeters of snow that sat on the ground when the temperature was above freezing played in an unending loop, all but confirming the government's hand in doctoring the weather reports. In another, a clever editor spliced together a Q-and-A sequence starring XX and all his demands, protestations, and reactions. The resulting portrait features the blinking, cringing, and wheezing of a terrified man with obvious knowledge of the massacre, doing everything in his power to control the situation.

I am both afraid and thrilled when snippets of the interview make it online. I cannot help but cheer that the truth will not stay buried, that my men will somehow find vindication. But the stolen tape is a time bomb. XX panics whenever a leak appears, certain that he and I will be arrested at any moment. We cannot sleep until he—or the government—is able to take it down.

May-ling kneels in front of BeiBei. "I'm sorry, sweetie. I really am, but we can't go into the water for your plane. Would you like Uncle-BaBa to make you another? An even better one?"

Uncle-BaBa is our new name for XX. As a favor to Hann, he agreed to stay and watch over BeiBei. In return, Hann had to relent on a number of points: The marriage would be in name only, as both XX and May-ling were eager to put an end to their bedroom time. XX is allowed to come and go from our home as he pleases. XX would manage the family finances without Hann's help and give him a monthly living allowance. And finally, the two brothers would dine together three nights a week rather than every night. Except for an active toddler in our bed, my marital arrangement has worked out better than I dared dream.

"No," BeiBei cries. "I want blue one." The lost plane was made with our last piece of blue paper.

"Listen," I say, pointing at a bush in the direction of a warbling flash of blue. We see long, white-tipped tail feathers before a bird hops forward. "See that blue bird?" BeiBei is entranced by everything blue these days. I tell him it is a magpie. "Did I ever tell you the magpie story?"

A worm twirls from the bird's red bill, and BeiBei is instantly captivated. He lurches after the bird, and it skitters, its cobalt-blue wings spread wide. I realize I shouldn't tell BeiBei the tale of the weaver maid and cowherd and their unlikely celestial reunions made possible by magpies. I don't need to remind him that he has little hope of seeing his father anytime soon.

Even though XX has wired BeiBei with a mic and Hann with spy-level listening devices, I turn and hold up a hand for Hann to maintain his seventy-five-meter distance. He is not allowed by law to have any contact with BeiBei. I'm glad to see he has already concealed himself within the cascading green of a willow tree. It breaks my heart that the sharpest dresser I know lives now in dumpy workman sweats.

We watch BeiBei stalk the bird until it flies away, a pied, notched-wing kite in the sky.

He returns to us. "I want my whistle, MaMa." XX bought him one recently.

May-ling unhooks it from around her neck and shortens the string before slipping it over BeiBei's head. We chuckle when he tells us he's going to call back the bird with the "dog" whistle. He toots a few times, and we point out a sparrow. It doesn't take long for him to scare it away too.

He runs back to us, eyes gleaming. "I'm going to help Uncle-BaBa find MaMa Dog."

"Wonderful," May-ling says. "Uncle-BaBa would love your help." BeiBei's memory of MaMa Dog has grown fonder by the day. We tried to convince XX to buy a new dog, a small housebroken one, but the suggestion only angers him.

I grab BeiBei before he runs off. "Remember: MaMa Dog has super-duper hearing. Use the whistle. She is too far away to hear your voice." XX fears that making it known that we are looking for an illegal stray could compromise us and the dog.

His whistle tooting in his mouth, BeiBei catches up to XX. "I help you, Uncle-BaBa." XX directs him to inspect under bushes and the occasional tree.

May-ling squeezes my elbow and leans her shoulder against mine. "Thank you."

I wrap an arm around her, and we begin to stroll again. "You don't have to thank me." I hold up a thumb for Hann, our all-clear signal.

"Oh, but I do," she says. "Instead of throwing a tantrum, Bei-Bei is helping XX."

"He's growing up. That's all." I kiss her forehead and lose myself in her comforting scent. "It is I who should thank you for loving me, for allowing BeiBei to love me." She circles my waist with her arms and plants a kiss on my cheek.

Despite the ongoing surveillance and threats, I marvel at how rich my life is with love, with possibility, with everything that truly matters. Not only have I a wife, I've found May-ling. May-ling, who defied all conventions to demonstrate her love to me. May-ling, who endangered her own safety in order to guarantee mine. May-ling, who makes me feel at home wherever we are together. I am of consequence to her, to a child, to two extraordinary men. I would go through it all again to be a part of this family.

I blush to remember that I once thought of marriage mostly as the physical act, my wife and me sequestered in bed beyond the reach of her other spouses. It surprises me how much I live for these Sunday walks together, for the hugs, the tears, even the snot of another man's child, for the protective antics of my new brother, for the ever-watchful eye of our guardian angel, for the quiet presence of a woman with whom I feel completely at ease. Throwaway moments like these are more precious to me than I could have ever imagined as a single man.

BeiBei darts back and forth between us, XX, and the greenery. After a half dozen circuits and still no MaMa Dog, he comes huffing and puffing back.

"I want another plane." He presses down on our clasped hands and hops. "A loop-de-loop!"

"Great idea," I say. "Let's ask Uncle-BaBa."

"No, BaBa!" BeiBei bounces on his toes. "You make airplane."

"I don't know how," I say. To elevate XX in BeiBei's eyes, May-ling and I have established him as Uncle Fix Anything, Uncle Trove of Knowledge, and more recently, the airplane-making expert. It's not far from the truth, and a productive and meaningful way for them to interact.

BeiBei narrows his eyes at me—he is becoming harder and harder to fool—and I hold on to his elbows for a little coaching. "How are you going to ask Uncle-BaBa?" XX does not tolerate brattiness.

BeiBei sways. "I want airplane."

"Politely, please," May-ling says. "May I have—"

"May I have airplane," BeiBei shouts.

"May I have a new airplane, please?"

"A loop-de-loop," BeiBei says, breaking free of my grasp.

He speeds off toward XX. "May I have loop-de-loop?"

"Please," I call out.

"Please, please, please!" He jumps, and I'm glad to see he's not tugging on XX. XX hates to be tugged on.

"Okay." XX tucks his dog whistle inside his shirt, lifts up the meat-bun-filled pockets of his coat, and sits down on a nearby bench. "Bring me paper."

BeiBei scampers back to us. May-ling riffles through the stack of airplane paper in her purse and pulls out a teal sheet.

"No!" BeiBei pushes it away. "Blue!"

May-ling sighs and thumbs through the stack that is full of colors he has previously rejected. "You know we don't have any more blue."

"I want blue," he says.

She fans out the papers as he shakes her. "You pick one."

398 ★ MAGGIE SHEN KING

I kneel down and get eye-to-eye with him. "Let's not keep Uncle-BaBa waiting. He really misses MaMa Dog. He is very nice to stop his search to make you an airplane."

BeiBei lingers over a green piece and then the purple.

"Maybe Uncle-BaBa can teach you and me to make one too," I say. "Who should we make our airplane for?"

BeiBei's eyes dart as he thinks. "I make it for Big BaBa."

"Yes," I say, "let's make one for Big BaBa."

May-ling combs BeiBei's hair with her fingers. "Big BaBa will love it."

In the distance, the willow branches ruffle in the breeze. It takes me a moment to locate Hann's face within it. I wish I could make out his expression. He notices me watching him and places his hands over his heart.

I do the same. I hold him in my gaze. I worry about how Hann spends his days without work and family. Afraid of what Hann's mandatory counseling sessions and the *Pursuit of Happiness*–type games might unearth, XX has refused him all information about the battle file. He regularly supplies Hann with mind-control exercises and spells out in no uncertain terms that Hann must train twenty minutes every day in order to stay in our lives.

I have tried to convince Hann to teach a ballroom dancing class at my studio—there's quite a demand for it and he could use the company—but he said he hasn't the heart to dance anymore.

When I prodded him about his emotional state, his understandably bitter and rageful demeanor, he said that unlike him, I have everything to lose, that I must focus on tomorrow and leave yesterday to him. My job is to give BeiBei a happy and secure home and raise him to be a strong and principled man. Hann is unreachable for days at a time and will not speak to me about his activities. I am both frightened and gratified that he could be fomenting some sort of rebellion with Dunn or someone we do not know.

May-ling touches my cheek. "Are you all right?" She is ever vigilant of the darkness in my moods.

"Of course." I smile and give her a reassuring nod. Her solicitude invariably makes me think of Lee Gwang and the part I played in his ending. True, it was him or me, but in my heart of hearts, I know that I could have chosen not to play that night. I could have opted to be a grown-up, a real man. I take a deep breath and ask Lee again for his forgiveness.

I hope I've finally grown up now.

When BeiBei still cannot decide on a color, I wonder aloud about Hann's favorite color.

BeiBei turns to May-ling. "What is Big BaBa's favorite color?"

"He loves you so much. I think he will love whatever color airplane you make him."

"When will Big BaBa come home?"

May-ling catches my eye. She checks her watch for possible listening devices in our vicinity—XX continually outfits us all with the most up-to-date gadgets and software—before leaning down to whisper into his ear. "Why don't we put this airplane in your next letter, and you can ask him yourself?"

Hann is not allowed to correspond with BeiBei, but we have decided this is a law we will go on breaking with handwritten notes. Hann needs all the small acts of defiance we can dream up, and BeiBei needs his father.

"But I want him now." BeiBei pouts. Tears glitter in his eyes. "Why won't he come home?"

May-ling kneels in front of him, and from behind, I brace his shoulders with my hands. Hann appears so alone and desolate in the distance. I try to convince myself that he is one of the fortunate ones, that unlike my men, he gets to live. If he continues to play by the rules, he might see his child grow into a man.

It enrages me that criminals in prison are allowed family visits, yet Hann, a loving father, respectable businessman, and contributing citizen, is cut off from his son for the rest of his days and forced to live against his most basic nature. How could BeiBei become whole in such a world?

May-ling says, "Your big baba may not be here, but he is always watching you. He is working very hard to make the world a better place for you, for every one of us, a place where everyone matters, where everyone can be free."

I sigh and give BeiBei a hug and a squeeze from his father. I can't escape the fact that despite our seeming freedom, our ability to partake in these idyllic walks, we too dangle by a thread. Our own country has ruled our love for each other—my love and respect for my teammates—unnatural. Criminal. The discovery of a mere dog tag could do us in.

BeiBei begins to whimper.

"I know you're very sad." May-ling's eyes ache with our child's pain.

I marvel at how she is not afraid to acknowledge BeiBei's hurt.

"I want BaBa now." BeiBei thrashes and throws off my hug.

May-ling says, "I miss your baba too. I know he wants to be with you now, more than anything in the whole world."

I sense tears from both mother and child. "How about green?"

"I don't want green," BeiBei cries, and I'm relieved he replies to my question. It takes our combined wits these days to distract him. We're afraid he will forget his father and equally afraid when he remembers.

"I know!" I say. "We should make Big BaBa a black plane. Spy planes are black."

BeiBei scrunches his nose, unconvinced. May-ling offers a sheet of black to him.

I say, "Black allows spy planes to hide, so they can sneak up on the bad guys and catch them."

BeiBei sniffs before snatching up the paper. "Big BaBa and I will catch bad guys." He flies toward XX on the park bench, the rectangular paper fluttering from the end of his fingers, his sadness temporarily jettisoned.

May-ling and I both exhale.

"Make me please a spy plane, Uncle-BaBa." BeiBei climbs onto the bench and perches on his knees next to XX, hands tucked in his lap.

XX studies him for a moment. "Good boy." He taps BeiBei's forehead—his version of a pat—taken aback no doubt by our boy's politeness.

"Can loop-de-loop plane be spy plane?" BeiBei asks.

"Loop-de-loop is an aerobatic maneuver, not a kind of plane," XX says while he folds and smooths the black paper. "Stealth fighters are designed to escape enemy detection. It is not designed for showy aerobatic performance."

May-ling joins the two to translate XX's explanations into terms BeiBei can understand. As BeiBei listens with rapt attention to the features that a spy plane needs in order to soar high above the clouds and defy radar, I feel as if I've been granted a glimpse of our future, one in which XX and BeiBei can learn to accommodate and even appreciate the other's idiosyncrasies. I look forward to a future in which our household nurtures not just Bei-Bei, but another boy or a girl—and the rest of us too—toward the best and true versions of ourselves. A future in which our family not only comes together but seeks each other out to choreograph our own brand of familial bliss. This is my most fundamental wish. This is a future that is worth protecting for *all* my fellow country-men and their families.

I imagine Hann, Dunn, XX, and other patriots circling in stealth, fighting toward a day when no one can be devalued or abandoned as excess, a day when Hann can come home to us, a day when everyone can walk tall and be who they are without fear. A day when one man would never have to kill another in order to stay alive. I bow my head and mouth yet another apology to Lee Gwang.

"BaBa," BeiBei calls out as he carefully stands up onto the bench. In his hand is a dark, wide-winged plane poised on the verge of flight. "Watch me!"

He launches his plane—without undue effort this time—the caution he takes around heights providing just the right amount of lower-body restriction.

"That's it!" I cry.

His spy plane rides the breeze, and XX's design glides high and true. May-ling holds BeiBei's hand as he bends his knees and hops down. He races off after his plane, his stride nimble and carefree. He is soon out of our reach. "C'mon," May-ling says, pulling XX to his feet. It takes him a second to decide to oblige, and when he does, she throws an arm across each of our shoulders. We laugh and scamper as she propels us after our child, encouraging us to catch up.

I hope that we can.

ACKNOWLEDGMENTS

I am much indebted to two lively communities of writers
and the best combinations of therapy and writing group:
**M. P. Cooley, Nita Gill, Colleen Ollee,
Lou Moore Selchau-Hansen, Kate Curry, Carol Pollard,
Casey Cameron,** and **E. B. Vandiver**
and
Kate Phillips, Heather Stallings, and **Lane von Herzen.**
Over the last decade, their critical eye and helpful advice
shaped my writing. Their unflagging support sustained me
through the peaks and the many valleys of this business.

Thank you to my wonderful agent,
David Fugate,
for believing in this book.
Thank you to my most magnanimous editor,
David Pomerico,
and the highly professional team at Harper Voyager
for taking a chance on me.
This book is better because of all of them.
I feel incredibly lucky to publish under their care.

Thank you to my early readers and dear friends
Linda Stroud, Jocelyn Dunn,
Lily Hurlimann, and **Shanda Bahles,**
who gave me much needed reality checks, encouragement,
and the occasional golf tip
to sharpen my game and focus my writing.

Thank you to
Connie Tamaddon, Andy Shen, and **Laurie Elvove**
for so graciously sharing their design sensibilities with me.

Thank you to my parents,
P. Y. and **Grace Shen,**
Whose love and encouragement made all my pursuits possible.
Thank you to
Sidney, Emmy, Jenny, and **Roger King**
for their warmth and generosity over the years.
I count my blessings for marrying into this family.

Thank you to
Matt and **Chris**
for making it a joy to be their mother,
for providing a sounding board for my writing,
and for cooking me gourmet meals while I worked.

And finally thank you to my beloved
David,
who has loved and supported me in every way
and given me the ultimate gift,
the luxury of time and mental space
in which to pursue my work.

I am grateful to you all.

READING GROUP DISCUSSION GUIDE

1. The one-child policy was adopted in 1979 to help China reduce its population to an "ideal" 700 million in order to alleviate social, economic, and environmental problems. What other forms of social engineering were carried out in this book for the public good? Who is valued under a government that espouses China First?

2. By the year 2030, China's one-child policy and its cultural preference for male heirs will have created a society overrun by 30 million unmarriageable men. More than 25 percent of men in their late thirties will never have married. Is it more immoral to violate the traditional notion of marriage or to deny tens of millions of men the love of a wife and family? What might be another solution to this problem?

3. In a society where marriageable men outnumber women in the millions, it seems logical that the scarcity of women would elevate their social status and role in society. What went wrong for women in this book? Are Compatibility Tests advantageous for them? Can you think of a societal group in which women grossly outnumbered men? How did that affect the balance of power?

4. During the eighteenth and nineteenth centuries, polyandry (marriage where a woman has more than one husband) was practiced in rural China to help impoverished families pool resources and avoid the breakup of property. The elites of the Qing Dynasty considered the practice immoral, yet emperors kept concubines and wealthy men had multiple wives and mistresses. Why do you think polyandry garnered such opposition?

5. Hann was forced to live contrary to his most fundamental nature. How do you feel about him lying to May-ling and creating a sexual outlet in his badminton team?

6. By requiring him to marry and become a parent, XX's family also forced him to live against his nature and his wishes. Was Hann right to interfere with so many details of XX's day-to-day life? Was it for XX's own good when Hann tried to encourage him to conform to social norms? To what extent should families of productive and independent adults like XX intrude upon their lives?

7. How do you think polyandry affects BeiBei and other children in such family units?

8. Privacy was of the utmost importance to XX. He insisted that his new spouse maintain a discreet digital footprint, yet he felt no compunction about planting a bug on Wei-guo, training cameras on his family in their apartment, or developing mind-reading algorithms that could be used on the public at large. Is he amoral, mercenary, or a modern-day hero?

9. What devices did the author use to build this fictional world? Did you find the world believable?

10. *An Excess Male* was narrated from four alternating points of view. Whose story was it? How would the story change if it was told only from Wei-guo's or May-ling's point of view?

Excess males were not the only unintended consequence of the one-child policy. To read a short story from Maggie Shen King about another segment of the population that was victimized by this social engineering measure, please visit: https://MaggieShenKing.com/companion-story-invite

MAGGIE SHEN KING grew up in Taiwan and attended both Chinese and American schools before moving to Seattle at age sixteen. She studied English literature at Harvard, and her short stories have appeared in *Ecotone*, *ZYZZYVA*, *Fourteen Hills*, and *Asimov's Science Fiction*. Her manuscript *Fortune's Fools* won second prize in Amazon's 2012 Breakthrough Novel Award contest. She lives near San Francisco, California.